ALE

MW01133916

CHOICE

A NOVEL BY EDMUND MARLOWE

First published 2012

Copyright © Edmund Marlowe 2012

The Author asserts the moral right to be identified as the author of this work

ISBN 978-1481222112

To every boy who has felt as Alexander felt

I: Hopeful Discoveries

The farther we penetrate the unknown,
the vaster and more marvellous it becomes.
   Charles Augustus Lindbergh, *Autobiography of Values*

Alexander Aylmer was thirteen and a quarter when he arrived at the King's College of our Lady of Eton beside Windsor, or just "Eton", as England's top public school was better known.

"With his intelligence, lively curiosity and imagination, he is just the sort of boy who will benefit most from all the opportunities Eton has to offer," said the final report of Mr. Osgood, his prep school headmaster. Though it was customary to find something nice to say about a boy on such an occasion, in his case neither this nor the other things his parents read that caused them to flush with pride and happiness were more than the truth.

After writing that, the headmaster had paused in deep thought before adding a more unusual insight. "Never before have I met a boy his age who always turns out to have a reason for everything he does." The other side of the coin was that this often led him to be dangerously uncompromising, but there was little point in saying so now.

He was not just gifted though. "His cheerful disposition, exuberance and evident good nature have won him the hearts of masters and boys alike. He will be sorely missed," Mr. Osgood had concluded without exaggeration. The headmaster had got to know him much better than most of his boys. He had seen what a rewarding and rather overwhelming gift the bestowal of Alexander's friendship could be, though he had also worried sometimes that it involved unrealistically high expectations.

What Mr. Osgood could not say in his report, though he had overheard masters' wives talking about it in gushing tones, was the one most immediately obvious thing about him: he was breathtakingly good-looking, striking enough to turn heads when he came into a room full of parents who had not seen him before. A little above average height for his age with a good figure and flawless complexion, his features were clear-cut with

1

quite high cheek-bones, a straight nose and long-lashed, deep-blue eyes. His hair was dark blond, thick and nearly straight.

In some respects Eton was more like a university than a school, and to a boy fresh from the small and enclosed environment of a prep school, it was both daunting and exciting, almost a new world.

For one thing, it had much of its own language. Alexander's father had been at Eton too and had taught him some of the stranger new words and customs he would need to know. So he already knew that the term for which he had arrived on this warm, September day was the "Michaelmas Half", that the schoolmasters were called "beaks" and when one passed one in the street one had to "cap" him by raising an index finger to the side of one's forehead in memory of the days when the boys would have raised their top hats instead.

Though most of the boys would not arrive until nearly ten in the evening, when the Half officially began, the parents of the new boys were told to bring their sons much earlier, so Alexander and his parents arrived at Peyntors, as his house-to-be was called, at four.

He had already been there once in July, when he had passed Common Entrance and at last known for certain he would be going to Eton. Thus he had already briefly met his housemaster, Mr. Hodgson, a short, stocky man in his late forties with receding hair and spectacles. His father had explained that it was the housemaster who ruled over a boys' house and was usually the most important person in a boy's time at the school. He would oversee all his academic, sporting and other activities, and praise or punish him.

However, it was to see the dame, Mrs. Austin, that Alexander's parents first took him now. It was she who oversaw the domestic arrangements of the boys' side of the house, as opposed to the part the housemaster lived in. She was a friendly, efficient lady in her early forties and greeted them warmly. First, she introduced them to Miss Flaherty, the boys' maid for his floor, whose duties ranged from cleaning to waking the boys up in the morning. "She will be like your second mother here, after me," she concluded, and Miss Flaherty, a tiny woman of about

2

sixty with a wizened face, squirmed with delight. Everyone smiled, though he himself did not much like the suggestion that anyone could begin to be a substitute for his mother, however kindly meant.

Next, the dame took them to Alexander's room, where they checked that all the special items of furniture and clothing they had had to order for him were there. For the first time, Alexander got into his tails, the school's famous nineteenth-century uniform. The separate stiff white collar and white tie had to be attached to the shirt by studs, a complicated business to anyone not familiar with them, so Alexander's father showed him how and got him to practise so he need not fear making a fool of himself when he got up the next morning. He felt a moment of panic as he wondered what would happen if he forgot, and he tried hard to concentrate.

After that, his parents took him to open accounts at the local post office and at Rowlands, the school food and snack shop, where they had a last meal together. Hitherto, Alexander had felt more exhilarated than nervous, but as the appointed hour for his parents to abandon him in this strange new world approached, his confidence ebbed away and he could feel his heart thumping louder and faster.

One by one, the new boys were being delivered to Mr. Hodgson's study by their parents. Alexander's both shook hands with the housemaster, then his mother kissed him good-bye and his father gave him a smile of encouragement and they left. The boys sat on two facing sofas, nervously giving each other furtive glances. They knew they were going to be living together for the next five or so years and they wondered anxiously which of the others would be their friends and which they would dislike. A pale and weedy boy with a flat but kind face and striking, rust-coloured hair who looked more like ten than thirteen caught Alexander's curious glance and ventured a brief but definite smile. Alexander smiled back, relieved to know at least one of the others was friendly.

A good-looking, dark-haired boy was brought in by a plump mother with a magnificent hat. Mr. Hodgson went to the door with the mother and shook her hand as she left, then he turned to address the boys, who now numbered seven.

3

"Now, in a moment I shall be taking you on a short tour of the school to help you find your bearings. You may at first think it a little difficult to find your way around, but there is no need to worry; you will be surprised how fast it will all become familiar. But first you need to learn each other's names, as you are going to know one another for some time to come." He spoke slowly, his words and cadence evidently carefully chosen and much to his own satisfaction.

Each of them said his surname as the housemaster pointed his fountain pen at them in clockwise order.

"Bell, Sir," said the tallest boy loudly, suggesting a confidence Alexander was far from sharing.

"Macdonald, Sir," said the next.

"Macdonald mi. for as long as your brother is with us," Mr. Hodgson added.

"Yes, Sir," he replied with a nervous smile.

"Aylmer, Sir," said Alexander, looking directly at the housemaster, as he knew that for an awful moment all eyes were fixed on him.

"Parker, Sir," said a short plump boy with blond hair, as the fountain pen thankfully moved on.

"Bates, Sir," said a rather pugnacious-looking boy Alexander did not much like the look of.

"Churchill, Sir," said the weedy boy in such a high-pitched squeak that a few of the others smirked furtively.

Finally, the good-looking boy gave his name as Drysdale.

They set out for the tour. It was a large school by any standard with over thirteen hundred boys, who lived in twenty-five large houses spread out around the town. First, Mr. Hodgson took them down Keats Lane to the Lower Chapel, where they would have to go every morning between breakfast and their first "div" as a lesson was called. He explained that after that they would have to walk or run many times a day between their house and the schoolrooms, also spread out around the town. These were what they needed to remember first and he accordingly took them to next. They followed him in tense silence, all too afraid of making fools of themselves to dare attempt conversation.

Finally they came to School Yard, the large cobbled square at the centre of the oldest and most beautiful part of the school, just

4

as the great clock on Lupton's Tower chimed six o'clock. He showed them the mediaeval College Chapel, much the largest and most magnificent building in the school. He explained that though it had originally been built for the whole school to attend, there were now too many boys, so they would not be going there for three years unless they were among the select few chosen for the school choir.

"Tomorrow every new boy will have a short audition with the Precentor," he added. "Those chosen for the choir cannot refuse to join and the practices are very time-consuming indeed, so I would advise you not to sing too well unless you wish to find yourself singing a great deal more." This was very much to the point for Alexander, who had a fine voice and had been thoroughly bored by choir practice at his prep school. He wondered whether he could or should really try to sing worse than he was able.

So far, none of the boys had said a word since giving their names in his study, so Mr. Hodgson tried asking them a question. "This is the Founder," he said, indicating a bronze statue of a man holding a sceptre in the middle of School Yard, its shadow stretching far out behind in the dying sunlight. "Who can tell me who founded Eton?"

"Henry the Seventh," squeaked Churchill in a rush, and Alexander noticed Bell and Bates exchange furtive smirks.

"Henry the Sixth," said Alexander.

"Yes, indeed. Henry the Sixth," said Mr. Hodgson, the corners of his mouth quivering briefly with amused approval. It would seem the report Aylmer's prep school had sent to Eton had not exaggerated his historical knowledge. "And do you know in which year?"

"1440, Sir," he replied. He was glad to be able to impress Mr. Hodgson, but just a little worried the others might think he was a show-off, which he did not think he was, so he was relieved to see Drysdale give him a look of entirely friendly surprise.

"Yes," said the housemaster in a tone of confirmed approval. Aylmer was going to be an interesting boy to have in his house, he thought, as he led them back to Peyntors.

As they walked back, Alexander felt the dawn of hope that the friendly glance he had caught Drysdale giving him might be the

5

seed of a friendship, just as earlier he had wondered for a moment whether the smirks he had seen exchanged by the two others indicated an incipient understanding. From such tiny beginnings, great things could grow.

Thirteen-year-old boys are usually still quite adaptable, but Alexander settled into his new life even sooner than most. It was easier for him academically because his liveliness and intelligence made him just the sort of boy Eton beaks found rewarding to teach.

The first of his beaks to take special notice of him was Mr. Trotter, who taught Classics, considered the most important subject. Eton was rich in colourful schoolmasters, but Mr. Trotter, a tall distinguished-looking man in his fifties with a rather severe demeanour and glinting spectacles, stood out for his delightful eccentricity, though at first he appeared to be gruff and fairly alarming.

"Weed!" he would call out to a tough-looking boy called Meade, and repeat it louder in apparent exasperation until Meade understood he was meant. Similarly "Cook, I mean Baker!" would learn to respond to the former name as his pseudonym and Greene soon got used to being called Brown. During their first div, they wondered if he was a little mad, but watching carefully when they giggled in response to his mistakes, Alexander soon noticed the faint twitch of the corners of Mr. Trotter's mouth that alone in his deadpan countenance betrayed the intense pleasure it gave him to bring his class to life in this way.

His third Classics div of the Half was repeatedly interrupted by the noise of drilling the other side of the div room window. After a while, Mr. Trotter put down his Greek grammar book, strode up to the window and opened it.

"I do hope I'm not boring you," he boomed at the bewildered builder, closed the window and quickly resumed his discourse on pronouns as if oblivious of the tittering of the boys.

The next div, he suddenly interrupted their Latin construe to command them to write down the Seven Wonders of the World, though they had never been taught them. He would give a sovereign to any boy who got all seven, he said. Each boy then

6

had to mark his neighbour's answers and announce his own score. Nought, one or two was the invariable score and elicited mutterings of feigned incredulity at the ignorance of modern schoolboys on the part of Mr. Trotter, until Alexander said six. Alexander caught the beak's slightly puzzled look, as though the glass of plonk he thought he was sipping had turned out to be fine claret. After that, he became a special target of Mr. Trotter's attention, but under the veneer of raillery, he could sense the man's warm interest in him.

Some of the more conventional boys were a bit put off by the frequency with which Alexander had opinions and tastes which were unfamiliar to them, but otherwise it was easy for him to make friends fast, as he was friendly and unpretentious as well as good-looking. Other boys tended to feel instinctively they could trust him.

Much his closest friend did indeed turn out to be Rupert Drysdale. They got on with each other immediately. As they had little in common apart from good looks, it was an attraction of opposites. Alexander loved learning, at least in some subjects, of which his favourite was ancient history. Rupert, who was of only moderate intelligence and lazy, thought that was dead boring, but felt a bit guilty about not being more like Alexander. His own passion was motor-racing, which Alexander secretly thought rather pointless, but all the same, the people who were involved in it looked terribly glamorous and he wished he were more worldly-wise like Rupert. Rupert's father had been an admiral and First Sea Lord who had had to resign his posts because of a sex scandal thought to have endangered national security, whereas Alexander's was a judge. Both boys looked up to their fathers, but Alexander wished his was a bit more fun-loving, as Rupert's sounded, and Rupert wished his was a little less notorious.

One of the more dramatic changes for a new arrival was of course finding that instead of being a big boy as he had recently been at prep school, and perhaps a prefect too, he was now very much a little boy and dwarfed by the eighteen year-olds. There were a few much older boys with whom Alexander remembered being friendly at his last school, but whereas before they had just seemed a bit bigger and more knowledgeable, the intervening years seemed to have turned them into a different order of being. One entered Eton still entirely a child and left it already a man. Until only half a generation ago, this natural difference had been heavily emphasised by the power structure of the boys' houses. The boys in F, the first academic "block" or year, had had to "fag" as personal servants to a member of "the Library", the senior prefects of the house, boys in A or B; the house captain had exercised an authority over them that even extended to caning for serious breaches of the house rules. Caning and fagging had been gradually whittled down until they had disappeared entirely three years earlier, but the memory of them still lay in the air; both the Library and Debate, the junior prefects, could still mildly punish boys who broke the house rules by assigning them some tedious task such as an essay about their misbehaviour or gardening for the housemaster.

After their first week, the Library gave the new boys their "colours test", so called after the combination of colours each of the twenty-five houses used as their sporting emblems when they competed, such being part of the test. More usefully, it was also a detailed test of their geographical knowledge of the school, as every boy really did need to learn fast where to find each school building, playing field and boys' house. The test was also a rite of passage. Grossly exaggerated rumours of the punishment that would follow failure were fed to the naïve young boys, so they were more than usually nervous of the boys in the Library when they queued up outside the door. Their examiners set out to amuse themselves at their expense. For example, they asked Simon Churchill whether Lupton's Tower was up Judy's Passage "at the moment," and guffawed with laughter at his confused and impervious innocence of the innuendo. However, it was good-humoured and they all passed.

Simon became very attached to Alexander, largely because Alexander was the only new boy who was too kind to make fun of him. Some of the others had made him the butt of their jokes from their very first evening. He had an unfortunate propensity to increase the ridicule by talking about subjects he was generally considered hopelessly immature to understand. Alexander guessed he probably did it in a misguided attempt to convince

8

them he was not such a baby. Once, when they were talking about the short stories they had just written for Mr. Hodgson in their weekly div with him as their tutor, Simon revealed he had written about getting stuck in the desert with a girl he had got pregnant. Alexander did not think he could get a girl pregnant yet either and said nothing. For a few days he was the only boy Simon could talk to without ribald jokes being made. A witty older boy coined the nickname "Lusty Rusty" and soon Alexander was about the only one who still called him Simon.

Simon's babyish appearance and squeaky voice were hardly improved by a lisp. Soon afterwards, he made the mistake of describing to two of the boys most inclined to tease him how his male labrador liked to jump up and hump his leg. "Sometimes he gets so excited he is litewally jwipping with sperm," squeaked Simon, and the expression reverberated through the house for weeks afterwards. Alexander laughed at that, but it still saddened him to see Simon mocked, because he knew better than the others how very good-natured he was. Fortunately, much of the mockery took the form of sarcasm and passed Simon by. His would-be tormentors were often baffled by his ability to take all but the most absurdly insincere compliments at face value.

As the boys' houses had been modernised, one by one, their kitchens and dining-rooms had been closed down, and their inhabitants had been sent instead for their meals to Bekynton, a gigantic canteen of typically seventies hideousness, but fortunately quite well hidden; the dreamlike beauty of the school with its ancient buildings and vast playing-fields being one of its outstanding features. Most of the boys in JRH, as Alexander's house was most often known from the initials of their housemaster, were thankful, in at least this respect, that Peyntors had not been modernised. It was both more intimate and more convenient to eat in their own house, and the food was reputed to be better too. "Boy's dinner", as lunch was known, was the most formal meal, as it was attended by Mr. Hodgson and his wife. The boys had to await his arrival, then stand up while he came in and said grace. The dishes were then passed down the long table. The presence of adult authority obviously placed

9

some restraint on the conversation. Breakfast was brief and chaotic, and supper too was loud and jolly. Once the house captain had said grace, the roar of fifty voices in animated conversation would start immediately as everyone rushed off to the long sideboard to help themselves.

One evening still fairly early in the Half, Rupert, having finished piling food onto his plate, turned round rather suddenly to go back to the dining table just as another boy reached out for something on the sideboard. His plate was knocked out of his hands and smashed on the floor easily loudly enough to cut through the din. For a second the room quietened, and then a long groan arose from many voices, causing Rupert to blush. Alexander, standing nearby, smiled sympathetically, but, to the astonishment of both, the groan was immediately followed by a chorus of "Mooooody! Mooooody!", then the room erupted into laughter. Alexander saw the whole house had joined in except the new boys, who looked puzzled, and a few boys sitting around Henry Moody, a boy in D, who were struggling to keep a straight face.

"Oh, shut up, it's just not funny," they saw Moody expostulating angrily to the nearest boys who had joined in. "You're all so pathetic."

"What was that all about?" Alexander asked Michael Bell, who had just been chatting to a boy in E the other side of him, as he sat down.

"Apparently most of the times any one breaks anything here, it's Moody, so everyone's taken to just assuming it's him, even when they know it's not."

The one aspect of life at Eton that Alexander greatly disliked was football, compulsory up to thrice a week. It was not that he disliked all sports, for he loved swimming, skiing and long bicycle trips, but that the team spirit football was supposed to engender was lost on one of his individualistic tastes. The more some of the heartier boys enthused about it, the more he was put off. Though it was a nuisance familiar to him from prep school, it was more competitive at Eton because the boys were always in the same house team. As a result, the hearties often tried to force him to share their eagerness, which only increased his aversion.

10

Whenever he was forced to play, he tried to alleviate the miserable tedium with daydreams, though these were hard to enjoy when the weather got seriously cold and they were constantly threatened by the ball coming his way, adept as he had become at avoiding it.

As he hated it and was no good at it, it seemed to him both a complete waste of time and unfair that he should be made to play it, so he used his imagination to get out of it as much as possible. He redoubled his interest in the piano and found other options to fill his time so that it appeared his piano lessons could only fall when football matches were being played. This soon reduced the threat to once a week, but even that he initially felt impelled to try to avoid.

Twice it happened that the boy in charge of posting the announcement of a game and those due to play was late to do so. Alexander noted the exact time he had been able to conclude from the notice board that no game was on, and promptly disappeared. The first time he did this caused irritation. The second time, it appeared he had gone too far. He provoked real antipathy for the first time and found himself summoned to Mr. Hodgson's study. Though he thought he was ready with a reasonable explanation, Hodgson was too shrewd for him.

"Why do you mind playing football?" he asked unexpectedly, leaning back in his chair, as if inclined to have a friendly chat.

Alexander was taken aback. He realised the question deliberately bypassed his prepared defences, but Mr. Hodgson had always seemed reasonable and his instinct to be frank was strong. "There are so many more useful things I could be doing, Sir, and what's the point when I'm never going to be any good at it?"

Hodgson lost his patience then. As it happened, he did not much care for team sports himself, but he was careful to conceal it because he knew it was his duty to take an interest in such an integral part of boarding school life. If someone of his intellectual stature forced himself to give up his time to go and cheer his house teams on when there were important matches, it was insufferable that this wilful thirteen-year-old thought his time was too valuable to join in what every other boy did.

11

"Now. You listen to me," he said sharply, sitting up. "You will play football whenever you are asked to, whether you like it or not, and you will find yourself in deep trouble if for any reason whatsoever you do not turn up for a match when your name is on the list. Is that understood?"

"Yes, Sir," replied Alexander, quite shaken by Hodgson's angry tone, but only after a pause, which though only momentary, was long enough for his housemaster to understand that though he admitted defeat on this specific issue, his obedience was not unquestioning..

Hodgson sighed deeply as soon as he was alone again. It was a shame he had had to be angry for the first time with this boy he had thought so good-natured and reasonable, but he now suspected there was a dangerous undercurrent to his character: it looked as though he would defy as far as he thought practicable any rule he thought unreasonable. Luck would be needed to avoid a serious clash in the future.

Peyntors was a very old-fashioned house, the most old-fashioned in the school and due for imminent renovation. It still had stone floors without carpets, irregular, narrow stone stairs and no central heating. Instead, each of the little rooms had its own fire-place with a bucket of coal. Every winter morning on their way to breakfast, the boys would take their buckets downstairs to the coal-room, and when they came back in the evening after their last div, they picked them up, already filled up by the odd-job man. After coming back from a long day through the cold, dark streets, lighting their fires and warming their hands against the growing flames had to be one of the highlights of the day. The coal buckets were a good size and easily sufficient to keep a fire going all evening.

Eton was unusual for a boarding school in that every boy had his own room, where he not only slept, but did his E.W.s, as their daily assignments of homework were called, and could be with his friends, though only at certain times. The rules were many, but there were as many ways of breaking them. For example, lights-out was at half-past nine for the youngest boys, but Alexander soon discovered that if he really built up the fire in his room just before then, it burned brightly enough for him to read

12

Your order of March 5, 2013 (Order ID 103-4912584-6350615)

Qty.	Item	Item Price	Total
1	**Alexander's Choice** Marlowe, Edmund --- Paperback (** P-1-Q36D71 **) 1481222112	$12.99	$12.99

Subtotal	$12.99
Shipping & Handling	$3.99
Order Total	$16.98
Paid via credit/debit	$16.98
Balance due	$0.00

V3

This shipment completes your order.

Have feedback on how we packaged your order? Tell us at www.amazon.com/packaging.

0/DSLzhOqcN/-1 of 1-//CVG5/std-n-us/7713697/0306-09:00/0306-00:58

in bed for at least half an hour afterwards. Once a boy in Debate burst into his room at ten, his officious eagerness to impose punishment written all over his face, only to look at the fire rather sheepishly and say "Sorry Aylmer, I thought your light must be on."

The year was 1983, and in anticipation of the new one to begin in a few months, Alexander's father had given him the famous book named after it as a going-away present. He got round to reading it in the firelight during his second month. It deeply impressed him, but much to his relief, George Orwell had got his timing wrong, as though there were signs England might eventually turn out as the novel depicted, it wasn't yet at all like that. Far from feeling the gloom the hero's fate might have induced, Alexander himself, when he at last finished the book, was bursting with enthusiasm for life and deeply excited by yearnings he was only beginning to understand.

Only two nights before, a most wonderful thing had happened: he had learned to bring himself to orgasm, and he was still exhilarated by the discovery. It was amazing that there could be such a fantastic sensation he had had no idea existed. It had come about by accident. He had simply become conscious for the first time that the generally pleasant feeling of playing with his organ intensified enormously when he kept it up long enough. Naturally, he had then kept going until he felt a spasm of delight and joy purer than any he had imagined could exist. Perhaps he could've done it months before and had been missing out through ignorance. He did not know.

The next day he had not forgotten his new joy and had looked forward all day to trying it out again. The mere thought had kept his spirits up through even the boredom of chapel. That night he had left his pyjamas off. It had been a new and delicious sensation to feel his body slipping naked between the sheets. He had turned on his torch under the blanket to have a first critical look at himself in his aroused and incomparably more impressive state. As his fingers went to play, he felt both surprise that he had not before taken a proper interest in his unexpected treasure, and a surge of fierce hope that there were other such unknown delights in life waiting to be discovered in the years to come. This time the climax had come sooner and he had noticed a drop of clear but sticky liquid appear. After that night, he never wore pyjamas again. It felt so much nicer being naked that he could no longer understand why anyone would want to wear the stupid things.

The discovery of this new joy naturally led fast to thoughts about its greater potential. He had already been taught that the purpose of his tool was future pleasure and procreation with girls, so he immediately became fascinated with them, aesthetically and physically, as had been practically impossible so long as sex was purely of theoretical interest to him. He longed more than anything to see a naked one, or just a picture of one, in order to better understand and anticipate the delights life now promised, but how? He was sure such pictures existed, because he had heard other boys talking about them, but where did they come from? Oh, why hadn't he listened more carefully? Again, he was surprised at his recent lack of interest. One had to be careful asking other boys this sort of thing, because they might know a lot more and make fun of one in front of all the others for being so backward.

Fortunately, Rupert was the boy in his year who seemed from his talk to know the most about the appeal of girls. Perhaps it had something to do with his father. Anyway, it was an example of that sophistication about worldly matters which had made him both more attractive and hitherto more intimidating as a friend.

Just recently, he had asked Alexander if he knew why all the boys' maids in the school were old and ugly.

"No," he replied intrigued, putting down the Rubik's Cube he had been toying with.

"Did you know James Bond went to Eton?"

"Yes."

"And did you know he was expelled?"

"No," he said in surprise. "What for?"

"For having it off with a boys' maid. Apparently in those days, which really means when Ian Fleming was here, they sometimes had quite young, pretty ones and Fleming had an affair with one too. Boys were caught several times, it must've been inevitable if an attractive woman was living in a house with fifty boys, so in the end they made a rule that boys' maids have to be over fifty."

Now that Alexander too was able to understand the fascination of girls, Rupert's worldly wisdom no longer seemed intimidating, just even more glamorous, so he wasted little time before broaching his question, while being careful to make it sound casual.

His misgivings about revealing his ignorance turned out to be unnecessary, as Rupert was simply delighted to find his friend shared his interest and chuffed to be his mentor in such a worthwhile subject. Both boys had long realised that Alexander was much the more intelligent of them, without of course being tactless enough to make it clear; the latter's newly revealed appreciation of Rupert's greater worldly knowledge thus established an equilibrium in their friendship which did much to cement it.

His enquiry was more immediately rewarded than he had dared to hope: with a mischievous grin, Rupert promptly pulled out the lower draw of his desk and lifted out several files to reveal a wad of glossy papers underneath. These turned out to be pages torn from magazines depicting totally naked people of both sexes and various ages, but mostly bronzed and fit young couples with children. They were walking and playing on idyllic beaches, their expressions happy, relaxed and without apparent hint of embarrassment. Astonished, and yet conscious of his thumping heart, he was unable to help his eye wandering in fascination to the tender, round breasts and most intimate parts of the young girls, all sights he had never beheld. He longed to peruse them without fear of his feelings being noticed; already he was aware of a stiffening that threatened to make a tent of his trousers and so belie his affected nonchalance. Turning slightly away from his friend, he gave the front of his trousers a short upwards tug that freed the evidence to jerk upwards from its dangerously horizontal posture and thwack into invisibility against the flat of his stomach. He diverted attention from this little manoeuvre by simultaneously asking with a disarming smile "Can I borrow these for a while?"

"Okay. Fine," answered Rupert with a knowing grin, "but bring them back."

15

As soon as he was alone in his own room, he pored over them with fascination. He soon decided which was the prettiest girl in all the pictures, a blond a year or so older than him. He tried to imagine what it would be like entering her and soon realised he wasn't going to be able to wait until lights out to relieve his excitement; he sat at his table, undid his flies and enjoyed his first wank to the image of a naked girl.

Calmer now, he returned to perusing the other pictures and considered the question which had been both baffling and exciting him since he first saw them. How and where could all these people be totally naked, looking so happy and free? Why had he never heard about such a thing before? A tremor of excitement went through him as he imagined being there himself with no clothes and no one minding. He imagined the beautiful girl was there too. They were throwing a frisbee back and forth. The girl missed catching and laughed, her teeth flashing white in magnificent contrast to her tanned skin, her blond hair blowing in the breeze. She couldn't care less that he was admiring her body and neither of them felt at all embarrassed by other people seeing them naked. Wow, what a fantastic feeling of freedom, of relief. Was there really a paradise like that? He didn't think the pictures could somehow be forged, but where could it possibly be? Would he be able to go there one day? It didn't look like England. In the end, the most likely explanation seemed to be that there was a secret country or island somewhere that only a few people knew about. It was a tremendously exciting prospect, not just in itself, but because it proved again there were truly wonderful things he knew nothing about just waiting to be discovered. The next day, he tried asking Rupert where the secret land was, but he seemed puzzled about it too. He yearned for someone who would know all the answers, but he couldn't think of any adult he would dare ask. He thought of his mother, but she would guess straight away that he wanted to go there, and what would she think? She probably wouldn't know anyway.

After a month or so of regular play, the drops of liquid that had concluded his first wanking turned to hot, vigorous jets. He wanked not only every night before falling asleep, but every morning on waking up and once or twice during the day too. If

16

he did not do it during the day too, his found his cock would stay stiff through his divs and it was quite impossible to keep visions of naked girls from invading his mind and destroying his concentration on even the most interesting lessons.

During one of Mr. Trotter's divs, Alexander was so lost in an erotic day-dream that the beak noticed he was not listening. Mr. Trotter got up from his desk and walked down the room while continuing to explain a passage from Caesar's *Gallic Wars*. Then he crept up behind Alexander, while making comical sweeps of his arms to heighten the anticipation of the other boys, and suddenly shouted in his ear, causing Alexander to jump with surprise, while the room erupted in laughter.

The novelty of both wanking and the naked pictures had worn off by now and he felt increasingly frustrated by his lack of progress in gaining enlightenment, until one Saturday in December when Rupert gave him exciting news: the next day his grown-up sister and some of her friends were going to take him out, and he thought her boyfriend was going to bring him some magazines with nothing but clear pictures of beautiful nude women.

He did not get a chance to see Rupert on Sunday evening, but the next morning, during Chambers, as elevenses was called, Rupert gave him a nudge.

"I've got them," he grinned mischievously. "Three. You can have one, okay?"

"Wow, thanks a lot. I can't wait," Alexander beamed back.

"Let's meet in my room after lunch."

"Okay."

As soon as lunch was over, the two boys ran up to Rupert's room together and Rupert brought out his treasure.

"Have a look through them all, but I'm keeping the one called *Playboy*."

There were women on the covers of all three magazines, though they were actually wearing skimpy pants rather than being nude. He opened one and leafed quickly past some advertisements and articles until he came to a full-page picture of a young woman wearing only tights, her legs spread invitingly open. His hands trembling with excitement, he turned the next few pages slowly. Then Rupert joined him and they

17

went through the magazines methodically, exchanging opinions on each woman's body. He could see why Rupert had chosen *Playboy*: more of the girls were beautiful, though there weren't so many full nudes, which he preferred. He soon decided he wanted the one called *Mayfair*, which had lots, and also had erotic adventure stories he couldn't wait to read.

Back alone in his own room and freer to linger on the most enticing pictures, he leafed through the Mayfair again. He allowed himself a few minutes to select the most exciting, after which he felt no doubt. It was of a dark-haired but very English-looking and beautiful nineteen-year-old called Lucy, a little reminiscent of his favourite actress, though sadly not that beautiful! She was on a bed on all fours, her bottom raised somewhat to emphasise its luscious curves, matched by those of her breasts, her face turned towards him welcomingly. He intended to enjoy this properly, so he carefully leaned the Mayfair nearly upright and open at that page, drew up his chair so he could sit under the flap of his burry, and undid his flies to release his long-erect cock. Then he imagined himself kneeling behind Lucy and plunging into the mound beneath the lovely buttocks. Only about twenty seconds later, he was shooting against the closed drawers of his burry in a series of splashes.

Then he resumed turning the pages and settled down to read with avid and practical fascination a section where a series of girls described how they were first seduced. His erection had never slackened, and though only ten minutes had passed, he knew he was ready for another wank. God it felt good! But his fleeting pleasure no longer made him feel happy, because he knew the real thing must be millions of times more satisfying. His lonely play was a regular reminder of the true fulfilment he was missing out on. When and how would he finally have it off with a girl? Did boys his age ever? Rupert thought so, and was optimistic that he would accomplish it himself within a couple of years, but Alexander was tormented with doubt.

The last week of the Half, snow settled on the ground and soon treacherous patches of ice had formed on the pavements, which the boys had carefully to side-step as they rushed between their "Trials", as the end-of-Half exams were called. The cold, dark evening following the last of them, Alexander trudged through the slush, clutching his notebook with a frozen hand, and torn between relief that Trials were over and worry he had not done as well as he hoped. Suddenly, he remembered with pleasure that, the day before, the dame had told a group of boys he had been hanging around with discussing *Worst Friends* that they would be welcome to watch the next episode in her sitting-room. It was a long-running television series and his favourite. It would begin in about ten minutes, so he began to run.

Afterwards, he went to the bathroom. As he washed his hands, he looked up in the mirror and smiled tentatively at himself, wondering whether the naked blond girl on the beach would find him attractive. He was not particularly vain and disliked boasting, but he could not help feeling some exhilaration and pride as he thought that in all honesty she ought to. He hoped she would agree that what he beheld in the mirror was a face of unusual beauty and grace. He saw a boy of thirteen with a dazzling smile of even, white teeth and luxuriant, slightly waved blond hair, and his naked chest and shoulders revealed a perfectly formed, boyish musculature. He probably wasn't nearly muscular enough yet to attract Lucy, but a girl near his age? Suddenly, Julian Smith burst into the bathroom, interrupting his reverie.

"Hi Alexander," he said with a friendly smile. Julian was three years older than him and had recently been elected to Debate, so he felt rather proud that he called him "Alexander" instead of "Aylmer". Generally, boys only used Christian names for their friends in their own year or a year or so off, and this suggestion of familiarity, so different from the tone of amused disdain older boys often used towards him, was flattering.

"Hi Julian," he replied. The first time he had thus replied, he had felt a little cocky using the older boy's Christian name, even though under the circumstances it would obviously have been most unfriendly not to, but they had said "Hi" to each other so many times now that he was long used to it. However, they had never said anything else to each other.

"What did you think about today's episode?" Julian asked. He had been one of the select seven who had chanced to be invited to watch *Worst Friends*.

"It was a bit depressing," he replied. "I mean it was so sad when Miss Isabella told Captain Charles she could never love him except like a brother."

"What do you think of Miss Isabella?"

"Oh, she's my favourite actress. I mean I know the character in the film isn't always very nice, but it's very well acted and she's so sexy."

"Yes, I agree she's ravishing," said Julian. "Do you know her real name?"

"Yes. Lucretia Pelham."

"Have you seen her in anything else?"

"No, I'm afraid not."

They chatted on for several minutes until the bell rang for supper time and they rushed downstairs.

Alexander felt pleased when he thought about their conversation afterwards. Julian was really nice. He had talked to him as if they were equal and seemed to take his opinions seriously. It had felt as though they could almost be friends. He had never had nearly such a long conversation with any other "upper" boy. Also, he couldn't at all explain why, but somehow he had begun to feel even more confident of his good looks while he was talking to Julian. It was odd. Now that he came to think about it, it wasn't the first time Julian's presence had in some mysterious way made him feel more self-confident, despite their having never spoken before. Apart from his mild pride that Julian called him "Alexander", he had never consciously thought about him before this evening, but now that he did, he wondered why he was so often in the bathroom. Also, why was he one of those who liked to hang around the lobby where boys stopped to chat, yet never seemed to say anything himself? It was all a bit mysterious, but never mind, there was so much in life he didn't understand yet and he just had to hope time would clear up the mysteries for him.

II: Escape from the Past

I will not cease from Mental Fight,
Nor shall my Sword sleep in my hand:
Till we have built Jerusalem,
In England's green & pleasant Land.
   William Blake, in the preface to *Milton a Poem*

If any of the boys who knew Julian Smith had been asked what he was like, they would have said he was a nice guy and probably have left it at that, because there was really nothing remarkable or different that anyone knew about him. He was kind, but quiet and reserved. He was intelligent, but only averagely so for a school from which the imbalance of demand for places with supply had long excluded the mediocre. He was quite ordinary looking, a little below average height with wavy dark brown hair and thick spectacles. He had friends, but no close ones.

If, however, anyone had suggested to Julian that he was just an ordinary Etonian, he would have profoundly disagreed, though he would not have said so, because he was deeply embarrassed by what he felt set him apart from his schoolfellows.

In the first place, there was his background. Etonians were probably no more or less snobbish than the average Englishman, but that could still be quite a bit, and exposure as a "yob" could bring misery to a sensitive child. About half the boys in the school had fathers who had been there, and most of the remainder came from families either as obviously upper-class or nearly so. Apart from some offspring of *nouveaux riches* spectacularly wealthy enough to make up for it, that just left some of the boys in College, the house for scholars, many of whom came from humbler backgrounds. However, they were generally proud or at least unashamed of their background, and indeed they had few grounds for feeling insecure, living as they did, grouped together as the intellectual elite of a school that valued excellence above all.

Julian felt himself to be possibly unique in that he was working class and neither rich nor academically brilliant, and he

21

was deeply sensitive about it, much more than he need have been.

His father, Alfred Smith, was not even English, much as he would have liked to have been, though his membership of the working class was the result of misfortune rather than birth. He had been born Alfred Wertheimber, one of the three children of Dr. Eduard Wertheimber, a distinguished and well-off professor of zoology at Heidelberg University. Dr. Wertheimber was of Jewish origin, but his family had converted to Lutheranism when he was a small child. As a young man in the early twenties, he had taken part in a well-known voyage of exploration in the Moluccas. When he came home to Frankfurt, he found himself to be a minor celebrity and invited to an endless string of fashionable parties. At one, he had met and fallen in love with a girl called Magdalene Pfennig. She was extraordinarily beautiful and impeccably Aryan. He did not hide his Jewish origins from her and there was no need. In her fashionable set, it was considered passé to be anti-semitic. His glamour as an explorer and his money were far more interesting. They married a month later. In the end, it turned out to be the worst mistake of his life, for he was an intellectual while her interests were limited to parties and fashionable clothes. They moved to Heidelberg, where he was soon made a senior lecturer, and had two daughters besides Alfred.

At first, they were reasonably happy, but with time and the rise of National Socialism their marriage began to fall apart. It was becoming less fashionable every day to have such a husband, and, one by one, all of Magdalene's old friends stopped answering her calls. As her beauty faded, the professor knew deep down that he had allowed it to cloud his judgment and they were really ill suited, but he would never acknowledge it. He believed in marriage and adored his children, who worshipped him and were far closer to him than to their mother, who had little interest in children and nothing of interest to say to them. When he was deprived of his job on racial grounds, in conformity with the Nuremburg Laws, their marriage was doomed. Even his wealth was drying up now.

Though Dr. Wertheimber had aspired to be a good German as a young man, he had never been a nationalist. Rather, the country he admired above all was England, where he had several zoologist friends with whom he maintained an extensive correspondence. The Great War had been deeply painful to him, though he had fought bravely for his fatherland, even being awarded a Knight's Cross with sword of the order of the Zähringer Lion for his valour. Afterwards, he had been the leading advocate in Heidelberg of restoring Anglo-German friendship, encouraging university exchanges and visiting England thrice himself.

Alfred and his sisters imbibed their father's ideas from infancy. They learned that England was better ruled than other countries because she was run by gentlemen who understood fair play. She had never had a violent revolution like the French or the Russians because English gentlemen played cricket with their peasants. Dr. Wertheimber had witnessed that for himself at the country house of one of his wealthier correspondents during his first visit. Above all, the English were far too reasonable to put up with being ruled by a vulgar fanatic like the Führer.

After losing his job, he entreated his wife again and again to let them all emigrate to England. One of his friends at University College, London had promised he could get him a job there, but Magdalene would not hear of it. She had always regarded her husband's anglophilia as a foible at best. She knew little about England and was interested less. It was terribly unfair of him to expect her, a true German whose only brother had died fighting for his country, to have to abandon her fatherland and relations to go and live someone where she did not speak a word of the language and would probably be regarded with hostility. One day, Alfred came home from school in tears with "Mischling! Mischling!" or half-caste ringing in his ears and joined in his father's pleas, and she lost her temper completely.

Against all his anguished entreaties, she moved out one day soon afterwards, went back to the safe tedium of her father's farming estate in Baden, and obtained a divorce. She had not been able to face saying good-bye to her children, and left while they were at school. Alfred was ten. His mother lived on more than thirty years, but Alfred did not simply not forgive her. He never spoke of her again in his life.

His father was arrested after the Night of Broken Glass, a few months later, and taken to Buchenwald. He came back after three months, but utterly broken in health as well as spirit. Alfred's elder sister Alice, though only fifteen herself, was already used to acting as mother to her younger siblings and now did her best to comfort their father, who was beyond looking after himself, let alone them.

Finally, as the war clouds gathered, Dr. Wertheimber roused himself from his despondency to write an impassioned plea for peace and took it to one of his old colleagues with pleas for urgent publication in the university journal. Three days later, a Gestapo van slowed down as it passed a crowd standing mesmerised before a large billboard announcing that Great Britain had just declared war. Then it ground to a halt before the block of flats where the Wertheimbers lived. The professor went quietly, though his children pleaded and cried in vain.

The Gestapo came back the next day. The officer in charge told them their father had hung himself in his prison cell the night before. Alfred never learned whether it was true or not. They were told they had to be taken into care now that they had no one to look after them at home. Alice did her best to reassure Alfred and their little sister Gerta and hugged them both tight all through the train journey that night. The next morning, they arrived at an enormous camp someone said was called Sachsenhausen. When they reached the head of the queue in the reception room, Alfred was told to go in a different direction to his sisters. He refused and clung to Alice until an SS man came up to him and knocked him flat onto the ground with the back of his hand. He lay there unable to move for a while, but he heard his sisters' screams as they were dragged away. He cried all that day, and the next, then he stopped.

He never saw his sisters again.

When Alfred looked back on his time at Sachsenhausen and Bergen-Belsen, whither he was transferred after three years, the only things he could bear to think about much were the things that had given him hope, the vital element in the will to survive. In his case, these amounted to his quasi-religious belief that one day his chosen people, the English, would come to punish the Germans for their crimes and take him to England, his father's promised land, and the preparation he made for his future there. His father had given him a good grounding in English, and all through the grim years of his imprisonment, he sought to improve it with whatever other inmates he found could speak it. It provided a distraction from the harsh reality around him. In the end, he had a good grasp of the language, though, since none of his teachers were English, his accent remained incorrigibly German.

The last few weeks were the only ones he could bear to think about in detail because the glimmer of hope he had felt had finally been realised. One by one, the cruellest SS guards tellingly disappeared and new recruits had to be brought in to replace them until the Allies arrived.

Nevertheless, however fine a saying "all's well that ends well" was when looking back on his past, it contorted how he had felt at the time. They had probably in fact been the worst weeks. The hope all the prisoners could not help feeling at the knowledge that the fall of the Reich was imminent was easily counterbalanced by new fears. Besides fearful rumours the SS intended to finish them all off rather than let them fall into the hands of the allies, a horrific epidemic of typhus looked likely to kill them all before they could be liberated. The prisoners were in fact dying so fast that any order for their extermination would have been superfluous. The problem of the guards was how to dispose of the bodies fast enough. They lay rotting everywhere, in piles on the ground, in uncovered ditches and in their bunkers where they had died, in many cases their bodies intertwined with those of the still just living.

One morning, all the prisoners like Alfred who were still well enough to work, were rounded up and assigned to spending the whole day methodically burying the corpses in mass graves. They had to avoid touching them, rotting and riddled with open sores as they were, if they were not inevitably to catch typhus too. Some were given blankets which they could wrap round the bodies to drag them along, but most had only odd strips of cloth, rope or leather which they had to tie round the dead limbs, their guards keeping now a certain distance to avoid contagion as they looked on. Alfred had still mercifully not fallen sick, but he was frightfully emaciated and faint with hunger. As the day wore on, his fear grew that he too would collapse and be left to die right there of starvation and cold. He survived the ordeal, but only to find it repeated the next day and the next.

On the morning of the fifth such day, they had just started their gruesome task, when Alfred noticed a jeep driving towards them. As it drew closer, he saw the uniforms were unfamiliar, neither SS nor Wehrmacht, and he let go of his strip of dirty cloth to stand up and stare in wonder and sudden hope.

The three SS men supervising them were facing the prisoners and had not noticed the jeep yet. Seeing Alfred momentarily idle, the Obersturmführer stepped towards him, drew back his whip and lashed him. The whip caught him in a diagonal line from his hip to his neck and he crumpled in agony. He was ordered to get up at once and go back to work.

The jeep suddenly sped up. The SS men could hear it now and turned round. It ground to a halt a few metres away. Soldiers leapt out of it led by their captain. Alfred again stood up to stare.

The young captain's face was pale and rigid with the shock of what he had just seen and he felt himself ready at any moment to vomit with the unbelievable stench everywhere in the camp.

"Stop that at once!" he shouted in English, and the language sounded like music in Alfred's ears. "You, all three of you, drop your weapons, and take their places!" he said angrily to the SS men, pointing at the prisoners who had all now stopped dragging the bodies and stood up straight. The five other British soldiers were pointing their sten guns at the SS, itching to use them. The two SS troopers did drop their rifles at once and their Obersturmführer dropped his whip, but otherwise they just stood still looking at the Englishman blankly.

"Sprechen Sie englisch?" the captain asked the crowd of prisoners in a strong English accent that caused Alfred to smile unstintingly for the first time in years. He was extraordinarily handsome, with dark hair and an open, honest and very English face, Alfred thought, rather reminiscent of the hero in the *The Divorce of Lady X*, the last film his father had taken him to see before Jews were banned from cinemas.

"I can a little," said Alfred eagerly, stepping forward.

26

"Jolly good. Tell these bastards to take your places burying the corpses, and get going at once." Alfred translated with relish.

The Obersturmführer's face whitened with rage. "Nein!" he said.

The captain drew his revolver The SS officer turned to Alfred, his fury heightened by having to address the Englishman through a Jew, and told him to say that neither he nor his men would do any such thing. Forced labour for prisoners of war was a violation of the Geneva Convention. Alfred thought he managed a reasonable translation.

"Tell him they are under martial law and any refusal to obey orders is mutiny," replied the captain immediately and Alfred duly translated.

"Nein, nein, nein!" said the Obersturmführer angrily.

The captain raised his revolver and cocked it, pointing it straight at the man's forehead. "Tell him to get started right now or I shall fire." The other British soldiers looked on in eager anticipation. They were all longing to be allowed to act on their shock and disgust at what they had seen.

This time the Obersturmführer did not wait for Alfred's translation. "Nein, Sie..."

The captain fired and Alfred saw blood begin to ooze out of the hole in the centre of the SS officer's forehead in the second before his body fell to the ground. The captain turned his revolver towards one of the troopers. Both troopers hastily bent down by one of the corpses to drag it off. The captain strode forward towards Alfred. It was lucky that the youth who could speak English, though shockingly thin, was one of the few who had no visible sores, boils or other signs of sickness, he thought, as he held out his hand, trembling from the shock of the action it had just performed.

"How do you do?" he said and smiled tensely. "I'm Julian Holland."

"My name is Alfred Wertheimber," he replied shaking the hand.

"Would you mind acting as my interpreter?"

"No, it will be my great pleasure," replied Alfred. At first, it felt strange being treated courteously by someone in uniform,

27

but he soon got used to it, as a camaradie between them developed quickly. They could hardly have had more different backgrounds, but that was just why they were so interesting to each other.

Captain Holland was shaken to the core by what he saw at Bergen-Belsen. He was only twenty-five and still impressionable, and he felt sure he would never get over the horror. He wanted to know more, to try to begin to understand what he could not. Many of his fellow officers could not wait to get away from the area, to try to forget all about it, but Holland felt an urge to do his best, little though that might be, to try to mitigate the horrors. He therefore applied for occupation duties at the nearby army camp whither the surviving inmates were transferred over the coming days.

For his part, Alfred felt in awe of the young man who, though not many years older than him, seemed to epitomise everything he had learned to idolise: modesty, courage, fair play, decency, honesty, in short the virtues of an English gentleman. He longed to know more about his life, how he came to be what he was. At first, the captain felt embarrassed by his interest. He knew himself to have had a privileged life which he had done nothing to deserve, and his story was anyway dull, but Alfred's fascination in it was so genuine that his embarrassment soon turned to amusement and he relented. Thus it was that Alfred first heard of Eton and Balliol, croquet and punting on the Cherwell.

One day Alfred asked him if he thought anything like the holocaust could ever conceivably happen in England.

"No, I don't honestly believe it could," replied the young captain earnestly after a pause, and Alfred believed him, not thinking his judgement was unduly affected by patriotism.

During the following year, the thoughts of almost all the inmates turned towards emigration and those who were luckier in their contacts began to be resettled. When Holland understood Alfred's determination to go to England, rather than the much more popular choices of Palestine or America, he helped him.

The reality of life in post-war Britain was not quite as Alfred had imagined. His education had been brutally terminated when he was eleven and there was little opportunity to do anything about it now that he was eighteen. Having no money, he was obliged to take the first work he could find, as a loader for a removal company. Affable and charming people like Holland had featured prominently in his dreams of life in England, but most of the people he came across in the East End of London, where he found himself living, were rather different. He often felt bitter that none of them understood him or had any concept of what he had been through. He was never able to overcome his strong German accent and was frequently called a "bloody kraut". But what was perhaps worst was that he gradually became aware that the gulf between him and his new compatriots widened rather than narrowed the more they were like the sort of people he had dreamed of. This came largely down to his lack of social graces. During his first couple of years in England, he found it impossible to break his concentration camp habit of grabbing food and wolfing it down with his hands as soon as it was before him. Gradually he became aware of the disgust this aroused in people who witnessed it, especially those more like Captain Holland in their manners, and he largely overcame it. All through his life though, he was unable to avoid a feeling approaching panic whenever the dishes of food were too far away from him during shared meals.

During his first three years in London, he and Captain Holland had exchanged occasional letters until at last Holland said he was coming home. They had always planned a reunion when this happened and Alfred looked forward to it immensely. At last, one chilly October day, he turned up as arranged for lunch at Holland's club in Pall Mall. He had of course never been to a gentleman's club before and had no idea what to expect. When he arrived, wrapped tightly in a great overcoat and scarf, he felt at once awed by the magnificent façade of the building. He went in and told the porter he had come to see Captain Holland. The porter looked at him askance, but sent a boy to tell the Captain. Meanwhile, Alfred looked around and saw to his horror that every single man there was dressed in a smart suit. He did not even have a suit and though he was wearing his best clothes under his overcoat, they did not at all resemble one.

"May I take your coat, Sir?" said the porter stiffly, as if he had read Alfred's thoughts.

"No thank you." Fortunately, at that moment Holland arrived.

"Alfred, my dear chap. How wonderful to see you again after all this time," he said, beaming with pleasure. "Do come through and have a drink. Wouldn't you like to take your coat off?"

"Oh, no thank you." It was well heated in the room they first went to and even more so in the dining-room. Alfred began to sweat profusely. Holland was as charming as ever and chatted away vivaciously. Alfred longed to open up to him like in the old days, but he found it nearly impossible to tear his eyes away from the tasty roast chicken on his plate. He cut it into tiny slices and forced himself to wait between eating each one, but he was still left sweating in front of an empty plate, while the loquacious Captain had hardly begun his. Holland sensed his discomfort and worriedly asked him again if he was quite sure he did not want to take his coat off.

"No, no thank you," he said again and glanced miserably at the three impeccably-dressed young men at the next table exchanging a flood of witticisms in their upper-class drawl.

Afterwards he felt wretchedly guilty at having been so dull-spirited at the longed-for meeting. Though Holland told him earnestly to invite himself again, he could never bring himself to do so, despite the great tenderness he still felt for his kind old friend. He knew that even if he saved up for months to buy himself a fine suit, he would never look or talk like the others in the club. It might just have been possible if only his family had emigrated before the war, but it was far too late now. The club became a symbol of the gulf between what he had always longed to be and what he always would be, and too painful a memory to bear reliving.

Thoughts of what was too late for him soon drifted to what might still be for his own child, if, as he very much hoped, he ever had one. Others might have easily dismissed such thoughts as idle fantasy if they were ever burdened with them at all, but though Alfred was poorly educated, he was highly imaginative, and the vicissitudes of his life had not inclined him to rein in his thoughts as to what was possible.

As the years passed and he came to terms with the fact that he would never be a weekend guest at an English country house as his father had been, a dream began to take hold of his life that he would one day have a son who not only would be, but for whom it would be a mundane aspect of his daily life. It was the most fitting tribute he could think of to his father, the person he had loved and looked up to most in his life, to make sure his own child, the only grandchild his father would have to carry his genes into posterity, would epitomise everything he had taught him to admire. When his son grew up to be like Julian Holland, then he would know that neither he nor his father had lived in vain.

He knew that if his dream were to be realised, it largely came down to having enough money, which was a tall order for a removals driver, as he soon became, but one thing he had learnt was endurance. He drove every shift he was allowed to and rented a small room in a boarding-house, so his expenses were minimal. After seven years, he had saved enough to open his own removal company with a little office, large van, a secretary and another worker. At times, he got worn down with loneliness or self-doubt and wondered if he was mad to be attempting something so fantastical, but always he would remind himself of how he had survived the concentration camps against all the odds, and he stayed faithful to his dreams.

More and yet more years of relentless hard work passed by, and he was nearly forty by the time he got married. Denise Smith was a plain woman with a strong Cockney accent, but she was impeccably English in her own way, she was practical and determined like him, and she had quite a good job with the Bermondsey social services. She had given up hope of marrying by the time she met him, as she was already in her mid-thirties, and she had always wanted a baby before it was too late. They could not say they were in love, but then neither of them was burdened with silly, romantic illusions. He accepted and approved of her continuing to have her own life. She found Fred to be a decent, hard-working husband, and they were happy enough together. She was a feminist and did not want to change her surname, and he was only too delighted to take hers, as he was sick of being thought German.

One thing he did not dare tell her was how terribly important to his aspirations it was that the baby they planned was a son. In a rare act of extravagance, he consulted an eminent specialist, who advised him that influencing the sex of a baby-to-be mostly came down to careful timing. He therefore restricted his amorous attentions to Denise to a few successive days of each month until his mission was accomplished. This did not matter to them, as sex had never been going to be a big part of their lives together, though she thought it a little odd that he had such sudden bursts of over-attentiveness.

Even before the baby was born or its sex known, Alfred had to put his name down for a tentative place at Eton if "it" were to have a chance of going there. The only way he could think of to achieve this with confidence of success involved tracking down and eliciting the help of a surprised Captain Holland, now an insurance broker in the City. He had been reluctant to do so, as it ran counter to his old dream of contacting him again only in another twenty years. He had passed many happy moments imagining himself turning up then at Holland's club, his grown-up son by his side, and relishing his old friend's astonishment when he introduced his son to him as a finished product of the best England had to offer.

Alfred had hoped the vast sums of money he envisioned spending on his child would not be needed for thirteen years, so he was put out to be advised in terms that did not really admit non-acceptance that it was impractical and "not done" to send a boy to Eton from a state school, however good a one. Fortunately, he was eventually able to find a prep school, albeit not of the best, that was agreeable to accepting his child for two years rather than the usual five.

Denise was entirely sympathetic to her husband's aspirations for their child, even though she had no illusions about the incessant hard work it would entail for him and the economies they would both have to make. Much of her thinking and time was devoted to the empowerment of women and the destruction of the old patriarchal culture of deference in favour of equality. As an emancipated woman, she had little more to win for herself, but winning for her child the opportunities that had for millennia been reserved for over-privileged toffs was immensely appealing.

As planned, Julian was their only child. His father had little to do with his early upbringing. He was out working every day, including weekends and some nights too. He now had a lorry as well as a van and three strong workers, but he always worked alongside them and pulled more than his own weight. They reckoned him as one of their mates even though he rarely went for a beer with them.

Alfred never spent money on anything he thought unnecessary and Denise spent little more. They never once went on a holiday or even just a weekend away. They had no car and no video player or any of the other electronic goodies virtually every family in Britain now had. They did not even have a television until Julian was seven, more than a decade after most households had one. Every penny possible had to be saved for Julian to go to Eton.

When Julian was four, like many middle-class parents anxious for their children's education, but unable or unwilling to send them to private schools, they moved to Wandsworth, a leafy suburb of London where the proportion of middle-class children was so high that Julian was bound to learn to speak in a reasonably posh accent. Alfred carefully encouraged Julian's friendships with children who had satisfactory accents and quietly discouraged the others. A shift was now underway in which of his parents gave Julian most attention. As Alfred's confidence grew that the necessary capital was going to be built in time, he allowed himself a little time off. He devoted it all to his son, both study and play, and relished every moment. Julian was the only person he truly loved and he had no hopes that did not involve him.

By the time he went to Eton, Julian fully understood and was in awed gratitude for what his father had accomplished for him. He also loved him deeply, much more than he did his mother. They were equally at home for him now, for his father took the weekday afternoons off during most of his school holidays, but otherwise they were very different parents. His father worked to live and came home for Julian, whereas his mother lived for her work. When she came home, she took good enough care of him in a practical way, but her mind was still focussed on her career, which had apparently started going unexpectedly well.

Proud of his father as he secretly was, after three years at Eton, Julian lived in terror of the other boys finding out too much about the social backgrounds of either of his parents.

In their house at school, there was just one public telephone the boys could use. If their parents wanted to talk to them, they had to call that phone and ask whichever boy happened to answer it to fetch their son.

When he was a new boy, his mother had called once. At tea time the boys met together in messes, small groups of friends, to eat cereal and biscuits, or sometimes scrambled egg, in one of the boys' rooms. As the new boys did not initially know anyone, their dame put them quite arbitrarily into two groups. It so happened that Guy Cowburn, the boy who answered Denise Smith on the telephone, was in Julian's mess. What was awful luck, though, was that Cowburn was a bully with a gift for turning other boys against his victims. For this reason, Julian had tried hard to make him think he liked him.

The next day, Julian had arrived after the others. He had run most of the way back from the schoolroom, and paused before the door to catch his breath before opening it.

"Sow, wot did yer suy to 'er?" he heard James Crichton ask.

"Owh, Oi just said Oi'll troi to foind 'im for yer," replied Cowburn.

The beginning of a horrid idea began to take shape in his mind, but he didn't yet make too much of it. They often tried mimicking different accents. Yesterday they had all been American. But, as he went into the room, he realised it must be aimed at him, because everyone suddenly fell into silence. James's face reddened and he looked a bit ashamed, but Cowburn and his best friend Peter Leigh were, on the contrary, trying to suppress their laughter. Julian felt his own face redden, as the silence continued. Leigh was bent over and had tears coming out of his eyes from his efforts not to laugh.

"Sow, 'ow's yer mum then, Smiv?" said Cowburn suddenly and very deliberately, cracking up at his own joke, and Leigh exploded into uncontrolled laughter. Julian did not know what to do. He could feel the tears coming and he knew he would not be able to control them for many more seconds.

"Oh crikey! I've left my essay for Mr. Rogers in the div room," he exclaimed, slapping his hand over his eyes as if in exasperation, but really to hide the tears that had already appeared, and he rushed out of the room and ran back to his own. There he went under his table, pulled the cloth down so he could not be seen in case anyone came in looking for him, and cried his eyes out. He could only stay there twenty minutes because he had another div coming soon. Afterwards, he somehow managed to make it to the bathroom without anyone seeing him. He washed his face thoroughly to hide the signs of his tears, and the cold water also helped him bring his emotions under control.

That evening, he cried again until his grief was exhausted and then he thought hard what to do. He would gladly have killed Cowburn, he hated him so much. He imagined what he would do if he met him alone on a cliff and sporadically pursued other fantasies of revenge, but always his mind returned to the central problem of what really to do. Soon Cowburn would spread the word around the house. Everyone would treat him with contempt for his whole five years at Eton. He knew he ought to be able to laugh it off, but he also knew he could not: it hurt too much. Had he been older and wiser, he might have realised that most of the boys would be merely a bit curious about his unusual background and the snobs would soon get bored of teasing him more than occasionally, but he was only thirteen.

He tried to think what his father would tell him to do. He even considered telling him, but he did not think he would really understand how much it mattered. His father was so sure of English gentlemen's fair play. If he did understand, it could only upset him, and anyway, what could he do about it? He guessed he would advise him to go to his housemaster. It was true the latter would be sympathetic and give Cowburn a hell of a blowing-up. Mr. Hodgson considered himself a socialist and immensely trendy for holding leftist views in the midst of such wealth and privilege, so Julian's cause was perfectly attuned to attracting his full support. But what could Mr. Hodgson really achieve? He would not be able to punish Cowburn because Cowburn would pretend his putting on an accent had nothing to do with Julian or his mother. Cowburn would hate him for ever,

35

and though he might fear to be too obvious in his persecution, every boy he knew would know within a day that he was a "yob" with a Cockney mother, and the mockery would always be ready to rise to the surface.

He thought too about leaving Eton and just going home, but not seriously. It was out of the question. Nothing would ever make up for the pain he knew it would cause his father, who had given up his whole life to getting him into Eton. Also, in most ways he liked the school very much and had himself great hopes for his future there.

No, there was only one possible solution, and deep down he thought he had known it all along. He would have to act really well, and pretend it had not been his mother who telephoned. She would be indignant if she knew, but she need never know.

The next day was a half day when the boys were free in the afternoon, so Julian spent it in his room practising again and again what he was going to do, and concentrating on how to control his emotions.

He went for tea deliberately late this time, to be sure all the boys in the mess would be there. Then he walked straight in and poured himself a bowl of frosties.

"Luyt agin, Smiv. Where've yer been, then?" asked Cowburn, and Leigh sniggered.

"Oi've just been down to Windsor to 'ave a look at the birds," answered Julian.

"Owh, and did yer meet yer mum there boi any chance?"

"Moi mum?? Wot the bloody 'ell 'as she got to do wiv it?" asked Julian, hoping he had managed to disguise any tremors in his voice.

"Well, it sounded loik she was missing yer so badly."

"Wot? You've spowken to moi mum?"

"Yea. Down't yer remember? She telephowned two duys agow."

Julian paused and contrived to look first puzzled and then as though comprehension had finally dawned on him.

"Oh now I understand! That wasn't my mother. That was my old nanny," he said in his usual accent. "Yer roight. She does spuyk a bit loik that." James gave him a friendly glance, but it was the look of disappointment on Cowburn's face that

36

convinced him his acting had been good. He finished his cereal and went out of the room.

That evening he telephoned home and beseeched his parents not to telephone again. He would call them regularly, he promised, but boys who got telephoned became awfully unpopular, as everyone minded going to fetch them.

That had happened three years ago, but so abiding was his fear that his parents might telephone again and ruin him irreparably by saying who they were too, that he really had called home at least on alternate days ever since.

At first, he had thought that perhaps it might not have mattered if it had been his father who telephoned with his strong foreign accent, but a tiny incident in his second year had confirmed him in his general wariness.

Julian was chatting to James Crichton, with whom he was by then friends, about the film *The Odessa File*, while they enjoyed a large tin of shortbread biscuits he was generously sharing with him.

"Some of my ancestors were Jews," said Julian, thinking it just a mildly interesting remark under the circumstances of talking about a holocaust film.

"Well, you certainly don't act like one!" replied James heartily, holding up a shortbread triangle as if to toast him.

III: Secret Yearnings

A mighty pain to love it is,
And 'tis a pain that pain to miss;
But of all pains, the greatest pain
It is to love, but love in vain.
  Abraham Cowley, *Anacreontiques*

Now a second difference between Julian and most of the other boys at Eton had arisen, and he feared it was just as serious. Julian was in love with another boy. He admitted that to himself, though he thought he might kill himself if anyone else knew.

The boy of course was Alexander Aylmer. He had noticed him immediately the Half began, and felt overwhelmed by his flawless beauty and gracefulness, his dazzling vitality and warmth. That first time he had caught sight of him, the unexpectedness of it had left him stunned, as if he had suffered a physical blow, and every further sudden intrusion of his presence hurt.

Since he was a new boy, Julian had been painfully aware of the greater prevalence of physical beauty at Eton than in Wandsworth, where he thought he had looked as good as the average boy in the street. Whenever he went home and encountered his old acquaintances, he was struck by how often they were gawky, short or flabby compared with what he had become used to. Centuries of breeding and healthy living had resulted in tall, fit and facially beautiful boys being plentiful at Eton, but Alexander stood out from the others far more sharply than they themselves stood out from the common herd.

It was an example of Julian's over-sensitivity that he was so ready to believe the other boys would utterly despise him if they knew the truth. There was in fact a general aura of mild sensuality between the oldest and youngest boys in the school, from which only the least sexualised of the older boys and the plainest younger boys were entirely excluded, but it was restrained by fear of what others would think and only rarely grew to self-conscious sexual longing. Alexander took this further, for he was an example of those very rare boys just so devastatingly beautiful that they aroused a latent pederastic urge in even many of their elders who had hitherto been entirely impervious to such attractions.

A more experienced observer of youths at play, himself emotionally detached from the scene, would have noticed a subtle change that came over some of the older boys whenever they found themselves in Alexander's sight and hearing: a greater tendency to bravado and jollity, an unconscious sort of showing off. And if the same observer had ever experienced the conscious feelings for a boy that Julian felt for Alexander, then he would know at once, better than they did themselves, to what cause such showing off should be ascribed. But Julian was inexperienced and far from detached, so he saw and understood nothing of this, and thought only of the difference between himself and the others.

It was not the first time he had fancied a younger boy, but it was the first time he had fallen in love. Once he had thought he just liked girls, then, when he admitted to himself his attraction to boys, he had thought of them as a supplementary taste, which had come into temporary prominence due to his living in an all-boys' school. It was only when he saw Alexander and reviewed his life in the light of his new passion, that he suspected he had unconsciously always preferred boys. Had not for him the boy of around thirteen or fourteen always been the summit of human perfection, combining as he did for just a few precious years the soft, tender sweetness and exuberant enthusiasm of the child with a carefully measured pinch of the heavy spice of manhood, and crowned as he was with a sexuality far more powerful than either?

Or alternatively, in debunking his former self-perception as someone fascinated by girls and uninterested in boys in favour of one that fitted better with his new obsession, was he rewriting his own history at the cost of the truth?

James Crichton, who was doing Russian for A-levels, told him a story about *The Great Soviet Encyclopaedia*. After Stalin's death, a man called Beria had briefly been the most powerful figure in the USSR and had therefore been accorded an extremely long article in the national encyclopaedia, which had to present the approved view of the time. Just as it was about to go to press,

39

Beria was overthrown and shot. Hence his biography had to be expunged too. Since it was too late to change the pagination of the whole series of volumes, they had appeared with the following article on the Bering Straits stretched to absurd length to include the pages formerly allotted to the abolished man.

It was a worrying idea that historical truth was so fragile, and Julian tried hard to remember how he had really felt.

When he was twelve, he had gone to stay for a few days in the summer holidays with his best friend of the time in wild countryside in Wiltshire. William Temple, his friend, had already told the boys in their prep school dormitory a sensational story.

William's oldest friends at home were a neighbouring brother and sister: Tarquin, aged thirteen, and Laura, aged twelve and on whom William had a crush. During the previous holidays, he had stayed overnight in their house. Early in the morning, before their parents awoke, he had gone into their bedroom to chat and found them together in Laura's bed.

"I was amazed," continued William, "but they didn't seem embarrassed at all. I asked if their parents knew and they said of course not. Then they said I did swear to keep it secret didn't I, so I said 'Yes, of course. You know you're my best friends. There's no way I would ever tell on you.' Then they told me everything quite openly. Every night as soon as they hear their parents go to bed, Tarquin climbs into Laura's bed and fucks her, then they sleep together and do it again in the morning, and their parents don't have a clue. I can't blame Tarquin because Laura is so sexy I'd give anything to have a go with her. I've often thought of asking Tarquin, but I haven't had the courage yet. Maybe I will." He paused for a while. "I just don't know if he'd mind. There's got to be a chance he wouldn't. After all, we are good friends."

The other boys in the dormitory had listened to the story in enthralled silence and Julian wondered what they thought. He himself felt awed that children near him in age were so much more advanced than him in experience, and a little jealous even of William for his possible opportunity.

Julian was in any case fascinated and looked forward with great curiosity to meeting them, which he did the first day of his stay. Not having a sister, Julian had not been sure how odd it was for a brother and sister to want to bed one another, but as soon as he saw them, he was well able to understand why, if any pair of siblings should feel thus tempted, this one would. Laura was pretty indeed, and Tarquin was easily the best-looking boy he had ever seen. It was agony imagining them entwined naked in loving embrace, so vibrantly beautiful that they made Julian feel like a toad.

He felt more jealous of them than he ever had of anybody in his life, but what he could not explain to himself when he thought about it further was that the jealousy he felt was more of the girl than of the boy.

They had gone to a lake and Julian had watched mesmerised as Tarquin stripped down to his pants and dived expertly in, his tanned muscles glistening in the sunshine when he rose to the surface. All four of them had raced across the lake. Tarquin had easily won and even Laura had outstripped Julian, hard as he had tried. Then they had had a foot race and Julian had watched miserably as the lithe body of the slightly older boy had shot ahead of him like a young god, further and further into the distance, his chestnut hair blowing in the wind behind him. Julian had never felt so inadequate and childish. He had not reached puberty and had never heard of homosexual love, and he wondered if what he felt was jealousy of Tarquin's beauty, agility and daring, as well as his sexual experience. There was no doubt he would love to have Tarquin's body instead of his own, but somehow this was not nearly enough to explain the deep, but suppressed longing that disturbed him for the rest of his time with them.

One had to be careful not to read too much into the past with the benefit of hindsight, but Julian also remembered the special excitement he had got the summer holidays of the next year, when puberty had dawned, of wanking in front of the full-length mirror in his bedroom. He thought at the time that the extra excitement had come from the mirror's help in filling in half of the picture he supposed he wanted to visualise of himself with a girl, but now he wondered if that had been an illusion.

As he had turned and turned to look at himself from different angles, had it not really been the narrow hips of his own lissom body that had excited him so much, the slender muscles that had grown just enough over the last year to hint at his new virility, that subtle but vital change in physique that had been part of Tarquin's superiority to him? When he admired his own erection, had not the real appeal been the beauty of his organ, stiff and silky-smooth, at that age of transitory perfection between the weedy immaturity of the eleven-year-old and the incipient grossness of the sixteen-year-old he now was? Or was he just imagining that now that he was in love with a thirteen-year-old?

Just after that, he had gone to Eton. He remembered how when Cowburn had mocked his mother, one of the things that had hurt most was that James Crichton had initially joined in. He had thought at the time that that was just because he liked him, though they had not yet become friends, but now he suspected that the special pain had been because James had been the best-looking of his fellow new boys in the house.

Throughout his first two years at Eton, he had been just as enthusiastic as the others about girls. He joined in their chat about sex, and he bought and shared girlie magazines like them. It was only towards the end of E, when he was fifteen, that he realised there was something sexual about his liking younger boys. Most of his friends then were in F, but he had not thought that had any significance. In the Summer Half, however, two new boys had arrived to form F delta, an extra mini block that formed the nucleus of what would be the real F block in the next academic year. They were therefore thirteen and one of them, Francis Ashcombe, was very good-looking, slim with blond hair and rosy cheeks, a sort of poor version of Alexander. Julian's friends in F acted as a bridge, enabling him to get to see quite a lot of Francis. He was a relatively stupid boy and their conversation was dull, so Julian only had to wonder a little why he admired him and relished his presence before he realised what it was about. He tried out an erotic fantasy about Francis, and though he was confused as to what he would like to do with him, there was no doubting his excitement. Just kissing and fondling would be fantastic and maybe something else would be even more so.

42

The following Half eight more new boys had appeared and Julian found he was already so used to the idea of liking younger boys that he had taken an immediate interest in which of them was prettiest. Over the course of the year, he fought against his shyness and gradually became friendly with some of them. He enjoyed their company, but never got near overcoming his nervousness around the really pretty ones enough to dare hint at his physical yearning.

Initially he assumed he was only finding himself attracted to boys because there were no girls around and he reassured himself that it was surely inevitable that some boys would feel so under such circumstances. The attraction was real and strong though, and he began to hope more and more that he would have at least one affair with a younger boy. It would be fantastically exciting and it would get it out of his system. Then, when he had left Eton, he would be able to enjoy having affairs with girls unreservedly, with no feeling that he had missed out on a special experience.

One day in the second week of the Half, Julian went into the bathroom and found Johnny Villiers, a boy in E, talking to someone hidden from view in one of the cubicles where the baths lay. The hidden boy replied and Julian realised with a thrill that it was Alexander. His heart beating fast, he abandoned his plan to go into another cubicle and went instead to a basin and slowly washed his hands. He listened carefully to the conversation, hoping for an opportunity to join in.

Suddenly the cubicle door opened and Alexander came out stark naked. Julian's heart jumped with the unexpected delight. It reminded him of the moment on his eleventh birthday when his parents gave him a racing bike, then by far the most expensive present he had ever received. Alexander began to rub his hair with his towel, and Julian feasted his eyes, knowing that any second Villiers would spoil everything. It was like a magical revelation and greatly enhanced by the boy's total innocence of the effect he was having.

"What are you doing?" asked Villiers, staring at him in amazement.

"What do you mean?" said Alexander, puzzled.

43

"Please, please just shut up, Villiers!" Julian wanted to scream, but did not.

"Anyone can tell you're fresh from prep school." Villiers chuckled condescendingly, and glanced at Julian with an expression that presumed the older boy would share his disdain for Alexander's innocence.

"Why, what's wrong?" asked Alexander in growing confusion.

"You've got a lot to learn about life here," replied Villiers a little more kindly. "You can't walk around the bathroom naked. It's just not done."

"Oh, I see," said Alexander, looking bemused and a little crestfallen as, to Julian's intense regret, he began to dress. Julian knew Villiers had guessed right from his own experience at prep school. There had been six baths there in one room and no one had thought anything of being naked in it. Now Alexander had been taught new shame and he would never again be so innocent in his natural state, thought Julian sadly.

It was the first time Julian had seen a naked boy of the age he desired since he had been one himself. He had wondered until then if he might after all find the real thing disappointing or even distasteful, but now he knew that boys were for him exquisite in the most intimate details of their anatomy, and that this one was perfect in every inch of his smooth, firm limbs. He could not imagine more beauty or grace.

He made every effort to keep the treasured revelation engraven in his mind, and its effect on the development of his erotic longings was immediate. His inhibitions and uncertainties dropped away like a prisoner's shackles under a blacksmith's blow. They were simply incompatible with his new knowledge of Alexander's body. He wanted now to do anything and everything with him that he had heard boys could do together. The gentle curves of Alexander's firm, lithe body were thenceforth the sole image that ever appeared when he wanked. He began to worry that if he could never have him, if he could not just once go all the way with him, he would never be able to get excited by anyone else or find any satisfaction with girls.

There was, however, genuinely a lot more to Julian's love than lust, strong as that was. His beauty alone excited more than that.

His most captivating feature was a smile enhanced by dimples so dazzling in its warmth that Julian found he was far from alone in being overcome by it. One evening, he followed Alexander into the coal room just as the boy exchanged words with the odd-job man, as grim and stony-hearted a man as Julian had ever come across. Julian missed what they said, but caught the end of the smile surely over-generously bestowed. Nor did he miss or fail to understand what he then saw in the man's uncharacteristically gentle expression: a feeling that his day had been made.

Julian soon realised that what was most moving about his smile was that it was a mirror to his soul. On every brief encounter with Alexander, he noticed more qualities that answered his deepest emotional cravings. Much of the appeal was again an attraction of opposites. Alexander's honesty and openness endeared him to Julian precisely because he himself felt so often the need for guile and secrecy. His beauty was more poignant to Julian due to his regret over his own plainness. Similarly, Alexander's exuberance answered his shy restraint, Alexander's brilliance of mind his own average one and Alexander's nobility his lack of it.

Even his names were seductive, proclaiming his beauty and aristocratic blood. Soon after Julian had admitted to himself his fascination with the boy, he went off to the school library to see if he could find out more about "Aylmer, A.M.C." as the school fixtures described him. He already knew there was a book there called *Burke's Peerage*, which listed a substantial chunk of the boys at school, along with all their families stretching back for centuries. He had come across it by accident a year ago and leafed through it in horrified fascination. If one book could encapsulate the biggest difference between him and his schoolfellows, the difference between him and what he would like to be, this was surely it. Afterwards, he had felt such a stab of envy whenever he saw the book sitting on its shelf that he had taken to averting his eyes each time he passed it. Early this Half, however, he had eagerly sought the book out and tuned its pages with relish. It was with triumph rather than chagrin that he found there really was an Aylmer family therein, for he had come to hope his secret love was as noble as possible, as if loving nobility could somehow ennoble him. The magic word

"Alexander" leapt out of the page at him. "Alexander Maximilian Christian, b. 27 May 1970." He already knew the date of birth by heart from the school fixtures. Alexander's grandfather was the 15th Lord Aylmer of Eryholme. The 1st Lord had been "elevated to the peerage" by King Henry VIII for his success in leading an expedition to capture the castle of Dalbeattie from the Scots in 1542. Even then, the family had been ancient, the pedigree positively bristling with mediaeval knights as it continued back to the first, a Sir Henry Aylmer knighted by Edward I in 1298. He in turn was preceded by the statement "The Aylmers deduce their descent from Athelmar or Ailmer Earl of Cornwall in the reign of Ethelred". As olde English as one can get, Julian supposed.

He wondered for a moment what his own English ancestors might have been doing in Sir Henry Aylmer's time. Perhaps they had known him. Was that not the age when surnames were just becoming fixed for common people? Perhaps an early Smith had been the blacksmith in Sir Henry's village, had made his weapons for him. A daydream began to take hold.

The blacksmith's son Julian was being sent by his father to the castle to deliver Sir Henry's new sword. The soldier guarding the gate told him to go inside as Sir Henry would want it inspected. He knocked nervously on the door to the kitchens, as instructed. The valet who answered said that Sir Henry was out hunting, but he would enquire if the young squire Alexander could receive him instead, as it was well known that his father trusted his judgement of weaponry. Ten minutes later, the valet returned to say the young master would indeed receive him in his chamber. It was his first time in the castle and he felt his heart thumping as he followed the valet up two flights of stairs and down several corridors. At last the valet stopped before a finely carved door and rapped twice with the iron knocker.

"Enter!" called out a clear unbroken young voice.

The valet turned the iron handle, opened the door a little, then stood back, indicating that Julian should go in alone. Trembling a bit, Julian did as he was told, and the door was closed behind him. Alexander was sitting in a metal bath steaming with hot water in the middle of a vast bedchamber nearly as big as his father's whole smithy. He was lit up by a beam of sunlight coming from the narrow, arched window. He was just stunningly beautiful, exactly the Alexander Julian already knew except that his blond locks were a little longer and perhaps even sexier now that they were damp.

"Thou art the blacksmith's son?" he asked and bestowed a broad smile on Julian. The dazzling white teeth thus revealed, together with his golden-blond hair and the creamy colour of his slightly tanned skin made a splendidly colourful contrast to the greyness of the iron bath and the bare stone floor that surrounded it.

"Ay, my lord."

"Pass me my towel," said Alexander, and though the words were commanding, no notion of addressing the lower orders in any other manner having ever entered into his upbringing, his tone was entirely friendly.

Julian walked across the room towards a chair with a towel draped over it, placed the sword on it, picked up the towel and turned towards the middle of the room to find that Alexander had stood up in his bath, his nakedness entirely revealed, though shimmering a little in the rising steam. Julian inadvertently drew in his breath quite audibly, such was his astonished delight, but if Alexander noticed either that or Julian's gaze momentarily fixed on the most interesting part of his anatomy, he showed no sign of it. Perhaps it had simply never occurred to him to consider what a mere servant thought, though his eyes bespoke sensitivity.

For a moment, Julian thought he saw clearly the smooth shaft and silky balls of the younger boy, so unlike the shrivelled and hairy man's things his own were becoming, then he remembered he was in the thirteenth century and they did not have spectacles in those days. Out of an unconscious fear that his fantasy would be spoilt by any lack of realism, he regretfully allowed his vision to blur, and he walked myopically towards the bath.

As he approached, Alexander stepped out of it, reached out for the towel and gave another dazzling smile as he took it from him. Julian could at last see clearly, but as Alexander was facing him and close by, he dared not look down. At last, he turned slightly away, and Julian allowed his eyes to wander a little. It was still too risky to stare where he really wanted to, but he let himself enjoy the boyish muscles rippling in the smooth, lithe body as Alexander dried his hair. The healthy glow of his flawless skin in the shaft of sunlight reminded Julian of the hot sunshine out of doors and he felt warmed despite the coolness of the stone chamber.

Suddenly he glanced at Julian and this time he appeared to have noticed the youth's admiration of him.

"Thou mayst dry my back for me if it pleaseth thee," he said gently, handing the towel to Julian. The latter was now trembling with excitement, not fear. Holding the towel with both hands he applied it gently between Alexander's shoulder blades, but his gaze was fixed longingly downwards on his narrow hips and exquisitely rounded, firm, little buttocks, their perfect smoothness interrupted only by a few glistening drops of water.

He was standing so close behind the younger boy that all his senses were filled by him. He inhaled deeply and took in the warm smell of boyhood mixed with an unfamiliar but delightful fragrance that also rose from the steamy water, doubtless one of those eastern luxuries recently brought home by the crusaders. He had to restrain himself from groaning aloud with desire.

"For the third time, I said the library is now CLOSING." Julian looked up in horror to see the librarian standing over him angrily. Everyone else had gone. He realised then that he had heard someone say something loud a few moments earlier, but he had been too lost in his daydream to take it in.

"Sorry, Sir."

Desperately as he longed to approach Alexander and somehow strive towards a familiarity that might one day lead to greater things, he could not find the courage or the words. He was too shy at the best of times and much worse with his secret love. One afternoon soon after the incident with Villiers, he had finally plucked up the courage to say "Hi, Alexander" as they passed at a landing. He had been afraid the slightly unusual use of a Christian name for a much younger boy would arouse someone's suspicion, but the reward he got for his daring, one of those heart-wrenching smiles, was so

48

overpowering that it left Julian feeling for a while that he should not give a damn what other people thought. Before long, though, his fear returned of what other people, and above all Alexander, would think. Though he had kept up greeting him since, he never dared to say anything more, and the sense of triumph he had originally felt on climbing that initial step towards friendship soon dissipated.

If he found himself in the same room as Alexander, such as the lobby or a bathroom, he would always stay if he had the free time to do so, waiting with a beating heart for an easy opportunity to join the conversation. He longed to make some cool remark that would elicit the boy's approval, perhaps even draw another of those smiles. In the dining room, he timed his forays to the sideboard to coincide with Alexander's. Just being near him, looking from behind at those golden locks, was a treat, and any kind of hope that he might somehow make progress was better than none. Sometimes he dreaded his encounters with Alexander almost as much as he longed for them, because of the terrible pressure he felt under to overcome his shyness, and the anticipation of his disappointment and self-contempt at failing to do so.

Julian was quite friendly with the house captain, Patrick Hurley. Though Patrick was in A and two years older, he appreciated Julian as one of the few boys who seemed to like him. He had also felt particularly sympathetic towards Julian since becoming house captain, when Mr. Hodgson had told him in confidence a little about Julian's unusual background. He had no serious friends himself, being rather dull and too earnestly absorbed both in his responsibilities as house captain and in his studies. He had just taken the Oxbridge exam, and having by no means one of the more brilliant minds in the school, he had had to study relentlessly to give himself a realistic chance of being accepted by Cambridge. Now that he only had a fortnight left at Eton, he felt a little sad he would be leaving without having established any of the close and sometimes lifelong friendships that his contemporaries had, so when Julian came to his room one afternoon on a trivial errand, Patrick was glad of the opportunity for a friendly chat.

"What are all those books?" asked Julian after a while, indicating four thick quarto-sized books with heavy black covers stacked on the floor.

"Oh, they're the JRH House Books," said Patrick.

"What do you mean?"

Patrick hesitated for a moment, wondering whether he should even tell Julian what they were. Hardly anyone knew of their existence and only the Library were allowed to read them. His predecessor had not said their existence was a secret though.

"Well, since God knows when, every house captain, before he leaves the school, has written a short note on every boy in the house, saying what he thinks of him. The books are supposed to be kept in the library, but I've brought them here for a couple of days because now it's my turn to do a write-up of the house. I wanted to have a look at the older books just to get an idea of the sort of things I'm expected to write about, but I haven't had time." Actually, he had read all the entries since Lent 1979, when he had been a new boy. Before that did not interest him.

"Can I have a look?"

"Well, I really shouldn't let you. Only the Library are allowed to read them, you see." He paused. He was aware that many boys thought he was a bore because he stuck to the rules, and very soon he was leaving. Also, the only book that really mattered was the current one hidden in his burry, in which he had been writing earlier. "Oh, all right, seeing as you are in Debate and those are all old volumes, but don't tell anyone I let you, okay?"

"Okay. Thanks," said Julian, sitting down to read in Patrick's armchair and wondering if any of the books he was being allowed to see were new enough to mention him. He found there was one which ended with Michaelmas 1980, his first Half. He had rather liked the house captain then, Charles Faber, though he had been in tremendous awe of him. It was strange to remember how impressively grown-up eighteen-year-olds had seemed to him then.

"<u>Smith</u>" his entry read. "A plain and timid little fellow, but keen to please and actually very nice if you get talking to him." With unsurprisingly mixed feelings, but anyway fascinated, he proceeded to read the other entries for his block, arranged in alphabetical order.

"Cowburn. I find him pretentious and two-faced and suspect he is a trouble-maker, but he seems to be popular with his block." Julian found himself warming to Faber again.

"Crichton. The most interesting boy in F. Friendly, sincere and intelligent, he will go far. A promising football player too."

When he had read all the entries for F, he turned back a few pages to see what Faber had said about Patrick Hurley.

"Hurley. A worthy fellow indeed, conscientious, hard-working and good at games. A pity he is so dull, but he will go far down a narrow path." Julian glanced at Patrick, feeling a pang of sympathy for him.

He put down the book and picked up one of the oldest-looking ones. "Summer 1954" headed its first page. As he began to read, he sensed at once that he was going back to an era to some degree lost. The language was that he had heard in old black and white films and he did not understand all the terms. He flicked slowly through the pages, reading excerpts here and there. It was intriguing to imagine what had happened since to all these boys, now presumably in their forties. He wondered what the most distinguished and pompous of them would think if they could read the disparaging comments of their elders at school. Still, it became hard to sustain interest for long in an endless succession of boys he had never known. He began to turn the pages faster and was just deciding it would be more fun to go back to the 1979 book and read about the block above him, when suddenly the words "prettiest boy" registered themselves in his mind and he froze. He had already turned the page on which he thought he saw them and turned it back excitedly, though half expecting to find it had just been his imagination spurred on by his longings.

"Granville. By far the prettiest new boy. Apparently still a virgin, a state of affairs perhaps unlikely to endure, as no less than three members of the library have confided in me their hopes for ending it. Should be interesting to see what happens." Julian read it over twice. He could feel his heart thumping with excitement and looked up nervously to see if he was being

51

observed, but fortunately Patrick was absorbed in whatever he was writing at his burry.

Julian had of course long known implicitly that there must at least occasionally have been sexual liaisons between boys at Eton and that he could not be the first to have lusted over younger boys. In his last week at prep school, his headmaster had had an informal chat with all the leavers about what they should expect at public school. The one danger he had warned them of was improper advances from older boys, any hint of which should be firmly rejected and reported to their housemasters if unambiguously attempted. No details of what was meant had been given beyond the implication that it was sexual and harmful, but that had been more than enough to inflame their imaginations.

Once he had settled into Eton, he had become aware through innuendo rather than expressed belief that any friendship between boys a few years apart in age was considered odd and open to suspicion of being sexually motivated. This was precisely what made him so frightened of what others would think when he egged himself on to show friendliness to Alexander.

What, however, he had never come across before was the merest hint of a confession by any boy that he found another sexually attractive, and this was what staggered him about what he had just read. It was all the more surprising in that it was written down by a house captain in a book he presumably expected other eighteen-year-olds to read. Did this imply he thought they would not think less of him for it?

Julian read on, fast but careful not to miss anything interesting. The next two entries held no interest, then he came to "Mordaunt. Another pretty little chap. Obviously gets on well with Adams, his fagmaster. Everyone suspects hanky-panky, but Adams isn't letting on."

Next came "Saunders. Earnest, keen to please and a promising cricketer, but sadly as plain as the boys' maids."

This was the last entry in the series, so Julian went back a few pages to read what the house captain in question said about the older boys, but though most of it was quite humorous, the sexual innuendo was limited to an ambiguous reference to one Graham in C as "a priapic frequenter of the railway arches."

The writer's libido only warmed up when he got to E block. There Julian found the most startling revelation of all:

"<u>Lovell</u>. Better known as "Lovely" or "the house tart". A blond of limited intelligence, but easy-going and of easy virtue and reputed to have been enjoyed by half the upper boys. I can vouch for several through confession. Sadly no longer wears a bum-freezer, but still lovely indeed."

Julian wished he could spend hours checking through all the house books for every reference to pretty boys, for this was a voyage of self-discovery as much as discovery of others, but Patrick was showing worrying signs of finishing what he was doing. It looked as though his reading was likely to be brought to an untimely end at any moment, so he knew he must ration himself severely. What he most urgently now longed to know was how often and how recently there had been boys like the house captain of 1954 and indeed himself. He returned to the volume that ended with Faber's write-up of his own block and worked quickly backwards through it, too fast to take much in, but hopefully slowly enough to pick up any key words like "pretty" or "fancy." He came across a few references to boys suspected of being queer, but otherwise disappointingly nothing. He quickly opened the other three books to establish which was the next back and resumed his now frantic search. Patrick had stood up and was gathering papers together. At last he struck gold again. It was Michaelmas 1967.

"<u>Chapman mi.</u> Rather shy, but popular nevertheless, he is quick-witted and a promising athlete. He is also much the comeliest lower boy. So far as I know, no one has scored yet, but Charlie Taylor, who has long had a crush on him, says he has decided to offer him fifteen guineas. I would advise acceptance: it is a good offer, as I have it on the authority of one who has been at the receiving end that Taylor is poorly endowed and it is all over quickly."

"Julian, I'm afraid I have to go now," said Patrick. "I hope it was interesting reading, but you will keep it to yourself, won't you?"

53

Julian had never closed a book with such reluctance. "Yes, of course. Thanks." He returned to his room, still stunned. He had heard the occasional rumour about boys in other houses whom he did not know, the participants always being referred to contemptuously as queers. When he had been a new boy, there had been speculation about an unusually warm friendship between one of the Library and a handsome fourteen-year-old in E, but no one had really believed it had been more than platonic. That was the nearest thing to a love affair he had heard of in his house. It was so far removed from the world he had just read about, where the older boys apparently confided in each other which of the younger ones they fancied or had already bedded, that it made his head spin. He would be far too terrified of being branded as a queer to hint at such an attraction in even the most oblique way.

"Queer" made him think of balding old men in raincoats sitting and leering on park benches, something as far removed from the beauty and purity of Alexander as he could imagine. The newer word "gay" was perhaps even worse, reminding him of limp-wristed men simulating ridiculously the opposite sex in the ludicrous hope of attracting a real specimen of their own.

It would be so unfair to be thought of as that, for the idea of doing something with a man filled him with disgust. It seemed obvious to him that boys Alexander's age, with their smooth, hairless and curvaceous bodies, fresh complexions, slim waists and silky hair were closer to women than men in their appearance, though somehow even more exciting. He felt sure the writers of the old house books must have felt the same way too, as the boys they were attracted to seemed all to have been in E or F.

Quite apart from cringing at the thought of being called queer or gay, he did not want to be labelled anything at all that would cause presumptions to be made about his tastes and aspirations in life, which he did not think were anyway very different from most people's. In the end, he wanted to meet a nice, understanding girl and have his own family. It was just for the time being that he had succumbed to a longing for something special and apparently only recently misunderstood.

54

He did not know whether to cry with joy at his discovery that others had desired younger boys and thought nothing was wrong with it, or with anguish that he seemed to have come to Eton too late, a decade or more after his only known soulmates had departed.

The feeling that he had been born at the wrong time deepened the more he thought about it. It made him feel more isolated than ever from his peers, but with this detachment came a greater freedom and determination. He had never been able to see how there could be anything bad about his love for Alexander, or of consummating it in the theoretical case that he was able to make the necessary advances and lucky enough to find them welcomed. His total lack of sympathetic company had nevertheless made him wonder whether the other boys would not be right to despise him, as he was sure they would if they knew about his feelings, even though he could not understand on what grounds. Now, though still terrified they would think and call him queer if they found out, he felt sure they would be wrong to despise him, both morally and aesthetically. His love was noble and good. The only legitimate objection to it could come from Alexander himself. Henceforth he would beware of their prejudices for practical reasons, but they would not trouble his conscience.

He could understand only too well why Alexander would be likely to reject him as a serious friend, let alone as a lover, as he did not feel remotely worthy of him; but now that it was clear in his mind that this should be a matter solely for Alexander to decide, he felt more than ever that it would be a betrayal of all his aspirations, of his very essence, not at least to present his suit to the best of his ability.

One day nearly three months after he first saw Alexander, he came into the lobby from outside, shaking the snow off his tailcoat, and noticed him amongst the boys chatting there. As usual when this happened, he stopped, both to feast his eyes and in the hope he might find a way of joining in the conversation, but unfortunately they were talking about *Worst Friends*, a television drama he found painful and irritating to watch, glorifying the class system as it did.

55

"Hello Ma'am," said all the boys as the dame came in.

"Good evening all!" she replied with a friendly smile. She had caught the end of their conversation. "As Trials are over tomorrow, would you like to come and watch *Worst Friends* afterwards in my sitting-room?"

"Yes," said several boys delighted. Julian noted the look of enthusiasm in Alexander's expression.

"Well, it starts at 6:20. But just the ... seven of you here. I can't fit the whole house in."

Now that at last Julian knew well in advance of an occasion when he and Alexander were going to be doing something together, he could begin to plan a conversation. The next evening, he followed him from the dame's room to the bathroom and paused outside the door listening, though he very much doubted he would be able to hear through the thick door whether anyone else was inside with Alexander. He was not sure if he would dare start a conversation if another boy was there. In that case, might it not be better to save the things he had thought of to say until a better opportunity arose? But what if there was not one? There were only a few days left until the end of the Half. He would hate and despise himself if he went home without having achieved even a single conversation. He went in.

"Hi Alexander," he said, relieved to find they were indeed alone. The flashing smile he got back warmed him immediately and he began to relax. As planned, he asked him what he thought about today's episode of *Worst Friends*.

"It was a bit depressing. I mean it was so sad when Miss Isabella told Captain Charles she could never love him except like a brother."

Julian felt a pang of jealousy of Captain Charles for so evidently having Alexander's sympathy, though he guessed it was Miss Isabella who was the main focus of his attention. Another question soon established that Lucretia Pelham, as it transpired the actress was really called, was his favourite, so Julian improvised that she was his too. As a matter of fact, he had to admit she was very beautiful, though such blatantly upper-class girls had never been his choice for amorous imagination; his fantasies of them were always spoilt by fear of what they would think when he took them home to introduce them to his parents. Nevertheless, he decided he would gladly make her his favourite actress now, so that they would have something in common of such evident interest to Alexander.

Alexander was so open and lively, and indeed fun to talk to, that the conversation went far more easily than he had dared to hope possible. He had feared before that he would run out of things to say and that it would grind to an awkward stop, but instead he felt immediate regret when they were interrupted by the bell calling them to supper.

Afterwards, however, when he returned to his room, he felt so elated by their conversation that he could not stop himself from walking round and round his room in little circles, relishing it all. It was real progress at last and he wondered what to do next. He resolved to learn as much as possible about Lucretia Pelham. That should impress him. The more he thought about it, the more it seemed an ideal subject for developing their friendship. No one hearing an enthusiastic conversation about a beautiful girl was likely to suspect that the real subject of Julian's romantic interest was his boy interlocutor.

Over the ensuing month of the Christmas holidays, Julian began to fret as to how he could find anything out about the actress. He was therefore thrilled with his good luck when, coming down to breakfast one day, he glanced at his father's *Sunday Express* lying on the kitchen table and noticed on the front cover "Miss Isabella's story: exclusive interview with Lucretia Pelham, page 6." His excitement grew enormously when he read that two years after being voted Britain's most beautiful teenager, she had at seventeen posed naked in *Mayfair*. That should certainly impress Alexander, if he did not already know it. Did Alexander even know what *Mayfair* was yet? Quite likely not, he thought . He did not think his block had got into girlie magazines until the end of F. He began to hope very much that he did not, as that would give him the opportunity to be the one to show him an exciting novelty. He longed to be the one who could introduce Alexander to the good things in life, of which he would surely find erotic pictures of beautiful girls to be one. His remembered his own confusion about sexual matters when he was thirteen. It was just the sort of subject where an older friend could prove his worth. He carefully tore out the newspaper page.

When they went back to school, Julian fretted over how to use his discovery to his best advantage. When he passed Alexander in a corridor, the greeting he got was at first a little warmer than before their chat, as though he was now acknowledged as an acquaintance, but though friendly, it was still fairly perfunctory, and he could not quite bring himself to dare just go to Alexander's room to see him. If someone else was there when he went, he would be too embarrassed to steer the conversation towards a proposal to show Alexander a *Mayfair*. Also, if he was unlucky, Alexander might be in a hurry to go somewhere, which would equally rob him of his opportunity. He could not think of anything else nearly as effective for initiating a friendship as introducing him to *Mayfair*, so he was desperate not to throw away the opportunity.. On the other hand, he could hardly carry the article about with him and give it to him when he first found him alone. It would look so contrived. He had better first mention the article in another supposedly casual encounter, and thus reawaken his interest enough for a follow-up visit to his room to be welcomed. As he was shy of doing even that in front of others, it took him a week to accomplish.

"Oh, Alexander," he said after they had greeted each other passing on the staircase one day, "I've just remembered. I found an article about Lucretia Pelham I thought would interest you. Shall I bring it to your room sometime?"

"Oh, fantastic, thanks very much," said Alexander with a dashing smile. "I'll look forward to it."

That boosted his confidence, but he still wanted to go there when Alexander was alone. The only way of being nearly sure of that was first to go past his room pretending to be on his way somewhere. This was difficult, as Alexander's room was in a passage of the first floor entirely occupied by boys in E and F. The only boy he knew well enough to drop in on the other side was Stephen Grey in E, and he not well enough to make frequent visits. Several times he went past only to find either that there was no answer when he knocked on the door or most often that he was talking to Rupert Drysdale, the last person he wanted to be there. He had long been aware that Drysdale was the boy in the house he would fancy most if there was no Alexander. Besides his usual nervousness in front of boys he was attracted to, he was intimidated by Drysdale's apparent knowledge of worldly things like *Mayfair*. Also, he did not have that immediate, warm friendliness that had made Alexander easy to talk to despite his radiant good looks.

Thus, if Julian's approach had not been witnessed, he always retreated immediately, but soon it happened that it was and he felt bound to go on to Grey's room with a trivial excuse for conversation. Finally, one day when he could hear no voices in the room as he approached it, he forced himself to knock on the door. Alexander answered and he went in. To his dismay, he saw at once that not only was Drysdale sitting reading a magazine in Alexander's armchair, but Churchill was there too, though he did not mind Churchill nearly so much.

"Hi Alexander. I've brought that article on Lucretia I told you about," he said in a rush, painfully aware he was blushing, and he saw the other two look up curiously.

"Oh, thanks a lot," said Alexander warmly and he began to read at once.

"Did you know she stripped for *Mayfair*?" asked Julian after half a minute, worried Alexander might read that before he got a word in.

"What's *Mayfair*?" he hoped Alexander would ask and he glanced nervously at Drysdale, but instead Alexander said "She was in *Mayfair*!! Wow! How amazing." Churchill got up and stood over Alexander's shoulder, peering at the large photo of the actress.

"Do you fancy her too?" Julian asked Churchill, hoping to retain control of the conversation despite his disappointment.

"Mmm yes, she's vewy pwetty indeed," said Simon.

"I'd give anything to have the issue with her in it," said Alexander.

"I know what!" exclaimed Simon. "One can order back copies of most magazines. We can have a look in a new one and see if it says anything about it."

"Yes, but even supposing we could order it, what if it comes in an envelope stamped "Mayfair" and Mr. Hodgson decides to open it?" asked Alexander.

"Lusty will tell him he was just doing some preparatory research in case he got stranded in the desert with her, won't you Lusty?" said Rupert.

"Oh vewy funny," replied Simon.

After their banter had continued a few minutes, Alexander finished the article and thanked Julian again. The older boy had been standing awkwardly by the door trying to think of something clever to say and now felt obliged to retreat while he could still do so gracefully.

Thus it came to pass that three weeks into the Half, Julian felt he had made no real progress at all and had relapsed into his familiar self-disappointment and despair, when unforeseeable happenings made him feel even sorrier for Alexander than for himself.

IV: A Thief at Large

The greatest thief this world has ever produced is Procrastination, and he is still at large.
Henry Wheeler Shaw, *Josh Billings' Wit and Humor*

After three years at Eton, Guy Cowburn was still a bully and a snob, and Peter Leigh was still considered his best friend. Follower would have been more accurate than friend, as their friendship was decidedly unequal. Guy initiated all their pranks, and his ideas and opinions were invariably adopted by Peter as his own. Guy's ability to dominate was mysterious, as he was slow in both body and mind. He was one of the least intelligent boys in their house and no great sportsman either, but dominate he undoubtedly did; and not just over Peter, though Peter was much his most faithful crony.

Ironically, but not coincidentally, Guy was actually the one boy in the house whose lineage was just as plebeian as Julian's, though his humbly-born Glaswegian father had made so much money as a building contractor that it was easier for Guy to delude the others with a show of extreme wealth.

One aspect of Guy's snobbery was a taste for very expensive, mostly tailored clothes accompanied by a biting disdain for those who were either uninterested or financially unable to dress according to his tastes. Unknown to him, this imposed a terrible strain on Peter, whose parents were both poorer than Guy's and less inclined to spoil their son. It was the only significant secret he kept from Guy, but probably wise.

He tried his best to keep up with him by skimping on everything most boys spent their money on, and pretences of having paid vast sums for things like haircuts in modelling studios he had never been near, but still he needed more to be confident of retaining Guy's full respect.

Already for two years, he had taken to supplementing his parental allowance by regular pinching from his mother's purse throughout the holidays, which he justified to himself on the grounds of his parents' meanness, unfairness even, in not giving him more. She apparently never noticed, and he began to feel more confident of what he might get away with.

One morning a week before the school broke up for the Christmas holidays, Peter came back to the house for a free period, a time allowed to some of the older boys a few times a week for studying in their rooms instead of attending divs. On the way to the bathroom, he passed Rupert Drysdale's room and noticed the door was wide open, which was unremarkable as he was probably the most laid back boy in the house. Peter had become deeply envious of every boy who was obviously much richer than himself, and Drysdale was also the richest boy in the house. Peter could see a very expensive-looking camera sitting on his table. Drysdale was getting a reputation for having newly-invented gadgets none of the other boys had seen before, and Peter could see several he could not readily identify lying around. The house was silent. It was quite likely in fact that he was the only person in it except the dame and boys' maids. The rooms had already been cleaned, so they were evidently busy elsewhere.

His curiosity got the better of him and he stepped in. He listened and realised the house was so quiet that he could hear the birds chirping the other side of Drysdale's closed window. He would be bound to hear if anyone came along, so he walked gingerly up to the table. He would love to have a camera like that. Guy would be most impressed. He wondered for a moment if it were practical to take it, but it obviously would not. It would be missed and everyone would know it was Drysdale's.

Then he saw sticking out under one corner of the enormous camera at least two banknotes, and he froze. The upper one at least looked like a £ 20 note. The temptation was immediate and obvious, so much so that he went straight off to his room to give himself time to make a decision in safe seclusion.

It only took three minutes. After all, Drysdale was so rich he might not even notice the loss, and if he did, he and everyone else would probably think he had dropped the money somewhere. He nipped down the corridor and into Drysdale's room, whipped the notes out with one hand while holding the camera steady with the other, and was back in his room less than a minute after leaving it.

On opening his hand, he found he had £ 40, half his allowance for a whole Half! That afternoon, he went for tea in Guy's room nonchalantly wearing a new silk shirt and tie that he remembered Guy admiring in a shop-window a fortnight earlier. The biggest thrill was knowing he had got it all for nothing.

All through the Christmas holidays, he kept reliving the thrill and easiness of it all, and by the time he came back for the Lent Half, he was looking forward to repeating the experience.

The first week back at school turned out to be frustrating. He had got carried away in his imagination and thought it would be easy to find more banknotes waiting to be snatched, but of course they were usually better hidden than that.

Most boys also did not leave their doors wide open, so he had no choice but to open them himself. He would then stare through the open doorway in every direction, hoping to spot a wallet, but he did not yet dare to go into a room to search. He used all of his free periods searching. He could not go anywhere in the house, as he was supposed to be in his room, so before setting off down any particular corridor, he had to have thought of a legitimate excuse for being in it, such as that it led to a loo. He concentrated on the younger boys' rooms, as they did not have free periods, but also tried to discover who in his own block had free periods when.

If he did see a wallet, he had decided he would snatch it straight away, but that week he did not, and he got so frustrated that in the end the first person he took from was none other than Guy himself, which was far easier. He knew that Guy was loaded, as besides just having received his usual generous allowance for the Half, he had been given £ 30 for Christmas by a godfather. He also knew Guy kept his money in his inner jacket pocket, so when one afternoon they were doing their E.W.s together in Peter's room and Guy set off for his own to fetch a book, leaving his jacket hung on a chair, it was dead easy to pull out the wallet and replace it in seconds. He did feel a bit guilty about taking from a friend, so he restricted himself to £ 10, which Guy could easily afford.

After that, he realised he would have to be more daring. Most boys kept their bank notes in wallets, and he reckoned a decent fraction probably left those wallets in jackets in their rooms when they had divs, rather than taking them along in their tailcoats. He would take the risk of briefly searching the room of any boy

63

he was on reasonably friendly terms with. He would leave the door ajar and listen out intently for anyone coming, and in the worst case, that someone came before he could get away, he would claim that the occupier had said he could come to borrow some particular item and bluff his way out of it.

In the week following, he gathered a total of £ 60 from four rooms, and the week after that another £ 95 from six.

Mr. Hodgson was in a quandary. Five boys had come to report to him that they were certain money had been stolen from their rooms. Initial enquiries had revealed another two who had not reported it and five who thought their money had probably been stolen. His house was buzzing with rumours and bad feeling, and he had not a clue as to who was the culprit.

He considered himself a shrewd judge of character. He was fond of claiming that no one understood boys better than he did. To him that meant he had no illusions about them, and to them it meant he had a jaundiced view of boys. At any rate, he decided he could solve this case by confronting every possible culprit face to face.

He made his announcement at his customary time after "Prayers", the twenty-minute session every evening when the house gathered together to listen to a presentation by one of the boys. He stood up and all ears were immediately attentive.

"I have some very grave news to announce. There has been a spate of thefts in the house in the last few weeks, and I must ask all of you to be very careful not to leave money or other valuables lying around and to report any further losses to me immediately. I do not yet know who the culprit is, but I shall soon. What I would like to say to him now is that if he will reveal himself to me without further delay, I shall listen to him with understanding and I shall not be harsh. All of you are now to remain in this room. I shall go to my study and I want each of you to come and tell me anything you know that might have any bearing on this case. You will come one by one in house order when the house captain calls you. You may return to your rooms immediately afterwards."

It did not go as Hodgson had hoped. No one confessed, and no one had seen anyone acting suspiciously. The closest thing he heard to that was a boy called Bagley's report that he had returned from a div unexpectedly early on the morning Macdonald ma.'s money was thought to have been stolen and seen a blond-haired boy he thought was Aylmer walking past Macdonald's room. However, he was not at all sure it was Aylmer, and even if it was, there was a bathroom at the end of that corridor to which he could quite legitimately have been going.

Hodgson did not believe it was Aylmer for a moment. The boy was too open, his face too obviously honest, childish in its innocence. When questioned, he had looked completely blank.

As for detecting signs of guilt in the faces of any of the other boys, there were two or three he had thought looked distinctly nervous, but he had to admit to himself that he had no confidence it was one of them.

After all the boys had been questioned, Hodgson had briefly summarised his findings, or rather lack of them, to his house captain, Anthony Burrows. They agreed to discuss the matter further after a break. He remained in his study in deep thought for half an hour, then he set off for Burrows's room.

Three doors down the corridor from Burrows's room lived an unremarkable boy in D block named Eddie Craven. As the time for his lights out approached, he set out from his room to go and brush his teeth and saw Hodgson go into Burrows's room and close the door. His heart leapt with excitement. Perhaps Hodgson was going to reveal the thief's identity. Just imagine if he could be the first to know! Everyone would be crowding around him, hanging on his every word.

No one else was around, so Craven crept up to Burrows's door, knelt down to undo his shoe laces, then pretended to do them up again.

"Ee ba goom!" he heard Hodgson say ponderously. "It seems that we have nothing to go on except for Bagley's sighting of Aylmer."

Suddenly someone came round the corner. Craven quickly finished tying his shoe lace, then ran off, almost dancing with excitement.

Inside the room, Hodgson was sitting in the house captain's armchair.

65

"I can't believe it's Aylmer, Sir. I don't exactly know him, but from what I've seen he's just not that sort of boy," said Burrows.

"Well, I do know him, and I am inclined to agree with you."

"Anyway, Aylmer was probably just going to the bathroom."

"Precisely. I fear I now have no alternative but to call on the expert advice of the police as to how we may learn our thief's identity. I shall keep you informed. Good night, Anthony," he said as he got up slowly and left the room.

At breakfast the next morning, Alexander thought that a group of boys in D were looking at him rather oddly and speaking in strangely subdued tones. What could he have done wrong? He surreptitiously examined himself to check he was properly dressed, then got up to leave, feeling a bit unnerved.

When he came back for lunchtime, it was much, much worse. He arrived late. The others still passing through the lobby seemed to be looking at him with dislike. His heart thumping, he walked into the dining room and sat down amongst the other boys in F. They too were looking at him with contempt, except for Rupert and Simon, whose eyes were averted.

Suddenly a hiss started up and spread across the room. Alexander glanced up to confirm that everyone was looking at him. He was terrified now and he could not stop tears coming to his eyes.

"What have I done wrong?" he whispered loudly at Rupert, who was seated two places away, but Rupert would not look at him.

"We've all talked about it, and we don't understand why you didn't just own up to Mr. Hodgson," said Michael Bell.

"Own up to what? I haven't done anything," cried Alexander in anguish.

"You know bloody well what, you filthy thief," said James Bates, one of those whose money had been stolen, almost shouting with fury.

It was clear enough to him now and hopeless. The tears started to stream down his face as he stood up and ran out of the dining room. He heard the roar of fifty voices in excited conversation erupt behind him. He ran straight up the stairs and all the way to Rupert's room and sat down on his ottoman, his

66

head bent between his trembling hands. He had to talk to Rupert and he could not see how he would dare go from his room to Rupert's once there were other boys in the corridors. There was silence now, because everyone else was having lunch. He dreaded the sudden end to the silence that would come when the boys surged out of the dining-room towards their rooms, but he longed to see Rupert. Surely, Rupert at least would believe him.

Suddenly the dreaded noise started up like a slow eruption. It would take Rupert a minute or two to reach his room.

"Oh God, please let him be unaccompanied," thought Alexander desperately. He was shaking all over as he waited.

The door opened without warning and Rupert walked in. His face went white as he saw with shocked surprise that Alexander was sitting on his ottoman. Alexander stood up.

"Rupert, I've never stolen anything in my life. Surely you at least know I wouldn't? I thought you were my friend." Then Rupert relented. He felt a bit ashamed now of having believed the other boys without even having talked to Alexander, and it was difficult to believe Alexander was lying. And he really was a good friend.

"Yes, okay, I believe you. But everyone else thinks you're the thief. They say you were seen."

"But I can't have been!" It was all too much for him. Evidently, Rupert had believed he was a thief, and even now it seemed he might not be certain. Nothing so unfair had ever happened. There was only one thing for it. He was a child and he needed his mother. She at least loved him and knew he was good.

He rushed out of the room and down the corridors and stairs. There were lots of boys around. Some looked curious, while others started to formulate some nasty remark, but he neither saw nor heard them. He ran out of the house, his vision blurred by his tears, then ran down Eton High Street and on and on, across the bridge over the Thames which separated Eton from the much larger town of Windsor, and only then did he slow down and begin to look out for a public telephone. Soon he saw one, but someone was in it, so he waited outside. It was a bitterly cold day, still early February, but he hardly noticed. At last, a woman walked out of the phone booth and he went in and

67

called home. The phone rang and rang. He imagined it ringing on its pretty wooden stand in the drawing room of their house in Chelsea, and wished so much that he was there sitting on the sofa talking to his mother. After two minutes ringing, it was obvious she was out.

Fortunately, it was a half day, so he was under no obligation to go back to the school until lock-up at 6:15. He wandered aimlessly around the streets of Windsor for an hour, then tried telephoning again without success. He resumed his wandering for another hour. Still no luck. It was getting dark now and the cold intensified, so he went into a bookshop. He soon found that no book could distract him from his misery, so he went out again, crossed the street, walked along the wall of Windsor Castle and turned into Windsor Great Park. There was no one about and it was pitch dark, in contrast to the brightly-lit streets. His tears had exhausted themselves and the silence helped him concentrate. He began to consider what he must do. He was running out of hope of getting hold of his mother before lock-up. He would love to just run away, catch a train to London, and never mind the consequences. His mother would certainly understand, and hopefully his father too. But he did not have enough money with him.

Who else could help him? Then he remembered the dame. She was kind and he thought she would be fair. If he could not have his mother or go home, any kind woman at the school was surely the closest substitute. That was what he would do then if he could not reach his mother. He timed his last call for a quarter to six to give him time to talk to her and still run back to the school in time. This time, he let the telephone ring for ten minutes before he put it down in despair.

When he got back to his house, he walked fast without stopping, looking down to avoid contact with anybody on the way, until he found his way down one corridor blocked by a big boy. He looked up to see the sneering face of Oliver Fisher, another of Cowburn's cronies.

"Been off pick-pocketing, have you Aylmer?"

There were two ways one could go up from the first floor to the second, where the dame's rooms were, so Alexander simply turned straight round and ran the other way. A flood of relief surged through him as the door to the dame's apartment closed behind him.

"Ma'am?"

The dame emerged from her sitting-room and suddenly Alexander's tears started flowing again. She had heard rumours and had a fair idea what the poor child's visit was about.

"Everyone's saying I...," he started.

"Yes, I've heard."

"I didn't do it!"

"I know," she said softly and drew him into her shoulder for a few moments. "Don't worry. I'm going to talk to Mr. Hodgson. You stay here. Sit down and make yourself comfortable. Everything will be all right." She went over to her television to turn it on, then left.

Alexander felt much better. He was safe here, and it was like a real home, sitting on a comfortable sofa and watching television. The dame came back after about twenty minutes and again reassured him that everything would be all right. Mr. Hodgson knew he was innocent and would say something to the boys. There was no need to go down for dinner. She would cook scrambled eggs, beans and toast for him here. However, the housemaster did want him to go to Prayers and she would take him down there.

By the time they went down, only a few boys were still rushing towards the common room and they fell into silence. She saw him into the room, then left, as she did not attend Prayers, just as Hodgson came in. Alexander kept looking down, and no one disturbed him. After Prayers, Hodgson again rose to speak.

"Now. It has come to my attention that one of the boys in this house has been accused of the recent thefts. I wish to make it quite clear there are no grounds whatsoever for suspecting this particular boy or, as yet, any other. If I hear of further such accusations, I shall take a very dim view of it indeed."

As soon as Hodgson had left the room, Rupert came over to Alexander.

"Hi Alexander. Where've you been all afternoon?" he asked and chatted on merrily. Evidently Rupert was determined to carry on with him as if nothing untoward had ever happened, and that suited Alexander fine. As they joined the noisy crowd

69

rushing out of the room, Alexander glanced quickly around and thought he took in a mixture of looks varying from definitely sympathetic to still suspicious, but the tension was gone.

He went into his room, followed by Rupert. Ten minutes later, they were still chatting when there was a knock on the door.

"Come in!" he said, suddenly a little nervous again. Michael Bell and James Bates entered looking rather stiff and formal for thirteen-year-olds.

"I'm sorry Alexander," said James, evidently much embarrassed, and held out his hand, which Alexander readily shook with a beaming smile.

"So am I," said Michael, as he did the same.

"Everyone told us it was a fact," said James, "so how could we know it wasn't true? Obviously, some burke got the wrong end of the stick."

They were entirely sincere. They had always liked him. His openness and generosity of spirit had made him one of the most popular boys both in F block and with the other boys who knew him.

The next day, it began to look as though the whole miserable business had never taken place, except that at lunch Alexander noticed that the group of boys who generally hung out with Guy Cowburn still looked at him rather malevolently.

The day after that was a Saturday, again a half day, so early in the afternoon, Alexander decided to go to the music schools to practise a new piece on the piano. He stepped out of the house into the adjoining alley way and found himself suddenly confronted by Cowburn himself. No one else was in sight.

"You think you've got away with it, don't you, you thieving little jerk," said Cowburn with a menacing sneer, advancing on him.

"I never stole anything!" shouted Alexander in indignant exasperation, but also growing frightened as he thought the much bigger boy might be going to hit him.

"Who do you think you're fooling? Hodgson had to say all that just because he hasn't got complete proof it was you. But I know it was and so does every boy in the house who matters and we're going to make life hell for you."

Suddenly Julian Smith emerged and walked right up to them. He was blazing with anger. Besides naturally sympathising with the object of his love, he was apparently the only boy in the house who had never for a moment doubted Alexander's innocence. It was not because he was besotted with him, but rather that Alexander's total guilelessness was precisely one of the things that had made him fall in love with him. He had never felt sorry for another being as deeply as he had for Alexander at lunch the day before yesterday. Immediately afterwards he had spent more than two hours looking for him in every place he could think of, longing to tell him he believed in him and would do his best to help establish his innocence, but he was nowhere to be found. Adding fuel to the fire in him, there was of course his own secret loathing of Cowburn since he too had so nearly had his happiness at school spoiled for good by the vile bully, when he was Alexander's age.

"Just leave him alone, you bastard!" he shouted at Cowburn. "How would you like it if you were accused of something like that without a shred of evidence? And if you have to bully people, why don't you damned well pick on someone your own age at least?"

Cowburn quailed. He was shocked by Julian's anger. He had never seen him at all like that before. He was usually so mild and conciliatory. Perhaps he might attack him. He had never been in a fight and avoided all kinds of confrontation unless he was certain of winning. Julian had hit the nail on the head there.

"Okay, okay, there's no need to lose your temper." He had been pissed off about the loss of his £ 10 and had been further pissed off when Hodgson let Alexander off the hook. It had been fun watching the little wimp run away from the dining-room in tears, so he had tried to convince himself as well as his friends that they should still regard him as the thief. Deep down though, he had known it was unlikely, and now that he had been given a shock, he recognised his own duplicity. "You've misunderstood," he added, glancing around nervously. He had never intended his encounter with Alexander to last until someone else came along. He did not want a reputation as a bully and it would be awful if Hodgson somehow heard about this. "All I was doing was trying to make quite certain it wasn't

71

Aylmer. I didn't think it really was. So just keep cool, okay?" He walked off.

Alexander hardly heard what Cowburn said, such had been the awed wonder and surprise with which he had been looking at Julian.

"Thank you," he finally said with a warm smile. He could hardly credit his senses that Julian had done that for him. His best friend had doubted him and everyone seemed to have turned against him, but Julian, whom he hardly knew, had stood up for him and seen off his worst tormentor.

"Where are you going?" asked Julian.

"I was going to the music schools, but can I come with you instead?"

"Shall we just go for a walk?"

"Yes, okay," replied Alexander delightedly, and they set off, chatting animatedly. Both had forgotten shyness in the happy delirium of their new friendship, the older boy marvelling that he had so unexpectedly won something so wonderful he had for many months longed for, and the younger boy marvelling that he had so unexpectedly won something so wonderful he had never even thought of. They walked to the other side of the school, on through the massive playing fields and then beyond through paths and meadows where neither of them had been before. They sat beside the river and talked of their likes and dislikes, their friends, Alexander's family, their pets at home, their beaks, their everything. They forgot about tea-time and when the cold and growing darkness finally drove them back to their house three hours later, they felt like old friends. Alexander accompanied Julian to his room to continue their conversation without either of them thinking about where they were going.

That evening, when Julian looked back on the day, he felt his stupefying and otherwise-unalloyed triumph mixed with a little trepidation that he had broken his carefully nurtured habit of staying on the right side of Guy Cowburn. What would Guy think of him after his open display of anger? He remembered how easily he could turn most of their block against him, and went to see him in his room. Guy looked up from his burry in some alarm when Julian appeared, but recovered his poise as soon as Julian apologised for having got carried away, and they

72

quickly made it up on the surface. When Alexander asked him the next day if he and Cowburn had spoken since their quarrel, he changed the subject, though he knew that the evasion was akin to a lie.

Within a few days of spending all their spare time together, Alexander felt sure Julian was the best friend he had ever had. He noticed his own growing self-confidence when Julian was around, a feeling that he could always be completely himself and need never worry about being thought weird or stupid, as he had to sometimes with most boys. Julian would never mock him. Even when he said things he thought a bit outrageous himself, Julian would smile at him approvingly.

One day he suggested they invent their own language so they could say things to each other without anyone else understanding, or did Julian think that was silly?

"No, not at all," replied Julian thrilled at the idea of any unique bond with Alexander, "but how?" Alexander had already thought of that. He suggested they use English with the consonants and vowels all separately pushed on one alphabetically, so that "Julian and Alexander" became "Kamoep epf Emizepfis." After a few days, Alexander knew about seventy words fluently, and though Julian could never keep up with him, they managed slow conversations.

Soon after that, Alexander confided in him that his greatest fantasy was one day to find and buy in outright independence his own island where he and anyone who wanted to live with him could live in total freedom. Julian said he would certainly like to live there too. The only person in whom Alexander had ever before confided that was his mother.

Miranda Drummond, the daughter of a housemaster, was one of the very few girls to be seen regularly around the school and, being by far the prettiest, was inevitably noticed by most of the boys. Every weekday at half past four, she would alight from her bus at the Burning Bush, the antique lamp-post in the centre of the school, just as the boys were streaming past in different directions to get back to their houses for tea. A few of the boldest and better-looking boys had taken to chatting her up as she strolled back home. She apparently was quite friendly, and soon a small but regular clique was to be seen stopped in conversation with her for a few minutes. Alexander had seen her quite often, though never close up, and confided in Julian that he had rather a crush on her. Though at thirteen and a half, she was a few months younger than Alexander, the boys flirting with her were all in the trendy set of the year above. He had not thought to try to join in until walking along one afternoon he suddenly saw her demurely chatting just a few yards away. By chance she turned her head momentarily and caught his stare. He smiled at once. She looked surprised for a moment, then smiled back, briefly but most definitely warmly, before turning away to answer the boy talking to her. Smitten and jubilant, he almost told Rupert at tea-time, but held back. Unless privately sworn to confidence first, Rupert might well spread the word for fun and soon everyone would be joking about it. He thought again how lucky he was that he now had a friend like Julian who would never do something like that and was besides so much more experienced. He told him that evening.

"So are you really going to talk to her?" asked Julian.

"Do you think I should?"

"Why not?"

"I don't know. I'd certainly like to try. If I met her on her own and she smiled like that again, I would, but I'm not sure if I dare when all those other boys are around. If only I knew one of them."

Now that Julian had got used to his triumph in establishing a close friendship with his secret love, his thoughts had begun to return to how he might make yet further progress towards his ultimate, amorous goal. Instinct told him to act without delay while all was going so well, but he would not trust it. He was terrified Alexander would drop him in horror if he knew his true feelings, so he told himself he was wise to be patient and try to make sure their friendship was central to Alexander's life before taking any risks. After all, he was happier than he had ever been just having for the first time a friend so close and entrancing, and they had all the time in the world.

On hearing about Miranda, he was at once overawed. No girl had ever smiled at him as Alexander described, though he was so much older. He was not in the faintest bit surprised it had happened to Alexander, as he was sure that if he were a girl, he would still be just as much in love with him. He wondered if there could really be any hope that a boy with a possibly mutual crush on a beautiful girl could be enticed to amorous dalliance with him. His pride in being Alexander's esteemed friend was increased by the addition of pluck to his other qualities, but mingled with a new sense of hopelessness.

Guy soon noticed that Julian was much with Alexander. At first it irritated him, as he supposed the new friendship had come about entirely due to Julian's intervention in the alley way and was thus a living reminder of his own humiliation. However, after a week had past and it looked from the amount of time they were together like more than an ordinary friendship, he reached different conclusions. He had never been attracted to another boy himself, but he was not blind to the obvious appeal a pretty boy like Aylmer would have to a pervert. He had thought it odd that Julian had got so stroppy. Why should he have cared? It seemed clear enough now though. His annoyance already mixed with a measure of glee, he soon broached the matter with Peter. Peter had been behaving a bit oddly recently, he thought, but he seemed to cheer up when Guy propounded his new theory and readily agreed with him. Soon the whole of their block was talking about it. Only James Crichton seemed entirely impervious to the scandal, but then he had always been partial to Julian.

"I just don't see what all the fuss is about," he said, much to Guy's irritation, for James was the only boy in their block who commanded sufficient respect to counter his influence.

It was not long before Julian himself caught on to the rumours. Coming into the lobby with Alexander one afternoon when several of his block were there, he was surprised that some of them fell into sudden silence and looked away from him. As he started up the stairs, out of the corner of his eye he saw Guy nudging Peter and smirking. He blushed deeply as he wondered miserably what they had been saying about him, though he thought he could guess the gist of it. At least Alexander, who was climbing the stairs ahead of him, seemed miraculously not to have noticed anything.

His greatest, most heart-wrenching fear was that somebody might say something to him that would put him off their friendship.

Soon the talk spread to the block above too. Geoffrey Hay, the captain of games, was one of the few boys apart from Julian who had admitted to himself that he had a crush on Alexander, though he was no more inclined than Julian to admit it to anyone else. In the Michaelmas Half, he had gently tried to make himself agreeable and had flirted vaguely with the idea of attempting to take things further. In the end, he had not. The risk of what others would think if he were too obviously friendly to a boy four years younger was much too great. He had already been expecting to be the next captain of games, the second most important boy in the house. He even hoped eventually to be elected to Pop, the elite group of school prefects distinguished by their colourful waistcoats and checked trousers, and regarded in awed admiration by most of the boys. This had not yet materialised, but he had long ago abandoned all thought of courting Alexander and indeed convinced himself that he had always thought it would be wrong to do so. He was therefore intensely indignant, as he described his jealousy to himself, when it appeared that a nobody in the block below had not only not shown his stamina in resisting the same temptation, but had successfully plucked the fruit and looked as though he might already have tasted it.

"Really Anthony, you've got to do something about it," he said to the house captain one afternoon in the library, a couple of days after the rumours had started to circulate.

"What can I do?" replied Anthony. "There's not a shred of evidence he might want to do anything improper, let alone that he already has."

"Oh come on. How many boys in C spend all their time hanging around with one in F?"

"All the same...."

"You mean you're just going to do nothing until someone actually catches Smith in Aylmer's bed?" Suddenly there was a knock on the door, although it was ajar. Drysdale came in and handed over some lines to Geoffrey, who had given them to him as a punishment for having his light on at ten the night before.

An embarrassed silence descended on the room, as they both knew that Drysdale was Aylmer's friend.

Their hopes that they had not been overheard were delusive, for Rupert confided the conversation to Alexander word for word the same day. His immediate reaction was shocked indignation on behalf of Julian.

"How can he say something like that? I swear Julian's never touched me. He's not like that. It's so unfair." Once he was on his own, however, he inevitably began to reflect at length on whether that could be something that Julian wanted. He had not really thought about it before. The only conclusion he was able to draw at once was that if it were so, it was in any case decidedly flattering.

Almost as soon as Alexander had come to Eton and had his first conversations with older boys, he had become aware of something indefinable that often arose in the atmosphere and made his heart beat a little faster. He could sense they liked him in a way they did not like Simon Churchill, for example, much as they sometimes amused themselves talking to him. Sometimes, when he had found himself alone with a boy in the Library, especially the more charming ones, this feeling in the air had become so intense that it became impossible to pretend any longer not to notice it. A moment would arrive when he realised the older boy knew he felt it, and usually he could not help blushing when this happened, even though he knew it would make their conversation falter.

He understood implicitly that the feelings involved were somehow linked to the warning his prep school doctor had given the leavers in a sex talk near the end of his time there. The doctor had told them frankly that some grown-up boys at public schools sought sex with the younger ones and they should ready themselves to reject firmly any advances on them. He had not explained though what the sex involved or why they should refuse it. Alexander remained thoroughly confused on both points.

The nearest he had had to any experience of sex between boys was as an unseeing witness of fumblings in his prep school dormitory. Some nights after lights out in his last year there, two particular boys had got into each others' beds. As it had been in the dark, and anyway under the blankets, he did not know exactly what they got up to. They had told the other four boys in the dormitory they were just practising for when they had girls, but he was fairly sure now that it had amounted to no more than mutual fondling. All of them had talked about sex quite a lot and he was fairly sure they would have known if one of them had been able to come. One of the two boys involved had urged him to join him in his bed and he had nearly accepted, out of curiosity more than anything, but he had finally held back for fear of exposing his ignorance and possible comparative immaturity.

His only other knowledge of homosexual practice came from Simon Churchill of all people. Simon read novels voluminously and was a mine of surprising information. One day a few months ago he had alluded to buggery as the thing that homosexuals did. Alexander had heard the word before without having any idea what it meant. Being alone with Simon, he had dared to ask what it was and he got a blunt explanation. He had been shocked that anyone would want to do that.

Looking back on it now he knew what other people thought, he reckoned there had always been that same aura of faint sensuality hanging over his early conversations with Julian, though it had not affected him noticeably at the time. Since they had become friends, he had noticed feeling even more confident of his good looks whenever Julian smiled at him, as if the smile was saying "you are beautiful." He had told himself that a smile was just a smile and couldn't really mean that, but now he rather thought it could. He decided it was quite likely that Julian had always hankered after him sexually, but he was still not certain and he had no idea exactly what Julian might want of him. Was it just fondling or did he really want to bugger him or do something else Alexander had not thought of? Julian was so good and kind that he could not believe he wanted anything bad or disgusting. It was all terribly confusing, but somehow whatever Julian did want must be all right.

However, little as he knew what Julian might want of him or what they might possibly ever do together, he did at least know for sure that it was none of anybody else's business. He was appalled by the threat to their friendship. Whether it was true or

78

not that Julian desired him, he might easily be made unhappy by knowing others suspected this. Julian might also fear that he himself could be turned against him. He could at least set Julian's mind at rest on that one, and he resolved to do so at the earliest opportunity. As he left Julian's room to go to bed that night, he paused by the door and looked him in the eyes.

"I want you to know I don't care what anyone says about you and me. I know you would never hurt me," he said, and met Julian's surprised smile with his own unusually solemn one.

Two days before Long Leave, Rupert came to see Alexander in great excitement, brandishing £ 40. He had just been summoned to see Mr. Hodgson, who told him the thief had confessed and returned all he had stolen. Rupert had been one of those who thought his money had been stolen, but had not been sure.

"But who was it?" asked Alexander.

"Mr. Hodgson wouldn't say." Rupert began to mimic Hodgson's distinct and pompous tone, a habit he had recently picked up from the older boys: "Now, there is no need to concern yourself with the boy's identity. He has been suitably punished and that is the end of the matter."

Only two boys ever did know what had happened: the thief himself and Anthony Burrows, who was sworn to eternal secrecy. With the assistance of the police, Hodgson had obtained a transparent powder, which he had sprinkled on a £ 5 banknote. Anthony had left the banknote on his table, visible from his door and left the door open. It took eight days to disappear. Then he and the housemaster had each taken house lists. Every time they encountered a boy, they glanced at his fingers and, if convinced that the glance had been adequate for the purpose, they ticked his name on the list. As it turned out, they had only ticked off a quarter of the names when Anthony noticed red spots on two fingers and the thumb of Peter Leigh's right hand. Summoned to Hodgson's study, he had confessed straight away and broken down in terror. In fact, he got off lightly, for Hodgson considered that the horror of being caught and the shame of having to face his parents about his crime were enough to teach him a lesson he would not forget, especially when combined with the certainty of immediate expulsion should there be the slightest repeat of his offence. Had he been exposed, he would have had to be expelled at once and his future prospects would have been ruined. The only condition Hodgson set was that all the money was returned with a list of which boys were owed what, and it was indeed returned in full once his furious parents learned what had happened.

V: Alexander's mother

Thou art thy mother's glass, and she in thee
Calls back the lovely April of her prime.
  William Shakespeare, *Sonnet 3*

It was Long Leave at last. Alexander was always tremendously excited to be going home. It was only for four days, but it was the only break lower boys were allowed in the term. They were allowed to leave their houses at school at 7 am. He ran all the way to Windsor Central Station to be one of the boys who managed to catch the 7:17 train to Paddington. He rang on the doorbell of their Chelsea house at about twenty past eight and then he was in his mother's arms.

Penelope Aylmer was still a beautiful woman, who did not look nearly her forty-four years. She had a magnificent figure, being 5′ 9″ with a waist of 21″, and was always elegantly dressed. Her hair retained its natural golden-blond colour identical to Alexander's. She had fallen in love with and married Hal Aylmer, then a successful barrister, when she was nineteen and he eleven years her senior, and she was still deeply in love with him. They had two elder children: Andrew, aged twenty-three and recently married, and Christopher, aged twenty-two and recently graduated from university. Alexander was her youngest by a long way, and she absolutely adored him.

She cooked him a delicious big breakfast while they chatted away, exchanging news, after which they played eight rounds of racing demon. Afterwards, she asked him more about his plans for the afternoon, as he had already told her he was going to meet up with Julian. He told her they were going to a film, though not what they had planned to do first. He had discovered that the *Mayfair* magazine office was in Chancery Lane and they had agreed to meet at the underground station of that name with a view to trying to buy the issue with Lucretia in it.

Penelope had not heard of Julian before and was always curious about Alexander's friends. When, however, she heard he was already seventeen, she became oddly disconcerted that they were evidently such close friends.

"Do the other boys your age have friends so much older?" she asked.

"No, I suppose not." Just a fortnight ago, he had supposed everyone would think he was right to feel proud he had won the friendship of an older boy, and though in the last few days he had learned that some of the nastiest boys had a poisoned view of his new friendship, he was quite put out to find that his mother was worried about it.

"Then what do they think about you going around with one?"

"I don't know really. I don't think anything."

"Darling, how can you be sure he doesn't want to do things to you, I mean …you know…?"

"Mummy, you've really got the wrong end of the stick" he replied a little indignantly. "I've been longing to tell you for ages, but it seemed awkward on the telephone because it's such a long story." He told her then the whole tale of how he had been falsely accused, ending with how Julian had stood up for him. She relented then, horrified by what poor Alexander had been through and genuinely grateful to this Julian she did not know. She could understand why Alexander was so enthusiastic about him and perhaps the older boy was just bowled over by Alexander's gratitude. Doubtless in due course, they would both want to go back to spending their time with their own age groups.

At half past two, he met Julian at Chancery Lane underground station. The *Mayfair* office was indeed just around the corner. They went up two floors and opened the door into what turned out to be a rather nondescript office. Alexander gazed in awed fascination at the wall the other side of the counter, along the entire length of which ran five shelves completely filled with identically-sized magazines, his hopes rising that every single issue was here.

"Er, is this the place to buy back issues of *Mayfair*?" Julian asked the woman behind the counter, reddening.

"Yes, it is. How can I help you?"

"Is it true there's one with Lucretia Pelham in it?" asked Alexander.

"Yes. Hang on a minute." After a little searching, the woman returned and placed a *Mayfair* on the counter. "Lucretia Pelham: Britain's Most Beautiful Teenager reveals all!" proclaimed one of the four headlines on the front cover.

Julian asked the woman about another issue he had decided to buy. He did not feel he could well afford to spend the money, but he did not want Alexander to think he did not share his enthusiasm.

"Wow! Look Julian! I've found her! God how fantastic!" whispered Alexander, holding the magazine open for Julian to see.

The woman returned with another magazine.

"Will that be all then?"

"Yes, thanks."

"That'll be £ 2.40 then." Julian paid her and told Alexander to wait when he started to bring out his own wallet. They ran down the stairs and back into the street. Julian handed over one of the magazines in its paper bag.

"A present!" he said.

"Oh thank you Julian," Alexander beamed at him, touched.

Then they found their way to the film they had told their mothers they were going to. Back at home, Alexander had to wait until he had said goodnight to his parents before he could take a good look at the photos of Lucretia. She looked rather shy. Perhaps it was just the contrast with the brazen vulgarity of most of the other girls. In other respects too, the comparison between her and the others underlined her finest features. He had never much liked *Mayfair*'s emphasis on enormous breasts. Lucretia's were small and firm and her whole body slender and delicate. How he longed to kiss and touch lips and breasts like those! He imagined the exhilaration he would feel if he could be naked with her, if she would accept his caresses, even better if she returned them. If she were to hold his cock in her hands, to show she liked it, if only any beautiful girl would do that, he would surely become at once and for ever after the happiest and most self-confident person in the world. But he knew it was an absurdly hopeless dream. If he were really to meet her and somehow get her to like him enough that he dared tell her how he felt, he could

83

well imagine how she would react from observation of her character in *Worst Friends*.

"Gosh Alexander, what a funny little boy you are," she would say with a lovely smile, ruffling his hair indulgently.

The next morning, Alexander was reading on the drawing-room sofa, when his mother came in and sat on the upholstered bench opposite. She was holding a magazine in her hand and he realised with a shock that it was his original *Mayfair*. He blushed deeply. He knew he had brought it home in the Christmas holidays and had forgotten to take it back with him, and he had been rather disconcerted not to be able to find it yesterday.

"Alexander darling, I found this under your bed. You left it there when you went back to school last time. Don't worry darling, I'm not cross at all." She paused, but he felt his face still to be hot and remained silent. She really was not angry about it. In one way, she was pleased: it was precocious of him to take such an interest in the fair sex when only thirteen, she thought. But she was also worried.

"Was it the Drysdale boy who gave it to you?"

"Yes...."

"Hmm. I thought it probably was." Alexander realised at once that this deduction must derive from Lord Drysdale's reputation. He wondered guiltily whether he should not make it clear he had been an eager recipient of the magazine rather than let his mother assume it could all be explained away as a hereditary moral blemish in his friend, but the conversation moved on before he could decide.

"Daddy and I had never seen a magazine like this before. We didn't know there were things quite like that, but we asked Christopher about it and he told us lots of his friends at Oxford had them, so I suppose it's quite normal nowadays.... But darling, you do understand, don't you, that no nice girl would appear in a magazine like that, not the sort of girl you would want to marry?"

"Yes, I ..." He stopped. He had wondered about this. He thought she must be right, except what about Lucretia Pelham? She was surely a nice girl. He imagined his mother would have to accept her as one of them if they were to meet.

84

"A girl like the ones in this would never really love you. When you get married and are ready to have children, don't you want it to be with a girl who has never loved anyone else, who has kept herself for you, so you can love each other for ever?"

"Yes, I do. I understand." He did believe her. That was what he wanted. He wanted to marry someone who was good, kind, beautiful and pure like his mother. Someone who would love him like his mother loved his father, and whom he could love like his father loved her. A virgin would definitely be better. Was Lucretia a virgin? He had no idea. But he did also know that he would most definitely like to screw her, whether she was or not. It might even be better if she was not, as he was a bit worried he wouldn't know exactly what to do and also he suspected there were exciting things one could do that he did not yet know about. He just wished he could explain that to his mother.

"Good. You know, if you like, I'm sure I could arrange for you to meet some nice girls your age during the holidays. I'll have a think who there is among our friends' children. Perhaps I could arrange a dinner party or something. Would you like that?"

"Oh yes, Mummy, thank you very much," he said enthusiastically.

"But darling, you really do understand that nice girls, the sort of people we know, they couldn't possibly want to do anything ..., you know what I mean, with you? That could only happen when you are much older, when you have fallen in love. Meeting girls now would be just to see if you could be friends. You do understand?"

He was silent. He understood the meaning of her words, yes, but he could not accept the terrible verdict they implied. It was so futile to meet girls if there was no hope at all that he could persuade them to go to bed with him. Sex was the whole point. It seemed that he and his mother lived in different worlds. He understood her world and he wanted it for himself when he got married, but that was so far ahead it did not bear thinking about. It felt a very long time now since he had thought of wanking as an unexpected and delightful addition to his life. It was just a way of distracting himself temporarily from what he really wanted. He longed to feel a beautiful being. Even more, he

85

needed someone to want his touch and to want to touch him. Above all else, he longed for the supreme acceptance of himself that he could only imagine coming from the joyful reception of his seed by someone he desired, and he wanted to know he could find that soon. Just the three months until he would be fourteen seemed a depressingly long time to wait, and the idea that another whole year might pass, that he might reach even just his fifteenth birthday without having had any sexual experience filled him with deep dismay. But he doubted he could make her understand this and it was too embarrassing to try.

"Alexander, you know you can explain your feelings to me. I just want you to be happy." He nearly answered her then, nearly told her how desperately he longed to "make love" to a girl, as he knew she would put it. He badly wanted to ask someone so many things and he was much closer to his mother than anyone else in the world. Also, he sensed she was hurt that he was finding it difficult to open his heart to her. He felt the opportunity slipping away as he desperately struggled to find the words, but they would not come.

"Oh well," she said sadly, "I'll always be here when you do need someone to talk to." He was becoming hard to understand at times, she thought, as she got up and went out of the room to make lunch, leaving the magazine on the bench and her son rather forlorn.

Soon afterwards, his father came home and his uncle Godfrey, a jolly man, came to lunch, which was fun, but he could not help feeling a slight aura of sadness hung over the rest of the day. However, on the morrow, a Sunday, both his brothers and Andrew's wife Sabina came over for the day, and everyone's determination to have fun left no room for any sad reflections. They went out to lunch at his favourite restaurant, the Asterix in the King's Road, and in the afternoon they played a long board game. For teatime, his mother had made his favourite walnut cake.

The next day was the last of Long Leave and he was alone with his mother again. The possibilities that theoretically opened led him to reflect again on their conversation. He was reminded sadly of how he had first begun to learn about procreation.

It had been nearly four years ago. He was ten and at prep school. A much older boy had teased him for not knowing "the facts of life" as he called them. Alexander believed him that these were extremely important mysteries, but repeated badgering of the older boy yielded no more information than that they concerned how he really came into the world and the advice to ask his big brother, who would know all about it, he was told with a smirk. He had done just that when Christopher came to pick him up from school one day.

"What are the facts of life?" he steeled himself to ask five minutes after they had driven off.

"What do you mean?"

"A boy in the top form at school said you would know what I meant if I asked you what the facts of life are" he said, growing disappointed.

"Well I'm afraid I don't. I'm sorry," answered Christopher, becoming a little flustered. Perhaps, however, he had told their parents, and this explained what had then happened.

One day the following holidays, he was sitting with his mother in their garden on a particularly fine day, when she asked him if he knew how babies were born.

"No."

"Well, when you want to know, Daddy can explain it to you." They got up to stroll around. After a few moments, she seemed to come to a decision. Perhaps the beauty of the day inspired her or the birds and the bees.

"Actually, it's nothing very complicated. I could explain it all to you now if you like." She paused. "Or if you don't feel like it now, you can ask me another time." He did want to know, but he felt somehow a little daunted. Perhaps he needed to get ready to hear something so important.

"Can I ask in a few days?" he said after a moment.

"Yes, of course you can, darling, but ask me when we're alone together. It's definitely not the sort of thing to ask in the middle of a dinner party," she said with a smile.

He had quickly felt regret at letting the opportunity slip and readied himself to ask her soon. Only two days later, he went to her in her bedroom and reminded her of her offer. To his great disappointment, she sent him straight to his father. His father had explained for about a quarter of an hour while he shaved in his dressing-room. It was all rather scientific and disappointingly dull. He thought he had grasped the central points that when it became time for him to make babies with his wife, he would somehow put his willy in her and a baby would start growing in her tummy and come out nine months later, but he was merely baffled by all the talk of eggs, uteruses and wombs. He felt sure he had missed some important, possibly magical point that he would have understood perfectly if his mother had explained it to him. It would have been much nicer too. As it was, he had had to wait nearly another three years until rumours in his school dormitory, finally confirmed by the school doctor, gave him a clear understanding of the matter.

Now he wondered whether history was repeating itself. He loved his mother terribly, and yearned to have a perfect understanding with her. In the end, he could not think of anything useful to say, but they had fun together playing racing demon again, and he felt that in time he would somehow find a way of saying what he wanted to. The next day, he was for the first time at Eton going to be playing a piece on the piano in a school concert, so he spent the afternoon practising it in the hall, while his mother sat nearby and did her embroidery. In the evening, his parents drove him back to school. He promised to telephone as soon as possible after the concert, to let them know how it went.

The concert went very well indeed. Julian was there, and just as Alexander was about to begin, he caught his smile wishing him luck. He played as well as he had ever done and was not conscious of any mistakes. The applause sounded truly heartfelt, and later several people came to shake his hand, including two of his beaks. He went back to his house with Julian.

Julian felt a bit awed at this new instance of the much younger boy's superior talent and still prouder of their friendship. He himself had never learned to play a musical instrument. It added to his feeling that some unseen force was somehow making everything in his life go right at last.

He had been happier than ever since Alexander had told him he did not care what others thought. He had spent the whole of

Long Leave thinking about it. Surely it must mean Alexander had heard that other boys thought Julian wanted to bed him, and he did not care if it was true. If instead he had meant that he did not believe them, he would surely have said so.

Did it not follow from this that Alexander did not see anything wrong with Julian desiring him? And when he had added that he knew Julian would not hurt him, could it not suggest he would be willing to let Julian make love to him because he knew Julian would not do so in a way that could hurt? The only worrying thing was the implication that there were things he would not do because they might hurt. Of course he never wanted to hurt him, but what might this exclude? He had a sinking feeling it might mean the one and only path to the supreme pinnacle of joy and fulfilment. Could someone possibly have told Alexander about this, and that it hurt? He himself had no idea whether it would or not. He knew girls hurt and even bled the first time they were taken, and though he thought that was because something had to be torn, it seemed at least possible that boys hurt too. That, however, was a problem for the future and with determination he would surely find a way. For the time being, he was happier than he had really believed possible because physical love with Alexander seemed genuinely to be within reach. He just needed to find a fortuitous moment. This evening it was obviously too late, Alexander's mind was on his success and he would be going straight to bed, but who knew what might happen tomorrow or the next day? And once what he most wanted had happened once or even just been agreed, then lights out would always thereafter herald the beginning of the day's most sublime joys rather than their end. Just imagining it made his head spin.

The next morning Alexander just missed having time to call his mother to tell her how well the concert had gone. He was longing to do so. Only she understood how determined he had been in practising his piece to perfection and he felt a surge of happiness as he imagined her delight. She had wanted terribly to go to the concert herself, but by rotten luck it had fallen on the eightieth birthday of her own old mother, for whom she had had to give a dinner party. Never mind, calling her would have to wait until the quarter of an hour between curfew and supper. That was a better time anyway, because she was much more likely to be at home then.

He got back to his house after his last div at ten past six and ran into Rupert. They chatted animatedly until a boy in Debate appeared and told them sternly to go to their rooms as curfew had begun. This did not lower his high spirits, for his only E.W. was to read a few chapters of *Great Expectations* for English. He had started to be gripped by it and happily looked forward to an hour's reading followed by the telephone call to his mother. He had just begun to hum contentedly to himself, when suddenly Mr. Hodgson came into his room.

Alexander looked at him in rather shocked surprise, as well as a little embarrassment at being caught humming. The housemaster was punctilious in his habits, and if he wished to visit a boy in his room, it was invariably in the hour after Prayers. For a second, Alexander wondered if the false accusations against him had been revived, but surely that was all settled and Mr. Hodgson did not look angry. His face was tense, but white.

"I am afraid I have some very bad news," he said heavily and paused. Now a rush of fear overtook Alexander.

"Sit down," Hodgson added more softly. There was a short pause, which seemed endless to Alexander, before he carried on. "This is the worst news a housemaster can ever have to deliver to a boy." He sighed and though he then continued quickly, Alexander's mind had already raced ahead, wondering desperately what was the worst thing possible that could happen. He realised at once that it could only be something to do with home and the idea of an accident had just begun to form in his mind, when Hodgson's next words struck him like a thunderbolt.

"Your mother died suddenly this morning."

His room seemed to recede into the distance and his sense of time to disintegrate. His head was swimming. It was so impossible to believe that he wondered whether he was having a nightmare. Surely it was only in nightmares that horror and fear were so intense. Perhaps he was going to wake up, but now he could taste the saltiness of the tears streaming down his face. He

90

had never tasted anything so real in a nightmare. They were falling so fast he could hardly see Mr. Hodgson, but he heard his voice as if from a great distance, sometimes muffled, sometimes booming.

He heard something about his father having telephoned, then more clearly: "He will be here shortly. I shall stay with you until he arrives." Then his head was swimming too much to hear, though he thought the housemaster was still speaking.

Someone kept reassuring him again and again that it could not be true, then he realised it was just himself. He paused to wipe away some tears because he needed to see what he was doing. He was trying to stuff clothes into his airline bag. Why was he doing that? Oh yes, he remembered now. Mr. Hodgson had told him to because he was going home. He must have heard him after all. He had no idea how much time had passed when he saw that the door was opening.

There was his father. His father was crying too. It was the first time he had ever seen that. He had not even known it was possible. It brought him nearer to his senses. It must all be true then. Mr. Hodgson had got up from the armchair and come to the door.

"I'm so sorry," he said quietly to Hal Aylmer, briefly grasping his wrist with downcast face, then he passed out of the room. Alexander was alone and face-to-face with his father.

His father stopped crying, though when he spoke he punctuated his sentences with half-sobs. He told him what had happened. His mother had been fine yesterday evening during the dinner party. After breakfast this morning, she said she didn't feel well. She thought perhaps she had an upset stomach, but it would not go away, so before going off to work, his father called their doctor for her. An hour and a quarter later, she telephoned him at his office to say it was much, much worse and the doctor had not come. He said he would call him again and come back home himself. The doctor was no longer in his surgery. He was on his way. When he got back home, he had found Dr. Evans waiting outside the door, having been unable to get in. They found her lying on her bed. The doctor went over. He asked if she was dead, and the doctor said yes. It was something called massive coronary thrombosis, which meant a heart-attack. No one knew the cause. It had nothing necessarily to do with her previous state of health. Perhaps she had bumped herself cooking last night and that had blocked an artery.

Then his father said they should go home. He followed him down the stairs and out of the house, in a daze. There was Christopher waiting in the driver's seat of the Mercedes. He drove them home. Alexander had lost all sense of time and passed the journey home in a haze. They stopped and Christopher opened the door of the house. For a moment, Alexander could not stop himself hoping his mother would come out into the hall to greet them, that it was all just a terrible misunderstanding, but she did not. Instead, there was Andrew, who greeted him sadly, and his grandmother, looking lost. All the same, he could not quite stop himself from stealing glances towards the open kitchen door just in case she was somehow in there, even though he knew it was silly, and he felt a new pang of despair when he finally got a chance to go in and see that it was empty. He knew he was at home and yet it could not be his home any more because the one person who made it home was not there and was never going to be again.

The next day, other relations came, and the next and the next and the one after that, just like they did at Christmas, but it was not Christmas and he had never felt more alone. Much of the time he felt himself to be in a trance, watching himself talking to his kind relations, not really part of what was happening. Then he found himself clinging absurdly to the fantasy that he was just a spectator and the Alexander doing the talking was only an actor playing his part in a horrific drama, and surely it must eventually be over and he would be able to go back to his real, happy life.

Though he knew he ought to accept the ghastly truth without question, when he lay awake at night he could not stop himself returning again and again to the fantasy that he was really asleep, that it was all just a nightmare from which he might at any moment wake up. He knew that if he did, the relief would be so enormous that he would not stay in bed, but would rush out of his bedroom and into his mother's arms. He would hold on to her tightly until he was quite sure she would not go away. If only.

He was told that however miserable he was now, he would eventually, with the passing of time, come to terms with the loss of her, but he had lost his sense of time and he could not really believe it.. Whenever anything happened that he could not cope with, it was his instinctive reaction to turn to his mother. His present despair was surely insuperable as it involved the loss of despair's only verified solution.

On the fifth day, they drove to somewhere called Golders Green far in the north of London for the funeral. In the chapel there was a coffin. Apparently his beautiful mother was in that wooden box. It was difficult to believe, but everyone else seemed to believe it, and the words of the priest implied it was so. Then the coffin moved off out of sight and apparently his mother was being burnt all up. He had been told that afterwards someone would scatter her ashes on the grass outside.

Only the closest relations had been invited to the funeral and they all cried as the coffin disappeared. After that a sort of depressed calm descended on them all. Then they all dispersed to their own homes. Christopher had moved back in with their father for a while, so Alexander left with them both. His father was going to take him back to school and would himself be going back to work the next day. They all had to try to learn to get on with their lives, he was told.

First, his father took him to a teashop, where he asked him what was going on at school. It was the first time in his new life that he thought about the future. It all seemed so petty. He remembered that Mr. Hodgson had said all the boys in F had to write a short story by the end of that week. He had been looking forward to it before, but now he had no idea what to write about.

His father told him of a famous saying by a writer called Robert Louis Stevenson that "it is better to travel hopefully than to arrive." Why not use that as the title, and write a story about a boy who set out to build a little boat, which got ruined just as it was finished? "Never mind!" said his father's imaginary boy at the end, "it was the making it that was fun."

Alexander said that was a good idea. He did think the title was an excellent one, but he secretly thought the story proposed was childish for someone his age and also missed the point of the quote, which was surely a sad one. He knew now that life was about much graver matters than boys making boats and the tone of hope with which the story ended rang hollow.

Meanwhile, in their house at school, on the evening Alexander went home, Julian had tried in vain to find him before dinner and was surprised not to see him either there or afterwards at Prayers, at the end of which Hodgson stood up to make a brief announcement.

"I am sorry to say that Alexander Aylmer's mother has died suddenly and he has been sent home for a few days," he said sadly and left the room. There was a moment's shocked silence and then an uncharacteristically subdued rumble of many voices. All of them could to some extent imagine how devastating a horror it would be to lose their mothers. Most of them were taken aback.

Whenever the subject was mentioned over the next couple of days, it was apparent that even the less sensitive boys and some who hardly knew Alexander were moved a little. A genuine look of sadness was to be seen in the goofy face of Oliver Fisher, for example, as he confided to his friends his remorse over his nasty jibes when they had thought Alexander was the thief. Guy Cowburn kept studiously silent whenever the topic of Alexander arose.

Unsurprisingly, however, it was Julian who was by far the most shaken. The first night, he lay awake for hours gloomily imagining Alexander sobbing in bed at home. The protective urge he had always felt around Alexander since they became friends overwhelmed him until he found he was almost in tears too.

Once Hodgson knew when Alexander was coming back, he went to see the dame to consult her over the arrangements they should make. She told him that Alexander, as even Hodgson unusually took to referring to him for the rest of the Half instead of "Aylmer", messed with Drysdale and Churchill, and she thought they were his best friends, so he went to see them. They were evidently keen to do what they could for Alexander, but rather nervous. He told them all they could really do was to be around to keep him company and try to treat him as normal.

He also consulted his house captain.

"Do you know if Alexander Aylmer has any particular friends apart from Drysdale and Churchill who might be enlisted?"

"Yes. Recently Smith seems to have been spending most of his spare time with him, Sir" said Anthony.

"Really. How has that come to pass?"

"I don't know, Sir."

It was most unorthodox, he thought. It was not the sort of friendship he would normally want to encourage, but now was hardly the time to hold to such scruples. He would have to adopt a middle course.

He went to Julian's room the next evening.

"Now. It has come to my notice that you are a friend of Alexander Aylmer. Is that right?"

"Yes Sir," replied Julian, wondering who could have told him. Even though he knew his source might well be a critical one, he could not help feeling a flush of pride that their friendship had gained such recognition.

"Well. As I am sure you can understand, this is a time when Alexander needs his friends about him, so I hope you will continue to stand by. However, if you really have his welfare at heart, you will make sure he also has time to spend with his friends in his own block. What is likely to benefit him most is to get back to an ordinary routine as soon as he is able."

"Yes, I understand, Sir."

On the drive back to school, Alexander was unable to hold back tears. As he and his father approached the boys' entrance of Peyntors, he wiped them away and steeled himself against more. Following his father into the lobby, he heard a loud rumble of voices which died down as soon as he came in. He looked up briefly to see several boys averting their gaze. Knowing himself now to be an object of pity, he felt more alone in the world than ever as he walked numbly up the stairs. Almost as soon as they reached his room, the dame appeared. His fear surged as his father bade him a sad goodbye, then Rupert and Simon came in. Despite their awkwardness, they were so obviously determined to sound cheerful as they chatted away about what had gone on in his absence, that he tried as hard as possible not to show his despair.

When they went down to dinner, Julian, who was already sitting amongst his block at the table, looked up in horrified fascination as Alexander came in. He had been wondering how he would look, but the change still shocked him. His face was blank and lifeless, as if all the joy and vivacity he associated with it had been wiped off like chalk from a blackboard, though still poignantly beautiful in its melancholy, and Julian's heart bled for him.

Afterwards, he went to his room. Rupert was already there and they did not say very much, but he thought Alexander seemed relieved that he had come, so he stayed until the dame appeared and implied they should all leave him to go to bed.

Over the ensuing days, he continued to spend most of his spare time with Alexander, but found they were rarely alone. Unlike the blissful fortnight when their friendship had begun, Drysdale and Churchill were usually hanging around, even accompanying Alexander to Julian's room. Every evening the dame came to see Alexander, and often Hodgson too, so Alexander stayed in his room after Prayers and Julian did not dare go there then in view of what Hodgson had said about leaving him time with his other friends. He had in any case abandoned all idea of furthering his amorous ambitions for the time being. He squirmed guiltily when he remembered his line of thought the night before Alexander received his devastating blow.

As the days rolled by, Alexander thought he was getting used to being unhappy. He still often felt himself to be just a spectator of his own interaction with others, especially his friends, and growing more distant from them as a result. It was partly because natural spontaneity had gone from their chatter. He knew they were acting, kindly trying to distract him because they felt sorry for him, while he was pretending to be distracted while really thinking about his mother. Once on the fourth day, he began to get genuinely absorbed in a chat with Rupert and started without thinking to tell him something related that had happened to his mother the year before.

"I think we should change the subject," said Rupert and Alexander realised to his dismay that talk of his mother was forbidden. He could understand Rupert, but it only made him long yet more to talk about her. He felt truer to himself with Julian, as Julian seemed rather to join in his sadness, leaving him freer to act as he felt, so the next day he quite deliberately told Julian a story about her and though Julian said nothing, Alexander could still feel his intense embarrassment. After that he never dared refer to her with any boy.

The only person who once mentioned her was Miss Flaherty, who came into his room to clean it one morning and caught him in tears.

"Don't be upset," she said in her strong Irish accent. "Your Mummy is in heaven now." Alexander did not believe in heaven, but he could not help feeling comforted for a moment by her simple certainty, and he smiled. It was a tremendous relief just to hear his mother spoken of at last, and he was grateful for that.

Otherwise it was only his father who talked about her and he only saw his father twice again that Half. On the first two Sundays after he went back, he dropped by to take him out to tea. He felt immensely relieved both times. Only his father shared his grief. Though he had always loved and revered him, he had never been close to him like his mother, but he felt more specially bound to him now that they were in the same boat.

When his father arrived the second time, he said he had more sad news.

"I'm afraid Gigi died the day before yesterday." The surge of relief he had felt at his father's arrival dissipated at once. Gigi was his old and beloved maternal grandmother. He felt momentarily stunned. He had had no idea she might die soon, though she was eighty and had been in poor health for as long as he could remember. He simply had too little experience of old people dying. He became quickly conscious, though, that the impact it was having on him was nothing compared to what it would have been before his mother died.

The only person he had known at all well who died before his mother had been his father's father when he was eight. His mother had come to his prep school to tell him. He had cried then, even though, as a revered patriarch who did not talk much

97

to little children, his grandfather had been a remote figure in his life compared to Gigi. But no tears came now.

Gigi's husband had been invalided by gas in the First World War and died when she was forty-two. She had refused to consider remarriage, having loved him too much, so she had been lonely for the second half of her life. Alexander had always been deeply touched by this. For many years she had been living in a lodging house for old ladies near their house in Chelsea so that Alexander's mother could visit her most days and attend to all her needs. She had made it abundantly clear that she doted on Alexander, who was usually the only one who went too.

"She simply lost the will to live after Mummy died," explained his father. "She had seemed to be coping reasonably at first, but it turned out to be a case of delayed shock. She had to be sent to a nursing-home. Uncle Godfrey went to visit her there most days and I went twice, but there was nothing that could be done for her. It was awful, I'm afraid. The worst thing about it was that right at the end she lost her belief in God. You know how her faith had comforted her all her life."

Alexander felt guilty that he was not crying, for he knew she deserved his tears. It seemed that he was failing in love for her, but he was too drained. Only when his father had left did he fully feel the yet greater loneliness of his life from the loss of her.

By this time, Rupert and Simon had started spending less time with Alexander. They found it hard whenever Alexander was subdued, especially Rupert, who had always been attracted to him by his warmth and liveliness. Julian was always hanging around anyway and Alexander seemed to need his company more than theirs. Soon they just left them to it, much to Julian's relief.

It was not long before Guy Cowburn noticed. One afternoon he was in Oliver Fisher's room together with Robert Williams, when James Crichton came in.

"Does anyone know where Julian is?" asked James.

"Where he always is, I should think, drying his little friend's tears," said Guy.

"For God's sake, Guy," said James hotly, "Hodgson told Julian to spend time with him. Don't you think Aylmer's got enough on his plate without you making nasty insinuations about them?" Cowburn raised his brows, but failed to catch Oliver or Robert's eye. He resolved at once to shut up. Clearly he was going to have to bide his time before a change of fashion might allow him to amuse himself further at Julian's expense.

Towards the end of the Half, Alexander was sometimes more like his old self and Julian could not help his old longings coming back. From time to time when they were alone together and Alexander still looked sad, Julian felt almost overwhelmed by the urge to take him in his arms. He was not sure if it was to comfort him or for his own happiness, or if indeed the distinction need be drawn, but in the end he never even nearly dared. With the lapse of time, his old briefly-held notion that Alexander might once have been ready for his amorous advances had come to seem excessively optimistic and he could not bear the idea that Alexander might think he was taking advantage of his grief.

One day they went for a long run together and when they came back, Alexander was in much higher spirits. When they were in Julian's room and their panting had subsided, Alexander looked at him with sudden seriousness.

"Julian, you know how we're best friends?" he said.

"Yes," said Julian eagerly.

"Do you think we'll always be?"

"Yes, I hope so."

"Are you sure you'll never change your mind?"

"Yes. Do you want us to swear to it?"

"Yes," said Alexander happily.

"Best friends for ever, then," said Julian holding out his hand, and Alexander took it with the first smile Julian had seen entirely like his old heart-wrenching ones. Julian felt that to try something just after that might seem like an abuse of Alexander's trust, but he felt a surge of confidence that next Half his dreams could at last come true.

Since Alexander first went to boarding school, his mother had always come to collect him at the end of the term. This time his father had arranged for a friend who had a son at Eton to pick him up. They took him to Hampton Court to pass the day, so it was late afternoon by the time they dropped him off and handed him the house keys which had once been his mother's. His habit of looking forward to going home at the end of term was so deeply engrained that his efforts to dampen his expectations were woefully inadequate. As the heavy front door closed behind him and its echo died, he felt overwhelmed with loneliness. He carried his suitcase through the silent house to his bedroom and though he knew his father would be home in only an hour, he lay down on his bed and was soon in tears. What he missed most by far was being hugged by his mother. He realised then that no one was ever likely to hug him. He did not think his father had ever held or kissed him, certainly not in his memory. He thought he could remember him holding his hand, when he was four or five perhaps, but that was the nearest to physical affection that had ever passed between them.

At last he heard his father's key in the door and rushed to meet him. His father seemed pleased enough to see him, though his greeting was a pale shadow of what his mother's had always been. They played a game of L'Attaque before dinner and then they went into the kitchen. His father put a pie the daily had left ready into the microwave and showed him how the machine worked. Their efforts felt very awkward compared to the apparent ease with which his mother had produced lavish meals. As they ate the pie, he told him what plans had been made for the Easter holidays and asked him if he had any ideas for the summer ones.

"No, I'm afraid not." He really could not imagine such a long time at home without his mother.

"I thought we might go to the seaside somewhere easy like Mallorca and ask Uncle Godfrey and his family to come too. What do you think?"

"Yes. That would be fun."

"And later on, I was thinking of renting a house in the country for a week. Andrew and Sabina and Christopher could come too. Aunt Olive has a friend called Mrs. Tweedie, whom I've met a few times and seems very nice. I was thinking I might ask her to come and cook for us. She's rather hard up you see, so she might be interested in doing it so that her daughter can have a holiday in the country. The only trouble is I've heard the daughter is awful, so I'm not sure."

His father gave him a list of the telephone numbers of relations who had offered to have him to lunch and told him to choose whom he wanted to see. In the morning, he telephoned his favourite grown-up cousin. She and her boyfriend took him to the cinema. All the relations he called were very kind and invited him to lunch repeatedly, but he did not like to accept too often, knowing himself to be a burden to them, so he was still desperately lonely and he longed for physical affection. He wished he had a sister. He had aunts-in-law and grown-up girl cousins, but he was not close enough to them for hugs or kisses by a long way. If they had kissed him, he would have been embarrassed, because he would have known they were only doing it because they ought to, not because they really wanted to. He wanted so badly to be wanted.

He would have liked to spend time with Julian, but he had been sent on an exchange to Paris for the first fortnight of the holidays to improve his French for A levels, and in the end they were only able to meet up once after that.

Some days he did not bother to get up until well into the afternoon, there being nothing to get up for. He just lay in bed reading. Every hour or so, he would interrupt his novel to leaf through his Mayfairs and wank. He thought about girls a lot. The craving he felt for the physical affection his mother had so liberally bestowed on him compounded with his sexual frustration to create an overwhelming longing for love, for total intimacy with another being. He longed to meet girls. He remembered sadly his mother's offer to introduce him to some these holidays. He did not see how his father could help him there even if he had been close enough to him to ask. He had anyway begun to doubt that meeting a girl his age could be the solution to his misery. He could much more easily imagine being happy with a girl several years older than him, someone still young and beautiful like Lucretia, but old enough to comfort and reassure him. The trouble was that, from everything he had heard, grown-up girls just weren't interested in boys his age.

Several days he went to the London Library in Piccadilly. It was the largest lending library in the world. He had been there a few times before with Christopher, who had been given life membership for his twenty-first birthday and had been utterly enthralled to be in a place where it seemed every bit of knowledge could be found. To give him something he was happy to do on his own, his father had now bought him his own life membership at a staggering cost of £ 1500. It was by many times the biggest present he had ever been given. There were only a few thousand members, many of them distinguished writers, and he was proud of being the only child there.

One of the first things he looked for was any book about the secret country where people did not wear clothes, but though there were nearly a million books and he checked the catalogues and spent long hours going through the topography shelves, he never found anything about it at all. Like everything he longed for most, even the possible means of finding what he sought eluded him.

If there was one thing he definitely liked about himself it was his name, Ἀλέξανδρος, defender of man. Obviously he knew he owed it to the good taste of his parents rather than to his own merit, but he was nevertheless proud of it. If he were not Alexander, then he would like to have had a much rarer name, as he was well aware of its great disadvantage, that he shared it with millions of others, but still he liked his name enough to think it easily worth that one failing. His main reason was not its sound or meaning, but its greatest bearer, indeed the greatest bearer of any name, Alexander the Great, unique among men of action for the imaginative splendours which inspired him and unique among dreamers for the things he achieved. He had been enchanted by stories about him since he was seven. Now he found that the London Library had a shelf full of books about the ancient hero, which led him to the discovery of a novel about his childhood called *Fire From Heaven*. He took it home excitedly, but then decided to save the pleasure for school.

His father arranged for them to spend Easter with his own mother. Old Lady Aylmer lived at Eryholme Hall in Yorkshire, with only her servants for company since she was widowed. She was eighty-four, but vigorous in both body and mind. Alexander was going by train four days earlier, so he would

102

have a full week there. He was delighted, for he loved his remaining grandmother deeply.

Even when he was much younger, she had taken him seriously. She told him what she thought about things other adults seemed to think he was too childish for. She also often asked his opinion, and when he gave it, she really listened, unlike some adults who just pretended to for politeness while their minds were half elsewhere. As a result, he always enjoyed their conversations immensely and had discussed many of his favourite historical topics with her at greater length than with anyone.

She was the very opposite of the aunt he disliked most, who always talked down to him as if he was a baby, while affecting to like children with gushing sentimentality. Recently he had reached the surprising conclusion that it was in fact the stupidest adults who had nothing to say to children. He was fairly sure his aunt would know nothing about Alexander the Great, if indeed she had heard of him.

It was thus at Eryholme that he spent the happiest week of the holidays, chatting to his grandmother, reading and going for long walks on the moors. Sometimes, when she was resting, he would go off with just her alsatian, Dulcie.

"Dulcie knows who I love most!" his grandmother had said two years before, when he came back from taking the dog for a walk on his own for the first time. "You're the only person she's ever gone off with without me." Naturally, his happiness playing with Dulcie had much increased.

His father drove them back to London on the afternoon of Easter Monday and only two days before Alexander was due back at school. He seemed subdued, so they fell into silence during the last part of the journey, by when it was dark. When they drew up near their front door, he turned off the engine, but made no move to get out, so Alexander sat still with him.

"Do you think I'll ever get married again?" he asked suddenly. Alexander paused, confused that his father apparently had such unexpected doubts over the course of his life that Alexander's opinion could help him know his own mind.

"No," he answered finally.

"Why not?" asked his father after a moment.

"Well, you loved Mummy too much, didn't you?" answered Alexander, feeling he was just stating the obvious.

"Yes," he said sadly, opening the car door. "I suppose you're probably right."

VI: New Beginnings

If you see a beautiful boy, strike while the iron is hot.
Say what you mean, take hold of his testicles full-handed.
But if you say 'I honour you, and will be like a brother,'
Shame will close your road to fulfilment.
   Addaios Makedonos in *The Greek Anthology* X 20

When Alexander went back to Eton for the Summer Half, the change was much more profound than the usual sudden difference between home and school.

The immediate changes of which he had known in advance were depressing. The dame, Mrs. Austin, whom he had come to regard as a real friend, had left to rejoin her husband, who had been working in Bahrain. The new one, Mrs. Baker, was older and much drier. Alexander felt the absence of a sympathetic female quite sharply.

Most of the boys soon decided that the worst thing about Mrs. Baker was her fat dachshund, which waddled along behind her nearly everywhere she went. Whether because the creature had already had some bad experience of young humans or whether it just sensed its lack of popularity with the boys, it was from the outset unfriendly to them and growled if one of them came too close. This inevitably much increased their antipathy. Fuel was added to the fire when on the third day of the Half, Robert Williams in C came back to his room to find the ugly creature had managed to pull the tablecloth off his table with all that had been sitting on it, notably the food stores of his mess, which it was greedily guzzling. He just managed to give it a good kick before it fled. The story spread in no time and soon it became a house sport to try to give the wretched animal a kick if it ever got left sufficiently behind its mistress for her not to know.

Another change was that his old English beak had taken a sabbatical to go to Italy. He had been put out when he had first heard that was going to happen, as Mr. Rice had been both easy-going and interesting and one of his favourite beaks. When he had his first English div, however, he found that the new one, Mr. Cavendish, was even nicer. He was cheerful, friendly and open, and seemed to learn all their Christian names in no time, though none of Alexander's other beaks had even wanted to know them. Perhaps the most invigorating thing was how very much younger he was than anyone else who had taught Alexander at Eton.   He looked about the same age as Christopher, though otherwise quite different, as he was tall and had dark hair with warm, hazel eyes that often twinkled. It felt pleasantly strange being taught by someone who came across as a big brother, rather than someone his parents' generation. His teaching too was invigorating. He had a rich, expressive voice and when he read a poem out loud, it came alive for Alexander as never before.

At the end of their first div with him, he told them to write a short story of at least one thousand five hundred words for Monday week. He pointed out that as it was Friday they had two weekends to do it, so he would not accept lateness and advised them to get going the next day. Alexander was a bit surprised by the sudden hint of strictness, which struck him as superfluous. This was not the sort of beak who had to threaten punishment to get one to do one's E.W.s well and on time. Rather one was eager to win one of the warm, approving smiles that often accompanied the twinkling of the eyes in his handsome face.

Alexander had never written anything that long and he was excited by the idea of trying to make it really good. He decided at once that he would use his father's still unused idea for the title. Rather to his disappointment, when he had got back to school after his mother's death, he had found that Mr. Hodgson had indefinitely postponed the story-writing he had earlier proposed. He started thinking of a story almost at once.

He found that the attitude of the other boys in JRH towards him had changed by some unspoken consensus.   The deliberate kindness they had shown him in the Lent Half had just disappeared as if it belonged to some fallen regime. He did not mind foregoing the pity as he had become irked by the hollow rapports it had led to, but he found himself suddenly with far fewer friends than he had ever had before. Rupert and Simon seemed not to have forgotten how withdrawn from them he had become, and to have gone their own ways. He realised it was largely his own fault for having spent so much of the last Half with Julian.

106

The switching of his principal friendship that had occurred was given a new formality the first morning of the Half, when Julian asked if they could mess together. Alexander was thrilled at the prospect of spending every tea-time with him and proud that Julian was willing openly to acknowledge him as his best friend. It might be the first time that a boy in F was going to mess in a C boy's room. Nevertheless, he did not want to hurt Rupert or Simon's feelings, especially Rupert's.

"No. That's fine with me," replied Rupert when asked if he would mind, and Alexander realised sadly from the apparent indifference in his tone how far apart they had grown.

Occasionally when he was alone and especially at night, Alexander still wept for his mother, but otherwise his zest for life and his self-confidence had returned and he knew he owed it largely to his friendship with Julian, the one friend he could rely on. Julian seemed also to have changed quite suddenly from the Lent Half, though not in the way others had. On the contrary, he had become much more attentive to him and in a tense manner that suggested he needed Alexander as much as the other way round.

Alexander soon found that the Summer Half had a quite different and much more agreeable character compared to the others. The natural difference of the evenings being light and warm was greatly enhanced by the special summer timetable. The divs began and finished earlier in the day and lock-up was not until eight instead of a quarter past six, so that even on the three days when they had afternoon divs, they had more than three hours free time between the last and lock-up. Another novelty he was enthusiastic about was that instead of playing football or the Field Game, he was going to go rowing on the Thames.

Alexander had known he was going to row at Eton since the year before last, when his father had first explained that the boys there were divided into wet bobs or dry bobs according to whether they went on the river or played cricket. They had gone to stay in the Lake District with one of his mother's close friends, whose son Philip Watson was her godson and one of the oldest tribulations in Alexander's life. He could hardly think of anyone he had less in common with than Philip, a goofy bully with an unpleasant jeering manner. Philip expressed contemptuous boredom with everything that interested Alexander and seemed himself to be interested only in cricket, which Alexander found one of the most tedious of games. Philip had an unsatisfactory home background with his thrice-married mother and Alexander's mother unfortunately took her godmotherly duties seriously, so he came to stay with them quite often during the holidays. Thankfully at home they at least did not have any cricket equipment, but now that they were staying with Philip, daily cricket practice was an obligation. Alexander longed to escape into the rather fine library of Philip's new stepfather, where there was no danger of Philip wanting to join him, but his mother told him it was his duty as a guest to indulge his host. He thus endured the tedium and the jeering at his alleged incompetence, while quietly longing to go home.

At last, one particularly fine morning, it was announced that they were going for a long picnic by a lake. He loved picnics. His father drove them to a particularly beautiful and isolated spot where a meadow with both cattle and sheep ran gently down to a deep blue lake shimmering in the sun. It was an unusually hot day and utterly peaceful, with no sounds except insects and birds to disturb the gentle chatter of the two mothers half-lying in the sun. Alexander's father went fishing, while Alexander escaped Philip to go wandering among the surprisingly friendly calves, and Philip sat on the grass, looking bored and cross.

It was then that his father somehow found a rowing-boat and proposed teaching them how to use it so they could decide what they wanted to do when they eventually went to Eton. Both boys were enthusiastic. His father showed them how to hold and move the oars. Alexander took to it straight away. He loved the swish of the parted water as it swept past and could sense its coolness in delicious contrast to the heat of the sun. Out on the beautiful lake with birds swirling overhead he felt closer to nature than in any other sport he had known. Soon they went back to the shore. His father got out and suggested they take turns rowing their mothers across to some woods two hundred feet away.

Their mothers climbed in and Alexander took the oars first. He took them across in long steady strokes and he could sense his mother was impressed. Reluctantly, he handed the oars over to Philip. When he first pulled on them, one bounced heavily against the surface of the water and splashed everyone, while the other began to get dragged under the boat. Philip pushed and pulled and heaved and eventually managed to extricate the oar. He paused and tried again, but the boat just went round and round in circles. His face was red and his eyes angrily averted.

"I really think you'd better let Alexander do it, darling," said Philip's mother as her embarrassment mounted.

"No. Alexander, no. Philip just needs a little time," said Alexander's mother. "He'll get the hang of it in a moment." But Philip did not get the hang of it and carried on going round in circles for another couple of minutes. Eventually he gave up and sulked while Alexander took them back to his waiting father. And thus had he become a wet bob in his heart long before he even went to Eton.

The first afternoon of the Half was a half-day and Julian agreed to accompany him on the river. Julian had actually given up rowing the year before last, but faced with Alexander's determination, he agreed to take it up again. He was certainly not going to throw away the chance of so many sunny afternoons with Alexander. By the time they got to the boat house, he had anyway been infected with his enthusiasm. As they arrived at the landing stage, they were amused to see James Bates, who was rather a show-off, step gingerly into his whiff for the first time and topple straight off into the water the other side. Alexander took to it as effortlessly as before, though the narrow little whiffs built for speed required more skilled handling than the boat he had rowed his mother in.

On the first Saturday they went to Queen's Eyot, an island four miles upriver with a clubhouse, which was the one place where younger boys at Eton were allowed cider or beer. Most boys never went further than that, but Alexander was soon dissatisfied and the following Saturday insisted on going all the way to Maidenhead, which was nearly as far again. It was a hot day and thirsty work, as they did not stop at Queen's Eyot on the way.

"Why don't we ask for a drink from one of the pleasure boats passing by?" suggested Alexander.

"We can't possibly," said Julian, embarrassed at the idea.

"Why not?"

Before Julian could think of an answer, a boat slowly chugged up level with them.

"Excuse me," said Alexander to the woman on the deck. "I hope you don't mind me asking, but might it be possible to have some water?"

"Yes, of course, dear," the woman replied, disappearing into her cabin. She soon returned with an enormous glass of orange juice. "Here you are," she said, stretching it out to him.

Alexander thanked her with a beaming smile and Julian could see she was well pleased with the exchange.

"Would you like one too?" she asked Julian and he accepted, though blushing deeply. It was yet another example of how much more daring Alexander was than him, he thought admiringly.

"You see? It wasn't hard, was it?" said Alexander. After that, he asked someone whenever he got seriously thirsty and Julian became quite thankful for it, as he never dared himself.

Another consequence of the long summer afternoons was that Miranda and her clique were to be seen quite regularly engaged in languorous conversation for an hour or more. There was a particular spot in the street where it widened out by Barne's Pool that had become their meeting-place. Alexander had never forgotten her, but had let his dream of joining her little group of suitors fall by the wayside during the miserable weeks after his mother's death. Now he felt emboldened again. One day he saw Johnny Villiers there and seized his chance. Johnny seemed to be a new adjunct to Miranda's set. It was not surprising as he was the trendiest E boy in JRH. Alexander was not friends with him, but it might be the best chance he would ever get. He crossed to their side of the street before he was seen, and contrived to run into Johnny as if by accident.

"Hi, Johnny," he said in a friendly voice, and stopped.

"Oh hello," said Johnny reluctantly, embarrassed at the invasion by a younger boy.

The other boys looked at him askance, as if to say "Who the hell are you?" but Alexander just brazened it out. If he could survive these awful first moments without being driven off, he should be able to stay on as long as he liked. After a couple of minutes listening to their desultory conversation, his nervousness subsided. He caught Miranda's eye and smiled bashfully. She smiled back and he detected looks of irritation in the others, but that did not matter now, he thought triumphantly. He stayed on for twenty minutes until he reckoned they were so used to him that he would dare to stop by again without the excuse of knowing Johnny. Then he caught Miranda's eye again and smiled good-bye.

The next day, he approached the group openly, his heart thumping.

"Hi Alexander," said Miranda with a warm smile. With a surge of exhilaration, he realised she must have asked who he was. Her greeting also served as her stamp of approval. After that, the others did not feel they could look at him as if he did not belong. He had effectively joined the club. The conversation was disappointingly dull, but for the time being he did not care much. It was enough that he could stand close to her, occasionally getting in a word or a smile while in his imagination he kissed and undressed her.

A few days later Johnny accosted him in their house.

"What do you think you're doing hanging around Miranda like that?" he asked snidely.

"Why shouldn't I?"

"You don't really think she would be interested in a boy like you, do you? You're just a child compared to her."

"She's the same age as me."

"You don't know anything about girls yet. Miranda's been seen with boys in B. You have no idea what she gets up to with them, do you?"

"What does she get up to?" asked Alexander, too fascinated to hide his curiosity.

"You'd like to know that, wouldn't you? Well, I could tell you some things that would surprise you, but I'm not going to."

Alexander was dreadfully tormented by this conversation. He had no idea if it was true or not. It seemed very possible. He

111

knew that Johnny was more sophisticated and knowledgeable about what went on around the school than him. Though he had never seen Miranda with a boy so much older, he had sometimes wondered if she thought him childish, especially when she talked about things like fashion that he knew nothing about. On the other hand, she seemed to like him nevertheless, so even if she had already been screwed by an older boy, as Johnny seemed to be insinuating, maybe she would do it with him too, if only he could get to be somewhere private with her.

After that, he felt more intimidated by the other boys, who were mostly Johnny's friends, but he did not let it deter him. The feeling of having been humbled was soon outbalanced by the awe he detected from many of his own block that they supposed he had managed to join the trendiest elite of the block above and flirt with Miranda.

Julian was the only boy Alexander dared ask if he thought what Johnny said might be true. From the beginning of their friendship, Alexander had simply assumed that Julian had more experience of girls than him, and Julian had not disillusioned him, fearing he would sink in his esteem if he did.

"I haven't heard anything about Miranda, but you'll know how far she's gone with another boy when you kiss her on the lips for the first time," he improvised.

Alexander always confided his successes in Julian, who responded with sincere demonstrations of admiration. Julian could not even contemplate daring to try to join the cool set of his own block, now jockeying for position to try to get elected to next year's Pop, let alone that of the block above. He was sure Alexander could achieve anything he wanted. He was a young god. His prowess made him more daunting, but it also made him even sexier.

Julian was determined not to let his awe of Alexander put him off pursuit of his greatest longing. His life hitherto seemed to him as useless as those of drones in a bee-hive, whom his biology beak said did nothing but guzzle honey until the magical day arrived of their nuptial flight high into the summer sky with their queen. Only when he released himself deep into his beloved, would he like the luckiest of the drones have justified his existence. He had come back for the new Half firmly resolved to do everything in his power to achieve this, and though he thought he had all the time in the world, his physical yearning was grinding down his patience and his determination to make progress soon was renewed. He had still not quite recovered the confidence he had had just before Alexander's mother had died that it would be easy to bed him. The lapse of time somehow made changing the tone of their friendship more daunting.

He wavered between thinking he should begin by making a confession of his desire and wondering if a gentle kiss would not be a more eloquent way of achieving the same end. Day after day he urged himself to do either and tried to find a suitable opening, only in the end to put it off until a tomorrow that never came. Once Alexander stood by his window, quietly watching a game of croquet being played out on the lawn below and Julian came to stand right behind him and a little to his side. He ordered himself to act, to move his lips steadily forward until they touched the boy's flawless rosy cheek. He drew closer and closer until he was within seconds of reaching the point of no return whence he had readied himself to swoop down unhesitatingly for the final inches. At last, he thought, his heart and loins throbbing, when suddenly Alexander turned his head and bumped into him, confused.

Unsuspected by anyone, Peter Leigh had long suffered from crushes on several younger boys, of whom Alexander was inevitably one, but he had always tried not to think about it. Guy, his most important friend, was rather strait-laced and would not be amused. It was typical of Julian, he thought, to make an undignified spectacle of himself and an example of why he was so pitifully an outsider in their block. His own traumatic experience of last Half had reinforced his belief that the only way to get along in life was to make oneself as agreeable as possible to the accepted arbiters of decent, sociable behaviour. He went back to the Summer Half determined to strengthen his credentials as one who understood these things and Julian offered him the means. He therefore took the lead from Guy in expressing disgust for Julian's presumed proclivities. Guy and

113

others were then only too happy to contribute their own ridicule once it was re-established as the in thing to do.

Geoffrey Hay was much more forthright in his criticism. Once Julian went into the Common Room, looking for Alexander, and found himself face to face with him.

"Looking for Aylmer, are you?" asked the captain of games with a hearty sneer in front of eight other boys who turned to listen with eager anticipation.

"No," said Julian.

"Can't let him out of your sight, can you?"

"I don't know what you mean. We're just friends. Mr. Hodgson asked me to keep an eye on him."

"That was months ago. He doesn't need a nanny now. What's it really about, eh?" A boy in D giggled.

"I really don't know what you're talking about" said Julian, feeling his cheeks burning hot as he retreated from the room.

Since Alexander had first surmised that Julian desired him, he too had often wondered what sex with him would be like, especially recently when he had sensed a renewed intensity when they were together.

He was not physically attracted to Julian. He was conscious of appreciating good looks in those of his friends who had them, such as Rupert, but that did not amount to a desire to do anything sexual with them, as he would definitely like to do with a girl. He could not see anything wrong with boys doing things together if they wanted to, but he felt no need for it himself. Julian was not even good-looking. All his physical presence evoked in Alexander was an immense fondness and feelings of trust, reassurance and gratitude.

On the other hand, his devotion to him made it difficult to imagine refusing him anything he badly wanted, including even the thing he supposed from what Simon had told him that Julian probably wanted. He trusted that Julian would not hurt him and he realised his initial shock at the idea of it had been because he had never before thought of that part of his body except in terms of its ignoble function. Now that he had thought further, he realised there was no reason why it should not have two quite independent purposes, as other bodily parts did. He definitely

114

had no wish to possess another boy himself, but he understood instinctively that this was not in question. He as the younger boy was the desired one.

As soon as the Half began, Alexander had started reading his novel found in the London Library, *Fire From Heaven* by Mary Renault. He decided it was by far the best novel he had ever read. Every fantastic episode in Alexander the Great's boyhood was recounted so credibly and yet so movingly. His favourite had always been the taming of Boukephalos.

As he had read the original story in Plutarch's biography of Alexander, when the ancient hero had been about thirteen, a horse-dealer had brought the stallion to sell to his father the King of Macedon for a great sum. The horse would allow no one to mount him and reared wildly whenever one of the King's grooms approached. At length, the King grew angry at having been offered such a vicious, unbroken beast and ordered him to be taken away, but then the young prince shouted out that they were losing the best horse, and all because they did not know how to handle him or dared not try. His father ignored him at first, so he persisted until the King felt bound to take notice and asked him if he found fault with his elders because he could manage a horse better.

"I could manage better this one at least," retorted Alexander. His father could not ignore such a public challenge and asked what he was prepared to forfeit if he failed.

"I will pay the price of the horse," Alexander replied without hesitation and all the courtiers burst out laughing. The King agreed a bet with his son, thinking that he needed taking down. Alexander took him by the bridle and turned him towards the sun, for he alone had noticed that the horse was shying at the sight of his own shadow moving around in front of him. He ran alongside him for a while, calming him, then vaulted onto his back with a light spring. Once he had got Boukephalos used to the bit, and the horse had lost his fear and become impatient to show his speed, he urged him forward into a gallop. The King and his friends looked on in an agony of suspense until Alexander reached the end of his gallop and turned in full control to ride triumphantly back. Then they had broken out into loud applause, while his father wept with joy and, when the boy dismounted, kissed him.

115

"My son, you must find a kingdom equal to yourself. Macedon is too small for you," said the King. For the rest of his life, Boukephalos never let anyone mount him but Alexander, who always rode him into battle until he was too old. Once after that, he was carried off by raiders and Alexander threatened to devastate their entire province until he was brought back.

Mary Renault told the story at much greater length and so movingly that it made him cry. She also made it the moment when began his lifelong best friendship with Hephaistion, whom he had hardly known before. When he challenged his father and everyone else had laughed or fallen silent, Hephaistion alone had stepped out in front, his eyes fervently wishing him success, and Alexander had caught his look.

In just the same way, had not Julian been the only one who had openly taken his side when others had been against him? He remembered too the day he had caught Julian's eyes wishing him success at the piano concert, though of course that, like everything in his life, was mundane and paltry compared to what his great namesake did as a boy. All the same, was Julian not his Hephaistion, the one person who understood him and on whom he could rely, just as Hephaistion had been for Alexander the Great?

A few days later, he reached the point in the novel where Hephaistion finally dared to reveal his desire for Alexander and they lay together. This transformed his thoughts yet further. If his heroic namesake, the greatest and bravest conqueror, had been willing as a boy to give himself to his bigger best friend, it could hardly after all be effeminate for him to do likewise. He must also have somehow misunderstood the sexual act itself more badly than he had imagined, for it was also impossible that one of Hephaistion's character would want something distasteful.

The novelist referred to the sex very delicately, but it was made fairly clear that his namesake had not been drawn to it for his own physical pleasure either, or at least not nearly so much that as to bring happiness to the friend he loved and who desired him so badly. Any reluctance he himself might once have felt at doing likewise now seemed shamefully churlish.

116

Having decided that making Julian happy by giving him whatever he might want sexually would be good and noble, he began to hope those wants were real, so that he could satisfy them. Having sex as boys could only have strengthened the bond between Alexander and Hephaistion and helped ensure they remained best friends when both were grown up and married. Sex would likewise cement his special friendship with Julian. He longed too to be held and touched by someone who loved him, especially in his most intimate parts. That really would be exciting.

Sometimes when he was alone with Julian, he thought from the way he looked at him that he was finally about to touch him or say something that would bring them together, but in the end he never did. Other boys were starting to make jokes about their friendship like before, so it was surely impossible that Julian had not addressed the question of whether he liked him that way or not. The most likely explanation was that he did not dare do anything because he was frightened of what he would think. He asked himself if he had done anything to put Julian off, but he could not think what. Sometimes he wondered if he should tell Julian bluntly that if he wanted what other boys suspected he did, he could have it, but his remaining tiny doubt put him off. If he was wrong and Julian had no sexual interest in him, he would feel disgusted and insulted by the suggestion. If only there was a more subtle way.

Alexander still dropped in on the little gathering by Barne's Pool most days, but he was getting increasingly frustrated. He could not think of a way by which he might ever contrive to be alone with Miranda, and he was obviously never going to get to kiss her otherwise.

Even striking up an interesting conversation with her seemed impossible. Once, a discussion started up about a historical film Alexander had seen and he had become genuinely absorbed in what they were saying. Then he had pointed out an inaccuracy he found absurd. Miranda just looked slightly surprised, but the others had glanced at him as if it was positively distasteful to bring something as academic as historical fact into their chat.

One afternoon, Jocelyn Kerr, the most sophisticated of her regular admirers, mentioned that he had been put on Tardy Book.

"What's that?" asked Miranda.

"It's the punishment here for being late for something," replied Jocelyn. "Instead of getting up at seven thirty like everyone else, one has to get to School Office before then to sign a book. I was just a minute late for my maths div this morning and I've been put on it for three days."

"You're lucky!" said Miranda. "I have to be ready at the Burning Bush for my bus to come at seven twelve every day."

That gave Alexander a brilliant idea. If he could get there just before then, he could be alone with her while she waited. The only problem was that he did not know if he could get out of his house that early. He went down to see the next morning and found that it was only opened at a quarter past seven to let any boys out who were on Tardy Book, so he searched around to see if there was any other way out. Looking in the coal room, which no one went into in the summer and adjoined the boys' entrance, he saw it had a sash window which opened horizontally from the top. He could get to it from the shelf beneath and it was wide enough for him to slip through. By the time he came back, the boys' entrance would be open.

He decided to go for it. He tried to think of what he could say when he arrived at the Burning Bush, then he decided it would be far easier if he gave her a present. If he brought her a box of chocolates, then she would know how he felt and he would not have to say much. Maybe, if no one was around, he could even dare kiss her on the cheek. The next morning, all was ready. It was already sunny, though still cold, as he set out, feverishly excited. As the Burning Bush came into sight, he saw with a thumping heart that Miranda really was there standing alone. When he got close enough for her to see that it was him, a look of astonishment came over her.

"Hello, Miranda. I just came to give you this," he said, handing the box to her. She looked briefly bewildered as she took it, then she looked at him with an enraptured smile.

"Oh, Alexander! Thank you so much," she said warmly. This was the moment he had been waiting for, his chance to kiss her.

He was near enough. Just one step. Glancing briefly at both sides of the street, he could see only two beaks walking, neither of them close by. He turned back to take the plunge, but just as he did so, he heard the swish of the bus as it appeared round the corner and ground to a halt beside them.

"Well, good-bye and thanks again. See you later," said Miranda at once.

"Yes. Good-bye," he said, trying not to sound dejected. He turned back to his house with a heavy heart, trying to console himself that at least she knew his feelings now. When he told Julian, he was surprised that his friend thought he had been so daring. He wished so much that he really had been.

He went to see her again that afternoon, but though she smiled at him charmingly, the conversation was as desultory as ever and he saw no sign that he had made any lasting impression until he left.

"He's so-o sweet," he heard her whisper loudly to Jocelyn, as he went off.

Alexander finished writing his short story for Mr. Cavendish, *It is Better to Travel Hopefully than to Arrive*, two days before it was due. He was sure it was by far the best thing he had ever written. Though his ideas had flowed easily, he had still taken a lot of time over it, working out the plot before starting to write and choosing his words carefully. He was much looking forward to his second English div of the coming week when Mr. Cavendish would hand their stories back to them. Though the beak had been entirely friendly, he had never yet been able to catch his full attention. He had seen his twinkling eyes fix with lively interest on boys around him, but only ever glance briefly at himself. With his short story, though, he was hopeful of finally arousing his interest.

He was thinking happily of this as he went up to his room during the Chambers just before the story was to be handed in. When he got there, he was a little disconcerted to see his door open, as he always left it closed. Going in, he saw chaos and knew at once that the dame's dog must have caused it, though it was no longer there. As had happened to Williams, his tablecloth lay on the floor beside broken shards of glass. To his horror, he saw that the sheets of his story lay also on the floor partly buried under a mound of smelly, soft, brown pooh. They must have scattered slightly as they fell, but only one was entirely free of the mess. He tried to pull out the bottom one of the others, but it was stained and soggy and began to tear as he did so. Then he saw the torn wrapping of his new packet of Bourbon biscuits the other side of the table, and remembered regretfully that he had refused to kick the horrid beast as it passed him on the stairs the day before, though urged by Bates to do so.

After a week and a half as an Eton schoolmaster, Damian Cavendish was more confident than ever that he had made the right choice of profession. There was nothing he would rather be doing and he was already confident he was making a success of it. His div room discussions had all been lively and he had not yet detected any signs of boredom in his pupils.

This very morning, he had received a touching indication he was liked. He had come back to the school from a weekend at home with his parents. Though he had left plenty of time, there had been an accident on the M4 and such heavy traffic that he had arrived twenty-three minutes late for his first, E block div. According to the school rules, if a beak was more than fifteen minutes late, the boys in his div could "take a run" to School Office, where they reported the matter before taking the rest of the div period as free time. It was a disagreeable black mark for a beak to have on his name, especially when he was new. Usually, the older, specialist boys, who tended to know their beaks better, would not take up the option, but he had never heard of the youngest ones resisting the temptation of rare free time. He had therefore despaired of finding the boys still waiting, and was immensely chuffed to find they were.

He well understood these nuances, because he had been a boy at Eton himself. He had been thoroughly happy there, mostly because he had been so popular with both beaks and the other boys. An Oppidan Scholar, as those who won scholarships but did not go into College were called, he had distinguished himself in just about every aspect of school life. He had ended up both in Pop and as captain of his house.

His house captaincy had been unorthodox, but highly successful. He turned a blind eye to breaches of the house rules that did not disrupt others, while a couple of the more officious boys in the Library prevented a collapse of discipline. Unlike most active House Captains, no one therefore resented him and his popularity was such that it was seen as anything but cool to arouse his displeasure. His evident compassion and good sense enabled him to end most trouble by simple reasoning. At any rate, his housemaster, who had had some misgivings about appointing someone so gentle and forgiving, was so pleased with the smoothness with which the house was run that he insisted on keeping him on for the whole of his last year, contrary to normal practice.

He had greatly enjoyed his time at Cambridge as well. He was genuinely impassioned with English literature, so the academic study had been no burden to him and he got a First without wearing himself down or unduly sacrificing the pleasures of undergraduate life. For him, much the greatest of those had been a steamy affair with a stunning tall and slender, blond girl called Dashka, which had gone on through the last half of his time there. He really did think she was the most beautiful girl in the university, he thought proudly, and he could tell from his male friends' envy that many of them thought so too.

It was very much she that had taken the initiative, though he could hardly have been more eager. Though she was a few months younger than him, she had been absolutely self-assured, as well as experienced, having slept with a small succession of boys and men since she was twelve. He in contrast had been still a virgin, though nearly twenty-one and a most reluctant one.

Since his early teens he had wanted to sleep with a girl just as badly as any of his friends did. He had kissed plenty of them at his friends' teenage disco parties. A lot of the boys and girls at those occasions had ended snogging on the sofas, and with his dark good looks he would have had to try hard to avoid being one of them, but he had never gone further before Dashka. He thought it must be because there was not enough of the seducer in him. He could not bring himself to try to persuade a girl to do something she did not appear ready for. It was only later, when he was experienced, that he realised he had been missing the

121

signals many of the girls had been giving off that they were hoping for more. And whenever it had been obvious to him, he had still held back through dread of being trapped with someone he did not truly love. He did not think he would have the heart to drop a girl, especially if he had taken her virginity.

With Dashka, it just happened. Remembering it in detail always warmed his heart. They spotted each other across a room at an undergraduate party. She smiled and he smiled back. Then she came straight over to him. She was vibrant and fun and they immediately liked each other's sense of humour. After twenty minutes, she took him by the hand to sit on a sofa. He started kissing her straight away, but in no time he could sense her greater experience and that she knew exactly what she wanted. Without anything having been said, he already knew that that night it was going to happen at last.

He could hardly remember exactly how they ended up in her room, for nothing was said about going there. It was like a trance. They stood kissing intermittently while she undressed them both, throwing the items of clothing behind her. Her figure was perfect and every bit as ravishing as her face. When she removed his trousers, she found the head of his cock had already broken loose of his pants. She smiled happily, seeing that it was the biggest she had known. Then she knelt down and briefly took it in her mouth, as if to give it the seal of her approval, while Damian gasped with delighted surprise. And then they had fucked. That was what she had called it and to recall it now by some prissy euphemism would convey a false impression. It would detract from the raw sexual fun that it had been.

He came quickly the first time in great shuddering spasms of ecstasy, and they lay together happily for ten minutes while he explored her firm and pert little breasts with his tongue. Then she rolled him over. Kneeling above him, she tossed back her long hair and taking his long, stiff cock in her hand, she guided it once more into her warm, damp well. She rode him long, hard and fast. After a while, she began to gasp in quick pants and suddenly he felt the hot moisture of her orgasm on his shaft. She slowed right down for a few moments, then sped up again. He could tell then from the tensioning of her body that she was about to come a second time, and just as he felt the wet heat again, he began to empty himself into her until the last of his essence was drained.

They remained lovers for the rest of their time at university and intermittently in London during the ensuing two months, she having joined the Foreign Office, as she had long planned. Then he had gone to Italy for six months and by the time he came back for his interview with the headmaster of Eton, she was already an attaché in Peking. They still wrote to each other occasionally. He still missed her. He missed the sex, the sheer fun of her company and the warmth of her friendship, but he did not regret that their new circumstances had pulled them apart, because he had always known this would happen sooner or later and that she did not really mind.

They had never acted towards each other as if they were committed. Her evident lack of expectation about their future was one of the things that had most made him realise early on that she did not need him. She lived as she made love, with energy and absolute self-assurance. She was too independent to need anyone. Their friends thought they were a perfect match, with their spectacular good looks and obvious enjoyment of each other's company. Even their names matched, Damian and Dashka. But their friends misunderstood. From early on, and especially whenever his passion had just been sated, he had sometimes felt strangely dissatisfied, as though his deepest needs were still unanswered.

He supposed that when he got married it would have to be a more old-fashioned affair. However beautiful she was, he could never really be satisfied by a girl who did not need him. He had so much to give if only he could find someone who wanted looking after.

It was linked to why he wanted to be a schoolmaster. He had often asked himself why it appealed to him so much to devote his life to teaching boys. It was partly that he loved their company because their exuberance and openness raised his spirits and made him happy and relaxed, but more than anything it was their sensitivity and vulnerability, their need for attention. He could not bear to see an unhappy boy without trying to do something about it and he could not see a happy one without feeling uplifted.

He doubted he would be anything like as valued or successful as a teacher of girls. He had not known any teenage girls well, but he imagined that the ever-present possibility of romantic feelings developing between them and a young man would always inhibit the natural development of easy friendship between him and a girl pupil. Also, never having been a girl himself, he did not know how they felt and therefore lacked the ready empathy he had for someone in whose position he had once been himself. As a man, he could not offer himself as a role model to them either.

He knew from experience that for boys he answered a need. Even when he was at prep school, younger ones had been drawn to him like a magnet. They came to him incessantly with their worries and fears, their hopes and uncertainties because they trusted him and believed he liked them. Part of the key to his success as House Captain had been that he knew even the shyest of the junior boys well, his urge to protect them aroused by their vulnerability.

His gift of hitting it off with boys had since then manifested itself whenever he met his friends' younger brothers, Dashka's brother Felix for example. The boy had always been over the moon when Damian came to stay for a weekend. Dashka herself had always thought the seven years difference in their ages meant he was not worth much of her attention. It was thanks to Damian and the time the three of them spent together on games and excursions that she had come to see how wrong she had been, so that a real bond had at last developed between the siblings.

By then, Damian had known he was going to be a schoolmaster, and preferably at Eton. His specific reasons for wanting to go back to Eton were simply that he missed it, having been so happy there, and his personal knowledge of the opportunities it presented. More generally, his intellectual vivacity and passion for literature and drama made him less suited for a prep school, where he would have had to teach boys as young as eight, or indeed any school where the pupils were not intelligent and enthusiastic.

He also believed strongly that his subject, English, was much better suited than any other for satisfying his greatest longing, to fill the heads of intelligent boys with ideas of beauty at that age when their minds were most open to absorbing them.

On his way back to his div room after Chambers, Damian remembered with pleasure that he was going to be collecting his F boys' short stories. Nothing could give him a faster insight into the character and intelligence of each of his pupils, he thought. One of the greatest pleasures of teaching F block was that they had no public exams, which allowed one much greater flexibility for this sort of thing.

As he walked in, the vibrant but piercing hubbub of twenty unbroken voices subsided into the deeper and subdued sound of the boys rising simultaneously to their feet.

"Sit down," he said cheerfully. "First of all, I shall collect your short stories, which I've been much looking forward to." He strolled through the room, picking them up one by one and reading out loud some of the more interesting-sounding titles.

"I'm sorry, Sir, but I've lost mine," said Alexander, when he got to his table.

This was just what Damian dreaded. He had known it was essential at the outset to establish some degree of discipline, especially with the younger boys, if he were to enjoy without problems the friendly rapport with his pupils that he saw as necessary for effective teaching. That was why he had uncharacteristically warned them against lateness the first day, fervently hoping he would never have to punish any of them. If he was soft now, he would lose control. This boy could not even be honest about it, he thought angrily. How could he lose a story? Evidently the other boys thought it unlikely too, for he heard a ripple of amusement and anticipation pass through the room. Why could he not at least have had the honesty to say he had not finished it in time and needed an extension?

He felt bound to look straight at Alexander then, though he knew it would make him feel more flustered. He did not know why, but he always felt a bit unsettled with boys that strikingly good-looking. It almost hurt to look at them and he tended to avoid doing so more than strictly necessary until he had established a natural rapport. This was therefore the first time he allowed himself more than a brief glance. He really was

125

stunning, the finest-looking boy he could remember having seen, and that made him feel even more miserable. Unlike himself, the boy looked calm. Evidently, he was completely unafraid.

"And just how did you come to 'lose' it?" he asked. Some of the boys laughed.

"Well, Sir, it was on my table and when I went back to my room this morning, I found that my dame's dog had pulled it off and shat on it." This time all the others roared with laughter, some of them rocking back and forth at their desks. It felt to Damian like ages passed before the room quietened down again enough for him to make himself heard.

It was exactly as he feared. The boy was openly mocking him with such a preposterous story. Damian thought he had an inkling then of why good-looking boys so unsettled him. They were usually cockier than plain boys, weren't they? It was as if they secretly knew the power they had on others and were challenging anyone to defy it.

He saw Alexander glance at the boy laughing at the desk next to his and smile. Then he knew for sure that his authority was being challenged and that he must fight back. He wished he could think of a sharp and witty retort that might put the saucy little coxcomb in his place without losing the good will of the others, but he was too angry.

"I think we had better discuss this when the div is over," he said, struggling to sound calm as he turned back to his own desk.

He fought hard to be his usual enthusiastic self and put his anger out of his mind until the end of the div, but he could not quite do so. He felt hurt and humiliated, and he knew he was not talking to the boys with his usual easy flair for inspiring them. He was introducing them to *Cider with Rosie* by Laurie Lee, which they were about to start. It was one of his favourite novels and he had been hoping to enthuse them with his explanation of what made it so good, to help them appreciate it more, but now he felt that everything he was saying fell flat. Alexander had ruined the lesson and that added to his resentment of him. He had tried hard with all his divs and it was so unfair that this one was being ruined by one boy. It was extremely rare for him to lose his temper and it never lasted long, but he knew he was going to once he was alone with him.

126

As the other boys rushed out of the room at the end of the lesson, he began furiously to scribble a note to Alexander's tutors in red ink. The normal procedure when a piece of work was disgracefully poor was to give the boy a "rip", which literally meant ripping the top of the paper and writing an explanatory note on it for the boy's tutors to read. Damian was not sure of the procedure when there was nothing to rip.

He half saw Alexander standing close by while he wrote, but he did not look at him directly until he had finished writing. Then he saw with a glance that the boy was still quite calm. He averted his eyes again as he felt his explosion coming, fearing he would not have the heart to carry on with his intended blowing-up if he should see it was inflicting any distress, unlikely as that seemed.

"This is disgraceful!" he thundered, "and I won't put up with it. I warned you clearly not to be late with this work and I gave you plenty of time to do it. I am putting you on tardy book, and you can also get this signed by your tutors," he said, ripping his sheet of paper as he did so, and handing it over.

Having got it over with, he looked up at Alexander, curious to see if his self-assurance was shaken.

To his astonishment, big tears had appeared in the deep, blue eyes. For a moment, they were held up by the long, curved eyelashes, then they began to pour down the beautiful face. The boy was silently sobbing, broken down by his fury. Damian's heart melted at once, and he felt appalled at what he had just done. He could not have misjudged the boy's character more badly. Now that he saw him close-up for the first time, he could see that he was as sensitive as he was good-looking. He realised then that he had not only totally misjudged his character, but that his story about the dog was presumably true too.

"The dog really did mess up your story, didn't it?" he said gently. The boy nodded silently, the tears flowing fast now and his sobs becoming quietly audible.

"Alexander, I am terribly sorry. I didn't believe you. It just sounded so unlikely, you see, though that's no excuse at all. I do believe you now. Please forget everything I said a moment ago." He was more disgusted with himself than he could remember being. He could tell now that Alexander was gentle and sincere.

127

He had looked calm because he had known himself innocent and trusted that Damian would treat him as such, instead of which he had abused him horribly. When he had smiled at the laughing boys, it had obviously been out of embarrassment or to acknowledge that the story was funny, as indeed it was when one thought about it. Damian had always prided himself on being kind and fair, especially with children, but he had just hurt an evidently very nice boy for no good reason.

"Please forgive me," he added lamely. Alexander nodded again, and, much to his relief, Damian saw that he was cheering up.

"Look. Do you think you can manage to write it out again before lock-up tomorrow, so that I can read it before the div on Wednesday, or will that not be enough time?" he asked gently, after a pause.

"Yes, I'm sure I can, Sir. I can remember everything I wrote."

"Good, well in that case, could you just drop it off in my flat? I live at number 135 in the High Street. The door to the street is always open. If you could just go up to the first floor and drop it through my letter-box there, that would be splendid."

He did not have to wait until the evening of the next day. He heard it drop through his letter-box while he was having breakfast. His curiosity about Alexander had been awakened, and he decided to read it as soon as he saw what it was.

It was a promising title, he thought, his interest increasing. Leafing through the pages, he saw that it was much longer than the minimum he had required, and he felt a new pang of guilt over his treatment of the boy. He began to read.

VII: It is Better to Travel Hopefully than to Arrive

A more celebrated instance is that of Alexander, who wept bitterly because he had no more worlds to subdue. ... for to travel hopefully is a better thing than to arrive.
  Robert Louis Stevenson, *Virginibus Puerisque*

Seven generations after the fall of Troy seven ships set sail from Corinth to find a new home. The city had become overcrowded, so it was decided that a new colony should be founded. The adventurers were led by twins named Xantholeon and Xanthippos, younger sons of the King, who wished to become Kings themselves. They sailed west over the Adriatic and past Sicily, but though they passed many fine spots for the founding of a city, they did not consider them, for the twins were insistent that they must find an uninhabited island large enough to feed a city. So they sailed on and on. At long last they found one.

They anchored by the shore and decided that the next morning each twin should lead a party of men to find the best possible site. Both returned the following evening convinced they had found it. Reluctantly, each agreed to look at the other's site, but in the end they could not agree and the men too remained divided. A terrible quarrel ensued which was threatening to grow violent, when Xanthippos invoked a curse on his brother and stormed off with his followers to his site in the north, and Xantholeon took the remainder off to his in the south.

Thus were two cities founded on one small isle. They never forgave one another and their descendants carried on the quarrel, which simmered and often flared into war whenever there was a dispute over some limited resource.

One stormy day five centuries later, the great gates of Xanthippos's city were opened and its King rode out at the head of his cavalry to meet the invading army of Xantholeon's heir. With him were his three handsome sons Melanippos, Nikaristos and Alexarchos. Only the youngest, Mikrias, was left behind, for he was only nine. He stood with his mother waving to them from the battlements above. All day the battle raged. The Queen never came down from the walls, but paced up and down there, straining her eyes for any sign on the horizon of how her lord's army had fared. At last a growing straggle of weary men, many of them wounded, emerged in the approaching dusk and told the sorry tale without the need for words. The Queen screamed and tore her hair. When one of the exhausted soldiers was brought before her and told how he had seen her husband fall with his two elder sons each side of him, fighting to the last, she screamed

130

again and pummelled her fists against the kneeling man, berating him for his cowardice in having returned alive in their stead.

No news of Alexarchos's fate came until the next day, when the enemy appeared before the city walls. The gates were closed and the enemy King soon saw to his disappointment that enough of the city's men had survived to defend them. So instead of attacking, they brought the captured boy out in front, so that his mother could see him clearly from the battlements. He stumbled as they pulled him along in his chains. When they stopped, he looked up at his mother in sorrowful despair. He was only fifteen. Then a burly hoplite got him on his knees with a kick, drew his sword, hacked off the boy's head before his mother's eyes and held it up towards her mockingly.

The Queen stood watching in stony silence. She would not give the enemy the satisfaction of seeing or hearing her grief, but in those long moments of iron-willed self-restraint was born a hatred and a fury that would consume its bearer's mind and never abate as long as she lived.

When the grieving people had finished the funeral rites for the many dead, the free men assembled and chose Mikrias as their King, his mother to be regent until he came of age. It would have been hard to do otherwise, for she had already taken charge of everything and had transformed herself in no time from a dutifully submissive wife to a woman who would brook no opposition from anyone.

Mikrias found his life transformed almost overnight. His mother lectured him sternly and repeatedly on how it was his duty to his fallen kin and his city to devote himself entirely to preparing himself for revenge. Any use of his time which did not further that end was wasteful and selfish.

His tutor, who had been sought in far-off Corinth to give the royal sons a broader education than anyone in their city could provide, was dismissed. Episthenes, the steward and most devoted servant of the late King, was so disconcerted by this that he dared to remonstrate with the Queen that she was acting against her late husband's wishes and that a King needed to know about a great deal more than war.

"Perhaps my other sons would be alive today if the time they spent with their tutor had been given to preparing themselves for battle. Spartan kings lead their armies to victory without philosophy and their stewards do not presume to meddle," she replied acidly.

She had decided to adapt what she had heard of the education of the Spartans, renowned as by far the most efficient and fearsome fighters of the age, for the upbringing of both her son and the other boys who must one day form his army. The gymnasiarch Kratinos, who had never tired of boring everyone with his stories of a year spent in Sparta in his youth, found himself suddenly fashionable and promoted to be royal instructor.

The young King was no longer allowed shoes or cloaks, whatever the weather. His soft, woollen clothes were changed for plain homespun, harsh on his skin. Blankets and musical instruments were removed from his bedchamber. His day began an hour before dawn with a march across the plain, a load over his shoulders, followed by black broth for breakfast, but never too much to stop him looking forward to more at supper. Until noon, the other boys his age were his followers in all their exercises, but then they went home to their tutors and their amusements, the Queen not having ventured to make the people give their sons entirely to the state, as in Sparta. For Mikrias though, the daily ordeal was far from over. There would be many hours more of running, leaping and hurling, followed by reading military histories until the sun was down.

When he was thirteen, Kratinos was replaced by Lysikrates, his father's general, who taught him strategy and made him plan and lead the exercises of the other boys himself. The sound thrashings once liberally administered were no longer needed, for self-discipline was by now deeply engrained in him.

Six more years passed before Mikrias decided he was ready to implement the vengeance that had become his life's purpose. By then, he was entirely the master of himself and his city, for his mother had died the year before, prematurely aged by years of bitterness and hatred. As she lay painfully on her deathbed, she made him swear an oath enforced with deadly curses that he would never rest while one stone of the enemy city was left standing upon another.

As the trumpets sounded and Mikrias's army marched out of the city and onwards south, his soldiers tried hard to banish gloomy and fearful thoughts. Many of them had lost fathers or brothers in the last great battle and they could not help wondering if they would see their homes and loved ones again. In contrast, Mikrias's spirits had never been higher, for he was about to attempt the one thing he was passionately determined on and he had not much doubt that he would succeed. The waiting was over at last and today he would be fulfilled.

When they were about thirty stadia from their ultimate destination and approaching the valley where their scouts told them the enemy's main force was waiting, Mikrias split his army in three. Most of the infantry and half the cavalry were sent straight on under Lysikrates, while a small contingent of infantry brought the siege engines to the enemy's walls by a circuitous route and Mikrias waited hidden well behind them with the better half of the cavalry. Lysikrates had protested that his strategy was too risky, that he might not be able to hold the enemy with so little cavalry, but he was overruled.

The siege engines were positioned facing the narrowest of the city's seven gates. After enduring bombardment for half an hour, the city's defenders grew sick of putting up with damage from such poorly guarded machines and sent out a force of hoplites to overrun them. The moment the gates opened, a signal was relayed to Mikrias, who emerged suddenly and charged down on them at the head of his cavalry. Taken by surprise, the hoplites panicked and rushed back to the gates, but they were too many to squeeze through fast and Mikrias bore down on them while the gates were still jammed open. Then he was inside

135

and the rampage began. The hoplites were cut down fast, flaming torches were thrown into the houses and soon the city was ablaze.

The main force of the enemy had already engaged Lysikrates and the battle was raging without much advantage to either side when smoke began to rise up from the city. Knowing what it signified, the enemy lost heart completely and fled in disorder, leaving their King to be cut down in a hopeless last stand.

It was all over very quickly then. Fleeing men with their backs to the enemy stood no chance. Those in the city who had not been cut down soon surrendered, while the women, children and old people were dragged out of the burning buildings. When the fighting had died down and all the inhabitants of the city rounded up, Mikrias ordered his soldiers to cut the throats of all the men. Their bodies were left where they fell for the dogs and birds of prey, while a sorry procession of women and children, their arms tightly bound, were led off to be sold into slavery.

Mikrias did not stay long, but before he left, he made arrangements for teams of slaves with battering rams to be brought to knock down any stones left standing, so that his oath was honoured.

News of the victory ran well ahead of the returning army and when that night Mikrias reached the same broad gates from which his father had ridden to his death ten years earlier, they swung open to reveal a main street already thronging with celebrating people. Cattle and sheep were being slaughtered in their hundreds to provide the greatest banquet ever seen. An hour later, Mikrias sat down in the great hall of his palace with his officers and the city elders. Its doors had been thrown wide open and great tables loaded with food and wine laid out all around the adjoining courtyard and square so that all men could join the feast.

When everyone had eaten to their fill, Lysikrates rose to propose a toast. He began by praising Mikrias as the one responsible for their victory, and modestly but truthfully disclaiming credit for himself. Then he turned to what had been accomplished.

"Our land and our island are now one. We have no enemy, no borders to guard. Most of the army can be disbanded tomorrow, for henceforth we have nothing more than pirate raids to fear. Our swords and spears can be refashioned into ploughs. Our sons can study philosophy instead of war." He raised his goblet out before him. "To eternal peace, my friends," he concluded heartily.

When Mikrias heard the words "no enemy" he felt a terrible misgiving, and each of the general's further phrases stung him further. What would he do tomorrow if he did not drill his soldiers? He could barely remember the days when he had done anything without them. He rose for the toast with the others, but his high spirits had evaporated and he moved his lips silently as they all repeated "To eternal peace" in one loud voice.

As the slaves refilled their goblets, the conversation turned to plans for the future.

"What are you going to do, Lysikrates, now that your fighting days are over?" asked the phalanx commander on his other side.

"Ah!" said the general. "It has long been my ambition to write a history of our island, though I never imagined I would be able to bring it to such a momentous conclusion." Soon they were debating the reforms of a long-dead king Mikrias had never heard of. Yawning, he turned gloomily to the young commander of his bodyguard sitting on his left, but he was discussing a new play that was all the rage. Mikrias had never been able to see the point in people dressing up and pretending to be someone else on a stage. It was too silly.

138

Soon he was overcome with melancholy. He could see no purpose to his life at all. There was nothing to look forward to but one day of aimless tedium after another creeping by in endless succession until he died.

"Mikrias, are you feeling ill?" asked Lysikrates anxiously.

"Perhaps a little, but it's probably just tiredness. I think I had better retire for the night, but please make sure everyone carries on without me." He rose from his chair and two of his bodyguard followed him out. When they reached his quarters, he told his servants he would not be needing further attendance and they left, whispering in shocked tones at his look of despair.

In the morning, they did not like to disturb him without a sign and the sun was already high in the sky when the steward called out to him. When he did not answer, they went in. A bloody sword was on the bed and beside it the King lay dead.

"Do you know what being 'Sent up for Good' means?" Damian asked his F div when they had settled down on Wednesday morning. They all looked blankly at him, so he carried on.

"Well. It's like a Show Up, but far more special. In addition to getting a card signed by your tutors, you have to take the awarded work to the Lower Master and then it gets lodged in the College Archives, to be kept there for ever. It's much rarer than a Show Up too. I had not expected to award one to a boy

139

in any of my divs this Half, but now I'm giving one to Alexander for his short story. It's not simply the best one, it's truly outstanding for a boy in F. I'm going to read it to you now, before handing you back your stories, most of which are excellent by the way."

When he had finished reading it to them, he summarised what he thought its best points were, and Alexander, who had blushed furiously when Damian had begun his story, found himself reddening again, though he was proud and happy too.

The story showed real dramatic flare, explained Damian. It was carefully composed. Right from the beginning, including even the title, subtle hints were given that made sense of the conclusion. The genuine feeling for a different historical epoch was also unmistakeable.

He meant every word he said. He had had to get the permission of the head of the English department to award a Sent up for Good, and he would not have taken a step so bold for a beak only a fortnight at the school if he had not been sure it was deserved. The only thing about it that hinted at all at the youth of its author was that it was a bit melodramatic, especially the ending.

The story also had one quality he did not mention to his div. He found himself affected by its sadness. He began to wonder how such a young boy, who with his intelligence and looks would seem to have everything going for him, could yet express so well the experience of sadness and despair. Perhaps one of his other beaks might know something, as they had been teaching him since September. Back in his flat, he looked in the school calendar to see who they were.

As he came out of School Hall at Chambers the next morning, he saw Henry Muncaster, whom he knew from his own schooldays.

"Hello, Henry," he said. "I was wondering what you make of a boy called Aylmer. I believe he's in your F French div."

"Oh yes. Very promising, I should say, though his performance suffered a terrible setback last Half, as you would obviously expect."

"Why?"

"Of course, you weren't here then, were you? Aylmer's mother died quite unexpectedly. He's a sensitive boy, I think. I should imagine it's still affecting him dreadfully."

That evening Alexander's father telephoned.

"I'm just calling to tell you that Granny died last night," he said sadly. "The funeral will be on Wednesday, but no one is going except your uncles and I." Alexander was stunned. It was such a short time since he had been with her and she had been so very alive then. He also felt stung by his father's matter-of-fact manner of breaking the news.

"But why?" he asked miserably.

"Why what?"

"Why has she suddenly died?"

"Oh, you know, she was very old. These things just happen at her age. Well, that's all I called about. Good-bye."

He spent the rest of the evening alone, telling Julian that he had to do his E.W.s, as indeed he did, but the truth was he was too miserable to talk and did not want to tell him about it. He remembered trying to talk to him about his mother and he could not anyway bear the thought of more pity.

Evidently his father thought he would not care very much, and that made him feel distant from him, because he did care terribly. Perhaps it was because he had not cried when told about Gigi's death, but he could not hold back his tears now. Once he had thought that really terrible things like the people one loved most dying were things that only happened to other people. Now he was nearer to feeling that it was his special lot.

He knew Julian had been put out that he had no time for him and he was sorry for that. It was a recurrent problem. He was enthusiastic about many of his studies and took pride in writing his essays well, but Julian was often dissatisfied with the time he devoted to them. He could not imagine how he would be coping if Julian had not become his friend. He would make up for it the next day.

The next morning, Damian had his final F div of the week. He saw that Alexander looked unusually forlorn and his heart went

141

out to him. He wondered if he could imagine how it must be for a child still so vulnerable and dependent to lose his mother. He shuddered at the thought of it happening to him now, and he was a grown man living on his own.

As Alexander was going out of the room afterwards, he called him over and asked for a word.

"Alexander," he said hesitantly, not sure how to say what he wanted. "I heard about your mother. I didn't know before. I just wanted to say that if you ever feel you need someone to talk to, well, you'd be very welcome to invite yourself to tea any time you like."

Alexander smiled gratefully. He was moved by Mr. Cavendish's kindness. He was definitely the nicest beak he had come across, but he knew he would not really take up the invitation. It would be terribly embarrassing asking him and then going along and sipping tea politely, knowing the man was just putting up with him out of kindness because he felt sorry for him.

He also felt a certain nervousness coming so much to his attention, much as he had wanted it. His hope of attracting it through his short story had been more than fully realised, as those warm, twinkling eyes now rested on him approvingly at least as often as on any other boy. His pleasure was muted though by fear he had aroused expectations of excellence that he was likely some time to disappoint.

On Saturday morning, Alexander came into Julian's room holding a paperback. Julian thought he looked uncharacteristically nervous.

"Have you ever read a novel called *Cider with Rosie*?" asked Alexander.

"No, I think I've heard of it, but I've never read it."

"I'm reading it for English. It's good. Anyway, there's this one passage I was wondering what you would think of. I'll leave the book here for a while. It's the second paragraph on this page," he said pointing, before laying it down open on Julian's table. "I've got to go. I'll see you later."

"Yes," said Julian, intrigued that Alexander had not simply waited for him to read it. Soon he went to pick it up.

"Our village was clearly no pagan paradise," the second paragraph began, "neither were we conscious of showing tolerance. It was just the way of it. We certainly committed our share of statutory crime. Manslaughter, arson, robbery, rape cropped up regularly throughout the years. Quiet incest flourished where the roads were bad; some found their comfort in beasts; and there were the usual friendships between men and boys who walked through the fields like lovers."

Julian was astonished. The implications of Alexander bringing the passage for him to read were so dizzying that he needed time to think them through. Was he trying to tell him that it was usual for men and boys to be lovers, which was what he hoped, or just that it was inevitable that when men and boys were friends some people would think they were acting like lovers? He decided he must wait and see Alexander's further reaction, but in the meantime his hopes once again soared that Alexander was ready for him to act.

The passage also threw him into the same turmoil that the JRH House Books once had. Clearly he was wrong to have supposed that sexual yearning for boys was something peculiar to public schools. It had been commonplace among ordinary people in the countryside too. He was stung afresh with jealousy. Why was he starved of this joy that so many others had known?

Then he reminded himself that it was his own fault he was starved. If he was not so contemptibly wet, he would by now have had Alexander, who was surely far more desirable than any of their rustic boys could have been. He knew he had let the growing mockery of Cowburn and others intimidate and put him off over the last week, but he should not have, because the criticism had only grown worse.

That afternoon they went on the river together, so it was not long before he had to go to bed that Alexander came to his room. Again he seemed nervous. Julian thought and hoped he was about to say something about the book, so he did not try himself, and in the end it was only as Alexander got up to go that he spoke.

"Oh, by the way, have you finished with my book?" he asked.

"Yes, thanks," replied Julian handing it to him.

"Did you read that passage?"

143

"Yes."

"It was interesting, wasn't it?" he asked, blushing.

"Yes, it certainly was." Before Julian could say more, Alexander said good-night and was off.

Upper boys were allowed to go home for two weekends each Half besides Long Leave and Julian was going to take one of his on the coming one. He thought rather guiltily that for the first time ever he was not particularly looking forward to it. It was not that he would not be glad to be with his father, of course he would, but that he dreaded being away from Alexander. Not only would it be two more days when he would have no chance of bringing his hopes to fruition, but it would be yet another milestone along the long road of his failure to do so.

He had approached Alexander physically in every way possible short of the overtly romantic and still he had not managed to force himself to dare cross that threshold. If he could not now, when would he be able to? He had a sense of foreboding that now that so many were against their friendship, if he did not advance, he might anytime be forced into irreversible retreat. So he set himself a time limit. He must do something before he went home. He must pluck up the courage either to kiss him or to tell him how he felt.

After his awkward experience of trying to move gently into an embrace with him while they were standing up, he decided it would be much easier to achieve sitting down. Next time Alexander sat reading on his bed or his ottoman, wherever there was room, he would sit down right by him if no one else was there. He would lean against him and gradually move his arm round his back until his hand rested against his hip the other side. Then he would very slowly move it onto his thigh. If Alexander turned round to look at him, he would take the chance to kiss him at once, maybe even on the lips. If he did not react, then he would gradually move his head towards him until his lips came to rest on his cheek.

Every Sunday evening, Jack Hodgson went to the rooms of each boy in F in turn, where he read their Sunday Qs. These were essay questions set by their Classics beaks, usually on a religious question, but occasionally something more broadly philosophical. They were so named because they were relatively long E.W.s designed to be done on Sunday and handed in on the Monday morning. It was in fact the only time he did go to the F boys' rooms. In truth he did not much care for boys, and especially not young ones who were mostly too naïve and silly to stimulate his interest.

Most people agreed he had a fine intellect, even by Eton standards, albeit a little spoilt by a plodding and overly meticulous approach to questions, but his own estimate of it was very much higher. He believed he should more properly have been employed as a professor at Oxford, where he had been an undergraduate, but it had been intimated to him that the foolish authorities concerned did not have enough sense of his abilities to be likely to give him a post there, so rather than face possible humiliation by trying for one, he had decided to bestow his genius on the boys of Eton.

He saw himself as a big fish in a little pond and he enjoyed that. He liked teaching too, especially when his pupils were the more intelligent boys, as the older ones at least were, for his subjects were classical, which only the highbrow boys opted for. Like most of the best teachers, he took pride in stimulating bright minds. It was only when it came to the pastoral side of his duties that his lack of sympathy and interest in boys as such showed.

The boys in his house understood all this well enough, and were in their turn ambivalent towards him. None of them felt any real affection for him. Most of them respected him, at least intellectually, though behind his back they enjoyed themselves mimicking his pomposity and stilted speech. Perhaps the most curious sign of their attitude was that while most boys in the school referred to their housemaster as "Mr. X" or "M'tutor", those in his referred to him as "Hodgson" or even "Jack" when talking to each other.

Eton housemasters were the cream of the teaching profession and most performed their duties assiduously. Many went far beyond the call of duty, expending tremendous energy for their boys' benefit, and these often kindled an affection on the part of their charges that was deep and lifelong. To get to know their boys and ensure their continued well-being, they tended to spend an hour or more of most evenings visiting them in their

145

rooms, so that no boy was likely to pass a fortnight without having a chat with his housemaster.

Hodgson was aware of this duty, but found it tiresome and painful because he had nothing to say to boys except on drily academic matters. He had therefore latched onto reading their Sunday Qs as the one regular way he could pass a little time in the F boys' rooms without the need to say much. In this sense, they were privileged, for once they moved into a higher block, Hodgson was unlikely to trouble himself to visit them more than once or twice a Half.

As with everything he did, he timed these visits carefully. He would spend six or seven minutes reading each essay carefully, then another one or two glancing over it while his mind was really focussed on thinking of some apposite and hopefully witty comment to make as he got up to go.

Accordingly, at ten past nine on the third Sunday of the Half, he went to Michael Bell's room, settled himself into the boy's armchair and held out his hand for the exercise book to be handed to him.

"Er, I'm afraid I haven't finished my Sunday Q yet, Sir," said Michael.

"Hmm. Well, let me read what you have done."

"Actually, Sir, I'm afraid I haven't started it yet. I'm sorry, Sir."

"Great Scott, boy! When do you think you are going to do it?"

"I was going to start it before breakfast, Sir, and then I was going to finish it during After Nine." Actually, Michael, who was as intelligent as he was lazy, did not care for getting up early and planned to leave it all until After Nine, the forty minute break before his Classics div. He knew he could scribble off something acceptable in that time.

Hodgson was now flummoxed. He had nothing ready to say and could not think of anything. His hands tautened on the arms of the chair and he sweated more than usual as his mind raced fretfully.

"I hope you will remember Aesop's tale of the tortoise and the hare," he said finally, as he rose.

Aylmer was now the only boy in F whom he had not yet visited, so he proceeded to his room only to find to his exasperation that it was empty. He saw that it was still only 9:12 and the F boys' bedtime was 9:30, so he might have to wait a quarter of an hour, but it was hardly worth going back to his side of the house to relax with his wife, as he wanted, so he decided to wait in Aylmer's room. He picked up an exercise book and began to read through it, though it did not contain the Sunday Q. When it was past 9:30 and Aylmer had still not come back, his irritation grew rapidly, but there seemed to be nothing for it but to wait and confront him about his lateness. After another six minutes had passed, he lost patience and stormed out into the passage. A boy in E appeared, evidently on his way back from the bathroom.

"Have you seen Aylmer anywhere?" he asked.

"No, Sir."

Once the boy left, there was complete silence in the corridor and he could see that no lights were shining under the doors of any of the rooms, so presumably Aylmer was somewhere quite else, perhaps with a boy in another block. Suddenly, Hodgson remembered his friendship with Smith. He had not thought about it since last Half.

He went straight to Smith's room on the floor above and burst open the door. Sure enough, there was Aylmer sitting on Smith's bed reading a magazine. Smith was sitting right beside him, even leaning slightly into him. One of his arms was behind Aylmer's back and Hodgson could see his hand resting gently against the younger boy's far hip. It could not quite be called improper, but it was very nearly so and certainly too intimate for the housemaster's peace of mind. Both boys stood up, evidently shocked.

"Now, what on earth do you think you're doing here at this hour?!" he exploded.

"I'm sorry, Sir. I completely forgot the time," said Alexander.

"Well, go to your room at once!"

"Yes, Sir," he said and left quickly. Hodgson turned on Julian.

"And what excuse do you have for having a boy in F in your room after his bedtime, and you a member of Debate?"

"I'm sorry, Sir. As he said, we just forgot the time."

"Well. If anything like this happens again, I shall have to reconsider your position in Debate." He left then and went

147

back to his side of the house. He badly needed to compose his mind.

He had often considered himself lucky that so far during his tenure as housemaster, there had been no homosexual liaisons that he knew of. He remembered well a brief talk the Head Master had once given on this topic to a group of actual and soon-to-be housemasters. He had told them that it was absolutely essential to keep an eye out and nip anything of the sort in the bud. To illustrate his point, he mentioned a letter he had received from the headmaster of another school asking his advice on how to cope with an outbreak of homosexual affairs. Apparently a few popular boys at the top of the school had started going to bed with younger ones without the authorities having a clue and in no time at all it had become the fashion, with almost all the boys forming couples. By the time the headmaster found out, it was on far too big a scale to be brought under control by punishment.

"I am afraid I had to tell him that the only solution was to close the school down for three weeks, write to all the parents and then start again. And that is what he did," the Head Master had concluded. "But you can well imagine what the parents thought of it."

It was just the sort of thing that could ruin a promising housemaster's prospects. On the other hand, the Head Master had also forewarned them of the other side of the coin. Too obvious a move against an isolated case of suspicious friendship would draw the attention of all the other boys to it. It would encourage any who had been tempted to indulge in the vice by making them realise they were not alone and give others ideas they had never had. The essential thing to know was how the other boys were already reacting.

The next evening Hodgson went to see Anthony Burrows in his room.

"Now. What can you tell me about Smith and Aylmer?" he asked.

"Just that they seem to be very good friends, Sir. Aylmer seems to spend most of his spare time in Smith's room. They mess together too."

148

"They what?!"

"Since the beginning of this Half, they have been messing together, Sir."

"Great Scott! Why haven't I been told anything about this before?"

"Well, I didn't know what to say. As far as I know, they haven't done anything wrong, Sir. I mean there are no rules about who can mess together, are there?"

"But surely this must have attracted comment by other boys?"

"Yes, it has, Sir."

"And what has been the general tenor of this comment?"

"Well. That it's rather odd."

Hodgson paused. He had never been able to talk to boys about intimate matters. He reddened a little as he struggled for words. "Do you, er, mean to say that they are suspected of … improper intimacy?"

"That's what some boys are saying, Sir."

"Who precisely?"

"Well, most of Smith's block, and Geoffrey believes it too."

"Anthony, you know I rely on you to be my eyes and ears on the boys' side of the house. You really should have told me, and I expect to be kept better informed from now on."

"Yes Sir. I'm sorry, Sir. But it could easily just be malicious gossip. No one actually knows anything except that they are obviously close friends."

The next morning, Julian decided to skip Chapel in order to finish his French EW. It was most definitely not allowed, but some boys did it quite regularly and he had recently done so a few times. He was finding it difficult to keep up with all his EWs now that he spent so much time with Alexander. He was sitting at his burry busily scribbling when suddenly and noiselessly Mr. Hodgson came in. Julian had no time to do more than look up in shock.

"Heigh ho. Heigh ho," said Hodgson slowly in a ponderous tone of affected sadness, his black leather shoes creaking a little, then he turned and left. It was the first time Hodgson had ever caught him breaking a rule. He had never even heard of his housemaster coming to check up on the boys at this hour. He

149

had little doubt that for the first time ever he was going to find himself on the Bill, as a summons to see the Head Man for punishment was called. Nor did he feel much doubt that, whatever the Head Man would think he was punishing him for, it was really something quite else.

He knew the dreaded summons would not come that morning as there was too little time left. He expected it to be the next day, and though he was not quite certain it would come at all, he could not help feeling a bit depressed for the rest of the day. His heart sunk when there was a loud knock on the door during his second div on the morrow.

"Come in!" said Mr. Philipson, his French beak. A member of Sixth Form Select, the academic elite of the highest block distinguished by the silver buttons on their waistcoats, stepped into the room. Summoning boys on the bill was much their best known function and a thrill of anticipation hung over the room as everyone wondered whom he had come for. Julian alone knew. He blushed.

"Is Smith in this division, Sir?"

"Yes," said Mr. Philipson.

"He's to see the Head Master at 12:15."

The next humiliation was having to excuse himself for leaving his next div early to go to Upper School, where the Head Man held court. He had never even met him before, though of course he had heard him speak. Mr. Allenby was an immensely imposing figure. His tall, upright bearing was so dignified that just passing him in the street was enough to inspire profound awe in the boys.

"Why did you miss Chapel?" he asked, looking down at Julian from his high desk, a Sixth Form Select boy standing in silent reverence on each side of the room.

"I didn't want to, Sir," said Julian nervously, "but I ran out of time and I knew I would arrive late if I went … I'm sorry, Sir."

"I see," he replied just a little less severely. "Well, at least it is your first offence, but nevertheless it is no excuse. You must learn that the honourable thing to do would have been to own up to being late. If you had done so, you would have been put on Tardy Book for three days. Instead, I am putting you on it for six."

150

Some boys took being on the Bill in their stride, regarding it as an occasionally inevitable consequence of breaking the many school rules that were there to be broken, but Julian was quite upset that his clean record was spoilt; because of the extraordinary sacrifice his father had made to get him into the school, he had always felt beholden to avoid trouble. Though he had always got on reasonably well with his housemaster and he knew the punishment was minor and no more than fitted the offence, he resented him for it quite intensely, because he saw it as being really an unfair attack on his friendship with Alexander. It was true that he wanted to do things with Alexander that everyone would think justified attack, but the fact remained that he had not yet and as far as anyone knew it was depressingly possible that he might never.

It was now Wednesday and time was running out fast for Julian to adhere to his resolution. He had grown rapidly more tense as the week advanced. He began to fear that because his nerves were on edge all the time, he was making himself unappealing company. He had not found another opportunity to sit close by Alexander since Hodgson had disturbed them on Sunday, and he realised that the problem with opening his heart was that he was never ready with the words when a suitable opening presented itself. What he needed was to find in advance a sure way of steering the conversation the way he wanted. Finally he came up with the idea of giving him a present too obviously big to be dismissed as an ordinary act of friendship. It was something he could ill afford to do, for he had less pocket money than most boys, but nothing else mattered compared to this.

Reluctant as he was to forego Alexander's company for any amount of time, he made excuses and slipped off to Windsor after lunch on Thursday. He had hoped to be back by three, but try as he did, wandering in and out of almost every shop in both the High Street and Peascod Street, he could not find anything that would do. He saw endless minor possibilities, but each was just too ordinary to hang his fate on. He finally wandered back in despair after five. Half way down Eton High Street, he noticed that the bi-weekly market was open, and decided he might as well try his luck there. As he feared, most of the things for sale were either hopelessly expensive antiques or useless gee-gaws. He was just about to leave, when he noticed a stall with a large assortment of coins arranged under a glass top. He saw that some of them were Roman and surprisingly cheap for such very ancient things. Suddenly he was struck by a brilliant idea.

"You don't happen to have any coins of Alexander the Great, do you?" he asked the stall-holder.

"Yes, I think I may have one. They're not especially rare." He dived under his table and emerged after a minute with a silver coin in a clear little plastic wallet. "Here we are. This is a drachma of Alexander, rather worn I'm afraid, but then it's only fourteen quid. This is him dressed as Hercules. I expect you know who he was, don't you?

"Yes."

"Ah well, then you'll probably know he had to do twelve tasks and killing a lion was one of them, so here is Alexander wearing a lion's skin on his head. I tell you what; I'll let you have it for twelve quid." He took it out of its wallet and handed it over.

Julian gazed at the fine features of the great conqueror in awe. It was absolutely perfect as a present. He could imagine Alexander's face lighting up enthusiastically when he gave it to him. He turned the coin over and saw the magic word "ΑΛΕΞΑΝΔΡΟΥ" clearly visible on the reverse.

He bought it for £ 11, which was going to leave him hard up for the rest of the Half, but he was far too happy to care. Now at last he could make detailed plans. It had to be perfect and he would need time, so he decided to wait for the next day, the very last before he would have failed, for he would be going home straight after Saturday morning's divs.

He needed to talk to Alexander somewhere where they could be sure of being alone and, if things were to go as he hoped, out of sight. The best he could think of was one of the many clusters of woods that broke up the outlying games fields, but how to get him there? They would not be free until tea-time, which left only three badly-needed hours until lock-up, so he needed a reason for leaving fast. Then he remembered sneaking off illegally to the cinema in Slough last year with two others. The road there went right past the biggest playing-fields and it was a far enough destination to mean they would have to hurry off after tea-time.

Alexander accepted his suggestion eagerly that evening. He had never been to the cinema while at school before, or broken a serious school rule with Julian. Once it was agreed, Julian began to formulate a detailed plan. He could hardly believe how easy it was to do so and he berated himself for not having thought it through a fortnight earlier.

He would give him the coin at tea-time, just before they rushed off. Alexander would still be elated when they approached the playing-fields ten minutes later.

"Alexander," he would then say. "Do you mind very much if we leave going to a film to another day? There's something very important I want to talk to you about in confidence." Alexander was too kind and would be too curious to refuse that. Then Julian would suggest a walk through the fields to somewhere private.

"Look," he would say when they had sat down together. "Do you promise never to tell anyone what I'm about to tell you?"

"Yes, of course," Alexander would answer.

"And if you don't like what I tell you, can you just forget all about it and carry on being friends like before?"

"Yes." He would be safe then. Alexander would never go back on a promise. He would pause, perhaps putting his hand on Alexander's knee and looking him in the eyes. The next bit was the most difficult, but he was sure he could manage it if he was ready, if he knew when and where and in what context he would say it.

"I'm in love with you. I have been for a long time. I can't help it. I love you more than all the rest of the world..... Do you mind that?"

He could not guess quite how Alexander would respond, but he was fairly sure it would *not* be with a "Yes, I do."

"Then can I kiss you? You can always say if you want me to stop."

"Okay," he would probably say with one of those warm smiles, and there might be a blush on his rosy cheeks. Then he would turn towards him and their lips would come gently together, the first time either of them had done that with anyone, and Julian would have found paradise on earth.

153

He went to bed that night convinced that at last his dreams were about to be fulfilled. He told himself that by the time he went to bed on the morrow, he would have become a different person, fulfilled and blissfully happy. He was so excited that he hardly slept at all. His excitement was most acutely sexual, as he saw his erotic fantasies about to be realised, but it ran much deeper than that, as he found each time that he relieved himself by hand only to continue tossing and turning in his bed instead of falling asleep.

In the morning, he was perturbed to find himself so tired, but soon his spirits rose. The signs were good. It was an unusually hot day for May, so easy to imagine them standing warm in some hidden wood while Julian gently undid Alexander's clothes, piece by piece, until his godlike beauty was entirely revealed in all its naked splendour.

At first everything went just as he planned.

"I've got a surprise present for you," he said at tea-time and placed the coin in Alexander's hand. At first he looked astonished, but soon Julian saw his expression turn to one of delighted wonder and he felt him guessing that he was staring at the face of his revered namesake. Julian saw his wonder turn at once to ecstatic excitement as he turned the coin over and beheld the inscription.

"Oh Julian, thank you! It's incredible. Where did you find it?" he said, tearing his eyes briefly away from it to give Julian an enchanting smile.

Soon they set out, but as they made their way through the school to the Slough Road, Alexander grasped the coin in his hand. At intervals he opened his fingers to look at it and Julian was so overcome with emotion that he had to fight back tears. Then he remembered that they were only about two minutes from where he planned to stop and his nervousness returned in a great rush. He should not have let himself get distracted.

"Julian, there's just one thing," said Alexander with a suddenly graver expression, as if a little cloud had appeared in the otherwise clear blue sky.

"What?"

"It would be better not to tell anyone you gave it to me," he said.

"Why?"

"Oh, well, you know what they're like. They'll all say 'Ha! ha! Julian's in love with Alexander,'" said Alexander derisively. "Not that it's any of their business."

At this first and unexpected mention of the word "love" between them, presented in terms of the accusations of others, Julian panicked blindly. Then he spoke words which, even before he finished saying them, he already regretted far more than anything in his whole life.

"But you don't believe them, do you? You know it's not true. I'm not like that. I mean, we're very good friends, best friends, but it's not like they think between us." He knew it was as diametrically opposed to the truth as could be, but immediate denial of love was the only shield he had ready in his armoury against the slurs of his enemies. Now, he had used it in stupid reflex reaction against the one person to whom he had been planning to confess the truth. As he said it, he already loathed himself for his cowardice and dishonesty and, above all, his being his own worst enemy.

Alexander did not answer him. He looked definitely put out and possibly badly hurt, Julian thought miserably. The more he thought about it, the more he realised how very easy it would have been to have instead taken the chance to present his suit. Why couldn't he have just said something like "and is that what you believe?" and wait to gauge Alexander's reaction. He tried hard to think of words to put it right, but they would not come. As he struggled, he realised they were already passing the point where he had planned to stop, and Alexander was striding purposefully on.

"Alexander, are you sure you want to go to the cinema?"

"Yes, why not?" he replied in a subdued tone so unlike his usual exuberant one.

"We could just go for a walk." He thought then of telling him that he had been talking nonsense, but that meant immediately implying that what the others said was true, that he was in love with him and it was too late now to do it the way he had planned.

"No, let's go the cinema," said Alexander decisively, before Julian could bring himself to take such drastic action, and they

155

strode on in silence past the vast playing-fields, from which the enticing smell of freshly mown grass wafted tauntingly.

At the cinema, Julian bought the tickets, as the film they wanted to go to was X rated. The usher saw and told them in a hush to go in quietly before anyone noticed that Alexander was so obviously too young. Julian was too miserable to do more than nod blankly, but Alexander shot the usher a smile that left him feeling well rewarded indeed.

Julian hardly took in the film at all, he was in such anguish. He could not think of anything he would not give to be able to go back an hour in time and have another chance. Though he had realised other boys might tell Alexander that Julian's feelings for him were as they indeed were, he had not before known that it had actually happened. He wondered who it was. He had not worried about it much since Alexander had told him he did not care what other boys said, but now it occurred to him that it was not only himself who had suffered from the malicious gossip and Alexander might have endured quite a bit of ragging too. Yet he had remained loyal.

It was only now that it was too late that Julian felt certain in his heart that Alexander had been willing to give himself to him all along. While he, a grown-up boy of seventeen had proven himself too cowardly to act, his young friend had daringly even made his offer of himself plain with the extract from *Cider with Rosie*. Anyone else would have accepted the offer of what he most longed for at once, but he had been too pathetically cautious to acknowledge the offer for what it was until it was out of his reach. Unless he could put things right fast, he knew for certain he would be tormented with regret and self-contempt for the rest of his life.

Once it was seven o'clock, Julian could not resist looking at his watch with increasing frequency, hoping fervently that the film would end in time for them to be able to stop on the way back, at least for a few minutes. He longed as a very minimum at least to be able to tell Alexander he had said things that afternoon that he did not mean and he needed a serious, confidential chat with him as soon as he got back after the weekend, but the film dragged on. It was twenty to eight by the time they were out of the cinema, so they only had twenty minutes to cover the two miles back to the school in time for the roll-call at lock-up and they had to run all the way.

The following midday, he set off for London more depressed than ever, knowing he had inflicted serious damage on all that he cared about without having done anything to redress it, and sick with worry that it might be irreversible. Now that Alexander thought he did not desire him, would he not abandon any romantic feelings he might have had for him?

VIII: Shattered Illusions

O, what a tangled web we weave,
When first we do practise to deceive.
  Sir Walter Scott, *Marmion* XVI 17

Peyntors
Eton College
Windsor
Berkshire SL4 6TY
Tel. (07535) 57823

Tuesday 15ᵗʰ May 1984

Dear Alfred,

I regret to have to write to you about a delicate matter, which I am asking you to discuss with Julian this weekend.

He has developed an unhealthy interest in much younger boys. Recently he has been monopolising the time of a boy in his first year. Even if this liaison is, as I hope, innocent, I fear no good can come of it. The boy in question suffered the bereavement of his mother last Half and needs to get back to normal life with others his own age rather than being distracted by an unsuitable friendship.

As I said in my last report to you, Julian's studies are going to require his full attention over the rest of his time here if he is to have a serious chance of gaining admission to Oxford and he should not be frittering away his days in this manner. Whether deserved or not, he has built himself an unsavoury reputation among his peers, which can do him no good either.

If his aspirations at Oxford are to materialize, he will also need to retain the good will of everyone concerned with his education here, so I am hoping you will be able to convince him that it is in his best interest to discontinue his attentions to this, or indeed other, younger boys.

Do please telephone if you would like to discuss the matter further.
   Yours sincerely,
   Jack Hodgson

Julian's face was scalding and his hands were shaking as he handed the letter back to his father.

Alfred had realised at once on receiving the letter four days earlier that the penultimate sentence was a veiled threat, and that was the only part he had really minded. It had always been an essential part of his dreams that Julian should go to Oxford or Cambridge, and it had become much more so recently. Over the years Julian had been at Eton, he had felt a growing unease that Julian was not integrating himself into the upper class in quite the way he had imagined he would. He did not seem to have forged any friendships that ran deep enough to be likely to withstand the wear of time. When Mr. Hodgson had suggested to him that Julian set his sights on a good red-brick university instead, he had inwardly recoiled in horror. He feared that if Julian failed Oxbridge, not only would the sort of degree that would guarantee him lucrative employment be beyond his grasp, but he would shatter the entire dream by failing socially too. He would make the wrong sort of friends and meet the wrong sort of girls. In short, he would revert to type, like an acrid wild apple rootstock onto which one had tried and failed to graft a succulent cherry tree.

   The suggestion that Julian was attracted to boys and possibly even having an affair with one did not bother him in itself, though it mattered how it was handled. He breathed a sigh of relief that Denise did not know about the letter. She would blow it up way out of proportion and want to send Julian to a psychiatrist. He could not think of anything better calculated to make a mountain out of a molehill.

   Why did the English get so worked up about sexual matters? He doubted they always had. He had a nagging fear that some terrible cultural shift was underway the full impact of which was not yet clear, like the hidden movements of the earth's plates before an earthquake. It was somehow linked in his mind with

159

Denise's frequent visits to the United States over the last few years, perhaps because he had once thought it was just the Americans who were so puritanical. Had not loathing of a more civilised tolerance been the whole point of abandoning England for the people who set up the first American colonies and set their ideological tone? And had not that same tolerance, that refusal to get unreasonably worked up about silly things, been the very essence of what his wise old father had brought him up to admire about the English. Nowadays, however, they seemed ready to lap up uncritically every American hysteria.

He could not understand the fuss that people made about homosexuality. He thought buggery unsavoury, but was it not inevitable, if the truth be faced, that one find anything sexual disgusting that one would not want to do oneself? Anyone could accept other people doing things he could imagine wanting to do himself, so if tolerance had any meaning at all, it must be putting up with them doing things that repelled one. He had seen too much suffering to be able to feel anything but sympathy for all victims of intolerance.

Besides, he had witnessed that a homosexual affair could be found to be beneficial under even the grimmest circumstances. His only real friend at Sachsenhausen, a handsome boy his age called Otto, had willingly given himself to a guard who showed interest, in return for extra rations and other favours, not the least of which was the rare commodity of kindness. Otto had told him all about it quite openly. He said it had hurt at first, but after that he had not felt anything much except immense relief that he had found this way of easing his life. The sex was almost nothing, an irrelevance compared to survival. Alfred had decided then that he too would willingly do the same if he attracted the favourable attention of a guard, and though it never happened and he had in fact never had the slightest experience of homosexuality, he had felt confident, as he knew Otto did, that if it did happen, it could make no difference to his interest in girls. Sadly, Otto had died, or he would surely now be a happily married man to prove the point.

Though homosexual acts seemed harmless to him, he did not feel quite the same about the gay community now thriving in London. He wondered if so very many men could really be living fulfilled lives so fixedly and fundamentally different from everyone else's. To be sure, there were some obviously effeminate men whose hormones perhaps only allowed them to take a passive sexual role, and he wished them whatever joys they could find in life, but what of all the others? He suspected that many of them had chanced to have some homosexual experience in their youth that should have been of no long-term consequence, but had found themselves trapped for life in a virtual ghetto by a society that insisted on categorising people according to a dubious notion of orientation. He questioned whether this orientation was any more real than the non-existent God in whose name his Jewish ancestors had passed centuries trapped in ghettos, or rather whether it was only made real by people's belief in it.

In any case, he was not for a moment prepared to accept that Julian might be fundamentally different to other boys. The idea that he might spend his life in the gay community appalled him as an unwarranted renunciation of the joys of family life and fatherhood, as well by extension of his own anticipated and well-deserved joys of grandfatherhood. Julian was only seventeen and provided any affair he might be having was treated as just an ordinary part of growing up, Alfred felt sure he would become a normal, well-adjusted husband and father.

It was essential to approach the question with openness and sensitivity if his son was not to end up either traumatised or indoctrinated into believing himself homosexual, but the dangers outlined by the housemaster were real too and this had posed a terrible dilemma, which he had finally decided was impossible to address until he could speak to Julian. For the same reason, he had decided it was premature to telephone Mr. Hodgson.

"Who is this boy?" he asked his son, as he put the letter back in its envelope.

"I think he must mean Alexander Aylmer," replied Julian, hoping the pretence of uncertainty would make his housemaster's assertions seem overstated.

"And are you in love with him, Julian?" he asked in as gentle a tone as he could, but Julian felt the directness of the question like a punch and reddened further.

161

"No," he lied. "Mr Hodgson is exaggerating. It's true I like him a lot. He's a very nice boy. But there's nothing unhealthy about it and it's very unfair to say that." He did feel it to be horribly unfair considering he had barely touched Alexander.

He had no idea what his father would make of the truth. He had hardly ever heard him make any reference to homosexuality, and then only as a matter of fact. He felt crushed by the possibility that he might now find him repugnant, in which case he must be dreadfully disappointed in him. His father had never been to a boarding school. Did he have any idea of their hidden tradition of older boys falling for younger ones? If so, did he realise that it had nothing to do with the sort of people who passed their lives homosexually instead of getting married and having children. He knew his father would be devastated if he thought Julian would not carry on the family, and since he had every intention of doing so, it was as much to protect him from unjustified sorrow as from his own embarrassment that he lied. He regretted it at the same time, for he loved him and longed to confide in somebody.

"Well, in that case, I think you really had better give this friendship up," said Alfred, still a little uneasy about interfering with any good friendship, but relieved that it seemed possible to resolve the matter without breaking Julian's heart. "You read what Mr. Hodgson said. It's just not worth it, is it?"

"But I can't, Dad. We're very good friends, you see, and after his mother died, I told him we always would be. He'll feel betrayed if I do."

Alfred sighed and paused in deep thought. He knew it was in Julian's interest to give the friendship up. He had so much to lose and so little to gain by it if love was not at stake. Despite what both boys might think now, there must be a good chance it would not endure anyway, especially with such opposition to it. Betrayal was a potent and loathsome concept though.

As often when Alfred considered questions of decency and honour, the image of Captain Holland crept into his mind. He was for the first time unwelcome there, but it was too late to shut him out. He imagined explaining the dilemma to him, pleading with him to understand that it was absurd to risk things fought for so hard on account of a children's agreement, but he thought he knew without asking roughly what the captain would say about this. "It's not on to let a chap down" would be the gist of it.

He very nearly relented then and asked Julian what he really wanted to do. Perhaps some compromise could be found. They could take the risk of deceiving Mr. Hodgson. They would have to be discreet of course and meet less often and in secret.

Julian was also on the verge of breaking down in his own way. The words began to form in his mind "Dad, I'm sorry. I lied to you. Please forgive me. I do love Alexander with all my heart. I can't help it. I'm sorry." And if he had expressed these words before his father went on, then the latter would certainly have changed his mind.

Alfred had finally reached a decision. His thoughts had gone full circle. Would this Alexander be at all satisfied with a compromise? There was no point otherwise. Then he remembered the housemaster's words about letting the younger boy get back to normal life. If Julian and he carried on in secret, he would not be able to do that. It was pointless, and the risk so great. Besides, the other boy was not his responsibility, he was his housemaster's. Alfred owed it to Julian, himself and his own father to be true to his dream. Having decided that, he must make it as easy as possible for Julian and keep any remaining misgivings he had strictly to himself.

"Julian, I know it's hard, but this boy is Mr. Hodgson's responsibility, not yours. Alexander's father entrusted him to his care and he has to decide what is good for him. You only have to decide what is good for you, and you don't really have much choice, because I don't think Mr. Hodgson will let you continue your friendship anyway. You need to think about how you're going to get a place at Oxford. Don't you care about that?"

"Yes, of course I do," answered Julian miserably. That was his weakest point, and it was then that he felt the battle was lost. His father had given him the very best education possible. He knew very well the sacrifices that had been made. That his father forbore to mention them now only emphasised his generosity. In aiming for a place at Oxford, Julian was going to have to expend some effort himself for the first time, and he could not see how he could possibly ever forgive himself if he failed and wrecked

163

all that his father had struggled for without having tried as hard as possible in every way.

"Then promise me you'll tell him that sadly you can't be friends any more."

"But I promised him to be friends for ever! How can I promise you something now that contradicts that? He will be so hurt, Dad," replied Julian, still unable to resist protest despite his despair.

"You can tell him that if you really have something in common, which is what a lifelong friendship is about, then you can be friends when you have both grown up and left Eton." Julian thought miserably how that would be far too late for what he wanted most, but he certainly could not tell his father that.

"Can you not see, my son, that you are being selfish to him too? If you are his best friend until you leave the school, what will happen to him then? You are stopping him from spending time with boys his own age, which is what he really needs."

"No, I'm not stopping him. It's his choice."

"Yes, sure, Julian, but has he thought about that? Have you pointed it out to him? If you really care about him like you say you do, you have to help him by thinking what is good for him."

Julian gave up then. Every time he tried to counter what his father was saying, he felt that he was exposing his own ingratitude, and all for a lost cause. "Okay," he said finally with a sigh, unable to look his father in the face for fear of revealing the extent of his anguish.

"Good. Truly, I am sure it is for the best." He paused. "I haven't yet told you that your mother still knows nothing about this," he said, looking quizzically at his son. The look he saw of shock followed quickly by relief confirmed that Julian shared his feelings about this. "I don't think we need worry about that now, but not telling her could have been very difficult, you know. If you defied Mr. Hodgson, he might mention it again in his school report or even on the telephone to her. Then she would be very angry with me for not having told her."

Julian shuddered. He immediately thought of the scene at the beginning of last holidays. She had found the *Mayfair* he had bought with Alexander. He had left it hidden at the bottom of a drawer, but she had tidied up and gone through everything in his room while he was away. The moment he had come through the door, he had known there was trouble.

"Julian, I'll talk to you in the lounge in five minutes," she greeted him with flashing eyes. When he got to his room, he sat on his bed, his mind racing to identify the likely source and his heart pounding with dread.

"How dare you bring this obscene dirt into our home?" she shouted when he went through, holding out the magazine by one corner of its cover, as if it really was a piece of excrement.

"I'm sorry, Mum," he said quietly, blushing and cringing.

"I just don't know where you get your dirty mind from. I can't believe a son of mine has been supporting the exploitation of women. Is this what they teach you at that school?" she almost shrieked.

"No," he said quietly.

"I should've known better. An elitist all-male institution like that was bound to be sexist too. I don't know why I went along with your dad sending you there. And after all we've done for you, this is what you do in return. Have you no conscience?" Julian remained silent. There was nothing that could be done but endure stoically until the storm subsided.

"Do you think that's what women are for?" she continued, calming herself a little to try to make him see reason. "Just objects for your gratification? Can't you see how demeaning it is to treat us like we're nothing but your sex toys, like we have no other qualities and can't have interests or careers of our own? Doesn't it trouble you at all that these women are being used? You think they're doing it for fun, but they have to do it for the money." The reminder of money refuelled her fury.

"Do you realise the £ 1.20 you wasted on this filth could have paid for a girl in Sudan to learn to read? Well, you listen here," she said, beginning to rip the magazine to pieces, the initial effort required causing her to puff up further. "If I hear of you buying something like this again, never mind contaminating my house with it, we'll know you've got too much money and we'll cut your allowance right down, so you can't buy nothing. Do I make myself clear?"

"Yes, Mum. I'm sorry," he said submissively, though he really thought her unfair and the more he had thought about it ever since then, the more ridiculous her reasoning seemed. Just because one admired a woman as sexually desirable, it didn't follow that one was not aware she had other qualities. Were boys who had posters of John McEnroe with his tennis kit on their walls degrading him by focussing on one aspect of him to the exclusion of others?

One might as well say that the election posters he remembered from last year depicting a triumphant-looking Mrs. Thatcher with a prominent Conservative-blue incarnation were exploiting her because they focussed on her only as a politician to the exclusion of other valuable sides of her personality. Why was it more demeaning to be thought beautiful than to be thought a clever politician?

The notion that the girls in *Mayfair* were exploited because they were induced to strip for money was even more ludicrous. How many people would do any job if they weren't paid? They didn't have to do it if they didn't want to, so how could it be exploiting them to accept their offer? If anyone was doing any exploiting, was it not rather the girls? They were taking advantage of their beauty to make money selling pictures of themselves, which they could only really do because boys like him at boarding-school had no other sexual outlet.

Despite his apologies, the atmosphere had remained frosty until his father came home, and he had been immensely relieved that he was off to Paris on an exchange the next morning.

That had not been the first uncomfortable encounter, though it had been the worst. Anything sexual had always been taboo. He had never been allowed to watch television until she had checked that the programme he wanted to see was "appropriate" for someone his age, which excluded not just films with "disgusting" kissing scenes like James Bond, that all his friends had seen, but many more, for "exploitative", perhaps her favourite term, included a host of sins besides lust.

Lust though was the worst. Three weeks after the *Mayfair* incident, James Crichton's parents had given a disco party for forty boys and girls in the basement of their house in South Kensington. Some boys went to them all the time, but it was the

166

first time Julian had been invited to one. His father had been delighted. It showed that Julian was getting integrated into the upper class at last and it was the first time he would meet the sort of girl he hoped he would marry, so he was in an unusually effusive mood, almost tipsy with pride in his smartly-dressed son.

"Don't get too much lipstick on your cheeks," he joked, as Julian was leaving. Julian caught the glassy look his mother shot his father and blushed.

She was the last person in the world he wanted to have to talk to about his "unhealthy interest." He had a horrid feeling she would associate it with this child abuse thing she seemed to be involved in. He was not exactly sure what it was because he only ever heard her mention it obliquely to his father and she certainly never told her son anything about it. All he knew was that it involved children, the "exploitation" and "power imbalances" that lay at the heart of most of her "issues", and that her views on it were considered very important, so much so that they were becoming significantly better off as a family. It was absurd, of course. Julian knew boys had been having crushes on each other at boarding schools since they were invented, and everyone who knew anything about it knew that it had nothing to do with "abuse", but he doubted his mother would be able to understand that, especially after her lecturing him on exploiting women.

"So, we can just forget about it, can't we?" concluded Alfred.

"Yes, Dad, thanks," said Julian relieved.

"But Julian, you do understand, don't you, that half measures won't work? As soon as you get a chance to talk to him, you will explain that, sad as you are about it, it's got to stop at once? That's the only way it'll work."

"Yes," he said, longing now to be alone in his agony. He felt an immediately intensified regret that he had bungled the day before. If he could only go back a day in time, if he had known what was going to happen today, then he was sure he would have been bold enough to declare his love. If it had been accepted, as he felt sure now that it would have been, and he had guessed about Hodgson's letter, he would without question have

167

visited Alexander in his room that night, and he felt equally sure that he would easily have persuaded Alexander to yield his virginity. If he had known that fulfilment, he would not now feel the terrible despair he did at agreeing to give the boy up. Just as the drone knew that his whole, otherwise useless existence was fulfilled by his single moment of bliss with the queen bee without regard to his immediately ensuing death, so Julian too would have cared far less what happened afterwards, sustained for ever as he would have been by the memory of having possessed Alexander.

He had no idea what he would have done this day if he had consummated his love, because everything would have been so different. He wondered fearfully if perhaps he really was selfish to the core, for it was despite knowing that lovemaking would have made any subsequent betrayal much worse that he knew his terrible anguish and regret would be less acute. Was he so rotten that he would have found it less hard to agree to betray Alexander, or would the triumphant self-confidence he was sure would have immediately transformed his personality have emboldened him to confess all to his father and defy the rest of the world? He fervently hoped the latter, but now he would never know for sure.

Alfred was of course very much happier than his son, but despite his apparent success in defusing the crisis, he too felt uneasy afterwards. It was not just the awful misgivings he had hidden while urging him towards a course of action which he knew in some ways to be terribly wrong. He could muster the same arguments again and again to set aside those doubts without allaying his profound sense of foreboding. He soon realised he had a nagging suspicion that Julian had not been entirely truthful about his feelings for the younger boy, and that some dreadful calamity, he knew not what, might somehow be the final consequence.

Though lower boys were not allowed home for the weekend, Alexander's father had got permission to take him out for the day on Sunday. In the meantime, he had plenty of time to think about Friday's events. He had been hurt that Julian had so readily denied being in love with him, and initially disappointed that their friendship was not to be cemented in the way he had imagined. He was also sad he was not desired and felt rather foolish for having thought he was.

However, after a while thinking about it, he told himself that he was being ungrateful for what he did have. Even if Julian was not in love with him, he must surely at least like him a lot, whether that counted as love or not. After all, he had sworn they would always be best friends and he had just given him the coin, which was enduring, tangible proof that he cared about him. He worried a bit that he had not shown proper gratitude when they had gone to the cinema and determined to be especially warm to him when they were together again. The really important thing was their friendship, without which he could not imagine coping. He could come to terms with missing the rest. It had only recently come to seem appealing and only then because he had imagined Julian wanted it badly. He himself might well not have liked it anyway.

After Chapel on Sunday morning, Alexander waited by the Burning Bush until he saw his father's dark red Mercedes drive up. When he got in, he was glad to find his father in a cheerful mood.

"I've got three pieces of news for you," he said as they drove off. "One is good, one is bad and the other I've no idea what you're going to think of. Which would you like first?" Alexander instinctively grasped that the last-mentioned was the most important, something momentous, though he had no idea what. He always liked to get bad things out of the way first.

"The bad news."

"I'm afraid we can't go to stay with Uncle Charles in the Summer holidays after all, because he has to go to Japan that week."

"Oh, that doesn't really matter." Alexander felt sure now that it was only the not-know-what-he-was-going-to-think news that was really important. He sensed that it might be daunting and that it would at least need a lot of thinking about, so he decided to ask for the good news next. He hoped it would be really good; good enough to keep him cheerful if there did turn out to be something truly worrying in the remaining news.

"Well, what's the good news then?" His father looked a little disappointed for a moment, then smiled and handed him a Mars bar. That was nice of him. However, it proved beyond doubt that his father was seriously worried he would be upset by what was to follow, and that did not augur well. As he opened the Mars bar, he also thought it reminded him somehow of his father's idea that he should write a story about a boy making a boat.

"Er, don't you want to hear the other news?" asked his father after some moments of silence, looking at him nervously.

"Um, yes."

"I'm getting married again!" he said excitedly in a rush.

Alexander had never been so astonished. It was so unexpected that it took his breath away. Questions darted around him like the swarms of little fish that appeared out of nowhere when one dived in shallow seas. There was no doubt, however, what the big question was: what about my mother?

"Well, what do you think?" His father was smiling, but evidently becoming impatient for Alexander's reaction.

"I, well, congratulations!" he said and smiled, feeling a pang of guilt that the seconds that had elapsed between the falling of the bombshell and his reaction might have hurt his father's feelings. "But what about my mother?" he wanted to ask, but did not.

He had simply assumed from everything his mother had told him about the uniqueness of his parents' love for each other, that neither of them could ever consider marrying someone else. Besides, he had always known from Gigi's example how people who really loved each other acted if they lost their husband or wife in middle age. Did this not mean that his father had not loved his mother nearly as much as he had imagined?

"So, you think it's a good thing then?" his father asked eagerly.

"Well,… yes," said Alexander, torn between the desire to make his father happy and guilt that his "yes" could not be entirely truthful, so long as it might in any way be a betrayal of his mother. "I mean I suppose so, but I don't yet really know for sure, how can I, when I know nothing about it?" When I do not understand because my world has been turned upside down, he thought. When a lot I have thought has been based on a false assumption. Ruefully, he remembered how he had thought his

170

father's question last month about the possibility of remarriage had been one of genuine self-wonder, rather than the prelude to this. How could he have been so naïve?

"No, of course. I must tell you everything. Her name is Janet Tweedie. She is a widow of forty-one, so just a little younger than your mother, and her husband died two years ago."

"Oh, do you mean the Mrs. Tweedie with the daughter who you said was a friend of Aunt Olive, the one you said you might get to cook for us in the summer?"

"Er, I don't remember saying anything about cooking, but, yes, she is a friend of Aunt Olive's and she does have a daughter of nine called Dorothy. In fact, you are going to meet them both today. They are coming to lunch." Alexander felt a heady surge of nervousness mixed with an incipient curiosity. It was so sudden. He needed time to think how to behave, as he had no idea. Then he remembered with relief that his father had said on the telephone that both his brothers were coming to lunch too. They must know better than him what to do, so hopefully he could follow their lead.

"Janet married late in life," explained his father. "I think it must have been because she was too choosy. Her husband died of multiple sclerosis only five years later. In fact, I think she knew he had it when she married him, which was remarkably brave of her. Anyway, I'm afraid she's been rather hard up as a result, so she hasn't been able to afford to send Dorothy to a private school. Sadly, it's not that unusual nowadays. We know several people with perfectly decent backgrounds who are unable to afford the fees. You'll find that because of the other children at her school, Dorothy has a common accent and rather non-U manners, but all that will change soon. She's frightfully bright, you know, and she's got a place at St. Paul's starting in September." An awkward silence ensued for a couple of minutes. Alexander felt still weighed down by his unasked questions, and then at last some of the answers came forth.

"I want you to understand that this doesn't mean I've forgotten Mummy," his father continued. "I could never do that or feel the same way about anyone else that I felt about her. It's quite different between Janet and I. It's just that neither of us want to spend the rest of our lives alone. We have both had a full existence already. This is just the concluding chapter of our lives that we wish to spend together." Put like that, it was at last possible to understand, and Alexander felt immensely relieved. He had come to understand loneliness only too well. Of course it must be a relief for his poor father to have sympathetic company, and it no longer seemed to contradict what he had been brought up to believe of the uniqueness of his parents' love. But his father had not finished yet.

"One thing we're agreed about though is that it's going to be terribly difficult to build our new life together if we have pictures and personal things lying around to remind us of each other's old husband or wife, so we're going to put all those away. I hope you can understand that just because there won't be pictures of Mummy up any more, it won't mean that I've stopped thinking about her." Alexander could see the point being made, but he was uneasy again. It did not quite fit with what his father had just said.

Why did pictures of his mother matter if his father's marriage with Mrs. Tweedie was to be quite different, a mere closing chapter? He knew that he himself could not care less if there were pictures of Mr. Tweedie around. It was simply nothing to do with him. Clearly then, he and his father no longer saw things the same way.

Accustomed though he was to respecting all his father's decisions, he could not now simply swallow whole the idea that his father's replacement of his mother was something good just because his father said so. He had to think for himself because their outlook and ideals could no longer be the same. His mother was and always would be his mother, dead or alive, but now she was no longer to be his father's wife.

They had relapsed into silence, so he brought up the subject of his grandmother, which had been foremost in his mind while he had been awaiting his father's arrival.

"I'm afraid Dulcie had to be put down," said his father. "She pined away as soon as Granny died and wouldn't eat anything, though Hopkins kept trying to feed her. Alsatians are like that. They simply lose the will to live when their owner dies, so we had to have her put out of her misery." The expedience of it rather shocked Alexander, and he reflected sadly that one by one

172

and fast the links with his old, happy life were steadily being severed, as if all continuity was bound eventually to be extinguished.

As they approached their house, Alexander felt increasingly both curious and nervous. He was fascinated to see what sort of person his father intended to spend the rest of his life with, and longed to see how his brothers had reacted to the news.

They arrived before Mrs. Tweedie. His father went into the kitchen, while he went into the adjoining drawing room, where he found his brothers talking.

"Isn't it *wonderful* news?" Christopher immediately asked him loudly, except that it was not a question, it was a challenge. Using his tone as an interpreter, the way his words really came out was "If you are not a total jerk, you had better accept and proclaim straight away how thrilled you are to hear the news."

"Yes" answered Alexander quietly in shocked and miserable obedience, while his thoughts lurched in the opposite direction. The bullying tone, reminiscent of Christopher only at his worst, dispelled at once his readiness to shelter under his big brother's ideas, for evidently there was no room left in them for consideration of the merest accommodation of what might be his own. He wondered if Andrew felt the same as Christopher. Andrew was just looking at him in neutral curiosity, so he thought that perhaps, after all, the less-known of his two brothers was the nicer.

Then they all went into the kitchen to join his father in getting lunch ready, but Alexander felt detached from his family. He realised with distress that he was bound by his different circumstances to be on his own. Andrew had his own life with Sabina and though Christopher might be supposed to be less emotionally independent of their family, he lived in his own house with his friends and the duty he had undertaken of being their father's companion for most of the weekends when Alexander was at school had clearly become a burden to him.

Suddenly there was a shrill ring from the doorbell and his heart jumped. His father went to answer it, the others following. He was at the back, so at first he could not even see Mrs. Tweedie, as they crowded around her, but eventually she emerged and said hello to him with a gracious smile. He gazed at her in fascination as he answered, and was just beginning to feel relieved when Dorothy appeared. She said hello to the others sulkily, but when she caught sight of him, she scowled and walked past him, as if to say "just because you're a few years older than me, don't think I'm going to treat you like a grown-up."

He knew his father was aesthetically fastidious, so he had wondered if Mrs. Tweedie would look like his mother, but she was very different indeed. Though two years younger, she looked a few older. Whereas his mother had been unusually tall, Mrs. Tweedie was very short, in fact one of the few adults he had already overtaken in height. She was dark-haired instead of golden blond. Penelope Aylmer had borne a warm, open expression. Mrs. Tweedie had a pointy nose and her face was, above all, shrewd. The nearest point of similarity was a slender frame, but where this had made his mother graceful, it made Mrs. Tweedie even smaller.

It was only when her daughter sat next to her at lunch that Alexander realised from the contrast that she had an elegance and refinement that matched her charm and easy manners and must be the source of her appeal to his father. In some respects, Dorothy was the spitting image of her mother. Watching them together, Alexander traced an identical profile, but the same features that looked delicate in her mother, looked coarse in her. She was plump and grim, and Alexander soon realised that her looks matched her character.

"Alexander, come and help me find something to amuse Dorothy," said his father, when they had finished clearing up after lunch. They went into his old playroom. Dorothy was already there playing with his old toys. She obviously knew her way around and Alexander wondered how often she had been there.

As his father pulled out one game after another from the shelves, Alexander looked at Dorothy curiously. He still rather hoped they might be friends. He did not mind playing with much younger children. In fact, Dorothy was the same age as his favourite cousin Charlotte, who was the nearest he had ever had to a little sister. They had always got along very well. She had come to stay with them on her own last

174

Christmas holidays. She had followed him everywhere like a puppy and he had enjoyed indulging her. Dorothy was obviously not nice like Charlotte, but he thought that if she liked playing with him, it might relieve some of the loneliness he had felt last holidays.

Dorothy looked up and caught his eye. He smiled, but she turned away disdainfully. Just then, his father produced a Monopoly set and suggested they play.

"No thanks," said Dorothy coldly in her sharp cockney voice, continuing her play. Alexander could see that his father was a little shaken, as he followed him out of the room. They went back to the dining-room and Alexander sat quietly listening at the table while Janet, as he had been told to call Mrs. Tweedie, made polite small talk with Andrew and Sabina.

Soon his mind wandered. He had never before come home from school without getting into real conversation with whoever of the family was around. He realised that for the first time ever, he was looking forward to going back to school. Everyone left in his family had their own lives now and did not need him. He felt far more alone at home than ever before and a sudden, fierce longing to have his own life too overwhelmed him. That could only mean Julian, his one true friend. Just as Hephaistion had stood by his ancient namesake and lent him strength when he too had trouble at home, so Julian was the one he could always rely on to be on his side and understand his point of view. They could live their own lives at school, and with Julian's wise advice, he would somehow work out what to think and do at home.

Alexander got back to school at eight. After supper, he went to Julian's room every quarter of an hour or so in the hope that he would be there, even taking the risk after his bedtime, but Julian did not come back until ten.

"Jimmu Kamoep," said Alexander in their secret language, smiling with relief.

"Hello," replied Julian with averted eyes and a slight frown, giving Alexander the unpleasant feeling that he thought their old game childish.

"How was your weekend?" he asked, trying not to show he was hurt. "You'll never believe what happened when I went home today."

"Look. It's after ten. We don't want to get into trouble with Hodgson again. I do need to talk to you about something, but we'll have to leave it until tomorrow. I'll come to your room after breakfast, okay?"

"Okay," said Alexander, terribly disappointed and with a sinking feeling. He had never for a moment doubted that he would talk to Julian about his father getting remarried that evening. As he went to bed, he felt a terrible gloom that he was still alone in his thoughts about it. Also, Julian had never spoken to him at all coldly before, and though he tried to tell himself that it was unintentional and Julian must have been tired, he could not forget the way Julian would not look straight at him. Deep down he knew something was badly wrong. He felt such a dreadful foreboding that he hardly slept.

It was getting light when he finally fell into a sleep deep enough to forget his worries. When Miss Flaherty reached his door on her daily round waking up the boys on the first floor, she had to knock thrice before he answered.

"Good morning, Mr. Aylmer. Are you awake?" she asked as always, poking her head round his door. The moment he first awoke, his customary enthusiasm for the new day had briefly surged forth, but by the time he answered her, it had been checked and entirely overborne by his memory of the last evening. He lay in bed another twenty minutes, trying vainly to convince himself he need not worry. He decided to miss breakfast and paced miserably around his room waiting for Julian, unable to shake off his feeling of dread.

When Julian at last appeared, he forced himself to smile enthusiastically, as if by welcoming him warmly he could put him off wanting to say anything disagreeable.

"Alexander, I'm sorry, but I've got bad news," said Julian, again looking down. "We can't carry on spending time together like we have been."

"What do you mean?"

"Well, Hodgson wrote to my father and said we should stop being together. He said I must spend all my time preparing for

176

Oxbridge and you should be with your friends in your own block. You'd better go back to messing with Drysdale."

"You mean you don't want to be friends at all?" asked Alexander incredulously.

"Look. I still like you, but no, we can't spend time together any more."

"But it's nothing to do with Mr. Hodgson. You promised we would always be best friends."

"Everything's changed since then. You know what people are saying about us. Anyway, I've promised my father now. It wasn't easy for him to get me into Eton and I can't let him down."

"That promise doesn't count. You promised me first. Even if my father and Mr. Hodgson and the whole world tried to turn me against you, I would never break my promise to you."

"Maybe it's possible that in a year or two, when I've left the school, we can be friends again, but not now."

"No, that will be too late."

"Well I'm sorry then."

"What's the use of saying you're sorry when you don't have to do it. You can just keep your promise and we can forget this conversation like a nightmare."

"Look Alexander, it's already decided. Can't you see that in the end, it's for your own good? Next year I'm leaving here and then it'll all be over anyway. So if you went around with me all the time and had no other friends left, what would happen to you then?

"But you just said yourself that we could be friends when you left! You're such a liar."

"If that's what you think, it's for the best anyway. I've got to go now anyway," he said, glancing straight at Alexander for the first time and opening the door. "We'll be late for Chapel."

"Wait, Julian! Wait! I'm sorry I said that, but please, please don't do this." Alexander was crying now. He knew it was childish and that if anyone knew he was doing it over a friendship they would think him hopelessly pathetic, but the last pieces of his world were falling apart and he could not help it.

"I'm sorry," replied Julian blushing and he left hastily.

Alexander stood stunned. As when Hodgson broke the news of his mother's death, he was at first incredulous. It was so far from his nature to let down a friend, to betray anyone for any reason that it was impossible for him to understand. Ten minutes passed before he realised he had missed Chapel for the first time. Often checks were made in Lower Chapel, so he might well find himself on the bill for the first time too, but he did not care. He sat down in his armchair and cried, then decided he must pull himself together and go to his first div. He sat through it in a daze until near the end, when he found himself unable to fight back the hope that Julian would relent. Perhaps he would come to him during the approaching After Nine. Surely Julian was too kind to go through with what he had said.

Back in his room half way through After Nine, Alexander allowed himself to believe for the first time that Julian was not coming back. He was all alone in the world. Yes, he knew kind people. Among the boys, Simon at least would not turn him from his door. Mr. Cavendish too had offered to talk to him and he knew his father, Andrew or even his uncles would concern themselves if they knew of his misery, but he had no use for pity or sympathy. He wanted only love and he could no longer bear the thought of life without it. No one really wanted him and all those nice people would get over it soon enough if he were run over by a bus.

He wondered seriously for the first time in his life what it would be like to die. Need it hurt? Perhaps if one could faint first, one would know nothing about it. Would not suffocation have that effect? He wasn't ready to die yet, but he was ready to experiment. He could try strangling himself to the point of fainting and if it was easy then he would know that at any time he could hang himself painlessly. He found a tie, wound it round his neck and tied it to his upraised metal bed. Then he pulled himself down towards his knees. When he could no longer breathe, he felt blackness overcoming him and then a rush of nausea. Quickly he stumbled to his feet and ripped the tie off, then he had to rush for the bathroom. He vomited into his cupped hands as he ran and then violently into the loo. When it was over, he went back to his room and saw that his tie was a wreck. He wondered a little fearfully how dangerous it had been.

By then, it was time to get ready for his chemistry div. He had forgotten all about his EW, simple as it was, just learning the abbreviations for the metals, but it was too late now. The chemistry beak tested them immediately. It was the straightforward sort of test he would never before have failed to get full marks in, but now he got twelve out of twenty and a rip, another first ever. He reflected bemusedly on how badly he would have minded before today.

He went back to his house for Chambers, but he could not face tea with the other boys and headed straight for his room instead. On the landing, he saw Julian approaching and stopped, his heart thumping. Julian glanced at him just long enough to take him in, then averted his eyes and walked quickly past with a cold expression, only a tiny hint of irritation in his eyes showing he had noticed Alexander.

Then Alexander knew that Julian felt nothing for him at all and was never going to relent. He had to run back to his room at once. He did not know how many boys saw his streaming tears. Safely in his room, he slammed the door. Anger at the unfairness of life compounded with his misery. He could not stand it any more. There was no further point in experimenting. He wanted his body to be as broken as his heart.

Without thinking much about it, he picked up his Swiss penknife and opened its long blade, feeling for it, as he could barely see through his tears. He knelt on the floor, took off his tails coat and pulled his left sleeve right back. The extendable chain of his cufflinks allowed it to be withdrawn nearly as far as his elbow. Then he clenched his fist and his teeth, pressed the blade hard against the veins just below his wrist, closed his eyes, drew his breath and took one long, hard swipe.

He felt a searing jab of pain and opened his eyes in shock. Blood oozed out, soon covering his palm and dripping onto the floor. After a while, his head began to swim and he thought he might soon faint, but what felt like long minutes passed without him doing so and then he saw the flow was slowing. His wrist stung sharply and he felt a new jab of pain when he jiggled it a little, but soon there was no doubt that the flow was stopping. The blood was even beginning to dry.

He realised then that he was not going to die, though anyone who saw him now would deduce that that was what he wanted.

Suddenly terror of being caught gripped him and drove all other thoughts from his mind. He had heard of people who tried to kill themselves being locked away in asylums. That would be even more horrifying than prison, as, in addition to losing one's freedom, one would suffer the unfairness and humiliation of being treated as mad. He knew he was not mad at all. No doctor could cure him of anything because the only thing wrong with him was that no one loved him and he'd been betrayed by the person he'd imagined might.

He must remove the evidence fast. He covered his wrist with a handkerchief, put his jacket back on to hide it, made his way to the bathroom and locked himself in one of the bath cubicles therein. He ran the bath tap and clenched his teeth against the pain, as he gently dabbed the wound. The slit was an angry red and wet blood reappeared as soon as he wiped it clean, but it no longer flowed.

He drenched his handkerchief in water and went back to his room. He scrubbed the blood on the floor as hard as he could, dumped the bloodied rag into a draw and covered the wound with a plaster the dame had given him for his rowing blisters. His wrist still throbbed, but he thought there were no visible signs of what had passed as he put on his jacket again and looked at his watch. He was already two minutes late for his English div.

IX: Greek Love in Theory

I cannot say what greater good there is for a boy than finding a good lover, or for a lover than finding a boy to love. Love, more than anything ..., implants in men the thing which must be their guide if they are to live a good life. And what is that? It is shame of what is shameful, and a passionate desire for what is good.

Plato, *Symposium* 178

Damian burst into his F div that morning with much more than his usual enthusiasm. Earlier, he had been to see Mr. Griffith, his own old housemaster, and now in his last year as one, and Mr. Griffith had invited him to produce his house play. It would not be put on until the Michaelmas Half, but all the essentials needed to be arranged soon. It was a tremendous honour for him as a new beak and a wonderful opportunity. The drama department at Eton was fantastic, and making use of it one of the best things about being an English beak. He had been longing for such a chance and had already thought about what he would do if one came his way, so when Mr. Griffith asked him if he had an idea for a play, Damian readily answered "Julius Caesar". His head spun with ideas all morning. One thing decided was to give it as authentic a flavour of classical Rome as possible, for which he was going to do a great deal of reading. In fact, he planned to spend the evening in the Porson Library, a large room in the old school buildings entirely devoted to ancient history.

The boys stood up enthusiastically as he came into the room. He was well established as a popular beak now.

"Good morning," he said with a smile. When they sat down, he noticed that Alexander was not there. It was nearly ten minutes before he appeared.

"I'm very sorry, Sir," said Alexander dully without explanation. Damian saw the others looking at him expectantly, no doubt assuming he would put him on Tardy Book, but he had seen his expression of hopeless despair, and in any case now knew better than to think he might be late without a reason.

"Okay. Sit down and come and see me at the end of the div," he said gently. He resumed what he had been saying, but could not help his attention returning to Alexander. The boy's face was white and he looked quite ill. All his movements were slow. Damian's own enthusiasm dissipated as he realised that Alexander was utterly forlorn. He felt fairly sure he had been crying, and realised that something more must have gone terribly wrong in his life. He kept glancing wonderingly at him, but all he could detect was blank despair.

It looked as though he urgently needed help or comfort, and Damian felt an overwhelming longing to offer it, but how? He thought of asking him to come for tea again, but he guessed that Alexander would just thank him like before and never come. Probably he would think that Damian did not really want him to, which was not true. He did not simply feel sorry for him. His desire to really help was absolutely heartfelt. He was an extraordinarily attractive boy in every sense. There must be hundreds of people who felt sorry for him. Plenty of them had probably made it clear and perhaps that did not help. Alexander probably did not want to be pitied. After all, what could anyone's pity do to relieve him? If only Damian could do something to draw him out of himself.

He wondered for a moment whether he had any commitments after divs that would get in the way of helping Alexander, if he could think of the means, but he had no plans except to go to the Porson Library, and he would gladly postpone his Roman research. Then he remembered how he had commended Alexander for the historical feel in his short story. The boy evidently knew far more about the ancient world than he could have learned in the classroom. Why not ask for his help? That would let Alexander know he was valued, not just pitied, and he would be far more likely to take the invitation up. The more he thought about it, the more he thought his idea excellent. It would give them something to talk about too and hopefully distract Alexander from his misery. He might even really learn something useful about ancient Rome. Then, maybe, if Alexander did need advice, if, as he suspected, some new grief had been added to his unhappiness, he might feel able to open up.

"I've been wondering if I could ask you a favour?" said Damian, when Alexander came up to his desk afterwards.

"Yes, Sir?" replied Alexander, utterly confused.

182

"I'm putting on a production of Shakespeare's *Julius Caesar* for RFG and I'm keen to make it historically realistic. The trouble is I don't know much about classical Rome, so I need someone who can advise me in private so that I don't make a fool of myself," said Damian cheerfully. "I'm just guessing from your story that you know much more about it than me, so I wondered if you'd mind helping me?"

"No, not at all, but I don't know how I can," replied Alexander, flattered despite his misery and confusion.

"Well, could you spare half an hour to come over to my place, and then we can see?"

"Yes, Sir."

"Excellent. Thank you. You couldn't manage after divs today, could you?"

"Yes, Sir. What time?"

"Straight after last school unless you want to have tea in your house first?"

"No, straight after is fine," said Alexander, quite relieved. He had been thinking earlier that he would never go for tea-time again. He could not face either asking Rupert to rejoin his mess or explaining to Miss Flaherty that henceforth he would be messing on his own. It would be much better not to have to return to his house then at all.

During his next div, his misery remounted as he knew that he would shortly have to go back and be in the same room as Julian for lunch. In the event, he sat through the meal mostly looking down, numb with misery. He could not stop himself stealing glances at Julian a few times, but he was talking to Crichton. Back in his room, he cried again, but he did not think of trying to injure himself. Having agreed to go to Mr. Cavendish's flat was an obligation that helped him get through the afternoon. He was grateful for his kindness and was not going to let him down. He felt a bit puzzled by his request, as he couldn't really believe he could help much, but he was intrigued and for some unexplained reason a faint glimmer of hope flickered and intermittently alleviated his misery a little as the appointment approached.

Alexander had never been in a beak's home before and was a little surprised to find it so comfortable and inviting. He had not

183

expected either that there would be packets of cereal and biscuits and a steaming pot of tea. Evidently Mr. Cavendish knew what Eton boys ate at tea time.

"Have you ever seen a production of *Julius Caesar*?" asked Damian once they were settled down.

"No, Sir."

"But you know a bit about the real Julius Caesar?"

"Yes, Sir."

"Would you like me to read you the most famous speech in it?" asked Damian.

"Yes, okay."

"It comes soon after Caesar has been killed. Mark Antony, who was his friend, went to see Brutus and the other assassins and pretended to be willing to be their friend if they would give good reasons why they killed him. Brutus, completely taken in, assured him of this and agreed to let him speak to the people at Caesar's funeral after he himself had explained his action to them." Damian caught Alexander's expression and stopped. "I'm sorry, you know all this already, don't you?"

"Yes, Sir."

Damian smiled. "Then you'll know that Antony also had to agree not to blame the assassins. So this is what he said, when Brutus had finished his speech and the Roman citizens had already been turned against Caesar. 'Friends, Romans, countrymen, lend me your ears: I come to bury Caesar, not to praise him....'"

Damian read it magnificently. Unknown to Alexander, he had been one of the best actors in the school in his time and had played the title role of *Macbeth* to great acclaim in the school play of his last Half. As he continued, Alexander felt transported back to the forum of ancient Rome. With each increasingly ironic repetition of "Yet Brutus says he was ambitious, and Brutus is an honourable man," Alexander was sure he too could feel the wildly changing emotions of the crowd. When Damian finally stopped, he felt vaguely disappointed for a short while. He realised he had momentarily forgotten his sorrow.

"Do you know if Antony really made a speech like that?" asked Damian.

"Yes, Sir. I've certainly read that he made a speech at the funeral that turned everyone against the conspirators, and he showed them Caesar's bloody and tattered clothes, but I didn't know what he actually said."

Damian explained that what he intended to worry about was not the accuracy of the events, which he had to present as in the play, but the anachronisms that would spoil the Roman atmosphere, like the references to Caesar wearing a doublet and a nightshirt.

"I doubt I can help, Sir, but I could try reading the play," said Alexander, now genuinely keen to do both.

"That's jolly kind of you. Well, why not? I'll bring you a copy on Wednesday. So you wouldn't mind coming here again to talk about it?"

"No, Sir. Not at all."

"When would you like to come then?"

Alexander thought at once that he would really like to come back the next day. He was dreading spending time in his house and he could muster no enthusiasm for going rowing all on his own, but he would not be able to read any of the play by then, so he would have nothing to offer. "I could come on Wednesday, Sir. If you're going to lend me a copy of the play in the morning, I could read some of it in After Two and come here after divs again."

"You're sure you don't mind missing tea with the boys in your mess?"

"I don't bother with tea actually," said Alexander awkwardly, blanching. Seeing how flustered he was, Damian guessed this was somehow linked to the source of the boy's grief. He knew that messing at tea was the time when boys regularly had fun chatting with their best friends and was dismayed that he chose to go without, but Alexander had stiffened, so he knew it was too soon to probe. They agreed on Wednesday.

As Alexander descended into the street, he felt once more enveloped in gloom. On his way back, he saw Miranda at her usual place, the other side of the street, but he was much too depressed to face her and kept his head down, hoping he would not be noticed by anyone in her group.

185

The next day was a half day. He hated being in his house, knowing Julian was so near, but he could not find the will to go anywhere else until he thought of going to School Library to begin reading *Julius Caesar*. He stayed there until it closed, his concentration frequently interrupted by long thoughts about Julian. His heart had lurched dreadfully every time he caught sight of him and he feared he might still cry if Julian cut him again. He was so lonely that he could not help hoping he might yet change his mind, but he did not think it would really happen, and his feelings for Julian were now mixed with a growing resentment that was a new experience for him. He thought that Julian was both pathetic and wrong to have let others turn him against him. No true friend could ever behave like that. There was no way anyone could have come between his Macedonian namesake and Hephaistion. He could never have done that to Julian, and he was sure he had never done anything to deserve being so let down. He must have been wrong about Julian's character all along. Much as he longed to have him back, he could not help despising him too.

He was still thinking this when he knocked on Damian's door the next afternoon, but was soon happily distracted into a discussion about *Julius Caesar*, which he had already finished.

"So how does the Rome depicted compare with the real one?" asked Damian.

"Accurately, as far as I know, but that's not much," said Alexander, still confused as to why Damian thought he might somehow be able to help. "I mean, like you said, there are a few odd things like clothing. I noticed hats were mentioned too, which I've never heard of people wearing in Rome, but the only serious differences I noticed are in the events."

"What are the biggest changes there?"

"The main one is that everything is made to take place in only a few days. There were really three years between Caesar's triumph and the battle of Philippi. Also, Caesar was killed in the Theatre of Pompey, not the Capitol, and I'm sure the triumvirs met somewhere in northern Italy, not in Rome."

"I see. All that will have been for dramatic effect," said Damian after a pause, awestruck that a boy in F happened to know all that. His guess as to Alexander's knowledge of ancient history was clearly an underestimate.

186

Alexander quickly sensed from Damian's expression and tone that he was being more admired than felt sorry for. He began at last to open up and became genuinely animated like his old self.

"What did you find most moving in the play?" asked Damian a few questions later.

"Caesar's shock at Brutus's betrayal. When he saw Brutus was going to stab him too and he said 'Et tu Brute? Then fall Caesar.' I hadn't realised before that it was in his heart that he gave up when he realised someone he trusted had turned against him," replied Alexander so sadly that Damian looked at him in surprise.

"So you don't think much of Brutus?"

"No, of course not. I don't see how anyone can. Caesar loved him like a son and he claimed to love Caesar and he did that!" said Alexander in a tone of withering contempt that struck Damian as wildly out of character for a boy usually so warm and gentle. He had been so vehement that they were both reduced to slightly embarrassed silence. Damian's suspicion that he had struck a raw nerve grew to certainty as he saw tears begin to appear in the boy's eyes before he turned away.

"I think you know what it's like to be let down by somebody you trusted, don't you?" he asked very gently.

Alexander hesitated, then nodded silently, desperately trying to hold back his tears. He knew his voice would break if he tried to speak and he was appalled at the idea of putting on a childish display in front of this man he now realised he admired a lot, who had been treating him so much like a grown up.

"Would I be right in guessing this has just happened?" asked Damian, sitting down on the sofa beside him.

Alexander began to break down, his whole body shaking with his sobs. He had tried hard not to think about Julian while he was here, but now he had been caught out doing so and he could no longer hide his feelings.

Damian longed to offer him physical comfort, to let the boy cry in his arms, but all of his upbringing, all of their upbringings, militated against it. What would people think? But they were alone together and no one need know. At last he could bear it no longer. He took Alexander's far shoulder in his hand and gently pulled. For a few moments the boy stiffened in surprise, then he went suddenly limp and let himself go. His head fell against Damian's chest, his eyes closed, but the tears fell freely from them and dampened the man's shirt. It was the first time anyone had held Alexander, had done physically more to him than shake his hand in the three months since his final day with his mother, and the relief was unbelievable. Having abandoned his pride, he thought only of the relief and lay quite still apart from his sobs for what must have been minutes.

"Can you tell me the whole story? Start at the very beginning," said Damian quietly, when he saw that the boy's tears had subsided and he began to fear the silence between them might revive his embarrassment. Then Alexander sat up and did just that, awkwardly at first, but fluently once he gathered momentum. He started with how Julian and he became friends, the story of the theft. One thing led to another and he got side-tracked into starting to tell about his mother. He realised and stopped.

"No. Go on. Tell me everything," said Damian tenderly. So Alexander did. It was the first time he had talked to anyone about what it was like when she died, how he had felt. Occasionally, Damian interrupted him with a question and Alexander was surprised by how often that elucidated something that had not been clear to him before. He carried on his story until the day Julian ended their friendship.

"Perhaps Julian was under some pressure more terrible than you know," said Damian, hoping to assuage Alexander's bitterness, while thinking he could understand it only too well. He too could not imagine himself ever letting down someone like that.

"It wouldn't have mattered if he was a true friend like he pretended."

"How should true friends behave ideally?"

"Like Alexander the Great and Hephaistion," answered Alexander immediately.

"Tell me about them," said Damian, both amused and intrigued by the boy's ready answer.

Alexander forgot his own grief then, as he got swept away recounting the whole story of the two friends, unwaveringly true to one another. He told how when they had invaded Asia, they had gone to Troy to lay wreaths together at the tombs of Achilles and Patroklos, the most famous pair of friends in Greek legend, how they had gone on to marry the two daughters of the last Persian King of Kings at the same time, how Hephaistion had died unexpectedly of an illness, and Alexander, mad with grief, had had hung the doctor who neglected to care for him properly, before dying himself soon after. He told Damian too about *Fire From Heaven*, the best novel he had read and which he had now finished. He recounted the author's explanation of how the Macedonian boys became friends. The only important thing he left out was how they had then also been lovers.

When Damian saw the passion with which Alexander told the story, as if he had been his namesake and was recounting his own story, he knew that he had seen Julian as his own Hephaistion. It was as clear as if it had been said. It followed also that Alexander had the same passionate and loyal nature as his ancient namesake. It was a nature he understood because he knew he shared it too, and he felt bound to him by that knowledge.

Damian sensed that besides feeling a dreadful loneliness it was appalling someone his age should suffer, his pride had also been terribly wounded by Julian's rejection of him. If he were going to be able to offer the effective friendship that Alexander clearly badly needed and he was now determined to bestow, he would have to be careful to let Alexander know he truly valued him. And indeed how could he not value such a friend? He knew that Alexander was highly intelligent, imaginative, sensitive and loyal.

Though Damian had never had homosexual inclinations, he acknowledged that Alexander's extraordinary good looks added to his charm as a companion too. Good looking meant just that and who would honestly not prefer to have good things to look at? Even in tears, he was stunning, the clear-cut luminous skin of his glistening cheeks emphasising his melancholy until Damian felt his heart might break. As for when he smiled, the colour of his hair and eyes reminded Damian of haystacks lying against the sky on a clear summer afternoon, hot, happy and pure.

Damian was therefore sure that for both their sakes it would be wonderful if they could spend a lot of time together. The problem this posed was that both of them had a heavy academic workload. He had to prepare for the next day's divs and very likely Alexander had E.W.s that he was running out of time to do. It was already seven o'clock. He would be rotten both as a schoolmaster and as a friend if he led him into trouble so soon.

"Alexander, I've really enjoyed having you here," he said, "and I'd like you to keep coming back. I fear there are very few people who have friendships like Alexander and Hephaistion, but if you like being here too and think we can be friends, I can at least assure you that I'll never let you down."

"Thank you, Sir," said Alexander, moved almost back to tears. "I would like that very much."

"Good!" said Damian with a big smile. "So, when can you come again?"

"Tomorrow," Alexander very nearly said, but he did not. He did not want to leave at all. The warmth he felt in Mr. Cavendish's flat was in increasingly stark contrast to the coldness outside. He had had no idea it would be possible for him to feel as relieved and calm as he did now he had told the beak so much that he had never told even Julian. It seemed that Mr. Cavendish really understood him. He was flattered too that someone so much older and more knowledgeable enjoyed his company. He was still anxious about intruding on his time though.

"Is Friday okay, Sir?"

"Yes, fine. The only thing is, I'm worried about stopping you doing your E.W.s. How about bringing them here? You could work at the table while I use the desk. Then you could stay until lock-up if you liked."

"Yes. Thank you, Sir," said Alexander enthusiastically. If only Mr. Cavendish had suggested that first, he would certainly have said "tomorrow" instead of "Friday."

Damian found it difficult to settle down to work when Alexander left. He was very pleased he seemed to have been able to alleviate the boy's unhappiness, but found it hard to stop thinking about what else he might do towards that end. Wanting to know as much about him as possible, he looked in the school fixtures to find his tutors and exact age. He was born on the 27th of May, so his fourteenth birthday was in only four days time! Hopefully, he would be going out with his father, as it was a Sunday, but if not, then it was surely entirely up to Damian to make the day happy for him.

The next afternoon, Damian went to the Porson Library to read about Rome for the second time. Walking round a bookshelf, exploring for new material, he nearly bumped into Harry Talbot, a nice boy in his C div.

"Hello, Sir," said Harry, blushing a deep crimson for some inexplicable reason.

"Hello, Harry. What are you reading?" asked Damian, surprised and rather put out that this usually friendly pupil was so disconcerted by their encounter.

"Oh, nothing really, Sir. I was just looking something up for my Ancient History div. I'm afraid I have to be off now," he added, as he hurriedly crammed whatever book it was into a shelf. Damian noticed that, as he did this, the youth had twisted the cover of the book away from his gaze and his forefinger had also hidden the words on the spine.

"See you tomorrow then, Harry," said Damian with some amusement, as he now realised Harry had desperately been trying to hide whatever it was he had been reading. As soon as the door of the library closed behind the fleeing youth, Damian turned to the shelf. He was intrigued by what book could possibly cause such embarrassment amongst these dusty tomes of ancient wisdom. He could tell at once which book it was, both by its dark blue dustcover and by the fact that it was only half pushed in, another book having fallen down behind it. *Greek Love* was its title. What on earth was that? Even more intrigued, Damian pulled the book out and leafed through it. By an Oxford professor called C.A. Jameson, it was evidently a well-worn book, especially in its illustrated middle section, which he saw to his astonishment was given over to ancient ceramic depictions of the love-making of men and boys. Though he had heard of this as a peculiarity of the ancient Greeks, he had never seen a visual depiction of an overt homosexual act before.

Damian had vaguely known a few homosexuals at Cambridge. Some undergraduates had come out as gay and there had even been a gay society. Several of the professors had also been

191

reputed to be that way inclined, and Damian knew that in at least one case it was true, for the man had made a pass at him one evening, after inviting him over to discuss his essay on Chaucer. Damian had hoped his abrupt rejection of the professor's advances had not upset him too much, as he had been a kindly and fascinating teacher, but he could not help his own revulsion at the idea of a man as the object of another man's lust. It was so incongruous.

Since Damian knew his own interest lay firmly in the opposite sex, he had taken very little notice of the homosexuals at Cambridge apart from that one unwelcome suitor, though he had equally shied away from taking part in his friends' private mockery of their often mincing gait and tones. He was full of sympathy for people doing their own thing, especially when it involved daring to be different. He had, however, observed enough of them to realise at once that what was depicted here in *Greek Love* was a very different phenomenon indeed.

The most startling difference was that all the couples so graphically depicted were men and boys, or occasionally boys together, but never men together. The incongruity that had made the little he had previously observed of homosexuality aesthetically distasteful to him was somehow missing here. The men depicted were all uncompromisingly masculine, another marked contrast to most of the homosexuals he had seen at Cambridge, with sturdy poses, heavy muscles and beards, while the boys were invariably in their early or mid teens, fresh-faced with hairless bodies and figures that were all, well ... boyish. He had to admit that man and boy seemed somehow to complement one another.

He turned to the title page and saw that the full title was *Greek Love: The Role of Pederasty in the Classical Age*. How could it have a role? A role implied a purpose and the frivolity of the gay relationships he had observed at Cambridge had been the other thing that depressed him about them. How could what they did compare with responding to the deepest instincts of any sexual animal by starting a new family with someone of the opposite sex? Much as they had tried hard to give an impression of having a good time, he had felt sure that a tinge of sadness underlay their gaiety and he suspected that its ultimate pointlessness was the cause.

192

Another extraordinary thing was how big the book was. He had heard before that the ancient Greeks loved boys, but no more than that, and it had never occurred to him that there could be so much to say about such a subject. He was fascinated now.

He glanced around the room and saw that he was alone. Div time had begun for the boys, so none were likely to come for some time, but another beak might and he did not want to be caught reading this book any more than Harry had. He pushed the books either side of the space where he thought *Greek Love* must belong enough to ensure it could be put back quickly, and began to examine it more calmly, while keeping his eyes and ears alert for any sudden movement by the door.

He turned the page and was amused to see on the next that the book had only been published the year before last, so its battered state was even more telling when compared with the almost pristine condition of many of the nearby nineteenth-century volumes.

He read for more than hour until he had reluctantly to tear himself away. By then he thought he had a fair understanding of the character of "Greek love", as some modern historians termed the intense love affairs between men and boys in ancient Greece. Otherwise called pederasty, meaning the love of boys, it was considered by most of the great philosophers to be the noblest form of love because it was love of the soul as well as the body, and society's most powerful means of bringing up a boy to become a worthy and virtuous citizen.

Greek men did not usually marry until they were thirty. Girls were usually about fifteen and were anyway strictly secluded both before and after marriage. Though prostitutes were widely available, sex for its own sake was considered base, and during at least the ten or so years before marriage, a decent young man was expected as a civic duty as much as for his own happiness to become the lover of a boy.

While it was recognised that some men had a preference between women and boys, that was simply a matter of taste. It was mostly assumed that all men were attracted to both, as indeed were most of the great men whose lives are known in enough detail.

Once a boy reached sufficient maturity to benefit from a lover's attention, twelve being the age laid down in states like Sparta that had rules about such things, he would start to be wooed by young men. The boy's attitude was supposed to be rather like that of a young lady in nineteenth-century England towards a prospective husband. He was not supposed to want sex with his suitor, but if with patience the man showed himself to be virtuous, admirable, truly in love with the boy and concerned genuinely for his good, then he would inspire both hero-worship and gratitude, and in due course the boy would give himself to him, body as well as soul. For the boy, it was so far from being considered shameful to accept a lover that failure to find one was looked down on, as it was assumed to be due to some moral flaw in his character.

Man and boy would then be known as lover and beloved, or in Sparta, as inspirer and listener. The man would transmit to the boy everything which they and society thought good and worthy of procreation. Some even believed that the sex helped achieve this physically, the boy taking in his lover's virtue with his semen.

As with the nineteenth-century girl getting married, certainly nothing would be said either before or after the boy's acceptance of his lover about sex being part of their affair, but it was tacitly understood that thenceforth the man would enjoy his beloved's sexual favours when and as he wanted, usually meaning possessing him in the most intimate way. No gentleman would ever speak of the boy's pleasure, as that would be an insufferable slight on his manliness.

The boy's honour or dishonour was always his lover's too. In Sparta, for example, a man was fined if his listener trembled in combat. The Sacred Band of Thebes, entirely made up of pederastic couples too loath to do anything dishonourable in their lovers' company to concede defeat, was invincible for a generation until cut down in battle to the last man and boy by Alexander the Great.

During the ensuing years of their love affair, the man used his example and the boy's longing to emulate him to instil virtue in him, further him in society and train him in everything thought best. In places like Crete and Sparta, where the custom began,

194

this would largely mean training as an athlete and warrior, but in others like Athens where men sought to perfect the soul as much as the body, the result was the most intellectually vibrant youth culture ever known. Damian had always been admired for his sporting and academic accomplishments as a boy at Eton, but he felt daunted by what he now read of the philosophical discourse of Athenian teenagers and the physical courage and prowess of Greek boys everywhere.

The sexual aspect of the affair would end when the boy grew facial and bodily hair, though a strong friendship would generally endure for life. In due course, the newly grown-up youth would change roles and in his turn seek out pubescent boys to love and train until it was time for him to marry.

Greek love was so far from having anything to do with modern gay homosexuality that the rare adult males thought willing to take passive roles were always harshly ridiculed as unmanly and degenerate. Equally, Greeks would think the wish to possess men sexually not only distasteful, since males were no longer desirable once they were hairy, but reprehensible, since it fulfilled no pedagogical or reproductive function.

As agreed, Alexander turned up with his schoolbooks after his last div on Friday and soon settled down to write. Damian noted with satisfaction that he looked very much happier than before. When Alexander had finished his work, they began to chat animatedly. It was their first long conversation since the boy had recovered his natural high spirits, and Damian found himself overwhelmed by him afresh. This time it was the sheer fun of his company that struck him, his enthusiasm and their laughter.

It was a hot afternoon, so they had both taken their tailcoats off. Alexander was walking about the room telling him a story, when Damian suddenly noticed a plaster on his left wrist, just above his watch strap. He pretended not to have noticed it for a minute while his head spun and the likely explanation for it engulfed him in horror.

"Alexander, can you come here a moment," he interrupted the boy. When he approached, Damian took his hands gently and turned them over. "What's this plaster for?"

"Oh, it's nothing really," said Alexander, blushing deeply.

195

"Can I see?"

"It's nothing. It doesn't matter," he replied, trying to withdraw his hand. He was severely embarrassed. His self-injury struck him now as pathetic and he could not bear to have his silliness exposed to the one person whose esteem he sought above all others. It was irrelevant too. He had passed Julian in the corridor after lunch that day. He had not attempted to meet his eye and had walked past as fast as Julian, and though he had felt pangs of sorrow mixed with resentment, thoughts of the coming evening with Damian had soon tamed them. He wanted to forget all about last Monday.

"Alexander, if we are really to be friends, you must be open and honest with me." He slowly pulled the plaster back and Alexander did not resist. There was a long thin scab. He sat holding the boy's hand in silence, too shaken to speak. He found it hard to hold back tears when he was deeply moved, and he was overwhelmed with horror at the attempted waste of such an exceptionally precious life, so full of promise.

"I was just playing around being silly. Please don't tell anyone. It really is nothing. Soon it will all be gone."

"I'm not sure about that. I think you'll find there'll be a scar, though hopefully only a very thin one. Look, I won't tell anyone, but in return do you promise that if you're ever unbearably unhappy about anything again, the first thing you'll do is come and talk to me about it."

"Yes, Sir," said Alexander with a relieved smile.

"You know, if you liked, you could come here most days. I would be very happy with that. It's up to you."

"So I can come all afternoon tomorrow?" asked Alexander excitedly, Saturday being a half day.

"Unfortunately, just tomorrow is not possible, as I have to go up to London, but after that. Are you going to be around on Sunday?"

"Yes, Sir."

"Well, come along after lunch then. But tomorrow, you mustn't sit around alone in your house. What about that old friend of yours you said you used to mess with, Rupert? Why not go on the river with him or something."

Alexander eventually agreed to ask Rupert, despite misgivings as to whether he would be willing.

196

That night, the more he contemplated the new prospect of spending at least a bit of every afternoon with Damian, the more his excitement grew. He would have unlimited opportunities to tell someone wise whom he could trust all about himself, his hopes and fears. Damian could advise him about everything, answer all his questions and tell him so much that he longed to understand.

One reason Damian had to go up to London was that he had decided to give Alexander a birthday present. The idea came almost straight away that the best possible one would be a book about Alexander the Great. It was clear that it would be deeply appreciated. Also, his friendship with Alexander had already reached a level that was highly unusual between a master and boy, especially a younger boy, and he realised it was no use pretending the sort of minds that delighted in finding fault with others would not draw salacious conclusions if they knew about it. Only he knew nothing of the sort had entered his thoughts, because only he knew the unusual circumstances. If anyone should find out he had given a birthday present to a boy, a history book for one who had expressed great interest in the subject seemed more likely to be understandable than anything else he could think of.

He went straight to Foyle's bookshop, said to be the biggest in the world, and looked for books about Alexander. Some popular-type biographies looked rather simplistic for a boy already knowledgeable of the subject, while others looked rather dry for a fourteen-year-old with their endless discussion of how to interpret the historical evidence and reference to the arguments of others. He decided to try the fiction department, but first, before leaving the shelves on classical history, he sought out the book *Greek Love*. What he had read was so fascinating and bizarre that he felt driven to learn more. If one cut out the sex, which was the embarrassing and unnecessary side of it, the ethos described was not very unlike that which inspired the teaching profession at its best. He could not keep going to the Porson Library to look at the book. Somebody might wonder what he was reading, worse they might ask. He did not dare ask the staff in Foyle's if they had it, so he decided to go through all the bookcases on ancient Greece. To his delight, he found it.

He felt himself blush as he handed it over to the woman at the classical desk, and did not dare meet her eyes, but he saw enough to see that she was a little flustered too. Unfortunately, this did not stop her from leaving it face up on the desk for several minutes, while she took his money off to the cashier's till. The book's secondary title *The Role of Pederasty in the Classical Age* was clearly visible to anyone passing by and he felt his face flushing hot as he imagined what anyone would think, especially anyone who knew him and that he was a schoolmaster. Could they possibly understand simple curiosity about such a subject? He looked around nervously and seeing that the woman was facing away from him towards the cashier, quickly stretched out his hand and turned the book harmlessly upside down. All the same it was an immense relief when at last she came back and he saw it disappear into a paper bag, which she folded over and sellotaped before handing it over to him.

He exhaled with triumphant relief, as he set off for the fiction department. When he got there, he found it was arranged alphabetically by author, so he asked the man apparently in charge if he knew of any novels about Alexander the Great.

"Well now, let me think.... The only one I've heard of was called *The Persian Boy*. It was a bestseller many years ago, I believe, so we should have it in stock. Oh dear, who was the author? Mary somebody."

"Not Mary Renault?" asked Damian with a rush of sudden hope.

"Yes, that's right! You should find it under R over there."

There were in fact seven novels there by Renault, including *The Persian Boy*, which Damian was delighted to see from the dust-cover was the sequel to *Fire From Heaven*, and told "the extraordinary but true story of Alexander's last seven years during which, before his death at thirty-two, he carried his conquests to the eastern end of the known world." It was narrated in the first person by a young Persian taken into his household. Damian did not think there could be a more perfect present for the circumstances.

Alexander spent that day upriver with Rupert, who had looked a bit surprised at his suggestion, but accepted so much more readily than he had expected that it seemed he was equally eager for a rapprochement. At first, they both avoided any allusion to the parting of their ways during the time Alexander had been so much with Julian.

As they approached Queen's Eyot, an unusually fast boat passed by and set off a wave that rippled towards them with alarming speed. Quite suddenly, Alexander found he was in water up to his waist, his whiff submerged below him. There was nothing for it but to drop into the water. The whiff turned over as it rose to the surface.

"Are you okay?" asked Rupert, speeding up towards him, a little worried.

"Yes, but Christ it's cold," said Alexander. It was the only time he had been in water with all his clothes on apart from the swimming test they had all had to take as new boys. He managed to turn the whiff over as Rupert reached him, but there was nothing Rupert could do to help him. He grasped the sides of the narrow boat with his hands and lifted a leg into it, but as he tried to rise up, the whiff turned over again. Then Rupert couldn't help giggling, and in no time both boys were laughing. Finally, Alexander mastered his vessel, and they set off for the hundred yards remaining to Queen Eyot.

They were only officially allowed one pint of cider each on the little islet, but one could often get away with more. Alexander was freezing and determined to dry himself out in the sun before going back, so they stayed over an hour and got second pints. When they had chatted uninhibitedly for a while, like in the days of their old friendship, Alexander told him openly how he regretted their having grown apart, and Rupert said they should forget it. Alexander reckoned then that they had sufficiently broken the ice for him to ask to rejoin their mess, but he stopped himself when he remembered how he had already spent three tea times that week. He had better not do anything that would hinder their repetition. That would be as demoralising as anything he could imagine at present.

They were a little tipsy by the time they set off back downriver. On the way back, they had to wait five minutes for the gates of Boveney Lock to open. Just as they did and Alexander rowed in, Rupert's whiff got swivelled around in the current. As he fought to turn it round the right way, the lock-keeper shook his head tiredly. It was near the end of his day and Saturdays were always the busiest with all the weekend boaters as well as the boys from Eton.

"Cor blimey!" he exclaimed at last to Rupert. "I'll eat my 'at if we 'ave to 'ave you as Prime Minister."

When Alexander's birthday arrived, instead of making him happy as it usually had, it just made him think about his ninth one, the only other on which he had been unhappy. Not only would there be not be the usual telephone call from his mother, but he would not talk to anyone who would even know that it was his birthday. His father had gone to Scotland for a long weekend to meet some of Janet's relations and planned to give him his present during the upcoming Long Leave. The revival of his friendship with Rupert was so recent that they had not had a chance to be reminded of such details of each other's lives. He did not have any other close friends at school anymore, unless he could really count Mr. Cavendish, but he could hardly tell him it was his birthday, even though he was going to spend the afternoon with him.

His ninth birthday had also been on a Sunday, as it happened, as well as one of the most depressing days in his life. It had been his first since going away to boarding school. He had been badly homesick the first year. The shock of being suddenly torn from the company of his mother and his comfortable home and finding himself in a harsh, unloving world of rules and punishments had been tremendous.

The worst thing of all was the food, which was so vile that lunch was the time of day he dreaded most. He would have been thrilled if he had ever been allowed to miss it, but even the boys' pleas to be allowed smaller portions were ignored. Once, he was left sitting wretchedly in front of his plate of semolina after the other boys had left. It was the most disgusting of all their regular dishes, a lumpy white sauce that looked for all the world like vomit. After five minutes, Miss Proudfoot, the school matron, lost patience and took him into her study with the plate.

There she forced open his mouth and shovelled it into his throat despite his choking.

Miss Proudfoot was the person he disliked most at the school, though he was not the worst sufferer at her hands. There was a boy in his dormitory who sometimes soiled his pants. Whenever this happened, Miss Proudfoot would hang them up over the door which all the boys had to pass through in order to reach their dormitories, inside out to show the brown stain better. This was to ensure the culprit an evening of remedial bullying.

Lights out was at a quarter past seven for the youngest boys, so they had great trouble sleeping. Alexander used to take a book to the door of his dormitory and open it just enough to let in a little light from the outside corridor. Unfortunately, his dormitory was right next to Miss Proudfoot's study. Once she burst out of it without warning while he was writing a history of the Roman emperors and she caught him. He was so frightened that he peed in his pyjamas for the last time in his life. She took him into her study and told him to bend over, then she took off her shoe and beat him with it.

At first, that had seemed a very small thing compared to the matron's confiscation of the notebook containing his Roman history, which he had been writing up for weeks with careful illustrations. He had thought she would throw it away, but the next morning he was summoned to the study of Mr. Osgood, the headmaster. If Miss Proudfoot was the foremost person who made life unbearable, Mr. Osgood was her antithesis. He had heartily congratulated him on his history and urged him to keep it up, merely adding as an afterthought and with a twinkle in his eye that he should stop at lights out. He could never afterwards think of Mr. Osgood without a strong feeling of warmth.

The boys were only ever allowed out on Sundays, when his mother always came for him, so it had been a wonderful stroke of luck that his ninth birthday fell on one. His excitement at going home usually began to climb after lunchtime on Fridays, the regular day for semolina. This time it was naturally far more intense, so his dismay was considerable when he woke up with a sore throat the next morning. By the afternoon, he felt dizzy too and he was sure he had flu. He tried desperately to hide it and avoided all the school authorities, knowing he would not be allowed home if he was found out. The stakes were even higher than just his birthday, because if he could escape detection until he was away, then he would be allowed to stay at home until he got well again.

When he got up on his birthday, he felt far worse. He thought he managed to avoid Miss Proudfoot noticing, but after breakfast he had to go for the weekly hour of letter-writing supervised by his French master, Mr. Rider, who soon noticed. To his immense relief, Mr. Rider guessed how things stood and promised with a wink to say nothing. As the boys rushed upstairs to change into their suits for Chapel, after which their parents would arrive, Alexander at last felt sure he was going to get away with it. To his consternation though, his suit had not been put out. When he went to tell Miss Proudfoot, she said he was ill. His protestations of good health were immediately met with a thermometer. He took it out of his mouth as soon as her back was turned, but she caught him and he was sent off to bed despite tearful entreaties.

When his parents arrived, they were allowed to spend half an hour with him, then they went home without him, and he was left lying wretchedly in bed for the rest of the day, except for occasional look-ins by the dreaded matron. It had been the most disappointing day of his life, but at least it had been exceptional. His present loneliness that now reminded him of it seemed likely to be something he must try to get used to. There was no longer anyone who cared about his birthday. Maybe there never would be again. The memory of his mother's love hung over him like a dark cloud all morning.

"Hello, Alexander. Happy birthday!" said Damian with a warm smile, when he opened his door that afternoon, and the boy's gloom dissolved at once into happiness. When he went in, he noticed at once that there was something in wrapping paper sitting on the table besides things ready for tea. His heart jumped with excitement as the likely implication struck him. Nobody at school had ever given him a birthday present before, nor had he heard of anyone else being given one.

Damian caught his look and decided to hand over his present at once. The pleasure of watching Alexander's reaction as he took in the subject of the book and its author was the most intense he had known for a long time.

Later, when they had both settled down to some work, Alexander felt his heart still pounding with happiness. The way Mr. Cavendish took such an interest in what interested him reminded him for the second time that day of Mr. Osgood. He realised then that not only was he the first schoolmaster since Mr. Osgood who had evoked strong feelings in him, but that those feelings were far more powerful. Mr. Osgood had been his father's age, a little wrinkled with receding grey hair, and had behaved towards him as a kind uncle, and though Alexander had been moved by his kindness and grateful for it, he did not want to be like him.

Mr. Cavendish was his brother's age, and lively and fun. Alexander very much hoped he would be like him: dashing, intelligent, tall, handsome, and presumably irresistible to girls. He himself was now fourteen and felt himself no longer to be a little boy. Over the last year or so, he had begun to find people of his father's generation a bit dull and old-fashioned. Mr. Cavendish was quite the reverse. He was full of new, sometimes quite revolutionary ideas that were to Alexander a breath of fresh air.

There were also unexplored possibilities between them that he could not quite put his finger on, but also had something to do with his no longer being immaturely innocent. Mr. Cavendish's presence evoked feelings in him that he had never known before he came to Eton. He realised now that from the first time he had seen him, he had felt that same indefinable tension he had noticed before during private conversations with certain older boys. At first, it had been as fleeting as all his early contacts with Mr. Cavendish, but he would never be able to forget how he had begun to feel after he had held him for a while on Wednesday. As soon as his tears had begun to subside, and the ensuing relief had freed his thoughts to consider his position in Mr. Cavendish's arms, a tingling sensation had coursed through his body, his heart had beat faster, and he had felt himself being rapidly overwhelmed. He could not imagine what would have happened if Mr. Cavendish had not so soon interrupted their intimacy by asking him to tell the story of his grief.

They were together this day much longer than ever before. When they had finished their work, they chatted at length until they began to feel like old friends. When Damian knew that time was finally running out, he went back to his desk.

"I have another little birthday present for you," he said, and handed Alexander a piece of gleaming, newly cut metal. "It's a spare key to this flat. I think it would be better if you didn't tell anyone I've given it to you, as they might misunderstand, but it's yours anyway. Now you can come here whenever you feel like it without asking me and treat it as your home. It may happen that sometimes I have to receive someone else here and will need you to go for a while, but I don't think it'll be often or for long, and I'll know in advance."

Alexander longed to hug him, but did not dare. He knew that sadly the physical comfort Mr. Cavendish had given him that once was never likely to be repeated for fear of embarrassment, just as he immediately took his point about not telling anyone else about the key.

"And don't worry about me telling anyone," he said when he had finished thanking him. "I do understand. I told you what people said about Julian and me."

There were only three days left before the Fourth of June, the greatest annual festival at the school. It was actually being celebrated on the last Thursday before that date, and marked the beginning of Long Leave. All three days, Alexander spent the time between his last div and lock-up in Damian's flat, which by the end already felt quite like his own home.

Though Damian had fully expected Alexander to make frequent use of his key, he had not anticipated him coming that much. When he left, nothing was said about when he would be coming back. It was only when he turned up as soon as he was free for the second day running that Damian realised Alexander was intent on spending all the time with him he could.

He worried a little what anyone would think if they knew an F boy was visiting him every day. Should he tell Alexander to come less often? If he did so now, Alexander would certainly be disappointed and might even feel let down. Besides, he was thoroughly enjoying having him around. They were doing nothing remotely wrong, so surely it was intolerable to compromise their happiness out of fear of dirty-minded people suspecting otherwise? He doubted anyone would know anyway. Alexander clearly understood the need to be discreet, and it was rare to pass anyone on the stairs up to his flat, as only two other bachelor beaks lived in his building. And if he should ever need to explain himself, he could.

The next day, Alexander noticed Julian still avoided him when they might have met, but the disappointment he felt in him no longer seriously saddened him. He asked himself if he would now swap the friendship of Mr. Cavendish for Julian's and a confident "no" sprung to his mind before he even considered why. Above all, he trusted Mr. Cavendish completely and knew him to be his true friend, which Julian had proved he had not been. Besides, he was more intelligent, livelier, wittier, far more dashing and handsome. He knew so very much more about life, so Alexander could get real answers to his most searching questions. He could trust implicitly in his advice too, for he was sure that Mr. Cavendish always had his best interests at heart. Now that he looked back, he rather doubted that Julian had.

Having found a better friend who valued him, he could not help feeling contempt for the cowardice of the inferior one who had not, and had betrayed their friendship for fear of what others thought.

It was hard to believe it had only been nine days since he had despaired of life.

The Fourth of June commemorated the birthday of George III, the school's most devoted patron since the founder. It was a splendid occasion, attended by the boys' parents and other relations or family friends, everyone dressed up, the boys with flowers in their tailcoat lapels. Hordes of girls also descended on Eton from their own nearby public schools. After the parents had had drinks with the housemasters, everyone picnicked on the playing fields, where the nouveau riche parents had set up ostentatious marquees beside their Rolls-Royces.

Alexander's father brought Janet and Dorothy, and also invited his favourite uncle Charles and his wife to their picnic. Afterwards, they were strolling back to the school to look at the exhibitions, when Alexander saw Damian approaching the other side of the road, and they smiled at each other. He knew now that Damian was his first name. He had gone to Alden and Blackwell, the school bookshop, to look it up in the *Eton Calendar* that very morning. It was unusual and awfully glamorous, he thought. He had already started to think of him secretly as Damian, though of course he would never be so impertinent as to suggest calling him it, but just knowing that he carried within him the theoretical power to call him in such a personal way was invigorating.

Alexander was assuming regretfully that they would not be able to talk, when Damian crossed over the road and went straight up to them.

"Hello!" he said to Hal Aylmer. "Are you Alexander's father?"

"Yes."

"I hope you don't mind me introducing myself, but I'm his English master. I just wanted to tell you how splendidly he has been getting along." Hal was definitely interested now. "He wrote a short story for me that was far better than anything I've ever read before from someone his age. I had it Sent Up for Good in fact."

"Well , it's very kind of you to say such nice things about him."

"Not at all. I mean every word. He is much my most promising pupil. I really think he has the makings of a great writer."

"What a charming man," said Hal Aylmer after Damian had gone, then turned to Janet. "It's terrifying how young schoolmasters seem nowadays, don't you think?"

Alexander was proud that his father was so pleased, but he felt a pang of regret that his father and everyone else could not be told the thing he was proudest of all about by a long way, that the young man was his very special friend.

When the day was over, Damian went home to his parents in Gloucestershire for three nights. He took *Greek Love* with him and read it all. By the end, he felt himself not only to be extremely well informed on the specific subject, but

206

knowledgeable on all sorts of other aspects of classical Greek culture.

He also studied the illustrations in the book. Most of them were only worth looking at once to add to his knowledge, but there was one he kept returning to, as it was not only unusually clear and realistic, but soon came to be for him a visual encapsulation of the whole phenomenon. It was of a drinking cup in the Ashmolean museum, and showed a man and pubescent boy in foreplay. The man was wearing only a cloak, which was swept back to reveal a fit, muscular frame and vertically erect cock, and his knees were bent, so that the naked boy could stand between them, their heads level. The man was fondling the boy's genitals, while the boy gazed lovingly into his eyes, his hand placed affectionately round his lover's head.

The first time Damian looked at it, he suddenly thought of himself and Alexander in those positions and blushed, though no one was in the room. He shied away from the picture then, almost angry with himself for having drawn such an unfair comparison, but he soon felt impelled back to it. He was too honest to delay long before asking himself whether he would like to be that man, if Alexander were the boy. Had the question been lying repressed somewhere in his subconscious since he had befriended him, perhaps even since he first saw him? He did not know.

Just as he could not find anything distasteful in the picture, which he found deeply moving rather than erotic, so he could not imagine finding anything about Alexander distasteful. He had of course never seen his body, but everything he had seen was too exquisitely beautiful.

Then he thought of himself in the Greek man's position. The idea of exposing himself like that to Alexander made his stomach churn immediately, and he felt nauseous as he imagined the boy's likely look of shocked disgust if he were ever to suggest such a thing. Nothing could be less erotic. The frightening spectre was firmly repulsed and he sighed with relief.

After that, he found himself able to return to *Greek Love* with a much clearer head. Deep down, he must have suspected his own motives before, for now he felt like a man justly acquitted. Could he have confused love of the body with love of the soul? He did not know if he loved Alexander at all. He was most certainly very fond of him. Was there a difference? If he did love Alexander, then presumably it must be love of the soul, and some would say that was the noblest love of all. In that case, could he not let himself go emotionally and give him all the benefits of Greek love, safe in the knowledge that his sexual feelings were chastely English?

He longed to explore these questions with someone he could trust not to misunderstand him, and realised that by luck the best person possible was at hand: his father. Not only did he feel secure enough in his father's love and esteem to be confident of being able to get to the point in delicate matters, but his father's sharp and uncompromising intellect could be counted on to cut through humbug and guide him towards the truth, unswayed by convenience or embarrassment.

Walter Cavendish lived quietly with his wife in their seventeenth-century manor house. Once he had been a radical. A passionate believer in freedom from as young an age as he could remember, as a boy at Eton he had quickly recognised fascism as the greatest threat to liberty ever. His disgust at the way most of his contemporaries allowed their narrow class prejudices to persuade them that Hitler was preferable to the reds, exasperated by his rebellious instincts, had driven him into purported communism.

Soon after leaving the school, he went to France. He never told his family he was going further, but he made his way to Toulouse, where he contacted sympathisers of the Spanish republicans and got himself smuggled over the border. There he joined the British battalion and fought with it for over a year until it was disbanded and he was sent home.

He learned two things in Spain that changed the course of his life. One was a deep love of the country. The other was a disenchantment with his leftist comrades. There were some interesting exceptions, but many of them were so bigoted and illiberal as to be little better than fascists. His disillusionment thereafter encompassed the entire drift of modern politics and society and he realised he was one of those unhappy men at war with the spirit of their age.

By the time he was sent back to England, the drift towards world war was evident to the perceptive and he enlisted several months before it broke out. Seven years of distinguished service later, he finally found himself free and belatedly obtained the place to read history at Cambridge that he regretted having foregone, for his mind was extremely sharp and his love of the past intense.

Aged thirty by the time he graduated, his longing for the Andalusian countryside had only grown with the passing years of absence and he at last found the means to go back. He soon managed to track down old friends, one of whom invited him to his village's annual fiesta. Watching the candlelit procession to the church that evening, he caught sight of the most beautiful girl he had ever seen, and found he no longer had eyes for anything else. His friend told him she was called Inés. She was sixteen and the daughter of a small, local farmer.

Looking back on his life that night, he realised that for much of it he had been tormented by indecision, but now at last he felt sure of what he wanted. Some certainty of happiness was within grasp. How could he not be happy if he could be the one to have that girl waking up in his bed every morning for the rest of his life? Nothing else was important. He knew his family would object to a match on the grounds that they were from different countries and, worse still, different classes, and he knew equally that their objections could only strengthen his resolve. He felt sure from her face that her heart and body were as pure as her background was simple, and he had only contempt for the notion that he ought to marry an Englishwoman.

After a short struggle the next day convincing his friend that he was serious, delicate negotiations began. Inés's parents made discreet enquiries, and despite his own lack of interest in social background, it did not harm his cause with them that he was the grandson of a duke. A number of chaperoned meetings were arranged.

"Sí" she said simply with a bashful smile when he proposed to her a fortnight later, only her sparkling eyes betraying her intense excitement. He was much relieved to discover soon afterwards that her parents had left the final decision firmly up to her. They married a month after that.

At first they lived in London and he tried jobs in the civil service and on a newspaper, but he was miserably bored by both, and did not need the money, having inherited a small fortune. Soon after their first child was born, he bought the house they still lived in. He dabbled in esoteric subjects that interested him ranging wildly from sigillography to mediaeval Spanish numismatics, and was indeed a leading expert in some of them, but the real focus of his life was on their four children.

Damian was his youngest, but the only boy and his happiness was always his very special concern. From his infancy, they talked about every subject without reserve. Though Walter had no regrets about his own adolescent rebelliousness and later withdrawal from worldly affairs, he was proud rather than bothered that Damian had so far succeeded spectacularly in society by conforming relatively with its rules. He gladly acknowledged to himself that it was because his son was a gentler and more amenable character. He gave himself credit for the way Damian had turned out only in so far as he believed Damian's integrity and broad-mindedness had been enhanced by his unwavering insistence on openness with him.

His son was so dear to him that he had worried terribly that this special intimacy would dissipate as Damian grew independent. The occasions when it became evident they could still explore the most delicate questions together, despite Damian very much having his own mind, were therefore a source of immense happiness and pride to him.

"Papa, I've been reading an extraordinary book called *Greek Love*," said Damian to his father as they strolled through the fields their last afternoon together. "It's all about the love lives of the ancient Greeks. Is that something you know about?"

"Not much, but enough to know it wouldn't go down well with Mary Whitehouse and the other dreadful moral campaigners we hear so much about these days. Greeks tended to prefer boys, didn't they?"

"Yes, exactly. What's extraordinary about the book I've been reading is that it shows how the love affairs between men and boys, which it calls Greek love, were responsible for what it calls the Greek miracle. Have you ever considered how odd it is that so many great men lived in such a small land over such a short period of history."

"Yes, vaguely."

"Well, Athens was by far the most populous state and at her peak had about thirty thousand adult male citizens, the size of small town nowadays. And yet at that time, living all together there, were philosophers like Sokrates and Plato, dramatists whose plays we still put on today like Sophokles, Euripides and Aristophanes, the greatest ancient sculptor Pheidias, the world's first great historians, Herodotos and Thukydides, not to mention all the statesmen and generals I'm sure you've heard of." He paused, worried that through his anxiety to make the most of such an important point, he might be losing his father's attention, but his glance was met with an encouraging smile.

"If one extends the list to include all of classical Greece," he continued, "the number of great men is simply astounding, men who laid all the important foundations of art, science, philosophy and medicine and whose ideas still influence the world today. Compare their numbers to those from any of the great empires with populations hundreds or thousands of times bigger and which lasted many times longer than classical Greece, and one is surely bound to admit that "miracle" is a fair description."

"Yes, now I think about it, it is extraordinary, but what makes your book think it had anything to do with liking boys?"

"First, because so many boys having lovers and so many growing up to be great men were both so peculiar to ancient Greece that it would be too much of a coincidence if there was no link between them. Secondly, because that's what the Greeks themselves believed. It was the whole point of encouraging love affairs between men and boys. Thirdly, the book also shows how the miracle took place in the various Greek states as soon as pederasty was institutionalised in them. Finally, what other explanation is there?"

"It sounds plausible, but if it's true, why hasn't it been generally acknowledged?"

"Apparently just because it's been such a taboo subject. Though modern historians of Greece have known perfectly well how important pederasty was, they've shied away from discussing it, sometimes with blunt statements such as that it's a

211

subject "unwise to pry into for our own equanimity" or "incomprehensible to the modern mind." That's why this new book is so amazing."

"That's certainly food for thought, but why should lovers have been more effective teachers of boys than professional schoolmasters like you?"

"Because it's when loving that people give of their best. The intense bonding involved drove the man to efforts he wouldn't otherwise be capable of, and inspired in the boy a willing acceptance of adult direction usually hard for adolescents."

"Isn't it a bit unrealistic though to suppose that every man who lusted after a boy would have been ready to give him so much love? Surely there must've been men who just wanted sex?"

"Yes, of course, but they're irrelevant to the book's argument. Such men could have sex with their slave-boys, if they could afford them, or otherwise in a boy brothel, or more likely in a women's brothel, since the bonding involved was most of the point of going with boys rather than women. The book's not saying sex never took place that fell short of the Greek love ideal, just that many Greek boys found the ideal and benefited enormously from it.

"But did these love affairs really need to be sexual? I thought Plato believed in, well, platonic love."

"Yes, that's exactly what I find so interesting. Plato believed that a love of the soul which had transcended sexual desire was the very highest ideal. Most love affairs then were sexual because most people found love without sex unappealing, but just supposing Plato's ideal could be achieved today, boys could get all the benefits of Greek love without homosexuality, couldn't they?"

"Damian," said his father with a gentle expression that mixed amusement with anxiety, "I don't want to pry, but are you meaning to tell me that you're putting this into practice with a boy at Eton?" Damian had anticipated this question and would in fact have been deeply disappointed if he had failed to provoke it, but he could not help being embarrassed all the same.

"There is a boy I've grown very fond of, and, yes, I do feel there's a lot I can do for him through a close friendship."

212

"And is it a friendship Plato would fully approve of?"

"Yes, very much I think."

"Were there affairs between boys while you were a boy at Eton?"

"I suppose there must have been some, but I never knew of any apart from some rumours."

"Well, homosexuality was rife there in my day, so maybe I understand it more than you. I don't think any harm ever came of it, or that it had any lasting consequences unless someone was caught. So there's nothing you need feel you can't tell me if you want to."

"I understand, but it's really not like that."

"So, this boy's not at all good-looking then?"

"Oh Papa!" said Damian, laughing and blushing at the same time. "Yes, I admit he is. Seriously, though, that doesn't mean Plato would disapprove. He actually commended appreciation of a boy's beauty as leading a wise man towards appreciation of his soul, and that sums up any influence this boy's looks may have had on me. I really can't think of him sexually at all. It's a great pleasure just to be able to help and inspire someone with a lively and open mind. I've been wondering if in fact ideal platonic love isn't just an intensely concentrated form of what inspires the best teachers."

"You're probably right. Things don't always turn out as one intends though. Whatever happens, I of course know you too well to doubt you'll do anything but good to your young friend. Just beware of the malevolence of a world that assumes most when it understands least."

X: The Bow of Eros Unleashed

Of all the gods, Eros is the most friendly towards men. He is our helper, and cures those evils whose cure brings the greatest happiness to the human race. I'll try to explain his power to you, so you can spread the word to others.

Plato, *Symposium* 189

Long Leave ended on the Monday evening, but Damian went back the evening before, as he had a lot of work to prepare for his divs. The Monday was therefore his first day in his flat for more than a week with no Alexander. It was only then that he realised quite how very much he had grown to enjoy his company. The boy had lit his flat up with his warmth and lively conversation, and now it felt dead. He had to force himself to do his work, but when in the evening it was finished, a gloom settled on him which he could only alleviate by thinking of Alexander's return on the morrow. It was this that finally made Damian realise he was hopelessly in love with the boy. To try to pass it off as mere fondness was ridiculous, even though he realised sadly that almost anyone who knew the strength of his feelings would give them an unfair sexual explanation and condemn them accordingly.

Not only must he hide his love entirely from the world, but it was unlikely he would ever reveal it to Alexander himself, for, if he did, he would be bound, for the boy's equanimity, to accompany his revelation with a plain statement of what it was not. It would be awkward to get the right balance and almost a desecration of his love to have to do so.

For the same reasons, he thought even more sadly that he would never be able to give physical expression to his feelings. He was strongly affectionate and his parents had brought him and his sisters up according to the warm Mediterranean mores of his mother's country, so they all hugged and kissed each other on the cheek whenever they met or parted, irrespective of their gender. It was terribly sad and frustrating he could not express his love for Alexander that way. Ironically, though the thought of the boy's likely disgust made the idea of sex repulsive, he missed him more than he had ever missed Dashka despite all his happy memories of their fun in bed.

His melancholy thought reminded him of the sadness of Alexander's story and he reread yet again the photocopy he had made of it. He knew he had made the author happy after all. It would be nice to give the story a happier ending too and somehow express his frustration with the world for its lack of understanding.

Meanwhile, Alexander too was longing to return. They spent all his Long Leave at Eryholme. His eldest uncle, who had inherited the estate after his grandmother's death, had not yet moved in, and his father took Janet and Dorothy too. The wedding had been set for the 30th of June, another month's time, to allow time for the honeymoon before the school holidays. It was thus Alexander's one chance to get to know them properly beforehand.

His father seemed to be falling over backwards to please both mother and daughter, especially the latter. Evidently, he had got to know Dorothy better over the last fortnight, for she responded to his efforts with a new familiarity which alternated between rudeness and an incipient awareness of the possibilities opened up by an indulgent adult. She was still cold towards Alexander, as if she saw him as a potential rival to be neutralised. He was dismayed because the unpleasantness sullied his happy and hitherto untarnished memories of the home of his grandmother, whom he found himself missing terribly again now that he was at Eryholme for the first time without her. He resented the intrusion too, considering they were in the home of his ancestors since time immemorial.

Janet was as gracious as before, except that the first morning he saw an ominous show of unsuspected steel. He came into the drawing room just as his father was asking Hopkins, his grandmother's old butler, to have a bedroom prepared for Christopher and his new girlfriend, who were also coming to stay for the weekend. As soon as Hopkins was gone, Janet told Dorothy in a firm tone to go and play in the garden, giving her a glare that sufficed to stifle dissent. Then she turned to his father.

"Christopher can't possibly stay in the same room as Rosie," she said.

"I can't very well stop him," said his father in a mild tone. "After all, they've already shared a room here together once." Alexander could have added that his mother had always let Andrew and Sabina, who lived together for a year before getting married, sleep together in their own home.

"I'm not arguing about it, Hal," she said in a shrill and determined tone. "I am not having my daughter staying in a house where an unmarried couple are sharing a bedroom. It's that simple."

His father looked quite shaken, but backed down at once. Alexander had never seen anything like it. His mother had never once spoken to his father in such a manner.

Upset as he was that such a disagreeable girl had been thrust inescapably into his home life, he could not help hoping he might feel less desolate if he could overcome Dorothy's apparent hostility and establish some degree of companionship. That was evidently what his father hoped from him too. She did not want to play a game with him, so after lunch he followed her to his grandmother's old television room, where she had already spent much of the morning. His father had forewarned him that she spent most of her time this way, and explained that poor Janet had had to bring her up thus as there was so little she could afford for her.

Alexander saw her switch the television on. A football match was being played and he wondered if that was what she had come to see, but after a minute she switched channel. He realised bemusedly that she did not know what was on and simply watched television for its own sake. It was for him a novel and initially rather intriguing idea. His family had always read about what was coming on in the weekly television magazines and decided together if there was something worth watching after dinner. Besides that, he had only ever watched the odd afternoon children's programme that his mother agreed was worth letting him take over the sitting-room for.

Dorothy, however, seemed to presume that by switching around between the four channels, one could always find something worth seeing. She did not care that the film she was

216

now watching had already started. It was an American disaster movie about people on a cruise ship. After an hour and a half, the selfish baddies had all drowned along with just enough others to allow for plenty of sentimental gush, the goodies had all been heroically saved at the predictable last second and Alexander felt quite relieved when it drew to an end. Perhaps Dorothy might want to do something else he thought, but no sooner had the names of the cast begun to appear than she got up to switch channels.

She eventually settled into a game show, something Alexander had never seen before, but after ten minutes he could bear it no more. The film had left him unsatisfied and his feeling of having frittered much of a sunny afternoon of his precious Long Leave had grown until he panicked at the waste. There was so much else to do.

He went out for a walk on his own to clear his head, then settled down to read *The Persian Boy*, which he had saved until then.

He found he had very little chance to talk to his father alone. When he did, he soon noticed that he tried to avoid referring to his mother, in sharp contrast to the last holidays, and both the times he did, he called her "your mother" instead of "Mummy."

Christopher was friendly enough, but they did not try talking of anything consequential. It was strange how everything warm and comforting about the notion of "big brother" was now so much more strongly represented by Damian than by Christopher.

He remembered how a fortnight ago it had been Julian whom he imagined offered him some kind of emotional independence from his family. He knew now that the relief and happiness he had felt with him had always been shallow compared to what he had found with Damian.

The lonelier he felt at home, the more he realised how happy and fulfilled he had begun to become in Damian's company and he surprised himself by pining for his flat almost as if it were his real home. It was comforting too to think of it as that. Every time his father made him feel peripheral to his new life, he would try to reassure himself with the idea that he too was beginning to have his own life, and he felt urged to get back to building it.

In the meantime, reading *The Persian Boy* soon became much the best antidote to his loneliness. It was even more gripping and moving than *Fire From Heaven*,. His fascination grew by leaps and bounds as the sensual direction of the novel became clear, as it very soon did. It was the story of a noble Persian boy called Bagoas, whose family were betrayed and murdered when he was ten, while he was castrated and sold into slavery. He was exceptionally beautiful, so when he was twelve his master started to rent him out for men's sexual pleasure. Soon he was resold to an unknown master of mysteriously staggering wealth, and handed over to a cultivated young man who trained him in the arts of lovemaking. At this point, the story began to take on a romantic note which spasmodically but surely grew to take over from the earlier theme of horror, for the young boy experienced both pleasure and a simple love in the arms of the young man, who in contrast to those who had enjoyed him before, was handsome, charming and highly skilled in bed. He was dismayed when the lessons were finally over and he was pronounced ready for the bed of his new master, who turned out to be none other than Darius himself, the last King of Kings.

Despite the absolute horror of Bagoas's earlier experiences, Alexander could not help feeling some jealousy of his later ones. To have men lusting after you and to be the sexual plaything of a King could be distasteful under some circumstances, but must at least have made for a terribly exciting life compared to the safe, drab monotony of an English schoolboy's. And what about when it was not distasteful? If it was pleasurable for a young eunuch to lie in the arms of a handsome young man, how very much more delightful it must be for a boy like himself, possessed of a raging sexuality. Imagine too if instead of it being just part of a training, enjoyed despite knowing that any love experienced could not be deep or lasting, the young man was someone one really loved? In other words, if for him, it was Damian?

It was only a while after he said that to himself that he suddenly realised what he had just implicitly acknowledged, that for the first time in his life he was in love. He had never felt remotely the same way about anyone else, so that must be what it was. He was surprised that he could have failed to realise earlier what was so blindingly obvious. He just had not tried to define his feelings before.

He wished desperately that Damian would love him too. He knew Damian liked him, but he wanted it to be far stronger than that, as strong as he could imagine, which was how he loved Damian. If only Damian would desire him as well, that would be almost unimaginably exciting, or more poignantly it would be so exciting that he should not imagine it because he did not think it could come true.

For a moment, he allowed himself to fantasise that Damian had read the juicy bits of *The Persian Boy* and had given it to him as a sexual encouragement, in the same way he had got Julian to read the passage from *Cider With Rosie*. Then he remembered that the book had been in pristine condition and Damian had only chosen it because of what he had said about *Fire From Heaven*. He remembered too how he had misunderstood that Julian desired him. Suddenly he felt presumptuous and foolish. He had probably misunderstood those tingling feelings he had had. The tensions he thought he had felt in the air were more likely just in his own mind.

Straight after lunch his first day back at school, Alexander rushed off with his books to Damian's flat. He burst in enthusiastically, then saw to his disappointment that it was empty. He went over to the table and picked up a note.

"Alexander," it said, "I have an engagement and won't get back until at least 3 pm., but make yourself at home until then. Yours, DEC."

As he sat down, he felt a new surge of pride that Damian trusted him enough to share his home. It was his first time alone there. Then the implications struck him. He could do what he liked. He longed to know everything about Damian and now he had a chance to look at anything without seeming to pry. The bedroom was the one room he had never been in. Why shouldn't he look? Damian had said he could treat the place as his home.

He went into it and saw a large framed photograph of a couple perched on top of a chest of drawers. The man was in his sixties with refined features and inquisitive eyes. The woman looked about fifty and he could tell at once that she must be Damian's mother, for she had the same warm, hazel eyes and charming smile.

He went over to the bedside table, where a heavy-looking book sat on some photocopies. To his astonishment, he recognised his own handwriting on them and he saw that it was his short story. Putting the book aside and picking up the photocopied pages, he was surprised to find they were followed by four more of contrasting blue ink in Damian's small, neat handwriting that he now knew so well. Could it be a very long commentary on his story, he wondered with interest. He turned to where Damian began. Oddly, the full stop which had followed the last sentence of his story "A bloody sword was on the bed and beside it the King lay dead" had been overwritten into a comma. He read on:

or so they feared.

"Oh my lord!" cried out the royal steward in despair, as he rushed to kneel beside the young King's body. He fumbled desperately for his pulse. "He is still alive! Fetch the doctor fast!" he shouted at one of the squires. He was only semi-conscious and had lost a tremendous amount of blood, but when the doctor came he found that the sword thrust had missed his vital organs. Provided there was no blood poisoning, he should recover soon with rest and good care.

All day Episthenes hovered anxiously around his master's chamber. Occasionally he went out into the ante-chamber to hear the latest tidings. The King awoke late in the afternoon, but lay in bed listlessly. The steward sat beside him, while his dressings were changed, and gently chided him for what must surely have been an act of momentary madness. Perhaps it had been brought on by some jealous god, hearing all the praise that the people were heaping on him. Later he told him how everyone was now calling him Damianos, meaning the Subduer, and the assembly wished him to be known by that name rather than

Mikrias, meaning the Little One, which he had so spectacularly outgrown. They were also bringing him the newly captured boy Alexandros, only son of his slain foe, so that he could kill him with his own hands or at least watch his dying moments, as he pleased. The King listened tiredly as if it were no concern of his, but he did not resist sitting up to eat a broth. Much relieved by the ease with which he ate it, the steward ordered wild boar and wine to be prepared. At last the King arose and paced weakly around his bedchamber, but he remained grimly silent.

The boy captive was brought in, naked, his arms bound behind his back by a rope which was reddened with blood where it had cut into his slender wrists. He stood before his conqueror, his eyes downcast. He looked about fourteen years old and was of ethereal beauty. Quite tall for his age with a perfect boyish figure and flawless complexion, his features were clear-cut with quite high cheek-bones, a straight nose, blue eyes and full, sweet lips the colour of watered wine. His hair was golden-blond, thick and soft, though partially matted in grime. He was covered in dust from head to toe. At last he-who-was-now-called-Damianos understood the minstrels' songs in praise of the beauty of boys, something that had hitherto eluded him.

Suddenly the boy looked up at him in blank despair and the young man knew at once that his life had changed for ever, without yet understanding why. He could see the streaks down the child's dusty cheeks that must have been made by tears since dried and felt overwhelmed by a great longing to see how much more beautiful the already-impossibly-lovely, grave face might be if its sadness were to disappear, if the rosy lips were to part and light it up with a smile. He realised that he longed for that more than anything else under the heavens.

Thus was the curse of Xanthippos lifted at last.

The steward saw the young man's admiration of the boy and was pleased. Most of the army had enjoyed themselves last night

221

and he had been disconcerted that his master had not. The enemy princess and two of the prettiest girls he had been able to have saved from the rampage had been tied up under guard outside the King's quarters, but he had gone in without taking any notice of them. He had not thought to bring a boy there too, as the King had never shown any interest in them before.

The steward was very fond of his master, and in some respects had been like a father to him. He had always regretted the narrow education the Queen had insisted on and missing out on boys was one of its consequences. He had seemed either not to know or not to care that while he conducted his incessant military exercises and read dry treatises of war, other youths of his age and class were spending languorous afternoons admiring the boys exercising naked in the gymnasium and flirting with those they fancied. He had known nothing of their joys and heart-aches as they pined after a beloved, competed for his admiration, won his first shy smile. Then the first sweet kiss on boy lips, subtly different from a woman's, unstudied and charmingly frank, followed soon by the headier delights. And from the first declaration of love, the pride of being hero-worshipped and emulated by someone good, beautiful and bursting with enthusiasm for life, of knowing oneself and being known as the one who, as it may be, inspired the bravery a beloved displayed in his first killing of a wild boar, the endurance that won him the boys' foot race in the city's Games and the modesty not to speak of it. All these pleasures the King's martial duties had robbed him of.

The Queen had regularly provided her son with girls for his bed, the first, one of her serving-girls, when he was fifteen, and he had just accepted them like everything else she arranged for him. Episthenes suspected that one reason she remembered to keep her son's sexual needs sated was to make it less likely that he would fall for a boy. The real love affair that might then have ensued would have been an unacceptably time-consuming diversion from the narrow path she had designed for him.

In any case, Episthenes decided that the enjoyment of this gift from Eros might be just the thing to snap him out of his strange mood. The boy was unquestionably ravishing. If he were not who he was, he would of course be auctioned off. The sale would replenish the royal coffers for months to come. Most of the great slave-traders would be coming to the island soon, drawn by news of the fall of an ancient city, its people for sale, and all would have bid for him. Possession of a boy that phenomenally beautiful could make a brothel in a wealthy city like Athens or Corinth a legend among connoisseurs throughout the Mediterranean. Alternatively, if the Fates had been kinder to him, he might have ended up as the catamite of one of the fabulously rich kings in the east. It was sad that such a beauty had to die so young and it would be a pity if he were not enjoyed before being sent to join his ancestors.

The steward gesticulated that everyone should withdraw from the King's presence. All present moved out of the room and the steward followed them, turning round to face the King with a bow as he began to pull the double doors closed.

"What are you doing, Episthenes?"

"My lord King. …. Everyone is rejoicing after the greatest victory we have known, and yet you alone, its architect, have still enjoyed none of its fruits. This boy here, he surely need not die at once. Some men would give half their fortune for a night with one so beautiful, and I thought my lord had noticed….Such rare gifts from the gods are meant for us mortals to enjoy."

"How dare you insult me so!" exclaimed Damianos angrily, after a shocked pause in which he took in the steward's meaning. "How could you, who have known me since I was a babe, assume that I was thinking about … that? Yes, he is beautiful, but has it not occurred to you … Oh, never mind for

223

now," he said exasperated. He was deeply hurt that the old man had thought he had just been thinking of the gratification of his lust, which had not occurred to him at all, and wanted to ask him if he thought that was all that beauty counted for and that the love it inspired had no other purpose, but stopped himself when he remembered embarrassedly that the boy was standing close by.

He looked at the boy again and suddenly realised that the new longing to which he had succumbed had given him new hope. Why should he not devote himself to trying to restore the boy's happiness? He did not doubt for a moment that Alexandros's soul was as beautiful as his body, so there could be no questioning the worthiness of the cause, only its chances of success. Having been responsible for the death of the boy's father and the burning of his home only yesterday, it would be no small feat to win himself a smile from those beautiful lips, but it was a new challenge and he felt sure that overcoming it would bring him true and lasting joy, unlike the old one his life had been devoted to.

"Order a basin of hot water and a clean cloth," he said, turning to his abashed steward. Then he picked up the knife that lay beside the platter of roast boar and gently cut through the rope binding the boy's slender wrists, careful that it did not cut further into his inflamed flesh. The gentleness of his touch was in sharp contrast to the way everyone else had treated Alexandros that day and he looked at the King wonderingly. He knew that his father had once slain the young man's, and his brothers too, and he had not imagined there was any hope of mercy.

Episthenes soon reappeared, rushing in his eagerness to appease his master, who dampened the cloth in the hot water and slowly cleaned first the lesions on the boy's wrists and then the dust from his face. The rosiness of his cheeks was now visible and Damianos felt a renewed awe of his beauty.

He turned back to the table, poured wine from the jug into his goblet, mixed it with water and held it out to Alexandros. "Drink!" he said gently. The boy was looking at him steadily now. Damianos's kind and sincere demeanour had fully sunk through to him and an indefinable hope had punctured his despair. Slowly he took the goblet, and as he drew it to his lips, he looked more trustingly into the man's eyes and ventured a bashful smile.

To Damianos it felt as though a great rainbow was arching across the sky.

Alexander's happiness grew in great surges as he read on, until by the end he thought his heart must burst.

He stood up triumphantly and paced fast around the flat, swinging his arms until he was nearly whirling. He could not have avoided knowing since he was small that people found him good-looking, but he had never thought to have it confirmed in such superlative terms, and by the one person in the whole world he most wanted to think that. He stopped in front of the mirror and gazed at his "impossibly-lovely face." It did indeed seem far more beautiful to him than it ever had before. He gave himself one of those smiles that Damian so longed for and watched the mirror light up with a new surge of triumph. He thanked God or whoever had made him for blessing him so generously and giving him a life so worth having.

His mind raced back over the story. Had Damian said he loved him? He had certainly said his life had changed for ever. Alexander was still piecing the evidence together, when he heard a key in the front door lock.

Damian came in and greeted him warmly. He went over to his desk to put his books down, chatting away as he did so about where he had just been, but Alexander heard none of it.

"Sir," he said quite loudly to interrupt him. Damian looked up a little surprised. "I've read your story, the one about me. I'm sorry, Sir. I hope you don't mind." Damian reddened and looked shattered.

"Alexander, please sit down," he said heavily after a pause, as he did so himself. "I have a lot of explaining to do." He tried to remember the worst things he had written, and blushed more deeply. "I'm sorry. You must have been badly shocked, especially by the disgusting things Episthenes thought."

"I don't care what Episthenes thought," said Alexander. "I care about what you thought."

"Ah. Well, that's just the point of the story, you see. It's not the same. A lot of men in those days did think like Episthenes, I'm afraid. You've probably never read about this."

"Yes, I have, Sir, a little anyway."

Damian blushed again. "I see. Well, there were also some men like Damianos in the story, who didn't think about boys sexually, but loved one all the same." He took a deep breath. "Like I love you."

For a few moments, Alexander was silent, not trusting himself to speak, he was so giddy with excitement. Then he feared he had let Damian down by delaying to respond to such courage. "I love you too," he said, also blushing. There was another pause. Damian's mind swam with exhilarated surprise and happiness, while Alexander could not help hoping Damian might now kiss him, despite what he had said.

"Alexander, that makes me happier than you can imagine," continued Damian at last, growing a little anxious that he had not quite fully made his point, "but I want you to understand you need have absolutely no anxiety that I will ever ask you to do anything like Episthenes would want. I'm not like that. You do understand, don't you?"

"Yes, Sir," said Alexander, disappointment clouding his happiness a little.

"You can't go on calling me "Sir." It's absurd now we know how we feel about each other. My Christian name is Damian. Do you mind calling me that?"

"No … Damian," said Alexander with a delighted smile.

"Of course we'll have to keep up the pretences of formality when we're not here. I think you understand that if other people knew I loved you, they would misunderstand and think I was like Episthenes, and that could lead to a lot of trouble."

"I know. I don't care what they think, but don't worry, I'll be careful."

"Good. This flat will be our own, special, little world, then, where normal rules don't apply."

They carried on chatting as usual after that, except that both of them felt themselves to be half in a trance, still incredulous that such happiness had unexpectedly come their way. When they tried to do their work afterwards, they frequently caught each other's eye and smiled affectionately, glad to reassure each other that what had passed between them had not been just a dream.

That night, Alexander read more of *The Persian Boy*, but his mind was still half on the rapture the day had brought him. He told himself that he ought to pity the novel's eponym, now that he himself had found true love, and for the most part he did, but when he read about Bagoas being summoned into the King's bed with a discreet signal, cuddled, kissed and taken, his envy was more intense than before. He could not help imagining himself in Damian's bed, willing slave to his own King, while Damian, wild with lust, kissed him all over, and he himself lay utterly submissive to his will and determined that his handsome lord should enjoy him to the full. Soon he was much too turned on to resist relief from his fingers, and came for the first time in his life to thoughts of a man rather than a girl.

Afterwards, he berated himself for diluting his happiness by burdening it with hopes that were unlikely to be fulfilled. Damian had made it absolutely plain he did not think of him that way, despite thinking he was ethereally beautiful, so presumably he was incapable of sexual attraction to boys. Alexander knew he had had a very beautiful girlfriend at Cambridge, for he had been told about Dashka and shown photos too. He hoped he would have a girlfriend that beautiful when he went to university.

When Alexander finished his E.W.s the next evening, he sat down on the sofa next to Damian, who had just settled down to read *The Times*. He rested his shoulder and leg gently against the man's. They smiled at each other a little shyly.

"Do you read a newspaper?" asked Damian.

227

"Sometimes at home."

Damian was reading an article on the front page. "Case for new laws boosted by pits strike," proclaimed the headline. The miners' strike had been going on for three months. Alexander had often heard his father on tirades against Arthur Scargill, the miners' leader. He thought it was rather dull, but began to read the article anyway, happy just to be close to Damian. It told how the government was planning to introduce laws to punish much faster and more severely any miners who threatened violence against people or property.

"Do you think that'll make the miners give up at last?" asked Alexander.

"I doubt it."

"But surely they can't really expect the government to pay them for ever to do something that's losing money?"

"No. Not for ever. Just until there's no coal left in their mines. There are real costs in closing down the mines too, or they wouldn't be putting up with trying to survive without pay. All the men in those parts of the north have been working in mines for centuries. There is no other work for them. If the mines are closed, they'll lose the only way of life they know and they'll soon find themselves living in ghost towns, dependent on government handouts and with no hope for the future."

Alexander was becoming fascinated. No one had explained that to him before. He wondered about the other things his father had said.

"But the government was re-elected by a large majority only last year. Surely, the whole point of a democracy is that everyone has to accept what the majority wants?"

"Yes. That's why the government has to bring in police from London to deal with the miners. They're frightened the northern police will sympathise with them. But do you think it's all right for us southerners to treat the northerners as we like, just because we are in the majority?

"No, I suppose not, but my father says they've all been offered generous payment if they'll accept their mines being closed, so they're being totally unreasonable. It's their own fault if they are suffering."

"So why do you think they're refusing?"

"Because Scargill's a communist and wants to bring down the government?"

"Perhaps he does. But why should the miners do as he says if they've been offered generous payment?"

Alexander thought about it for a while. He was beginning to feel he had been shamefully mean-spirited. Damian's understanding was so much broader than his. "Do you mean it's because they care more about their way of life than about money?"

"Yes, I think so. The government tries to imply they want to be paid ever more for working less, but I think you'll find their greatest fear is spending the rest of their lives being paid for not working at all. Don't you think it's noble rather than lazy to endure hardship for that?"

"Yes, I understand now. So you mean that what's really unfair is not closing down the mines one day, but doing it so suddenly? They should change things gradually, so people have plenty of time to adapt from the way they've been brought up?"

"Yes, that's about it." He had not thought it through quite so far before, but the unfairness of sudden change did seem to be the crux of the matter. Alexander's mind was so sharp that he had overtaken him. It was why it was so thrilling to be his mentor.

Alexander could see he had been badly misled. It was much more complicated than he had supposed, and also more interesting. There must be lots of subjects of which he understood little because he had only ever heard stuffy, narrow, one-sided opinions. It was what made talking to Damian so exciting.

The next morning Alexander received his Order Cards for the second quarter of the Half in three subjects and the effects of recently spending most afternoons doing his E.W.s in Damian's flat were already apparent. After lunch, he took them to be signed by Mr. Hodgson. First he handed over the least exciting one from his chemistry beak.

"Mixed results, but signs of improvement," Mr. White had written, and placed him ninth equal out of twenty in the class.

"Persevere!" commented Mr. Hodgson in red ink before initialling it and handing it back.

"Excellent. Seems to have gone back to his old self at last. Keep aiming high," said the note from his Maths beak, who had placed him fifth out of twenty-four, a big improvement on the eleventh he had been in the first quarter.

"Hitch your wagon to a star!" commented Mr. Hodgson on this.

Finally, he handed his housemaster the one he was most proud of, from Mr. Trotter, his Classics beak.

"Outstanding work. Better even than his first Half," it said, and he was placed top instead of seventh. Considering that in Classics Alexander was in F2, meaning the second highest div of the twelve or so into which F block was divided according to the boys' abilities in each subject, this really was remarkable.

"I see you have been saving the best wine till last," said Mr. Hodgson drily as he underlined "outstanding" in red.

He was in truth much better pleased than he let on. It removed any doubts that he had done the right thing in ending Aylmer's unsuitable friendship with Smith, not that he had had any serious ones. Self-congratulations were definitely in order, though he must not forget too how compliant Smith had been. That had been a great relief. Some sort of reward should eventually be due there. Anthony Burrows, to whom alone he had confided that he had written to Smith's father, said that Smith and Aylmer were never seen together any more. Indeed, the ending of the friendship had caused some comment throughout the house. Since no one knew the cause, it was generally assumed there must have been a quarrel.

However, it was by no means Mr. Hodgson's approval that Alexander craved most. Straight afterwards, he took his Order Cards off to Damian, who was thrilled.

"It's mostly thanks to you for all the help you've given me," said Alexander.

"Oh no, apart from that one trigonometry lesson when you were really stuck, I've only answered brief questions, and I obviously haven't been able to do your tests for you. I'll show you the Order Card I'll be giving you tomorrow."

"Almost consistently outstanding," it said, but he had come second, instead of first, as in the first quarter.

"Don't worry about your place. It's only because of your marks in that one test we did the day you first came here, and we know why that was. I don't doubt you'll come first in the end and be moved up to a higher English div next Half."

They had agreed always to discuss Alexander's work in English in Damian's flat. It was one of the rules they had adopted to avoid drawing attention to their unusual friendship in the classroom. The most important was that they must not smile at each other, for they felt sure that anyone who saw them do so would at once see and understand their love. Since they did not want to look at each other coldly, the result was that they generally avoided looking at each other directly at all.

Alexander knew that the main reason he was doing better was that he was now free to indulge his academic interests to the full without fear of any critical comment. When he had done his E.W.s during free time in his house, Rupert had sometimes complained mildly about him being a swot, and though Julian had never done that, he had often looked put out when Alexander wanted to devote time to his books. Damian, on the other hand, never gave him anything but encouragement.

His success only made him want to go further though. He knew that Damian had been an Oppidan Scholar and he began to feel a great longing to be one too, to be worthy of him and make him proud. To achieve this, he would have to get distinctions either in three Trials running or in four altogether. He did not want to say anything about it, as distinctions were extremely hard to get, being awarded to only about a dozen of the roughly two hundred and sixty boys in each block. Though he had got First Class, the next of the six possible grades in Trials, when he was a new boy, he had not been near a distinction, and last Half he had only got a Second Class.

Nevertheless, he had recently began to feel a genuine interest in subjects like maths and chemistry that had previously bored him and a confidence that, at least with the support of Damian to explain things he was still stuck on, he should be able to aim for full marks in every test he had to take.

Alexander had to interrupt his time with Damian that afternoon because Andrew and Sabina came to take him out to tea. It was the first time he had seen his eldest brother since the day their father had told him he was getting remarried. He remembered wondering then if Andrew might be more receptive than Christopher to how he might feel, and soon discovered that he was indeed.

"Daddy says you're going to move room at home," said Andrew, when they had settled down to a cream tea.

"Yes, he said Janet wants Dorothy to have the room nearest to theirs."

"That's what he told me too. If you don't mind about it, that's fine, but it occurred to me that you might well mind. It doesn't seem right to me that you should be turned out of the bedroom that's always been yours. How do you feel about it?"

"It's true I don't want to move at all."

"Would you like me to have a word with Daddy? I'm sure I can make him understand."

"Yes," said Alexander with a relieved smile. "Thank you very much." He was surprised and touched by Andrew's unexpected concern for him.

"Oh, there's something we've been meaning to ask you," said Andrew later with sudden interest, after they had run out of other family news and lapsed into silence. "What do you think about the age of consent, or do you even know what it is?"

"No." Alexander was long familiar with Andrew's penchant for suddenly introducing thought-provoking topics for debate, so he was quite intrigued.

"Well, there's a law that no one can have sex with someone under sixteen, however willing. I don't think it's meant to stop a girl your age from sleeping with you, but a woman who did could go to prison."

"But that's outrageous! It's none of anybody else's business!" He was horrified. It had never occurred to him that the government could possibly think of interfering in something so private.

"They think you need protecting against people who might try to persuade you to do things that may not be good for you."

"Why shouldn't I make up my own mind?" said Alexander, almost angrily. It was beyond belief that if he was lucky enough to persuade a girl like Lucretia to go to bed with him, some policeman would think he could interfere.

"Yes, well I'm not disagreeing with you," said Andrew, rather taken aback by his vehemence. "Sabina and I were talking about it, and we were curious to know what someone your age would think. Now we know."

They changed the subject, but Alexander's mind was in too much turmoil to take much in. He realised with a jolt of dismay that the law presumably also forbade Damian to make love to him, if he should ever want to. George Orwell's novel was obviously far closer to having been realised than he had imagined possible. How dare they! He resolved at once that if he ever got a chance to sleep with an adult, as he hoped more than ever he would, he would most certainly treat the law with the contempt it deserved.

When Andrew dropped him off at the Burning Bush, he strolled back towards Damian's flat in such deep thought that at one point he forgot where he was going and crossed the street for no reason. He tried to pull himself together, but he was so oblivious to his surroundings that when a loud and enthusiastic "Hi Alexander!" interrupted his reverie, he found he was only a foot away from Miranda.

"Hi, Miranda," he said, pleased by the warmth of her greeting. He had kept avoiding her during that terrible week before his birthday, and then he had forgotten about her. He had forgotten how beautiful she was too, he thought now, so he stopped, glad to find that his courtship seemed merely to have been interrupted rather than ended.

He tried hard to get involved in the little group's conversation, but it was about the new girlfriend of some pop star he hadn't heard of, and soon his mind drifted. He was looking forward to telling Damian about his conversation with Andrew, and hoping to get some explanation for something so unreasonable. Then it occurred to him that Damian too might never have heard of such a stupid law. Supposing he hadn't, and just supposing he ever did feel like doing something to Alexander, might knowing the law put him off? He didn't think Damian was the sort of person to submit to such injustice, but perhaps it was better not to take the risk. There were plenty of other things he was longing to ask him about today.

233

His mind returned to Miranda and her friends. They were still talking about the pop star. It was so-o boring. The familiar sense of going nowhere also came back to him. He looked at his watch anxiously. It was twenty to seven. He would have barely an hour with Damian. He thought longingly of how interesting their conversations always were and how free he felt to be himself. He fidgeted for a few minutes longer, then he couldn't bear it any more.

"I've got to go. I have to meet someone," he said to Miranda with a smile.

"Okay. See you soon," said Miranda, sounding a little disappointed.

Meanwhile, Alexander had been reading more of *The Persian Boy*. It had become even more gripping and that night he carried on reading in bed well past his bedtime. The vast Persian empire had already succumbed to Alexander the Great, and its defeated King Darius had been killed by his own generals.

Now he read how the newly masterless boy Bagoas chanced to come into Alexander's service. The differences between Persian and Greek customs were brilliantly conveyed through the boy's culture shock. Yet more brilliant was the unfolding of the King's attractive character, shown most movingly through the high value he placed on love and loyalty as opposed to material considerations or possessions, or even desire; though his fleeting glances suggested he found Bagoas attractive and the boy himself expected to serve him in bed, the King showed no interest in letting him. Finally, in a particularly touching scene, the King rescued him from danger, and Bagoas suddenly realised what had long become subtly apparent to the reader, that he was truly in love for the first time.

Alexander perceived at once that his position was analogous to Bagoas's, so when he read Bagoas's next thoughts to himself, "I will have him, if I die for it," he knew that Bagoas had spoken for him too. He put the book down then, knowing he had arrived at yet another important junction in his life, and soon he fell asleep to dreams of how he might achieve his goal.

In the cold light of morning, he remembered Damian's clear denial of sexual interest and had new misgivings. At least

Bagoas had had no reason to fear that the Macedonian King did not like sex with boys.

Then he thought more about how fantastic it would be to be physically loved by someone stronger and wiser he could trust to protect him. If they made love, they would have no more inhibitions and he could seek comfort in Damian's arms whenever he felt like it. He knew that when he was a man he would not need looking after. He hoped he would be like Damian then and that a beautiful girl would seek comfort in his arms. How proud and excited he would be! But that was for the future. Though he would love to screw a girl now, he was not ready to offer that protection and comfort yet, because he still needed it too badly himself. He was a boy, and would be a lost one if it were not for Damian.

His longing lent strength to the arguments for hope and soon confirmed his determination. He knew from Mary Renault's novels that men then liked both women and boys, both Alexander the Great's father and Darius having enjoyed plenty of both, and though so far as he could tell men nowadays seemed not to, that could be only because they were worried about what people would think. Damian had seemed so worried he might think he had sexual designs that perhaps it was just fear he might object that put him off. He needed somehow to let him know that he did not. On the other hand, he would have to be careful. It would be dreadful if Damian guessed what he wanted, but still thought that sex with boys was disgusting, like he had said Episthenes's thoughts were.

Alexander's self-confidence had returned with his happiness and he was as exuberant and good-humoured as ever. His old friendships in his house were recovering rapidly. At lunch that day, he was laughing with Rupert and Jamie Macdonald, when he chanced to look along the table and caught Julian staring at him melancholically. Julian looked away at once. It was strange, but it did not bother him. He hardly thought about Julian at all now, and when he did, it was with relief that their friendship had ended when it did, for otherwise he would have missed the fantastic things that had happened since. He looked back with a shudder on his former readiness to sleep with him just to strengthen their

235

friendship. When he thought of Damian, Julian's plain face, large nose and gloomy bespectacled eyes seemed quite ugly. He was surprised now that he had not been able to see clearly before that sex with him would have been a bit disgusting. It would have been shamefully demeaning to have lost his virginity to him rather than Damian. He found himself blushing and turned to Rupert, eager to banish memories of his old ideas from his mind.

During After Two, he read more of *The Persian Boy* instead of doing his E.W.s, even though he knew it meant he would have less time to chat that evening. He knew that Bagoas was going to seduce his King and he could not wait to find out how. Bagoas was incomparably more experienced and must surely have some tips for him.

It transpired that it took Bagoas six days. It was beautifully told, but it did not give him any ideas other than that he should attempt as much physical closeness as possible and look away to give Damian the maximum opportunity to gaze at him without embarrassment.

When he arrived in Damian's flat that evening, he asked if he could have a bath.

"Yes, of course," replied Damian, a little surprised, but happy that Alexander really was treating the place as his home.

As Alexander lay in the bath, he wondered what Damian would think if he knew about his fantasies, which had become decidedly graphic. He wanted Damian to screw him, to feel him inside himself and to know that he belonged to him completely. That had become the regular theme of his erotic imaginings when he wanked, as he now began to do. It was even more exciting doing so naked and separated by only a door from the unwitting lover of his dreams.

His passion relieved for the moment, he became more pensive. Actually he only wanted Damian to screw him if Damian longed desperately to do so. It was the longing he craved more than the act itself. He remembered anxiously how he had imagined it when he had first learned that was how it was done to boys. Though he thought now that he must have misunderstood, not least because he understood that the deep longing that characterised his ancient namesake was incapable of being directed towards any act that was not exalted, he worried that Damian might think as he had.

He had already decided he was going to have a bath every day, whether here or in his house. He wanted to be immaculately clean and fresh, ready for the day of his intended triumph, and also to make the very most of his looks to bring it closer. Now it occurred to him that it was up to a boy who was ready for his lover to go all the way with him to prepare himself with a special thoroughness in his ablutions that would nullify the slightest grounds for erotic misgiving.

He emerged from the bathroom spotless from head to toe, his luxuriant hair softly glistening, and saw that Damian was again sitting on the sofa. He picked up the *Aeneid*, which he had to prepare for Latin construe, and sat down beside Damian, pressed against him a little more firmly than before. Then he pretended to be absorbed in his reading. A minute later, he felt Damian's eyes on him, but though his heart beat triumphantly faster, he kept his eyes fixed on his book all through the man's perusal of him.

Damian was thrilled by the way Alexander snuggled up beside him to read his book. It was at least some substitute for his longing to hug the boy and kiss his cheek. What ecstasy that would be! He was achingly beautiful, and the thought of his lips on that rosy cheek was unbearably delicious. His heart pounded when he imagined the happiness of putting his arm round him as they sat.

He thought about it more when Alexander had gone. Though he kissed his family like that, he never longed for it so with them, much as he loved them. Why was that? There must be something different about his love for Alexander. Looked at from this new angle, his confidence that there was nothing erotic in his love was suddenly shaken. He lay awake that night wondering nervously if deep down he might after all have been avoiding confronting the truth. Had the plea in his continuation of Alexander's story to believe that his love was unsullied by eroticism really been entirely to the world, and not to himself too?

Damian found himself walking down a winding street. It was a hot, sunny day, but the street was so narrow and overhanging with merchandise that it was mostly in shadow. He was momentarily confused as to where he was, though he remembered he had just come out of his house. His bewilderment ended once he came out of the street into a small square where several streets converged. For a moment, he was blinded by the sudden bright sunshine, then his eyes adjusted to it and he saw on the colossal limestone rock above him, the Parthenon and the huge statue of Athene of the Vanguard, the gilded tip of her spear glistening brightly above everything. Of course! He was in Athens, his own city.

He passed round the bevy of slave-girls queuing to fill their pitchers with water at the fountain, turned right into the Street of the Bakers and presently found himself surrounded by the smell of freshly baked bread coming out of every door. He inhaled deeply. It was a beautiful afternoon and his spirits were high. The sights and sounds of the city were exotically elating and he felt proud and happy to be one of her citizens.

Suddenly, he saw Hugh Swinton, another boy in his F div, whom he knew to be quite friendly with Alexander, approaching from the opposite direction. For a moment, he felt confused again. Did Hugh belong here in Athens? Then he realised that obviously he must. He was Athenian, so everyone who belonged to his world must be here somewhere. That meant Alexander too and his spirits soared higher, as he recalled that he was on his way to meet him.

"Alexander is waiting for you in the Academy," said Hugh with a friendly smile. For a moment, Damian wondered whether he should worry that their friendship was known, but it seemed he need not.

"Yes, I know. I'm on my way there." The Academy was ten stadia outside the city walls, so he strode on swiftly. Soon he was in the throng passing through the double-arched Dipylon Gate and suddenly surrounded by the sights and smells of the Attic countryside. The road ran past one low-walled garden or olive grove after another. In the distance, the plain soon ran in all directions into terraced hills, behind which grey rocky mountains rose up majestically.

At last he passed through the Academy's gates into the large walled park and the colonnades in front of the city's largest

238

gymnasium came into sight. The arid countryside had suddenly given way to soft, green grass and, in every direction, he saw groups of youths and men, mostly young, sitting or standing under graceful plane trees. Many of them were listening intently to white-bearded philosophers. Inside the colonnades, Damian passed rooms in which he could see men and boys undressing and rubbing oil into their naked bodies and then there opened up before his eyes the rousing sight of the giant quadrangle of the gymnasium.

For a moment, Damian was surprised to see that everyone there was naked except the spectators, then he remembered that gymnastics meant "naked activities" and they were as they should be. The sight warmed and relaxed him. As if his thoughts had been read, he suddenly heard someone behind him speak up in a carrying voice, and he turned round.

"The godlike beauty of the good-looking young male is vastly enhanced when in its evenly-bronzed natural state, and justly inspires all sculptors, vase-painters, philosophers, poets and men of intellect more than any other subject," said a short man in his fifties with a pointed beard and glimmering, round spectacles. His face was that of one of Damian's Cambridge professors, and indeed Damian noticed some of his university acquaintances among the group of students standing and listening attentively. Nevertheless, he knew instinctively that the professor was really Professor Jameson, even before he saw the copy of *Greek Love* in its familiar blue dust-cover in the man's left hand.

"Gymnastics enhances the beauty of a boy's body by giving it perfect proportions and flexibility as well as giving him endurance and self-control," continued the professor earnestly. "That they are done naked also encourages appreciation of the young male's beauty, inspiring him in his endeavours to perfect it and inspiring his admirers with love, the noblest of the emotions. Athletic nudity is one of those things that captures the very essence of what it is to be Greek, in other words a civilised person. Only barbarians wear loincloths at sport, just as it is only ever they who object to philosophy or the love of boys. To be Greek is to have learned reason," he concluded, and Damian thanked the gods heartily that he was.

239

Now he found he was walking down a long promenade and he could see the boys' palaistra ahead. Groups of men were standing watching the wrestling. He approached and tried to wind his way to the front. Several of the young men greeted him and made room for him to pass. When he got to the front, he saw there were dozens of boys wrestling in pairs under the supervision of a trainer, their naked bodies covered with oil and dust.

Most of the spectators were young men of the upper class like himself, and Damian recognised the faces of some of the other younger Eton beaks among them, but there were also large numbers of pedagogues. Several were hovering around keeping watchful eyes on those of the boys in their early teens who did not yet have lovers, not that that was stopping some of the youths from trying to flirt with them. Many of the pedagogues, though, were sitting and chatting together at the back. Perhaps their charges were still too young to attract suitors, for Damian noticed further off some little boys with their own special trainer.

Besides the pedagogues, who were of course slaves, there were a few older citizens watching the wrestling too. One of them glanced around, recognised him and smiled in greeting, before turning back. Damian realised to his surprise that it was Mr. Griffith. The boys in his house had always suspected he liked boys more than schoolmasters were supposed to, not that anyone supposed he had ever thought to give physical expression to his feelings, and he would surely have been mortified if he had known what they guessed. Now, however, Damian saw that he was gazing without embarrassment at two handsome fifteen-year-olds locked in combat. Though the way he was looking at them could certainly not be called lascivious, and indeed it was impossible to imagine such a kind man succumbing to the kind of greedy lust the word implied, there was no doubting his frank appreciation as he watched the boys' muscles rippling in their dusty young bodies.

Alexander was nowhere among the wrestlers. Finally, Damian spotted him in the distance amongst eight other boys his age at the starting-line of the oval running track. As he made his way over there, he approached Harry Talbot strolling with his arm round Michael Stanhope, a handsome dark-haired boy in his F

240

div. It was obvious they were lovers from the way they were looking into each others' eyes. He remembered Harry's embarrassment at being nearly caught reading *Greek Love* in the Porson Library and wondered how he would react now to being seen by him in such an obvious display of intimacy with a younger boy, but both boys looked happily unperturbed as they greeted him.

Another small crowd was standing or sitting in the colonnades by the running track watching the boys as they prepared for the signal to go. As Damian approached, he saw one of Alexander's companions nudge him and say something. Then Alexander looked up at him and gave him a heart-melting smile, eye-catching enough to cause some of the spectators to turn round in curiosity. Most of them knew Damian at least vaguely, and for a moment he wondered again if he should worry that the warmth of their friendship was being so publicly displayed. His anxiety quickly gave way to exhilaration though, when he realised from the way most of them smiled at him and Alexander that, far more than just knowing and approving of their friendship, he was evidently already known to be Alexander's lover. They were all looking at him admiringly or enviously, or a mixture of the two. He caught a particularly black look from Tom Bradshaw, a short chubby beak of about thirty-five, whom he had never liked much and was nearly as far from the Greek ideal as could be imagined.

He wondered then whether he should not protest that being Alexander's lover did not mean his interest in the boy was carnal, that he was not that sort of lover, but to whom was he to say this? It did not look as though it was a distinction anyone would want to make. He suspected their looks of admiration and envy would turn to pity if he said that and he found he did not want them to believe it after all. Instead he fell into conversation about the coming race with David Wilkes, a likeable history beak only a little older than him.

Now he found himself looking at the boys crouching behind the red starting rope, their lithe, naked bodies glistening with oil. All was silent until the gymnasiarch signalled with a nod for the cord to be dropped and the boys shot off.

"Come on, Alexander!" yelled Damian as loud as he could, as the runners approached. Alexander suddenly sped up and moved ahead of the others. As the slender tanned figure flew close by him, Damian reflected that it was hardly surprising their affair had caught so much attention. Any fool could see that his beloved was the most beautiful boy in the city. As Alexander approached the finishing rope, he left the others further and further behind. He won easily, but it was clear he had driven himself to his limits, for he was bent down with his hands on his knees and his body heaving.

David gave Damian a congratulatory hug and several of the others turned towards him with admiring smiles, as if it had been him that had run the race, but Damian had eyes only for Alexander and ran over to him. He put his arm round him and Alexander leaned heavily on his chest while gradually recovering his breath. When he stood up at last, Damian kissed him on the cheek and the boy shot another of his heart-wrenching smiles into his eyes. Damian took his hand and they strolled across the gymnasium together and into one of the rooms where athletes were having the oil and dust scraped from their bodies. Alexander lay down on his stomach on a spare table and Damian picked up a strigil.

Damian's exhilaration had grown steadily with his realisation that in this wonderful city that was evidently their home his and Alexander's love for one another was something that, far from needing to be hidden, was widely acknowledged and approved or envied. However, it was only when he drew the strigil slowly along the smooth flawless skin of the boy's firm slender limbs and saw the oil that had caused them to glisten luxuriantly thus retreating to reveal the delicate texture and high colour peculiar to adolescent skin in bloom that he felt suddenly confronted by Eros. Then he realised that his love must be erotic too. Other people could be wrong in their assumption that he enjoyed the sexual delights that were normal for the accepted lover of a beautiful boy, but there could be no mistaking the body language of the boy. The slightly mischievous smile of pleasure Alexander gave him as he turned over for Damian to scrape the front of his body showed not the slightest doubt, not just that his lover desired him, but that that desire was already openly acknowledged between them. So it must be true. He realised then that Alexander really was the most erotically desirable

242

being he had ever set eyes on, and, in recognising this simple truth, he felt that a great burden had been lifted from his soul.

When Damian had finished with the strigil, Alexander drenched himself in a bathing fountain, put his chiton back on and drew up water from a well for them both to drink. Then they strolled back to the city. Damian's happiness grew again as he realised from the boy's exuberant chatter that they were going to be spending the rest of the day together and on their own. They had agreed to go off into the wild of Mount Lykabettos. Damian knew of an isolated shrine there to Eros, the god who inspired love between men and boys, and they had had resolved to thank him with a libation. They carried straight on until they came to the Agora, the great market at the heart of the city, where they bought a flask of wine, then they turned towards the Acharnian Gate.

Damian quickly became aware how different it was to walk through the city with Alexander than it had been on his own. In every street he noticed men turning their heads to look at the boy, mostly discreetly, but some even pausing to stare. Whenever they took in that Damian was accompanying him, they would glance him over too. Generally their looks were envious, but Damian saw that they were also tinged with a respectful awe, almost as if he were an athletic victor, and he could not help feeling a surge of pride. He knew they knew what victory he had won and that they supposed he must have done something to deserve it. He had won the heart of the most desirable boy in the city, one who could have chosen any man as his lover and they knew no boy of such evidently good breeding would succumb to a man whose virtues were in doubt.

Proud as he was, he felt bad for Alexander, who was evidently still unable to accustom himself to so much attention, though he must have been subjected to it for a year or two by now. Damian saw him blush several times at some of the indiscreetly lustful looks and gestures directed at him by some ungentlemanly citizens, so it was with relief that they left the city behind them.

Time must have passed, for now they were quite far up Lykabettos and the steep steps leading to the shrine came into sight. They stopped and looked down the way they had come. The whole city lay below them. Even the great steep rock of the

Acropolis, crowded with colourful temples, looked almost flat from where they were. Behind the city, they could see the Long Walls stretching down to Piraeus, and beyond that the deep azure of the sea going into the horizon.

No one else was about. Alexander sat down on a rock and smiled happily at Damian, who sat down beside him. He could tell from the way Alexander then moved his face towards him that he assumed his lover was going to start kissing him on his waiting lips. His heart thumping, he put his arm round Alexander's shoulder and gently they came together. The feel of the boy's moist, warm lips as they met his gave him a new jolt of excitement. He moved his tongue forward a little and immediately that it touched the boy's teeth, they parted to receive it. Then Alexander's tongue gently but most deliberately touched his, and he thought he might burst of the happiness that surged through him. His tongue began to move playfully with the boy's, which responded at once. After a minute, he withdrew to catch his breath for a moment and looked about him, his heart still pounding.

He could not help his eyes tracing a steep little path that meandered down the hill from where they sat. It seemed to end not far from an unusually large olive grove that he could see in the distance was deserted. He glanced back at Alexander and saw that the boy had caught the direction of his gaze. Alexander gave him one of those intoxicatingly warm smiles that were his special gift and lifted his hand to Damian's cheek as if to reassure him that it was agreed they would soon be going there, while a hint of jest came into his sparkling eyes that seemed to be chiding him gently for his impatience. Then Damian knew for certain that something was soon going to happen so exciting it hardly bore thinking about. He had no conscious awareness of what it would be in detail, but he must somehow know without thinking about it, for it was evident that the boy was anticipating the repeat of intimacies they had already shared.

They had not yet made their sacrifice to the god, so they went up to the shrine and together they solemnly poured their wine over the altar. They sat again and resumed their embrace. The sun was still high in the sky, so they had most of the afternoon. Damian told himself that every moment of it should be savoured, and bade himself concentrate again on the pleasure of their tongue-play, but struggle as he might, he could not stop images of the olive grove and all that it promised from invading his mind. Soon they paused again, and this time Alexander took hold of his hand as if to say he agreed that it was time to go.

Then they were springing down the narrow path together, hand in hand, on and on. As they slowed down near the bottom, they came to an isolated hut, outside of which stood a wizened old man supported by a crooked walking stick. He gazed at them knowingly, then nodded approvingly as they greeted and passed him, as if to say that of all the hundreds of couples he had seen passing this way in his long years, they made one of the finest.

Damian put his arm round Alexander's shoulder as they strode the last hundred paces to the grove and the boy inclined his golden-blond head against his chest. They carried on into the middle of the grove, where they were overshadowed by twisted and gnarled trees that looked so old they might have been the original gift of the goddess Athene that had won her the patronage of the city at its foundation. Damian let go of the boy, who moved on a little before turning round, so they found themselves facing each other a few paces apart. It was refreshingly cool here and the chirping of the crickets, which had been almost deafening in the open, had slowed right down.

Alexander stood calmly, gazing into his lover's eyes with an expression of totally trusting love that said he was waiting. Damian looked down at the boy's body and took a deep breath as he contemplated the beauty of the firm slender limbs almost glowing in their smoothness. They both knew what was about to happen, so he was not embarrassed to let his beloved see his longing as he looked at where the boy's blue-edged white chiton fell half way down his thighs concealing his most intimate parts by a only a few inches. Damian was burning for them to be revealed and had almost decided to undress at once, knowing that Alexander would then follow suit, when he reminded himself again that they had all afternoon to celebrate their love. He should fight his excitement and draw out their pleasure as long as possible. So instead, he moved up to him and bent down towards his mouth. Alexander put his arms up around his

245

lover's neck as their lips met yet again. Damian moved his left hand down to the lower hem of the boy's chiton, then slowly up inside to fondle the treasure it still concealed, his fingers tingling in anticipation of its hot stiffness, and ….

"Rrrrrrrrrrrrrrrrrrrrrrrrrr." Damian fumbled frantically to turn off the alarm clock beside his bed, desperate to restore silence before the last beautiful image in his dream faded from his mind. It was still vivid and overpowering and he tried to fix it there, but he knew he could not. When he tried to recall early parts of the dream that he assumed he could reconstruct, he found they had already almost entirely disappeared. He was reminded for a moment of an illustration in his boyhood book of Greek myths. It was of Orpheus, who had descended into the underworld to fetch back his dead young bride Eurydike and so charmed the god Pluto with his music that he allowed her to follow her husband back to the world of the living on the sole condition that he did not look back until they were there. At the last moment, he had been unable to resist the temptation of turning his head to make sure she was still following. The illustration had shown Orpheus holding out his arms in a hopeless endeavour to catch his wife's as she receded sadly back into the dark depths for ever.

He lay back on his bed breathing deeply, overwhelmed with sadness and hopeless longing to return to his dream, until he became aware that one thing that had not faded at all was the intensity of his sexual excitement. He did not need to feel or see his throbbing organ to know that it remained as rigid as a poker. His mind was thrown into turmoil as the implications struck him. He wondered whether he should resist the obvious temptation, but found he was too aroused to be able to think straight. Added to this was an urge to limit the intense disappointment his clock had inflicted on him by enjoying the only poor substitute there was for the joys it had robbed him of.

He did not know what he would have done in his dream if he had not been interrupted, so he simply concentrated on what he could still remember or imagine of Alexander standing in the grove waiting for him and after a few strokes with his fingers, he came copiously and, for the first time in his life, to thoughts of a boy rather than a woman or girl.

246

He had to get up and get ready for the day then, but his mind was in turmoil all morning. He realised he had almost certainly crossed a threshold in his understanding of himself and there was no going back. His impatience mounted as the afternoon approached, for he was tormented by niggling doubts he must resolve if he were to have any hope of settling his thoughts. He wondered if his dream could have deceived him. Was it at all possible that when the real Alexander turned up, he would not after all find him desirable? He doubted it very much, but it was not until Alexander walked through his door that the idea was at once dispelled for ever.

The longing he immediately felt was exactly as it had been in the olive grove except that now it was accompanied by despair instead of excited anticipation, for he knew that the change in his feelings, or his understanding of them (and he was not sure if there was a meaningful difference) could make no difference to the shock Alexander would be likely to feel if they were ever to be revealed. Instead of bringing them closer, which was whole point of Greek love, his longing had opened a chasm between them.

At first he tried hard to restrain himself from gazing, but by good luck Alexander soon picked up a book and sat down to read. He looked down without interruption, apparently entirely absorbed in the book, so Damian was able to feast his eyes on his beauty as much as he liked and thus further his self-knowledge.

Looking across at him on his sofa, he felt sure that if the famous Helen of the Fair Cheeks were to sit beside him, the face that launched a thousand ships would be outshone by Alexander's as easily as the moon is outshone by the sun. Indeed, he could not imagine any face that could be more than a faint reflection of his as a model of human loveliness.

He wondered what trick his mind could have played on him these last weeks to blind him so. Nothing he saw was new, so he must until now have been looking at Alexander through an optical illusion induced by some distorting lens that had just been dropped. He had known Alexander was stunningly beautiful from when he first saw him and for some time he had acknowledged the tremendous power of his beauty to attract in certain ways, but he had failed miserably to acknowledge its absolute mastery of all his senses.

It was time to make amends to Eros for his disrespectful inattention to him by admitting frankly the charm of what he offered, however impossible it remained to accept his gifts. He knew now why his heart would thump if he could kiss those flawless rosy cheeks, as it did not when he kissed his parents or sisters, and he could sense the fire in his loins that would burst forth if only he could instead kiss the sensuous lips and move his tongue forward between the perfect ivory teeth to meet the boy's.

He saw clearly at last that there was a sublime bloom to Alexander's face that he could not define, his hair was as soft and silk-like as a beautiful girl's, his cheeks as soft and smooth, his bones as fine, his eyes as sparkling and long-lashed, his lips as full and sweet, and his waist and wrists as slender.

It must have been simply his assumption that a boy could not be erotically attractive for him, latterly aided perhaps by a will to see his love as "innocent" that had shielded him from conscious physical longing for Alexander. It had been a prejudice or simply a misunderstanding that a boy could not be erotically enticing like a girl.

Alexander had felt at once that Damian was looking at him a little strangely when he arrived. Twice he glanced at him to find him looking at him, only to look away embarrassed when Alexander met his eyes. Then he remembered Bagoas and seizing his chance, sat down with a book in full view. As on the day before, he felt a surge of excitement when he knew Damian's eyes were upon him, but this time he sensed triumphantly that his gaze was more intense as well as far longer. He stayed reading on the sofa for an hour, hoping Damian might join him there, but though he felt his eyes never left him for long, he stayed at his desk.

Eventually, Alexander went to the table to write an essay. From time to time he got up to pace around and they had several short conversations. The more often he looked at Damian, the more he felt sure Damian was looking at him differently today. It reminded him exactly of the feelings he had had before of being better-looking when Julian and some other older boys had looked at him. The feelings which had made him feel desired.

The trouble was he had been mistaken about Julian. Or had he? Was it possible that Julian had desired him, but was so cowardly that he had gone out of his way to lie about it despite the encouragement he had been given? The more he thought about it, the more likely it seemed.

When Damian at last finished his work and went to sit on the sofa, Alexander waited a few minutes to join him. As on the day before, he sat quite firmly against his side, but this time, instead of accepting him there, Damian stiffened at once and moved away a little. Alexander was acutely disappointed. What could he have done wrong? He had thought he was making progress at last. Whenever they spoke, though, Damian was as warm and friendly as always.

He went back to his house that evening thoroughly confused. The next day was a Sunday, so he could spend almost all of it with Damian. It was essential to find a way of being sure whether or not Damian desired him. Soon he had a plan.

He put off its implementation until he came back from lunch. He wanted to have plenty of time ahead just in case it was as successful as he hoped. When at last the time came, he went for a bath. Then he steeled himself to dare come out of the bathroom in only his pants. Pretending nonchalantly not to be able to wait to ask Damian something he had just thought of, he stepped out into view. He dried his body languorously, turning himself this way and that, but with his face well away from Damian's, then he slowly dried his hair with a towel, his arms raised to give a full view of his torso, chatting away all the while.

Finally, he went up to the mirror and carefully combed his hair. Leaning forward slightly, he caught sight of Damian in it without his knowing and saw his eyes wandering over his body with such a look of desperate longing as dispelled his last doubt. His heart leapt triumphantly and he turned towards him, hoping they might come together at last, but Damian blushed and looked away, though continuing the conversation.

Disappointing though it was that Damian seemed determined to resist, it was dizzyingly exhilarating to know he had such power to excite him. It made him feel like a god. He felt tingling sensations course through his body, but he had severely

249

underestimated how much the knowledge that he was desired would turn him on and he had to go back into the bathroom promptly and at an awkward angle before Damian saw the only-too-obvious bulge in his pants.

When he came back dressed, he tried again to get physically close to Damian, but found that the more he tried to flirt with him, the more withdrawn he became. It was frustrating, but he had made too substantial progress to let it get him down, besides becoming wiser about love and desire.

He was beautiful, Damian desired him and life was full of promises of happiness.

It was the first time Damian saw Alexander's body. He told himself miserably that he should not look, but his eyes would not obey him. Even across the room, the boy's whole figure radiated beauty. He tried to restrict his interest to the sight of the perfectly proportioned smooth limbs and naked, boyish torso, all of which made him ache with longing to kiss and stroke him all over, but he found that Alexander's pants, which were of the short close-fitting variety that narrowed to a single inch midway across his hips, inexplicably but irresistibly dragged his gaze towards them and the idea of what they hid.

The bulge in the front of the pants was too indistinct in shape to help his imagination much, but at the back they followed the curvature of the boy's firm, little buttocks except that the crevice between them was only hinted at. He found himself severely taken aback by the exquisite shape of it all, and wondered why it had such an effect on him. He knew from *Greek Love* that it was through that boyish crevice that Greek men most often sought their bliss, for Professor Jameson had discussed at length the often ambiguous evidence as to what they did to boys in various times and places. One of the things that put him off gays had been imagining them doing that too, but he found to his surprise that, try as he did, he could not induce any distaste in himself when he thought of Alexander's bottom being penetrated. It was too fresh and pure and its smallness evoked too much tenderness. He shuddered as he realised the shocking direction he had allowed his thoughts to wander and forbade himself to think about it again even in his fantasies.

250

He wondered gloomily what Alexander would think if he had any idea of the agonising effect he had on him. For a fearful moment, he thought Alexander might actually have noticed and understood his passion, but thankfully it seemed he had not, for when he had returned dressed from the bathroom, he had carried on chatting enthusiastically, his high spirits evidently unchecked. After all, how could the boy guess, when Damian himself had denied the sexual element of his love only five days earlier.

His self-understanding was deepening at a bewildering pace. Having taken in that it was the distinctly boyish features of Alexander's body that moved him most, he could no longer delude himself that he was erotically exciting *despite* being a boy, as had seemed possible when only his face had been considered. Too much of him was exciting *because* he was a boy.

To feel like that, he must, like the Greeks, be a lover of boys as well as of women. They were different flavours, each delicious in its own way, but quite compatible. He had failed to realise this before simply because he had assumed he was not homosexual, knowing that he was attracted to women and was not remotely attracted to other men. Though it seemed now that it should have been obvious, he had not even considered that he could be attracted to boys without having the faintest sexual interest in other men, because he had not heard pederasty spoken of nearly enough to become conscious of that as a possibility. The omission struck him as very odd considering its historical prominence.

During his English div with Damian on Monday morning, Alexander found it impossible to look at him without remembering his look of longing the day before and getting an erection every time he did. They could not go on like this, it was unbearable, but what should he say or do?

He was walking fast down Judy's Passage to get to his next div the other side of the school, when he suddenly saw Julian approaching from the other direction. He was already used to passing him in light-hearted silence, so he was quite shocked when Julian came towards his side of the alley.

"Hi Alexander," he said with a quiet smile.

251

"Hi," replied Alexander in astonished reflex reaction just before they passed each other. He began to chide himself for friendliness towards one who had treated him so badly, but soon decided there could be no harm in simply acknowledging Julian. He did not matter any more. The important thing was that everything had worked out well in the end. It was a relief to let the past rest.

His next div was History, and more specifically ancient history, generally his favourite subject by a long way, but his mind wandered all the same. The young beak who was teaching it, Mr. Noble, did not seem very interested and Alexander got the impression that he himself knew the subject better.

Besides the problem of how best to tackle Damian's reluctance to act on his evident desire, he was increasingly worried about his birthday. Almost as soon as Damian had given him a birthday present, Alexander had got out of him that his own birthday was only seventeen days later. He had been delighted at first that he would have a chance to reciprocate, and had silently rejected without hesitation Damian's warning that he should not give him anything. He loved giving things to people he was fond of. He had not thought of anything suitable until last Wednesday, when he had had his weekly Design div in the School of Mechanics. They were allowed to practise metalwork and it struck him that a ring would be suitably romantic when they had just declared their love. He was making it from little rods of flattened bronze intertwined, but already it was getting tarnished and now it seemed woefully inadequate to express the depths of his love. How could he find something to show that with a boy's pocket money and only two days left? If only he could, it might provide a special opportunity to bring his dreams to fruition.

Mr. Noble paused and referred them to chapter twenty-one of their textbook, *Britain and the Ancient World*. They were doing Julius Caesar. Alexander's uncle Charles had given him a beautifully bound edition of Suetonius's *Twelve Caesars* last Christmas, and he had recently reread his account of Julius in case it might help Damian's play. It was so much more lively and interesting than the modern, dull textbook. He wondered what the point was of rewriting history just to leave out the really interesting parts, though as it happened, he had been surprised that even Suetonius had left out the story of how Cleopatra had introduced herself to Caesar. Where had that come from? It was a clever idea, and had surely changed the course of history.

Suddenly, Alexander was struck by an idea as brilliant as it was outrageous. Surely, the best he had ever had, he thought. It would be two birds with one stone and impossible to miss.

Damian went to his divs on Monday with a new curiosity in his pupils. He needed to confirm that beautiful boys in general were as attractive to him as beautiful girls, as he imagined logically must be the case since recognising that Alexander's boyishness was part of his erotic appeal. Looking at those boys in his E and F divs whose good looks he had before found mysteriously disconcerting, and even a couple in D, it was at once mysterious no more. They were simply as sexy as the most ravishing girls, though even the best of them were but dull shadows compared to the boy he loved.

Remembering how he had always loved the company of boys and got on with them so easily, it struck him that trying to dissect love into different categories was missing the point and obscuring the truth, as foolish as cutting a living person's body into pieces and then discussing whether the head or the heart had been more important. It had certainly misled him about himself. Sexual desire was really just one inextricable part of one's personality, influencing and being influenced by its other components.

Over the weekend he had regretted his erotic yearning for Alexander because of the chasm between them that he felt had been opened by its hopelessness, but the more he thought about it now that he understood it to be an integral part of his love, the more he realised it was a force for all that was good and valuable in him, for he could not honestly doubt that his love had brought anything but good to the boy. He could not regret it because to lose it would be to lose the most valuable part of himself.

The fleeting image of Mr. Griffith in his dream sprung to his mind and he thought of the other beaks he had had as a boy at Eton who had stood out as special, the ones who had acted for their pupils far beyond the call of duty, the ones like him who cared deeply about their happiness and success, as opposed to those who just liked the sounds of their own voices. Could they have given so much of themselves if their emotional existence had not revolved around boys? Many of them had probably gone through their careers as innocent of conscious erotic longing for their charges as he had been until the day before yesterday. After all, his sexual innocence had only ended because odd circumstances had brought a boy of spectacularly rare beauty into close friendship with him. Others again had probably acknowledged their romantic longings, at least deep down, and resigned themselves to the hopelessness of their being fulfilled, as he was now doing. He thought of Mr. Rideout, his favourite English beak, a fountain of kindness, a bachelor whose flat had always been a popular refuge for every kind of boy yearning for sympathy. Had there not always been a hint of sadness behind his warmth that bespoke of the same frustrated yearning that he now felt? The Greeks were right that the lovers of boys were the greatest force for their good.

With the modern benefit of understanding natural selection, he had thought the Greek pederastic ethos through to its logical origins and conclusions. As *Greek Love* revealed there had historically been many societies, not just the Greek, where a taste for boys was considered commonplace and in some circumstances commendable, it followed that with an unprejudiced upbringing many, or perhaps most, men had a latent capacity for such love. To thus endure, pederasty must have had an important role in furthering the survival of the species during those hundreds of thousands of years in which human nature was formed, otherwise it would have been eliminated by natural selection. Classical Greece had made its benefits dramatically clear, and so diluted, but nevertheless important, benefits of a similar kind must have been felt by any society in which it was practised on a lesser scale.

It was easy to imagine what those benefits could have been in even the most primitive tribes. Boys could not compete against men in an age when physical strength and practical skills were what counted, and only the fittest survived. Prepubescent boys did not need to, because their fathers could protect them and provide for them, but how were they to get from this state of dependency to one where they could successfully compete against other men? Who would teach the adolescent boy how to hunt and fight rather than devoting the time to his own benefit? In theory, it might still be the father, but in reality many boys would have lost their fathers before reaching puberty and the paternal instinct towards teenagers was not often sufficiently intense. In any case, the Greeks had shown that the job was most effectively done by lovers.

Hence it followed that any tribe in which the pubescent boys had older male lovers would have a survival advantage over one in which they did not.

Having thought about it long and carefully, Damian felt sure that sexual desire for boys was therefore both essentially good and natural. He realised sadly that if only they had been ancient Greeks, if the whole ethos of society supported him, and if the value of his love being sealed were generally understood, then Alexander too would almost certainly see its value. If only that were the case, he would undoubtedly now declare its full nature, and, if its sexual element was welcomed, he would in the best conscience act on it.

If Alexander had been Greek, he could not possibly have been shocked that a man desired him and it was most unlikely he would see anything distasteful about it at all. Damian thought about the Ashmolean cup. He looked longingly at his picture of it every day. He certainly found it erotic now and that made him realise that what was so moving about it was that it was so innocently erotic. The man's naked excitement before his beloved was revealed both to him and to the viewer of the cup without sign of either shame or glee. It was hardly possible that a boy who had grown up with such a charming cup in his house could see sex between a man and boy as anything but beautiful.

Sadly, though, it was Damian's fate to be a twentieth-century Englishman in love with a similarly encumbered boy, and the thought of Alexander's possible incomprehension, disappointment in him or even maybe revulsion if he were to let him know how he felt was enough to turn his stomach. He would never risk that.

255

XI: Greek Love in Practice

Do you really think ... that it is weakness that yields to temptation? I tell you that there are terrible temptations that it requires strength, strength and courage, to yield to. To stake all one's life on a single moment, to risk everything on one throw, whether the stake be power or pleasure, I care not -- there is no weakness in that.
  Oscar Wilde, *An Ideal Husband*

During the morning of Damian's birthday, Alexander had a div with him and found himself suddenly much more nervous. He had of course endlessly gone over the pros and cons of his plan, but it felt different now on the very day and seeing him enthusiastically talking to his div without a clue as to what was soon going to happen. After ten minutes, Damian set them some exercises on the novel *Tom Sawyer*, which they had just finished. They were quite easy questions, but Alexander found it difficult to concentrate. He glanced frequently at Damian, trying with a thumping heart to imagine how he would react to what he planned. It was very hard to know. Sometimes he told himself he was mad even to consider it, but then he would remind himself that he had little to lose: Damian loved him and would surely not turn against him even if he did do one really outrageous thing. Then he would turn his mind to how he hoped it would turn out. His heart would start pounding and his excitement would mount until he thought he might come in his pants without even touching himself.

He arrived at Damian's flat after his last div at five. When he reached the door, he paced quickly up and down steeling his nerves for a minute. Finally, telling himself it was too late to get another birthday present, he let himself in. Damian looked up from behind his desk and smiled. He had guessed Alexander would give him a present despite what he had said. He knew his incorrigible generosity and just hoped it would be something small the boy could easily afford.

"Happy birthday!" said Alexander with a warm smile.

"Thank you."

Alexander came into the middle of the room and forced himself to go on. "Damian. I have a surprise present for you, but I need to get it ready. Do you think you could wait in the bedroom until I call?"

"Yes, okay," said Damian thoroughly intrigued, as he got up and went to the bedroom door. He could tell that Alexander was nervous, which just made it all the more mystifying.

"Wait, Damian, wait!" Damian stopped by the door. "I need to explain. The thing is I want you to unwrap it on your own, so when I call you, wait twenty seconds for me to leave before coming in, okay? I'll come back when you've already opened it. Don't worry. You'll understand soon, okay?" he said with a pleading smile.

"Yes, fine," said Damian. He did not think he had ever seen Alexander so nervous.

"Look, you might not like it, but please don't be angry if you don't," he beseeched.

"I'm sure I'll like anything you give me."

"No, really, you might not."

"Well, I promise I won't be angry."

"And you promise you won't come in until I call?"

"Yes, don't worry." He smiled reassuringly, went into the bedroom and closed the door firmly behind him.

Alexander leaped into action, allowing himself no time for hesitation. As quietly as he could with speed, he moved Damian's side table off the large rug that lay in the middle of his sitting-room, took out a letter he had prepared and positioned it carefully on the floor. Then he whipped off all his clothes except his pants, rolled them up into a ball and placed it out of sight behind the sofa. He paused for a few seconds, listening intently for any sounds. The next bit was the most terrifying and had to be accomplished very fast and efficiently indeed. It was really too late to stop now anyway, he told himself. He pulled off his pants, dropped them on top of his other clothes and took quick silent strides to the edge of the rug, along which he lay down. Then he picked up his letter and rolled himself round and round inside the rug until he guessed it was all rolled up. Next he pushed the letter out, lay it on top of the rug and drew his arm back inside. He lay there until his long deep breaths had subsided into silent ones. Then he called out.

Damian had been sitting on his bed, completely unable to come up with any guess as to what Alexander's present might be. He told himself not to get excited lest he betray any signs of disappointment when it was finally revealed. When the summons came, he counted silently to twenty before going in.

He saw at once that his rug had been rolled up and was just wondering what on earth that could have to do with the present, when he noticed a sheet of paper on it. He guessed just as he picked it up that Alexander must have used his rug as a wrapping. The present must be huge then. That would explain why he had not been able to prepare it before coming here.

"To Damian," he read, "whom I love with all my heart. This birthday gift is for you to enjoy in every way that you can think of, from Alexander."

Damian's head began to spin. He realised he did not want to torment himself wondering what it might be. He wanted to know before he could have time to think more, so he knelt down quickly to unravel it. As soon as he began to pull the edge of the rug up, gently in case it contained something fragile, he sensed an irregularity in its shape and then a limpness that in a short moment registered itself in his mind as signifying life. By the time the boy fell out of the rug and onto the underlying fitted carpet, he had already guessed that it was Alexander himself inside, though he was still in a whirl of confusion as to what wrapping himself into a rug could have to do with his present.

When he took in that Alexander was entirely naked, his astonishment was for just a second or two boundless. Then he understood. He too knew the story of Cleopatra's seduction of Caesar. His head was spinning and he wondered if he was back in the world of his Athenian dream, for the sensation was so similar, that of his deepest yearnings being answered beyond what he had considered imaginable in the real world. In his confusion, he tried to compare the Alexander who lay before him with the other naked one from whose body he had cleansed olive oil in the gymnasium, but he could not recapture any visual detail of that boy, though some of the feelings that this one physically evoked seemed somehow familiar to him.

His entire body seemed almost to glow in its delicate smoothness and clean good health. What he had previously concluded as to his facial skin being in a sort of sublime bloom applied to his whole body. Everything was also perfectly proportioned and slim, yet all the limbs were firm and gently curved. Descending from the utterly beautiful face that he knew so well, he saw a slender neck and narrow shoulders leading to graceful arms in the upper parts of which muscles just showed as they did around his chest and thighs, their small, round, boyish size nearly overwhelming him with a sudden, tender, protective urge. Below the chest, the gentle tapering of his body towards the waist was almost imperceptible until he half rose on one arm to give just enough of a side view to appreciate the inward curve of his lower back, and hint at the exquisite curve of the firm little bottom mostly hidden behind the narrow hips. Between these he saw at last what he had so longed to see without believing he ever would.

Here he had not known much of what to expect and the Greek vase paintings were not detailed enough to help. The thought of playing with the gross, hairy genitals of a man was almost enough to make him retch, and though he expected something much finer in a fourteen-year-old boy, he had wondered whether they might still put him off just a little. It was not so. They were as hairless as the rest of his body except for a sweet little mound of soft dark blond down just above his cock. The smooth twin orbs dangled deliciously behind an equally smooth, uncut shaft that tapered exquisitely down to the end, except where the domed shape of his hidden glans just visible through the foreskin lent it a delicate bulge. Though manifestly smaller than Damian's own, it was evidently virile, and indeed evidence of its virility was rising and growing fast before his eyes. It was this that snapped him out of his reverie.

He did not know how many moments had passed while he had been absorbing the sublime sight before him, and only now noticed that he had in the meantime sat down on his sofa, while Alexander had half risen on one arm and was staring into his eyes with a mixture of hope and fear. Suddenly, an idea of what must have gone through the boy's mind to make him do this came home to him. Not only had Alexander made a move that was incredibly daring considering it could surely only have been a guess on his part that Damian desired him, but he was willing

259

to let him "enjoy him in every way" just to make him happy. Tears came to his eyes and dampened a little the fire that had arisen in his groins.

"Alexander," he said, smiling through his tears, "you have no idea how moved I am by what you've done, but I'm afraid there are many things you don't understand." Seeing Alexander's crestfallen look as he sat up, he paused, torn in two and lost for words.

"Do you mean you don't find me attractive in that way?" asked Alexander fearfully.

"No, I do….. It's true. You guessed right. I didn't realise it at first. I'd never had any feelings like that for a boy before. But now, at least with you, it's different. I do find you very, very attractive. I'm sure you are the best looking boy in the school. If only things were that easy."

"You mean you think there's something wrong with men having sex with boys? That's just a stupid, modern idea," said Alexander derisively. "You told me yourself that some ancient Greek men did. Alexander the Great certainly slept with boys and so did his father and lots and lots of other great people in those days and they all thought it was good."

"Yes, I know." It was uncanny how Alexander too had been brought to think like this by Greek ideas. He was reminded again of his dream and it added to the whole unreality of the situation.

Alexander's eagerness and his own delirious excitement at the prospect of such happiness so easily in reach were such a powerful combination that all Damian's instincts told him protracted resistance was not only mad but churlish, but still he forced himself to consider quickly the possible objections. That the law should be obeyed for its own sake was the easiest to dismiss. He would not feel bad disobeying six hundred and fifty self-serving politicians who presumed to tell others what they could not do for their own good, because it was none of their business and he did not owe them anything. He did feel bad that the school would feel let down by him if it knew, because he owed it his job. Nevertheless, was it not wrong of any institution or anybody at all, however good its intentions, to impose a blanket ban on the fulfilment of needs and longings arising from

260

hearts it neither knew nor understood, or even cared about except in the abstract? In seeking to forbid something so deeply personal and private to the two people concerned, even the school was acting beyond what ought to be its business. For that very reason, no one should ever find out.

Though he was daunted by the idea of embarking on something the world was bound to misunderstand and react furiously to if it knew, he felt it would be cowardly and dishonourable to give in to this fear, if it were fear of doing the right thing. He owed Alexander courage and the truth, and the truth was that it would be the right thing if Alexander truly wanted it for himself, rather than to please him. It was only this he thought at all doubtful.

How could he get Alexander's reassurance about this without giving him the false impression that he was not longing to accept his gift more than he had ever wanted anything? Thoughts about Alexander's exquisite naked body still seated tantalisingly before him and the boy's willingness for love-making kept invading his mind and evoking an image of the boy in his arms far too exciting to concentrate on anything else for more than a few moments at a time.

Fortuitously, just then, nature came to his rescue. His body spoke for him with the part of the male that cannot lie and Alexander's answered him with the same incontrovertible candour.

Feeling his erect cock straining in his trousers, he glanced down for a moment to see that the bulge was only too obvious. To his momentary mortification, he saw that Alexander had followed his glance, and the boy's eyes had widened. He would have blushed had not the boy's own cock immediately risen in response from half-mast to stand in firm and indisputable refutation of his last misgivings. Then Damian laid them aside at last and, giddy with happiness, signified his eager acceptance with an excited smile.

Alexander understood at once that he had won. His eyes sparkling and his whole body throbbing with excitement, he got up and sat down on Damian's lap, putting a hand round his shoulder and pressing his head firmly against the man's chest. It was his first physical affection since the day three weeks ago that their friendship had really begun, and only his second since the day he had unknowingly said good-bye to his mother for ever. He lay there quite still listening to the beat of Damian's heart, while Damian put his arm round him and kissed his thick, soft hair. Then he moved his fingers gently through it.

Alexander was certain then that he was happier than he had ever been. He knew that a day would never pass in which he did not remember his mother or feel warmed by the memory of her love, but this was something more. His mother had loved him because he was her son and that had been enough when he had been truly a child, but well before her death, he had felt a deep longing to be loved for himself, just because he was attractive, fun and good. To be loved to the full, including in bed, and with that thought he finally looked up.

"You are really certain you want this?" asked Damian, understanding.

"Yes….. But I don't know what to do. Please promise that you really will do everything," entreated Alexander, sitting up and looking into his eyes. That was as far as he dared go towards making it clear that he wanted Damian to go the whole way, that he wanted them both to be fulfilled.

"Okay," said Damian in a hush. Then Alexander gave a short tug on the lapel of Damian's tailcoat. Damian understood and smiled. There was something amusingly incongruous, he thought, about having a nude boy in his arms while he was fully dressed in his tails. "I'm just going to the bathroom for a moment."

He washed his face in cold water, but still felt just as light-headed with excitement, then he looked at himself in the bathroom mirror and wondered why he had thought he would feel less bashful stripping off here. He reminded himself of Alexander's courage and undressed anyway. He began to open the bathroom door when he caught sight of his erection in the mirror and was overcome with shyness. He could not just walk out in front of Alexander like that. True, Alexander was also erect, but his own was so much more prominent. Alexander could never have seen anything like it. He wrapped a towel around his waist and went out.

For a moment they both looked at other a little shyly, the delay having broken their spontaneity, then Alexander flashed one of

262

his dazzling smiles. Damian smiled back warmly, sat on his sofa and beckoned Alexander to sit beside him. He put his arm round him and cuddled him as he kissed his forehead and his cheek and then, softly, his sensuous warm lips. Then he drew back and with his other hand gently stroked the boy's smooth leg from his knee upwards. Alexander shot a hard look at the bulge inside Damian's towel. He wanted the towel removed. It was time for him to see, but Damian instead moved his hand further up his thigh, his fingers making little circular strokes. Alexander's excitement mounted rapidly as the caressing hand came within inches of his balls, but he didn't want Damian to touch his organ until he was naked too. He moved his hand along the upper edge of the towel and gazed pleadingly. Damian paused for a moment, then stood up, undid the towel and dropped it decisively onto a nearby chair.

"Wow!" Alexander could not help exhaling softly. He was mesmerised, such was his astonishment at the enormity of the thing that rose up from Damian's groins to his navel. The nearest he had ever come to seeing a man's cock was in Rupert's pictures of the secret country, but they had not been at all clear and certainly not erect. He had known from the bulge that Damian's would be big, but he had never expected it to be that huge. He gazed at it in awed fascination as Damian sat down and began gently to kiss him again.

It reminded him of the stallion he had seen on his prep school leavers' trip to a stud farm. The boys had looked forward to the visit with titillation, as it had been explained that that meant a farm entirely given up to the breeding of race horses, and it was implicitly understood to be a practical follow-up to the quiet sex talk the school doctor had given them in little groups the week before. As they were shown around, various stallions were being led about the place, and the group of thirty boys giggled in amusement at the sight of the stallions' massive long organs swaying between their knees almost like third legs. To conclude the visit, a stallion was led out to a field where a mare was waiting. When the stallion saw her he started neighing loudly. As he got near, he suddenly reared up on his hind legs until he was nearly standing, his front hooves pawing the air wildly and his eyes mad with excitement, but it was to the beast's almighty

263

cock that the eyes of all the boys were glued. It had reared up wildly like its owner along most of the body's great length, the purest and most magnificent image of masculinity that Alexander could imagine. Disappointingly, the mare had backed away, she and a stable boy in a tug of war over her reins until the proprietor explained regretfully that she was not ready yet and they would have to give up.

Damian's cock only reminded him for a few moments of the stallion's because of its massive size compared to his own, a difference far greater than those between their other parts, for otherwise it was incomparably handsomer. Where the stallion's had been bestial and grey, Damian's was as straight as a thick knobbed poker and of the same fair skin as the rest of him. At its base was a mound of dark hair, a trickle of which rose in a straight line to his chest, where more dark hair spread out in contrast to the nearly hairless fairness of most of the rest of his body. The splendour of it all was enhanced by a lean muscularity far more prominent than in his own boyish frame.

Alexander did not feel desire for the young man's superb body, rather it was what he desired his eventually to be, but he felt in awe of its magnificence and overwhelmed by its manliness. It made him feel childish and he realised more than ever how inadequate girls like Lucretia would be bound to find him compared to Damian. It did not make him feel as he imagined a girl would feel, but it did make him feel how very different he, as a boy, was from a man, that boy and man were almost different sexes, and he felt a sudden, enormous relief. He had worried a bit that in accepting a sexual role with a man in some ways similar to that normally played by a girl, he would somehow have to subdue his sense of his own masculinity. Now that he could see how very different their supposedly common masculinity was, his boyish and Damian's manly, he realised there was no conflict. It might be unmanly to take a man as one's lover, but it would not be unboyish.

He was so thrilled by the flattering homage to his own beauty implied by the giant thing's standing in rigid attention before him, that his heart was thumping with excitement by the time Damian picked him up in his arms and carried him into his bedroom. He lay him gently on the bed, then lay down beside him and kissed him on the lips again. This time he did not withdraw and the boy's eyes widened in surprise as he felt the man's tongue push into his mouth to meet his. He had seen men and women do that in romantic films, but he had had no idea it would feel so incredibly intimate. After Damian's tongue had moved gently around his for a while, he began to respond. It was as if their tongues were dancing together except that Alexander had never heard of a dance that brought such relief. He could feel the residue of his pent-up loneliness, built up over months and then steadily eased as their intimacy had grown, the lack of love that had weighed him down, being finally drained out of him through their embrace, until it was all gone and he was free at last.

Then Damian's hand returned to the boy's leg and repeated its former journey. As it reached the point where it had been interrupted before, Damian gently withdrew from their embrace. He cuddled the boy in his right arm, as he cupped his silky balls in his left hand and then began to fondle them. The difference in the size of their organs evoked a sudden extra tenderness in him as he explored the boy's. His own was circumcised and he had never before seen an uncircumcised one at all clearly. Thus it was with some curiosity that he gently pulled back the foreskin until the glans was exposed. Alexander writhed with delight, then suddenly, despite the precaution he had taken of wanking earlier in the afternoon so he would not get too easily excited, he could hold back no longer. Just as Damian's fingers began to stroke his shaft, he felt the rush coming and seconds later his love juices began to spurt forth, the first shot so vigorous that it reached his shoulder. Damian, though taken by surprise, used his many years of experience wanking himself to prolong Alexander's pleasure by gradually slowing down and softening his strokes until the last of the crystal liquid had been coaxed out.

Alexander lay back hardly moving, deliriously happy with the intimacy of his first orgasm brought on by another. Damian, however, was a little baffled. He did not know, because Dashka had never done it to him, just how much more pleasurable than wanking oneself it was to be wanked by a lover. A mere wank seemed to him a feeble thing for Alexander to remember from their first time in bed together. Fortunately, Alexander's excitement seemed hardly to have abated and Damian began to plan greater pleasures for him to come shortly.

After a few minutes in which Damian just kissed him tenderly all over, Alexander began to worry that perhaps Damian was hoping he would do something, or why had he not yet begun seeking his own fulfilment.

"What do I do? Please tell me."

Damian understood then why the boy was growing anxious and that the time had come for him to accept his birthday present as he had promised. He already knew what he was going to do, for he had been doing it regularly in his erotic fantasies since soon after his Athenian dream. He copied the pictures he had seen in *Greek Love*, depicting what the learned professor called intercrural copulation. It was what Greek men did with boys who were not yet ready to be fucked. Unfortunately he did not have the olive oil they used, but Alexander watched in fascinated suspense as Damian took some skin cream out of a little pot he brought from the bathroom and smoothed it out over the full length of his massive shaft as it stood in rigid anticipation of the pleasure to come. He still had no idea whether Damian intended to go all the way with him or whether it was even possible for something so huge to enter him. He knew only that he gladly acknowledged Damian as his master in all things, he longed to give him pleasure and trusted Damian's judgement completely as to how best to obtain it.

Then Damian went down on all fours above him, his knees either side of Alexander's lower legs. He tickled both the little testicles with the tip of his tongue, moved up his still stiff shaft and kissed his naval, thereby giving Alexander a sensual tickle which caused the boyish muscles of his chest and stomach to clench and ripple. Briefly his tongue then explored the boy's tender nipples and the deliciously hairless armpits, before moving to the sweet lips, which opened to welcome him. Alexander had learned fast and his tongue played gently with his lover's as if they were old friends.

Damian was breathless with desire for the boy now. Kneeling back for a moment, he gently moved the boy's thighs together. Shifting his weight from his hands to his elbows, he moved his knees forward until he lay horizontally above Alexander and his cock descended between the boy's warm, slender thighs. With another, slight shift he moved it up to rest firmly along his beloved's smooth perineum and began gently to draw back and then again forward until he felt Alexander's hard tool pressed hotly between their stomachs. He sighed deeply with happiness, then began to thrust steadily back and forth. All too soon, he felt his climax approaching. He paused, buried his nose in Alexander's hair and inhaled its fragrance. He licked and nibbled an ear-lobe, then the nape of the quivering boy's neck, but the longing for release after so much pent-up longing was overwhelming. He resumed his thrusts and only slowed down as his erotic juices gushed forth in blissful waves.

Alexander recognised at once the warm wetness between his legs. With a burst of exaltation at having proved his value as beloved by bringing his lover joy, he clasped him round the neck and their mouths joined in another long kiss.

Alexander was still totally stiff and Damian soon decided he was ready for a much more special memento of their first love making. He remembered his surprise and ecstasy when Dashka had first fellated him. The sheer naughtiness of it when he had taken in the fact that he really was not only in her mouth, but that she intended for him to remain there until he came, had exhilarated him until he almost wanted to laugh with joy. Now he would bestow exactly the same joys on Alexander.

He repeated his previous exploration of Alexander's body, but in the other direction, and more briefly. As he reached his cock, he drew the foreskin right back with his fingers, so that as the throbbing organ slipped deliciously between his warm, moist lips, his waiting tongue could move to meet the exposed glans. His cock was still just small enough that Damian could take it all in without discomfort despite his lack of experience as the giver of this delight. Each time he felt the hot hardness thrust along to the back of his tongue and as the tip of his tongue applied delicious pressure on the most sensitive part of the boy's shaft, he remembered so vividly the sharpness of his own pleasure when it had been his cock receiving the same loving attention in Dashka's mouth that he was sure he could feel and partake of his beloved's ecstasy. The boy began to make urgent little thrusts upwards into his throat and Damian guessed he was near coming. He remembered then his own growing curiosity and excitement as to whether when he came Dashka would withdraw to avoid oral insemination, but she had not. She had already tied her hair back out of the way with a band, so he had had a full view of her face as he came. The only signs she gave of what was happening were the swallowing motions of her throat and a gradual slowing down as if she were luxuriating in the taste. She had just carried on calmly and intently at her task without any change of expression until his last drops had been brought forth and imbibed, while he lay there trying to credit his senses that the ecstasy he was feeling and seeing was real. So he now did exactly the same to Alexander. He wondered what it would taste like, but when he finally felt the warm gush into the back of his mouth, he could only make out a faint flavour of the sea, too indistinct not to be overridden by the fresh intoxicating smell of boy that he was inhaling through his nostrils. His overriding sensation, which brought him joy and relief as he swallowed his beloved's nectar, was simply of drinking love.

Alexander lay back, drained of his seed and momentarily of his energy. His body felt weightless, as if it had achieved everything it was designed for. For the first time in his life he self-consciously knew himself to be physically fulfilled, and for a minute he had no room in his mind for anything but wonder. Then he remembered the one who had brought him such unimagined joy and he turned himself over into his arms. They lay quiet and calm together for a long time after that, both satisfied simply to contemplate their happiness.

Eventually Alexander stirred.

"How about some tea?" suggested Damian.

"Okay." They went out of the bedroom, Alexander first. Damian stood by the door for a moment, wanting to savour the beauty and grace of the boy's body until the last moment of his nakedness. Alexander stopped suddenly in the middle of the room, remembering that his clothes were in a bundle behind the sofa. He realised he did not want to put them on at all. It would be bringing down the curtain on their theatre of joy. Could they not be free together like in the secret country? They had already made the flat their own, special world. He looked at the table with the things for tea on it, wondering what Damian would think if he just forgot his clothes and went straight to pour himself a bowl of Frosties, then he gave Damian a quizzical smile. He knew that Damian had intuitively followed his line of thought when Damian smiled back warmly and came to the table himself, instead of the bathroom where his own clothes lay.

They sat down together on the sofa, both feeling a renewed exhilaration at their unfamiliar freedom. For several minutes they ate silently, speaking to each other with happy smiles rather than words. Then Alexander grew pensive and began pacing around.

"By the way, how did you know all that about Greek men sleeping with boys?" asked Damian curiously.

"Most of all from *The Persian Boy!*"

"Seriously?"

"Yes, the boy of the title was a real historical character who was loved by Alexander the Great."

"Did it actually say they went to bed together?"

"Oh yes, very much so. You should read it. It's easily my favourite novel now."

"Thank God I didn't know that before, or I'd never have dared give it to you."

"There were lots of affairs between men and boys mentioned in *Fire From Heaven* too, but it wasn't a love story, as *The Persian Boy* is really. I got the impression that it happened so much then that any realistic novel about ancient Greece would have to mention it. Is that true, do you think?"

"Yes," said Damian simply, and they both fell back into deep thought.

With another burst of happiness, Alexander suddenly became conscious again of their nudity and remembered that at last he could dare ask about the secret country, but there was something else he was confused about and wanted to know even more badly.

"Damian, is it really true there's a law telling people they can't have sex until they're sixteen?" asked Alexander.

"Yes," said Damian sadly, though a little relieved that Alexander already knew. "I'm afraid it is. If we were found out, I would get sent away from here. I could even go to prison."

"But it's so unfair there's a law like that. It's just none of anybody else's business! What do they know about you and me?" The injustice of people he did not know having the right to tell him what he could or could not do with his own body rankled with him so much that a sense of moral triumph was added to his fulfilment, but it did not relieve his indignation. "Why should I have to wait until I'm sixteen for something I badly need now?"

"Actually you can only sleep with a woman when you're sixteen. You're not allowed to sleep with a man until you're twenty-one."

"But it's incredible. That's so old!" he said disgustedly, then he remembered that today Damian was twenty-three. "I didn't mean..." he began, but then he caught Damian's smile of understanding and they both laughed. "But why does anyone want a law like that?"

"They would say that you're not old enough to consent, that you don't know enough about it, so somebody older might persuade you to do things you wouldn't like."

"But it's not true. I did know enough to feel sure I would like it, and I was right."

"Well, I agree that anyone who met *you* and said you didn't know your own mind when you said you did would have to be either stupid or deliberately pig-headed, but they would say that other boys your age are not so sure what they want."

"Oh come on. I'm sure any of my friends, if someone asked them to go to bed with them, would know whether they wanted to or not, at least once they'd thought about it."

"Well, I'm certainly not trying to defend the law. If I'd thought it might be wrong to sleep with you, that you might get hurt, then I wouldn't have. I'm just trying to explain how they think. They would say that not all boys are like you and your friends. There are some who are backward or ignorant who could be fooled into thinking they wanted something that they didn't really."

"I find that hard to believe, but even if it's true, it doesn't justify stopping me when I do know what I want."

"I agree, but unfortunately they think it does, especially nowadays. It's like the new law that you have to wear seat-belts in the front of cars. If you are going for a slow drive down country lanes, you are no longer allowed to decide for yourself that the pleasure of not feeling constrained is worth the minuscule risk of getting injured. Or, … tell me, when you were at prep school, were you allowed to climb trees?"

"I don't think I ever tried. Actually, yes, I do remember a friend being blown up for climbing one once."

"Exactly. That's how a friend told me it is now. He said that no schools can allow it any more in case a child falls. You see, when I was at prep school, we were allowed to and I'm pretty sure no boy ever hurt himself. Even if he had, everyone would just have said that was part of life and growing up and learning how to do things without hurting yourself. But nowadays, safety is everything, and happiness and freedom must always give way to it."

There was a long pause then. Damian felt subdued, while Alexander was lost in his thoughts.

"It still doesn't make sense," Alexander suddenly said animatedly. "Supposing you were my big brother instead of my lover …" The novelty of using the word to describe what Damian now was to him stopped him in his tracks. They had both been so absorbed in their discussion that their recent joy had slipped to the backs of their minds. They both smiled, dizzy with happiness at the reminder of how their lives had changed.

"Just supposing you were my brother," continued Alexander after another pause, "and instead of taking me to your bed, you took me skiing, no one would object to that would they? Even though they knew that I could very easily break a leg skiing and possibly even get killed. Nor would they make much fuss about my consent. Even if I'd been reluctant to go initially and you'd had to convince me that it would be fun, they'd think that was fine as long as I wanted to go in the end. They would just think what a good brother you were to take me. And if I'd never been before and didn't know exactly what it'd be like, everyone would think it much better that you were an experienced skier of twenty-three who could help me avoid getting hurt rather than another fourteen-year-old. So why all the fuss about sex, which brings far more happiness?"

271

"I don't know," said Damian finally. "You're right. I haven't explained it." He wondered wistfully why indeed people couldn't share Alexander's simple acceptance of sex and be happy. Why did they look at it so negatively? Why did they consider only the possible harm of accepting it and never the harm of avoiding it when it could be bringing so much good, so much love and joy? Or was it fear of happiness itself? He was still puzzling over it when Alexander asked his other burning question.

"Damian. Have you heard of a country where no one wears clothes?"

"I've heard of primitive tribes that don't, but not whole countries."

"Well, Rupert has some pictures of people who definitely look European walking along beaches, swimming, sailing and playing other sports and all totally naked. I'm sure they can't be primitive tribes, but they don't look at all embarrassed about being naked. They just look happy and free."

"I think you'll find they're nudists, people who go on holidays to camps where they don't have to wear clothes. There's a funny depiction of a nudist club in one of the *Carry On* films, but it didn't look nearly as impressive as what you're describing. I doubt Rupert's pictures can have been taken in England. I've heard there's a lot more of that sort of thing in some European countries, but I'm not sure where exactly."

"How does one find out?"

"I don't know, but I'm sure I could. I take it you want to go there?" said Damian with a smile.

"I would if I could go with you," replied Alexander shyly. He hesitated, then his enthusiasm took over. "If you could see the pictures, you'd understand. The people look so carefree. Can you imagine how fantastic it would feel if we could be like we are now on a beautiful beach and other people were too and no one minded?"

"All right, you have me intrigued now. I've no idea how or when it might be possible, but I'll definitely find out more about it."

"Do you think that in a country where people were that free, they'd still mind about us loving each other?"

272

"I don't know," said Damian with a pensive sigh.

As they had chatted on, both of them had moved around the room. From time to time, Alexander sat in his lap, glorying in the constant availability of physical intimacy, then he would lie back with his head resting on the sofa's arm, so that he could look into Damian's eyes as they spoke. It was then that Damian thought he found what it was that imparted the special bloom that made a well-favoured pubescent boy's skin so exquisitely comely, apart from its delicate texture and high Renoiresque colour. Though the only obviously visible hair on his body was the soft little mound above his cock, on close observation there were extremely fine, colourless little hairs on much of his body that added to the silkiness of his skin's texture.

Often when one or the other of them grew animated, he would stand up and pace around. Every time that Alexander did this and turned away from him, Damian found his gaze drawn longingly towards his exquisitely curvaceous little bottom. After all, so many forbidden things had already been done, there could not be much harm in merely thinking about what made a boy's behind so enticing. Even proportionately, it was much smaller and more shapely than a woman's. Though it curved delightfully outwards behind, a boy's hips were barely wider than his waist, which gave his bottom the effect of being also much rounder and more delicate than a man's or woman's. He did not remember being especially excited by Dashka's bottom, though it was as perfect as the rest of her figure in its obviously feminine way. Nor could he imagine having any desire to penetrate it. Allowing himself though to imagine fully for the first time what it would be like to slide right into the warmth between Alexander's firm, tender, little buttocks, he realised it was the most exciting thought he could conjure up, mixed guiltily as it was with horror of what Alexander would think of him if he knew.

Suddenly he became aware that he was fully erect again and, knowing the specific cause, became flustered. Alexander giggled happily when he saw Damian's newly heightened excitement. He took him by the hand and led him to the bed, where he lay down on his back and pressed his thighs together, his own cock now stiff with anticipation.

273

The next day, they had all afternoon together. After their first round of love-making, Alexander brought up another question that had evidently been very much on his mind.

"Damian, do you know about the Rosebery Prize?"

"Only that it's the lower-boy history prize and very prestigious. I never tried for it myself."

"Tell me honestly, would it be pointless for me to try for it?"

"No. Why should it?"

"Aren't prizes like that almost always won by tugs?" asked Alexander using the slang word for the scholars in College.

"True, but not always always, and as I've said before, I think you're as intelligent as them and could have been one of them if you'd tried as hard in all your subjects as in the ones you like."

"Also, it's open to all lower boys. What hope could I have against tugs in D?" he asked, and though he did still feel daunted, he could not suppress his happiness at Damian's encouragement.

"Hmm. I don't deny it would be a gigantic challenge, but why not try if you'd like to? Much depends though on whether you're really interested in exactly what you'd be writing about."

"That's just the thing. One of the ten questions to choose from is about Alexander the Great. Otherwise I'd never have even thought about entering for it."

"That is a fantastic stoke of fortune!" exclaimed Damian, suddenly electrified. "You must certainly go for it!" He stood up. "What is the exact question?"

"Why did Alexander the Great inspire men so much?"

Damian began pacing about, collecting his thoughts for a minute, while Alexander watched patiently. The invitation to try for the prize and the choice of questions had been posted on his house notice-board early in the Half and time was now running out, but initially he had not thought he had a chance as a non-scholar in F and he had simply felt a pained regret that one of the questions was so much to his taste. When his friendship with Damian had begun, he had been tempted to ask him what he thought of him having a go, but he had held back for fear of coming across as presumptuous suggesting that he might have a chance. Then he had forgotten all about it until yesterday.

274

"I think one needs three things to write a superlatively powerful essay," said Damian. "The first is to have a subject that interests one passionately. If you are not really interested, you will not be able to interest anyone else, and if you don't believe strongly in your own conclusions, you won't be able to convince anyone else. You have all that. You are passionately interested in Alexander the Great and you do believe strongly in his greatness. Secondly, one needs to be able to write clearly and beautifully, as you have already shown you can in 'It is Better to Travel Hopefully than to Arrive.' Thirdly, one needs to apply vigorously logical reasoning, and I know you're capable of that too, so you have everything needed to win. Tell me what story about him inspires you the most."

"Probably the taming of his horse Boukephalos."

"Yes, I've heard that one," said Damian. "But tell me why."

"Because he showed such courage. Though he was only thirteen, instead of just listening to the opinions of his father and the others who should have known best as to whether Boukephalos was a good horse, he made his own judgement. Then he dared to stand up alone for what he believed against the anger of his father for his presumption and the laughter of the courtiers for his folly. And by taming the horse, he proved he was right and not presumptuous or foolish. He was someone people should always have faith in."

"That's brilliantly explained," said Damian impressed. "So what I would suggest you do is go through all the things Alexander did that you think inspired people and decide how they were inspiring or which inspiring quality they demonstrated. You have named courage as one. Can you think of any other examples of that?"

"Yes, lots and lots. For example, when he was besieging a city in India and he thought his soldiers were being half-hearted in the attack, so he ran up one of the ladders and jumped down the other side to fight the enemy in their city all on his own. He was very nearly killed then, but it made his soldiers follow him as hard as they could and capture the city. Or when he was leading his army home through the Gedrosian desert and his soldiers were beginning to die of thirst, and one of them brought him the first water they had

275

found in days in a helmet, and he refused it until enough could be found for all his followers."

"Good. Now you need some other inspiring qualities with examples of them. Tell me another good story about him."

"What about Alexander and Diogenes?"

"I don't know that one."

"Well, Diogenes was a philosopher who lived in Corinth and was famous for his independence. Alexander went there to be made leader of all the Greeks after he'd defeated those who rebelled after his father's death. Lots of famous people came to see him, but Alexander was disappointed that Diogenes didn't, so he went to see him instead. He found him sitting in the sun and asked him if there was anything he could do for him. Diogenes said "Yes, could you stand aside and stop blocking my sunlight?" When Alexander went back with his friends, they all mocked Diogenes, but Alexander said "You can say what you like, but if I were not Alexander, I would be Diogenes.""

"You're making me understand very clearly why you feel so strongly about him. You just have to do the same with the reader of your essay. Why do you think his behaviour with Diogenes is inspiring?"

"I suppose because it shows that when he'd become a great man, he could still appreciate the qualities of others who most people thought weren't important and he didn't let rudeness to himself blind him to what really mattered."

"Alexander, you really don't need any help from me. The material for your essay is already there in your head. I promise you that if you try hard enough, think about it, organise it carefully and perhaps bring in some references and quotes from the original sources to back you up, you could win the prize," urged Damian excitedly.

He had not mentioned that as far as he knew such prestigious prizes were invariably won by Oppidan Scholars, if not by tugs. He knew that all the runners-up for the prize would be declared in order and he genuinely believed in Alexander's brilliance. He was therefore determined that he try for it and at least come near enough winning to be officially noticed, and all under his own steam. After that, the boy would have to be willing to believe that the sky was the limit to what he could achieve.

Alexander quickly realised the greatest benefit of sex, beyond the sheer pleasure and joy of it, was the loss of inhibition with one's lover, both physical and social. In both ways, he was already far less inhibited with Damian than he had been with his mother, the one who had given him the most love before, and that could only have come about through sex. It was hard to feel embarrassed by anything physical with Damian after such intense intimacy, and he availed himself to the full of the possibilities this opened up. He knew himself always to have been an affectionate child, but only now did he realise just how badly he had needed physical affection. He never tired of the sheer joy of being able to sit in Damian's lap and know he was wanted there.

He also felt freer to be himself with Damian than he had ever felt with anyone before, and though this loss of social inhibition sprung from his confidence that Damian loved him, it was sex that had sealed that confidence.

If there was one fly in the ointment, it was his feeling that their love had not been consummated in the way he understood it could be. He longed to belong to Damian as a matter of physical fact, which he felt instinctively could only be accomplished one way, by a physical fusion in which the lord of his heart would through his dominant role become lord of his body too. It might hurt him and he had no idea if it would bring him any physical pleasure, but that hardly detracted from his longing for it. If the physical pleasure were all Damian's, his own eagerness for it would enable him to prove his love, and giving to the one he loved promised greater fulfilment than anything.

Later on the second day of their love-making, Damian lovingly stroked his bottom and ran a finger lightly along his crevice, making him tremble with excitement and anticipation, only to take him between his thighs again. He was badly disappointed for a few moments, but dared not say anything. He was not nearly sure enough Damian saw things the same way as him. If he did not want it, then it was presumably because he thought the act distasteful. The uncertainty as to whether Damian desired him that way was thus his one remaining cause for inhibition.

Alexander's inhibitions with Damian were in any case breaking down so fast that every day he found new questions for him that had lain submerged under his conscious thought and now came bubbling to the surface. He finally brought up the one that had hurt him most, that he had tried not to think about because he did not know the answer and dreaded what it might be.

"Damian, do you think girls should have sex too before they get married?"

"If they're sure they want to," replied Damian, looking up from his desk to see Alexander standing tensely. He realised at once that the question had not been lightly asked. "Who's told you they shouldn't?"

"My mother," said Alexander shakingly, and Damian reined in his high spirits at once, readying himself to guide them over thin ice. "Well, sort of anyway. She said I should marry a girl who had kept herself for me if I wanted to be truly loved."

"And do you think she thought you should keep yourself for marriage too?" asked Damian, wondering if this was why Alexander seemed upset.

"No, I don't think so, not necessarily anyway. My brother Andrew lived with a girl for three years and then with another one for another year before he married her, and she never seemed to disapprove of what he did. But I could tell she thought the girls were really making a mistake, that they were letting themselves down. She was very fond of the first one, so it made her think it was a bit of a pity." He fell silent, but Damian knew there was more. "But she did also say she'd introduce me to some girls my age who were children of her friends, but that they'd definitely not want to do anything with me, she meant sex, and she asked me if I understood that me wanting to meet them should have nothing to with that, that I'd have to wait until I was much older for that."

"So what did you say?"

"I didn't say anything," answered Alexander miserably. "That's just the thing. I couldn't think what to say. You see, I wanted so desperately to sleep with a girl. Now it doesn't matter much, because I have you. I mean I'd still love to sleep with a beautiful girl, but I don't mind now if I have to wait a few years. But I did mind then, so I couldn't just say I accepted it'd be years and years before it could happen. Can you understand that?"

"Yes, easily."

"Well, I didn't know if she would. Maybe she'd think I was vile to feel that way. Anyway, I didn't dare, but I couldn't lie to her either. So I said nothing. Then she said I could explain my feelings to her, that she just wanted me to be happy, but I still couldn't think what to say. Then she got up and went, and she looked so sad. I think she thought I didn't love her or trust her. And that was the last conversation about anything that mattered that I ever had with her. I thought I'd get a chance to make it up to her, but she died a few days later."

Some tears escaped as he said those last words, and he had to wipe them away. Damian went to him at once and held him tightly until his sobs had subsided, then he drew him towards the sofa and they sat down. He gently stroked his cheek, then took him by the shoulders to command his attention.

"Alexander. Listen to me. You must never think like that again, because it's not true. You did love and trust your mother completely, didn't you?"

"Yes."

"Then she knew it, because your feelings show. I promise that no one who knows you well would doubt your sincerity and she knew you better than anyone. Just being a little sad that you found it hard to explain something very awkward to her doesn't mean she doubted your love. Okay?"

"Okay."

"I don't believe she would have thought you were vile to want so badly to sleep with a girl either. She had three sons, for goodness sake, she must have known what boys are like, and you said she didn't blame Andrew. It sounds clear though that if she'd had a daughter, she would have discouraged her from sleeping around before marriage, so very likely her friends are the same with their daughters. I should think that's why she tried to warn you against hoping for anything from them."

Alexander had not thought of it that way. He felt very much better, suddenly relieved of a burden that, hard as he had tried to conceal it, had been wearing him down for months.

279

"And do you think my mother was right that girls should keep themselves for marriage?" he asked after a long pause, his former tone of anguish now changed to one of lively curiosity.

"It's very hard for a girl to do that nowadays, at least in England, unless perhaps she marries soon after leaving school, because all her friends, as well as young men taking an interest in her, will expect her not to. Not forgetting how fantastic sex is too."

"But if she did, would it be better?" Alexander was fascinated, as no one apart from his mother had ever discussed such questions with him. He knew of course that Christianity disapproved of pre-marital sex, but he did not think that explained his mother's viewpoint.

"Yes, I suppose so, usually anyway, as long as she still found just as good a husband. I suspect your mother was right that in that case she would love her husband more and he would be likely to love her more in return, and they would both be happier, which would of course be far better for their children too.."

"So in that case, you think we should marry virgins?" asked Alexander with a shy smile.

"That would certainly be my ideal. The trouble is there are so many nice girls now that aren't and it's harder to find nice ones that are, at least for the right reasons."

"Is it just because they've invented the pill that girls don't wait any more?

"Yes, I think so really. The trouble is that a lot of modern advances make people unhappy by strongly tempting them to do things that ultimately harm them. To give another example, there are now huge numbers of people in rich countries like America who are making themselves fat, ugly and unhealthy by eating too much, and millions of others who only avoid it by tormenting themselves with diets, so I wonder whether people weren't happier when they didn't have to make that choice, when they had to put some physical work into getting their food and then ate what they had found without worry."

"Yes, I see what you mean. But why should women become less likely to love their husbands if they have slept with someone else before? I really can't believe that when I get married, I'll love my wife any less because I've slept with you."

"No, neither can I. I think men and women have different roles, so they can't behave the same way and remain in harmony with their own natures. A woman has babies, and if she and her child are going to have a good chance of being well looked after, both she and the child's father need to know for sure who he is, which would be impossible if she were promiscuous. So women have evolved a monogamous nature. In contrast, there's never any doubt who a baby's mother is. As long as a man has got the means of supporting all his children, human survival is best ensured by him having lots, which would obviously be much harder if he only ever felt inclined to sleep with one person."

"But isn't there a contradiction if boys feel the urge to get lots of girls to sleep with them, and girls feel they should refuse them unless they're getting married?"

"Yes, but then many of nature's masterpieces are balancing acts between opposing forces."

Some days, when Alexander got to Damian's flat before him, he would undress and have a bath. If Damian had still not come back, he would hide naked behind something and wait for Damian to find him, in titillating evocation of their first day as lovers, but usually they waited until they were together to undress. It was more exciting that way. But once they had rid themselves of their clothes, they never put them back on until Alexander had to leave, no matter how many times they had made love. When their lust was sated, then their nudity stopped for the moment having a sexual dimension, but became to them an important expression of their freedom from shame or embarrassment, much as Alexander had dreamed when he saw Rupert's nude pictures, as well as allowing them to take unrestrained aesthetic delight in the beauty nature had bestowed on them. Damian never tired of simple, visual absorption of Alexander's naked beauty. Sooner or later, though, the delight would become more than purely aesthetic. Desire would creep back into Damian's admiration of the boy and Alexander never failed to be turned on by the signs of it.

On half-days, Alexander always came straight to Damian's flat after lunch, but on the three days of the week when there were afternoon divs, there was an hour-long interval after lunch called After Two when boys were supposed to be in their rooms doing their EW.s.

"Can't I come here then too?" asked Alexander the evening he finished his essay for the Rosebery Prize. "Mr. Hodgson never checks to see that we're in our rooms." A silent pause followed. "It would be so much easier, because then I could just leave my books and things here all the time," he added, but caught Damian's look and they both smiled, acknowledging the better but unspoken reason. After a whole night and morning apart, neither of them found it easy to think straight by two o'clock.

"On one condition," replied Damian finally. "That on those days, you go back to messing with your old friends before coming on here."

"Why don't you want me here then as well?" he asked, surprised.

"I do want you here then and all the time, but even more I want you to spend a bit of time with your old friends too. You have time for everything. If you've already been here during After Two, it won't hurt to postpone coming back for another half an hour. Please believe me. In the end, you'll be happier if you keep them as well as having me. I bet they miss you."

Damian turned out to be right, as usual. Rupert and Simon had missed him, as became evident from the alacrity with which they welcomed him back. They had not got on particularly well in his absence. They had only ever come together to mess with Alexander.

Sometimes when Alexander lay on his stomach or his side, Damian would caress the smooth, soft skin of his small, curvaceous buttocks with his hand and move a finger longingly along the crevice between them. It was not just because it was all so exquisitely lovely. He now ached with longing to fuck him, but he could never bring himself even to mention it as something that a man could do to a boy, despite all their talk of Greek love. Though he was as happy as he had ever been, he thought increasingly that he would never achieve absolute fulfilment or the summit of bliss except inside his beloved, and he could not help hoping just a little that Alexander might one day guess what he longed for from his worshipful caresses and somehow come to like the idea.

When Alexander finished reading *The Persian Boy* and lent it to him, the first thing he did was to seek out the sex scenes, fervently hoping at least one of them would describe clearly what Greeks did to boys, but the writer was reticent and left the specifics to the reader's imagination. If only Alexander knew about it, he would at least not be severely surprised that that was what his lover wanted. As it was, he was too frightened that Alexander would be shocked by the act at the same time as guessing that was what he wanted.

Alexander was passing Barne's Pool on his way to Damian's flat after lunch one day when he looked across and saw Miranda and her group. The last few times this had happened, he had carried on his way unnoticed by her. He was still much too excited by his imminent arrival at Damian's flat to want to delay it for any reason. Sometimes he had caught the eye of one of her group, but they had always looked away without acknowledging him, evidently only too glad to be rid of their juvenile competitor.

This time, however, it was Miranda herself who caught his eye and loudly called out "Hi Alexander!" in her sexy, girlish voice. He crossed over, reminding himself that today he had the whole afternoon ahead to spend with Damian. It was a shame to give up for no reason what he had built with Miranda. For the first time, he felt oddly calm with her. She still seemed just as desirable and he still thought it would be fantastic to sleep with her, but he found the desperate urgency he had felt before was all gone, and he even felt rather ashamed that he had seen her in such purely sexual terms.

Miranda was talking quite animatedly about a film she had seen on television the evening before, and the others were listening politely.

"Oh, you're talking about *Paper Moon*, aren't you?" asked Alexander excitedly.

"Yes, that's right! You saw it too?"

283

"Not last night, but I have before. It's definitely one of my favourite films.

"Me too," enthused Miranda, giving him now her undivided attention. "Didn't you think the ending was so moving?"

"Yes. It was so depressing when Moze dropped Addie off with that awful, cloying aunt who treated her like a little child, and such a relief when she ran away to be with him again."

"I know. As soon as the film ended, my father asked me if I'd have stayed with Aunt Billie, and I answered "no way" without even thinking about it. I felt so jealous of Addie though, being so free and having adventures with a man who treated her as an equal."

"That's *exactly* how I felt about it too," said Alexander, looking at her with new respect, while reflecting that with Damian he had now found just that, except that, unfairly, they couldn't go around together openly.

It came home to him then what a very nice and interesting girl Miranda was. Suddenly remembering the other boys standing around in awkward silence, he felt a rush of sympathy for her. He felt certain now that she was still a virgin. He imagined how hurt she would be if one day she were really to give herself to one of the boys who lusted after her and then find how shallow his feelings for her were.

He felt he now understood such things much more clearly and he could see that the boys who chased Miranda had two motives. Some of them were drawn mainly by lust, but for most of them it was the appeal of being seen as cool and trendy. One could tell the difference by whether a boy spent most of the time ogling Miranda or whether he kept glancing at passers-by to see who was noticing him. In either case, he felt sure that she could not rely on any of them to bind themselves to her if she let them have their way.

He realised that, much as he would still like to sleep with Miranda, there was no way he could bear to commit himself to her now or anytime soon either. He had Damian, and needed him far more, and even when he was grown up at university, there were adventures he wanted to have before tying himself down. He hoped that, like Damian, sooner or later he would meet a beautiful girl with whom he could go to bed without fear of letting her down, but he did not think Miranda was such a one, not yet at least.

The love of man and boy was such an easy solution to the dilemma posed by his mother. Girls might spoil their chances of finding true love if they slept around, whereas he was sure his chances could not be thus affected. Boys needed sex so badly as soon as they reached puberty, and they needed to experience it without having to make a lifelong commitment for which they were not ready. What could possibly be better then than a love affair with someone more experienced that must by its very nature eventually be grown out of?

When he excused himself from Miranda's company, he felt sure from her smile that she did not simply like him, but that they had at last established some kind of understanding, the beginnings of a bond of real friendship, unlike anything she had with the other boys.

After that he stopped by to chat once or twice a week. On other days, when he was in more of a hurry to be with Damian, he simply smiled and gave her a little wave if he caught her eye, and she did likewise.

Alexander sat on the bed shuddering with pleasure, his left hand on Damian's shoulder and his right on top of his bent head, as his lover knelt between his knees, intent on his amorous task. He knew he was about to come. He felt a great fountain welling up within him, still dammed but ready to burst forth. It was their seventh day of lovemaking, but Alexander was still surprised by how much more intense and above all prolonged his ejaculations into Damian's throat were compared with those induced by wanking. He wondered whether time slowed down because of the intensity of the pleasure, but even if it did, he was sure they took longer too. After his first hot fluid shot forth, he seemed to have time both to relish the continued working of Damian's lips and tongue on his shaft and to anticipate the ecstasy of his second spurt before it came, and then, when it did, to repeat the same pleasure again and repeatedly again until he was drained. Then Damian took his cock out of his mouth and lovingly licked it clean of the last drops of nectar.

He lay back on their bed for a few minutes, happy, relaxed, and, as usual after fellatio, momentarily exhausted, while Damian lay beside him, an arm around him, their legs intertwined. With each passing day, his suspicion that Damian wanted to go all the way with him had grown until he was nearly sure. Since Damian's manual play had first suggested interest in his bottom, his strokes had grown longer and more playful, the finger pressing a little deeper into his crevice, back and forth, but still he showed no sign of wanting to explore it with his cock. Alexander would have offered himself quite plainly if only he could be absolutely certain that was what Damian longed for, but he could not bear to take the risk of suggesting something that might possibly be distasteful in his eyes.

He stirred a little when he felt his excitement reviving and watched Damian rise up in response. Soon his lover was kneeling between his feet, his cock standing erect against his stomach, its head hiding his navel, and glistening with baby oil. He was still in awe of its massive man size. Damian bent down and kissed him gently in the mouth, then rose up again. Any moment he would stretch out over him, rest his lower arms under Alexander's shoulders to support his weight, his cock would descend between Alexander's warm thighs and he would begin his gentle, regular thrusts. Alexander anticipated the thrilling tingle along his perineum, especially each time the cock drew near his opening. If only it would go a little nearer. If only Damian would go right in, but even if he wanted to, he wouldn't be able suddenly to do that, because he was lying on his back. Unless...

He felt a sudden burst of courage and decided that what he could not or dared not offer in words, he dared to make a clear offer of with his body. He took hold of his legs under his knees and drew them back towards his chest, knowing that this would expose the cleavage between his buttocks to Damian's full view.

Damian was astonished. He felt a thrill of excitement surge through him at the unexpected invitation. He could see the tiny slit of an opening, just a little rosier in colour than the rest of the ivory-coloured crevice, the utterly smooth hairlessness and delicacy of it all contrasting with his own manhood like black and white. He had worried a little what it might look like, but now he could see that every intimate detail of Alexander was erotically enticing, and he was more excited than ever in his life. His cock was only a foot way from the little flower-like orifice and throbbing to accept the invitation to enter, like a tormented soul suddenly before the gates of heaven, but he forced himself to tear his eyes away, sat back and sighed deeply. He was deeply moved that Alexander loved him so much that he was willing to give him that, to give him everything. He felt a lump in his throat and almost sobbed with emotion. But nevertheless he could not accept if there was any chance it was self-sacrificial, offered only to please him.

"Alexander, are you really sure you want that?"

Alexander put his legs back down. He was nearly sure that Damian longed desperately for consummation of their love, but his pride and his anticipated happiness with the intended gift of his virginity craved certainty before admission of his own longing.

"Will you promise to tell me the truth?" he said looking intently into Damian's eyes.

"Yes. Of course."

"If you knew I really wanted it, how much would you want it?"

Damian thought for a moment. The only answer he could give was the plain truth.

"If you really wanted it and I knew you would like it too, I would want it more than anything in the world."

"Then I definitely want it," answered Alexander happily. Damian fell into silence, so after some moments, Alexander knelt before him and rested his head sideways on Damian's shoulder. He moved his left hand down to cradle his lover's balls, then slowly moved it up along the long, hard shaft. "Really. I am longing for it," he said, and Damian finally believed that Alexander's desire for it was for himself too, that their wishes and hopes were one. His excitement remounted. But one obstacle remained.

Such was the discrepancy in size that it was only the instinctiveness of his longing combined with his understanding it was the time-honoured means of consummation that made

287

him believe it even possible, and he feared it might not be easy. "It might hurt. I don't know," he said plainly.

"Try!" said Alexander, deciding that he did not care if it did. He wanted it too badly now that he was sure Damian did too, and his determination was unshakeable.

"You promise to tell me if it does?" said Damian gravely.

"Yes."

"Are you ..."

"Damian. I want it. My life is mine and this is my choice."

Alexander sat up and kissed Damian's lips, then lay back, and again drew back his legs, this time holding them firmly in place by clasping his arms round them..

Damian could still hardly believe what was happening. There really was nothing at all that he had ever wanted more than this and yet he had not dared to hope it would ever happen. Slowly he knelt down again, cupped the silky smooth buttocks in his hands, then gently parted them with his thumbs like a delicate fruit until he was able to nudge the head of his cock exactly into place, lightly nestled against the inviting little aperture. The boy moaned quietly. Then Damian straightened his arms, his hands flat on the bed either side of Alexander's shoulders, and pressed his cock forwards as gently as he was able. For about ten seconds nothing seemed to happen at all. Just as he became a little anxious that he might frustrate the consummation of their love by coming before he could gain entry, he sensed Alexander's sphincter yielding to him a tiny bit, then gradually faster, then suddenly his glans slid right in. He was firmly wedged inside Alexander's hot, tight passage. He gasped with ecstasy. Man and boy were one.

Alexander had felt just a delicious tingling sensation when Damian's cock had first nestled firmly in his opening, but as it began to make progress some pain had arisen and briefly but sharply intensified as it made its triumphant entry. He gasped loudly. Then Damian stopped quite still to make sure that Alexander was not hurt. Seeing the anxious look on his face, Alexander flashed a reassuring grin. The pain had receded surprisingly fast , and all he felt now was his own triumph that this man he loved was in him, that he was truly Damian's boy.

Damian was relishing every second, despite his enduring feeling of disbelief that something so wonderful could really be happening. He now resumed his progress into Alexander, but again very, very slowly, to be sure of not hurting him. As their stomachs drew close, he could feel Alexander's stiff cock pressed against him like a hot rod. Finally, he was in up to the hilt and could feel his warm balls resting deliciously against the cool smoothness of the boy's buttocks.

As Damian had pushed further and ever further into him, Alexander had began to feel that his breath was being squeezed out of him. Perhaps it was not possible for him to take it all. It was just too big. He clenched his teeth, fearful he might dissuade Damian by crying out, then intermittently began to gasp for breath. When, however, Damian came to a rest, his breathing slowed down again and soon his anxiety subsided into first relief and then triumph. The awesome knowledge that every inch of that great long shaft was now inside him thrilled him to the core.

After a pause of a few moments, Damian pulled back and back, then slowly tunnelled back into him. This time, though Alexander still felt a little breathless, he knew he could take it and was relaxed enough to begin to feel an entirely new and unforeseen kind of thrill, physical as well as emotional, which increased every time his lover drew out and journeyed back in. After several thrusts, he forgot the pain, relaxed his fingers, which had been digging into his legs, and thought only of the bliss. Each time Damian slowed to a halt after pulling back, Alexander felt his whole body crying out for his return and gasped with pleasure as he did. Then he realised he was going to come any moment, and as his lover's tool began its next descent into him, his crystal liquid shot across his chest in two long spurts followed by several shorter ones.

Damian had felt Alexander's sphincter as a tight, hot band sliding deliciously up and down his shaft, as he slowly thrust in and out of the boy. As Alexander approached his climax, it gave his cock a series of quick convulsive hugs, jolts of added pleasure. Never having possessed a boy before, he did not realise what they signified, until he saw the ensuing shots of creamy fluid from his beloved's sweet tool. His heart soared with joy, for he had not known this would happen, and then he felt his own climax coming. He fell on the boy as he felt himself pumping his liquid love into him in long sweet surges of pleasure. They rested still for a minute in calm elation, then Damian raised his head from its position beside Alexander's and they kissed lovingly and at length, both their tongues moving gently. All this time, Damian's cock was still resting in Alexander's soft, warm passage, its juices spent. Finally, he withdrew, lay down alongside the boy and clasped his body to his own long and tenderly.

They lay together in silent wonder. Damian pondered the enigma that he had just performed elatedly and without the slightest physical qualms an act he had thought of as repugnant until he had imagined doing it to Alexander. Real experience had finally also taught him that he had been right to have no qualms. It had been pure in its exquisite joy, for it had brought him the greatest physical and emotional fulfilment he had ever known and he felt sure that the beautiful boy nestling quietly in his arms felt the same way.

The distaste he had once felt for what he now knew to be the supreme act of love between a man and a boy was quite unfounded. It could be called a misunderstanding except that he suspected the horrid falsehoods about it, that it was necessarily at all painful for the boy or unclean for the man, had been deliberately perpetrated by early Christians and fostered down the centuries as a practical reinforcement of Christianity's violent rejection of the ancient world's happy acceptance of pleasure in general and boy-love in particular.

He also knew that it was an entirely natural act. This followed logically from his earlier realisation that pederasty was a natural kind of love. It was what nature impelled men to want from boys so that they could be bound to them. To put it with the bluntness that clarity called for, the sexual instinct of men was to fuck, so if it was natural to desire a boy, it must also be natural to want to fuck him in the only way there was of doing so. Therefore it must also be natural to find a boy's bottom especially attractive, which explained why he had found Alexander's so. He had been impelled by natural selection to

290

appreciate that it was one of nature's most exquisite masterpieces.

This also explained why, though he had found Dashka extremely desirable and her lovely bottom an integral part of her beauty, its shape had not aroused him as Alexander's did. Nature's purpose in demanding that men desire women was procreation and the raising of a family. Women's wide-hipped bottoms were designed precisely for that purpose and not so that men would want to do something with them that would thwart rather than further it.

Alexander's thoughts were less precise, but deeper and dreamier. He felt solemnly sure he would never see the world the same way again, without being sure why. Perhaps it was that he knew he had come as close to another human being as was possible and he felt thereby at last complete. He thought about it on and off all through the rest of the day, and fell into peaceful slumber that night, feeling he had accomplished something that could never be taken away from him and that his life must always be the richer for it.

All through the next morning, he was still in a trance. He felt a fierce pride that Damian's seed was within him, that he had been consecrated to his god. As he walked through the street on his way back to his house during Chambers, he wondered whether everyone else could see the change in him. If only they could be told.

"I have a lover! I am Damian's boy!" he longed to be able to shout out with elation. Just imagine how fantastic it would be if they had lived in ancient Greece, and could walk hand in hand, acknowledging all the friendly and admiring glances, and ignoring the envious ones without worry!

Suddenly, his reverie was interrupted by Julian coming up to him from behind. It was strange how he popped up out of nowhere. The same thing had happened only yesterday. Since that time they met in Judy's Passage, Julian always greeted him when they passed one another, and though Alexander still resented him, he was too happy to be cold and always said "Hi" back. Yesterday, Julian had told him a story about another boy as they walked back. Alexander had not really wanted to listen, but in the end it had been funny and they had ended up chatting in a quite friendly way. Thinking about it afterwards, he told himself it was mean and pointless to be unfriendly. He remembered Julian standing up for him against Cowburn. He still had the ancient coin too. He would never be able to respect him again, but he could at least be friendly.

Julian seemed keen to chat again now, so Alexander started to tell him something funny that had just happened in his classics div with Mr. Trotter, when suddenly he saw Damian right ahead. He wondered if he could say something to him, but felt constrained by Julian's presence, though he could not help smiling with all the happiness he felt. As he looked into Damian's equally smiling eyes, he was relieved to read in them that Damian understood another boy was with him. He wondered if Damian guessed who Julian was.

"Who was that?" asked Julian.

"Mr. Cavendish. He's my English beak. He's incredibly nice." It felt strange talking about Damian as if he were just a beak. Just mentioning him made him feel proud and happy.

"Oh, I see," replied Julian, looking oddly put out.

When he saw Damian later, Alexander asked him if he had noticed the boy he was talking to when they passed each other in the morning.

"Yes, I saw there was someone with you, though I'm not sure if I really took in his face. Why?"

"It was Julian Smith."

"I see. So have you gone back to being friends?"

"No way! I don't know if I should even talk to him, but he's suddenly started coming up to me in the street and talking to me as if he'd like to be friends again. I'm not sure what I should do."

"Hmm. I know he doesn't deserve anything from you, and there's no reason to spend any time with him if you don't feel like it, but it can't do any harm just to be friendly. After all, we have everything now, don't we? You can afford to be generous."

"Yes, that's just what I was thinking too, but I wasn't sure. I'll do as you suggest."

That week, Alexander received his Order Cards for the third quarter of the Half. Hodgson was astonished by how vastly improved they were, even though they had been heralded for three weeks by almost daily Show Ups for his E.W.s. He was now top of his div in four of his six subjects. Mr. Trotter suggested that he was heading towards a distinction in Classics Trials and Mr. Banks, his Maths beak, said he had never seen such sudden improvement.

Hodgson was genuinely delighted. If Alexander kept it up, perhaps he really might get a distinction, and he told him so. This sudden academic flowering of a boy who had certainly been promising, but never seemed likely to be one of the school's greatest scholars, would reflect on him very well indeed. It was most timely too, as the only Oppidan Scholar presently in his house was leaving at the end of the year. The housemaster had worried a little that he should have been paying more attention to Alexander considering his bereavement; this Half he had not visited the boy in his room any more than the others in F and so he had had no idea how he was now coping. Clearly though, his slight anxieties were unfounded and his approach had been the best one.

The boy could certainly not have put in so much hard work if he had been wasting his time with Smith. Thank goodness he had found out about that and acted promptly, or none of this would have happened. It could have been very awkward though if Smith had not been so compliant. What could he do to reward him? Then he remembered that that evening, Anthony Burrows would be coming to see him about the upcoming election to the Library. Three boys in C were to be chosen. As housemaster, he decided who was eligible for election and could at his discretion control the outcome by fixing the number of votes or blackballs required in consultation with his house captain. Smith would after all be a good choice for the third one. He was obviously a sensible boy, and had never caused trouble before either.

By then, Alexander and the other essayists for the Rosebery Prize had received a summons to Lower School to hear who had won.

The large room was humming with subdued conversation when he arrived. His heart sank as he realised that for the first time he was in a minority not being dressed in the distinctive gown of a tug, or a King's Scholar as they were called formally. He recognised two of them from his divs, but otherwise there was no one in his block at all. The room was dominated by a group of tugs in D, who sat together at the front. He felt their eyes on him as he walked in and wondered if in their muttering they were mocking his presumption. Forlornly, he looked for a seat on his own a few rows back, where most of the other oppidans were. As he waited, he felt, for the first time since Damian had convinced him to try for the prize, that he had been silly thinking he stood a chance.

When everyone seemed to have arrived, Alexander estimated there must be over thirty boys. Perhaps they were not all contestants, for they had been told they could bring a friend along. He had wished terribly that Damian could come with him, though of course they both realised resignedly that there could be no question of thus putting their friendship on public display. Now he guessed that in fact the only boys who had really brought a friend along were the older tugs who expected at least to be named as runners-up, for surely not quite so many of that group could be essayists.

At last the Lower Man appeared with a kindly-looking man in a tweed jacket, whom he introduced as Professor Sawyer from Durham University, who had set the questions and judged the essays, and was now going to announce the winner and nine runners-up. They were to be named in reverse order, starting therefore with the tenth best essay.

"The winner should come up here when he is announced," continued the Lower Man "though he will not receive the £ 40 prize today. He will be summoned to see the Head Master for that later, and his name will be duly inscribed on the list in the Marten Library. Professor Sawyer...."

The professor cleared his throat with a grunt and adjusted his glasses, while arranging the papers before him. Then he made a short speech about the general quality of the essays, of which Alexander did not take much in.

"Please, please let me be the tenth," he thought, as everyone in the room looked up at the professor expectantly. It would be such a relief to have got some recognition for his effort and it would after all be quite an accomplishment, he thought, considering how intimidating the competition was.

"The tenth best effort is by Marsh KS," said the professor at last. He then proceeded quite fast through the list of names, saying just a sentence or two on each essay's merits and shortcomings. "Ninth is Pemberton,... eighth is Jones OS,... seventh is Bright KS,..." Alexander's heart sunk, each name coming like a new blow. When the professor pronounced Smithers KS to be sixth, Alexander decided he had only one, slender chance left, it was not worth hoping he might have made it to the top four.

"Fifth is Lumsden OS," continued the professor, but Alexander hardly heard what he said for a while, he was so disappointed. He had so badly wanted to prove himself worthy of Damian's faith in him. Perhaps it was after all best that he could not be here. He knew Damian would comfort him, but he would certainly be bitterly disappointed too. Alexander had probably been silly too thinking he might get a distinction in Trials.

"The runner-up is Goldwinkel KS" Alexander was just conscious of the professor saying. "He is being Sent up for Good for a brilliant analysis of the causes of the French Revolution, which takes in most of the important points." Alexander saw one of the tugs in the front row shake the hand of another one, a spindly and very spotty sixteen-year-old. Then the whole group of older tugs turned their heads to glance round the room at those behind them with puzzled expressions on their faces. Alexander had just guessed they were wondering who could possibly have beaten them, when the professor went on.

"And the winner is Aylmer, also Sent up for Good ...." Alexander's head swam deliriously for a moment and though he could hear the Professor was speaking, he did not take in his further comment. Then he saw the tug in F two seats away lean over and whisper urgently to him to go up to the slightly-raised dais.

He walked there in a trance. He was vaguely aware of the applause and of shaking the hands of the Lower Man and the professor, but in his mind he was already elsewhere. He was opening the door to Damian's flat and shouting to him "I won!" and watching his expression of incredulity give way to one of delight, and Damian was raising him up in a tight hug and swinging him slightly to and fro, and his heart was pounding with happiness.

And so it came to pass that afternoon.

The Summer Half was moving inexorably towards its close. When Damian and Alexander had been lovers for a fortnight, they realised they had barely another fortnight left. Their talk turned increasingly towards the summer holidays, which initially they were both dreading. Damian had a long-standing arrangement to spend three weeks in Siena, which he thought of cancelling, but decided not to when they discovered it would mostly coincide with the fortnight Alexander's father was taking him and his new family on holiday in Mallorca.

They would have loved to go to the continent together and seek out a bit of secret country, where they could stroll naked on beaches or hills during the day, unafraid of meeting anyone they knew, and lie in each other's arms at night. They looked too dissimilar to be brothers, but they could surely pass themselves off as half-brothers. They discussed the excuses Alexander could offer his father for asking for temporary care of his passport and for being away for at least a few days, but they could not think of anything that might not be checked up on, especially as Alexander had found that his prospective step-mother was nosy. It was far too risky.

They therefore limited their hopes to days they could spend together. They decided it was also too risky for Alexander to come to Damian's flat during the holidays. It would be too hard to explain the oddity of it to anyone who might recognise him. That really only left London. Alexander wished more fervently than ever that his father was not remarrying, for otherwise they could have spent daytimes in his home that would be as diametrically opposite as was imaginable to the lonely ones of the Easter holidays.

In the end, Damian decided the best solution was to confide in his best friend from Cambridge, Adrian Stafford, who was working in the City and had a little flat to himself in Fulham, not very far from Alexander's house. Adrian was broad-minded, easy-going and witty. He would definitely be surprised and might tease him mercilessly, but Damian was certain he would at least not betray their affair and thought there was an excellent chance he would let them use his flat for their trysts. It would probably rather appeal to his romantic imagination and his mischievous sense of fun. He had said he was coming down to Eton to spend an evening out with Damian before the end of the Half, so Damian steeled himself to tell him everything then.

Having settled on this plan, the holidays soon sounded far more appealing. Alexander would tell Janet he was spending the days in the London Library and instead he would meet up with Damian in Adrian's flat. Between their lovemaking, they would visit cinemas and museums. Thinking about it made Damian realise just how frustrated he had become that he had never been able to take Alexander out anywhere or show him anything beyond the narrow confines of his flat. At last he would be able to give of himself to the one he loved in ways he had always longed to, but never really had. In London, they would be free to go just about anywhere together. If they mischanced to run into anyone they knew, it would be easy to pretend they had just run into each other by luck. It would still be irritating they had to pretend at all, when they were both immensely proud of their love for one another, but it would be a big improvement in their freedom together. They could even go off into the country in Damian's car for walks and picnics. Maybe just once they could also take the risk of spending a night together, something they both craved. Adrian was bound to be away at some point and Alexander could surely claim at short notice to be sleeping over at a school friend's home without serious risk.

The three weeks apart was going to be very hard, but once they had realised the possibilities for the rest of the holidays, they began to long for them so much that Damian said they must restrain themselves from getting too carried away in their expectations, at least until he had confirmed Adrian's acquiescence.

On the last day of the month, Alexander went to his father's wedding in an old church in the City. He had initially slightly dreaded it, fearing deep down that celebrating his father's new marriage might somehow be disloyal to his mother's memory, but now he no longer really cared. Damian had made him feel much better about it. He could not entirely agree with his argument that his father's wish to remarry so soon was a tribute to how happily he had been married to his mother and must therefore have loved her. The second conclusion did not follow from the first. One could be made happy simply by having one's emotional needs and physical comforts attended to by any competent provider. However, when Damian pointed out that his father had the same need as himself for love, he had felt churlish in not having been more enthusiastic that his father had found his new road to happiness. He was now unreservedly happy that it was so, because he too had found his own road. He was very lucky to have it at fourteen though, and could not help thinking a little wistfully that since his father knew nothing about his new, emotional independence, he might have waited a little longer before embroiling him in such change.

In any case, when the day came, Alexander found it easy to give himself up to helping make the day happy, and was charming to Janet and her relations. Hal noticed with surprise that Alexander had changed dramatically for the better. It was odd, but he was much relieved, having worried a little as to how Alexander was going to fit in. Several of his friends complimented him on how unusually grown-up his youngest son had become. He knew they were impressed with how well he had brought him up. He could justly feel considerable pride as a father.

Alexander was even able to maintain a gracious equanimity when faced with Dorothy's provocation. She came up to him suddenly during the reception and took a pretty, gold-capped fountain pen out of her bag.

"Guess who this used to belong to?" asked Dorothy. Alexander thought he could have guessed who from her expression of mocking triumph, without being able to remember it as his mother's.

298

"I've no idea," he replied in a feigned tone of slight curiosity, concentrating hard on the fact that the next day was a Sunday, so he would be able to spend almost all of it with Damian. "Who?"

Dorothy seemed to change her mind over what she had been ready to say. "Well anyway, it's mine now. Your father gave it to me."

"Lucky you," said Alexander with forced enthusiasm. "It looks like a really good pen." That remark seemed to change her at once, and she became genuinely a little friendly for the first time.

After the reception, his father and Janet set off for Heathrow. They were off for their honeymoon for ten days in Bali, and coming back just in time for the school holidays. Mr. Hodgson had given Alexander permission to stay out until eleven, so his brothers took him out to dinner before Christopher drove him back to school.

Since the day Damian had recommended Alexander to be friendly to Julian, it had become more and more apparent that Julian regretted having ended their friendship, at least as completely as he had. The older boy had even come to his room a couple of times to chat. Though Alexander had no intention of going so far as to reciprocate, he had been true to his plan of indulging Julian's overtures.

Nevertheless, he was wary of Julian's perseverance and a bit put out when, one morning, Julian even came to his room during the forbidden hour of After Nine. His forced smile as he came in reminded Alexander of the way dogs yawn when they are nervous, and increased his foreboding. Finally, it all came out that Julian was hoping they could go back to their old intimacy, as if nothing had happened. Alexander tried to deflect him, but he would not be put off.

"Can't we be special friends like we used to be?" he pleaded mournfully. "I'm sorry I broke my promise and treated you like that, but I'm ready to go back to the way things were between us and I'll never do that again, whatever anyone says." Alexander could sense that it had taken him great courage to say it, but he did not let that make him hesitate in his reply.

"No, it's too late," he replied at once, appalled at the idea of giving up to Julian any of his time with Damian. "We can be ordinary friends if you want, but it could never be like that again." He regretted having to hurt Julian, though his memory of the agony Julian's betrayal had originally caused him was still vivid, but it was the simple truth and there was no point in obscuring it. He was also a bit annoyed and could not help a little of his exasperation showing in his voice. Could Julian really not see that it was impossible that he ever trust or respect him like in the old days when he had never imagined him capable of letting him down so badly?

Between lunch and After Two that afternoon, one of the leavers, the boys in B who were not going to be attempting the Oxbridge exam in November, held a quick auction in the Common Room of those of his belongings that he did not want to take on to his new life. He had an erotic calendar of sexy models Alexander had already glimpsed with admiration, so he decided to wait until it came up before going off to be with Damian.

His fascination with girls had not abated, but the accompanying despair and urgency had been replaced by calm admiration. He could now face patiently the likelihood that it would be a few years rather than a few months until he lay with his first girl.

His old worry that he would not know exactly what to do had also disappeared. He felt that when he finally met a girl who definitely desired him, he would be able to bed her with confidence, even if she was a virgin. Perhaps the biggest difference was that he thought he would be able to detect the signs of her attraction to him, whereas before he had always feared he would never know. Then he would be able to respond to them. He reminded himself again with a thrill of pride that he knew far more about love and lovemaking than any of the other boys in F, possibly more even than any of the leavers. He would know how to bestow the gentle caresses which might gradually arouse the girl's desire to the point that she longed for his firmer touch, and then on until her mind was completely made up to yield to him and her body yearned for his. He would be able to understand and empathise with her responses to those caresses

300

because he too knew how it felt to be at the receiving end of a man's passion. Once rid of her clothes, he would know how to kiss and lick and fondle, and, if she were a virgin, to reassure with a profusion of further gentle kisses until she was panting for him to enter her.

Also, Damian had utterly convinced him now that he was desirable, and that girls would fall for him. Life was going to be fun. He became conscious of his stiffness thinking about it and that reminded him of all those recent months when he would have had to go off to the bathroom for a wank. What a miserable business, and how lucky he was now. He smiled inwardly as he considered that in only half an hour's time, Damian's warm, moist lips would be sliding deliciously up and down his cock, his tongue gently playing around the most sensitive area beneath his glans, and his life-giving juices would be pumping into his lover's throat rather than falling in sterile sadness onto the cold floor of the bathroom, as he had deduced was the only paltry relief available during the daytime to his schoolfellows.

There was a murmur of anticipation when the bids for the calendar began, which gave way to ripples of amusement as the bids went higher. Soon only Alexander and Johnny Villiers were left. Alexander was determined and had saved up a good chunk of his allowance for the Half. When the bids went above three pounds, the amusement turned to laughter and bawdy jokes began. Alexander would have been embarrassed a month ago, but now he could happily joke about himself with any of them. Let them see his foibles! Whatever they might think of him, he had won himself a lover. They had no idea what they were missing out on. He could be truly himself at last, for it was enough.

Johnny gave up at £ 4.10 and Alexander shot off to put the calendar in his room before bounding happily off for his hour of love.

XII: Second Thoughts

There is a tide in the affairs of men,
Which, taken at the flood, leads on to fortune,
Omitted, all the voyage of their life
Is bound in shallows and in miseries.
  William Shakespeare, *Julius Caesar*

Meanwhile, Julian had passed the six weeks since he ended his friendship with Alexander in dreadful emotional turmoil. He was far more miserable than he had been during the months of nearly hopeless longing that had preceded their friendship, or indeed any other period of his life.

At first, his guilt over having hurt Alexander so undeservedly, combined with the need to steel himself to stick to his resolution, made him an unpleasant subject he tried to banish from his thoughts. It had been a nasty shock the very first morning, only three hours after undergoing the trauma of telling him, to see Alexander standing on the landing, staring at him with nearly tearful eyes as he approached. He must try harder to avoid him, he thought, as he strode past with averted eyes, irritated by his own guilty feelings.

His agonised regret over his failure to act when he had had the chance never abated. The more he thought back, the more convinced he became that Alexander had been ready and willing, and so he had ruined his happiness for no reason. Most of all, he regretted their last day together, and his anguish was further sharpened by a new thought that Alexander could even have been deliberately giving him an opening in telling him other boys said he was in love with him.

From the very outset, he found he was incapable of forgetting his physical longing for him. This hurt most of all because, though he was nearly sure he could have gone to bed with Alexander if he had been less cowardly, he had never thought himself worthy of such bliss with a boy so far above him in good looks. Quite possibly, he would never in his life find a boy the right age willing to sleep with him, and certainly never one nearly that beautiful. There was nothing he would ever be able to do to make up for it.

It was eight months now since he had had an erotic fantasy that did not involve Alexander. He tried hard to re-interest himself in girls and bought himself a *Playboy* for that purpose, but it seemed so dull that it was hard to understand how such pictures had once turned him on. Girls compared to boys as water to wine now, so when he found he could not build any excitement about them, he tried in desperation to think about other boys, anything to rid him of his longing for Alexander.

Rupert Drysdale was very handsome, active and boyish to the core, his dark hair in beautiful contrast to his fair skin and vivid dark blue eyes. He was easily the finest-looking boy in F apart from Alexander and seemed less innocent than him, which made it easier to imagine him acting lasciviously. Several times when Julian lay in bed stiff with frustrated desire for Alexander, he tried wanking to the image of himself with Rupert. Rupert did excite him far more than a girl. He imagined him naked and ready to be mounted, his head turned back towards Julian with a naughty smile of excited anticipation, but always as Julian's climax approached and his self-control waned, the dark hair turned golden-blond and the face changed to that sincere, trusting one he knew so well.

If only he had told his father the truth. He constantly reassured himself he would make a habit of it thenceforth, but that was no consolation. It was too late.

After two days, he could no longer deny to himself that he also missed Alexander's company terribly. He realised he had been a much closer friend than any other he had ever had. He had forgotten how very dull and lonely his life had been before Alexander lit it up. Alexander's vitality and enthusiasm had breathed life into him and given him expectations of daily emotional and intellectual stimulation, the importance of which he only fully appreciated when it was gone. Though Alexander was inevitably more naïve than him in some ways, there was no doubt he was much more intelligent. He knew he had never deserved such a friend, and yet, with absurd irony, Alexander had looked up to him. No one else had ever sought his opinion so eagerly or so delighted in his esteem.

After four days of successfully avoiding him, he suddenly saw him approaching in the corridor one afternoon. There was

303

nothing for it but to stride on without taking any notice, but as they passed each other, Julian realised that Alexander had done just the same. He had not slowed down and he saw in the corner of his eye that his gaze was also averted. Julian found his feelings surprisingly mixed. It was a relief that Alexander no longer sought an encounter, but also hurtful. When he wondered why, it came home to him just how irrecoverable what he had given up was fast becoming. Alexander apparently no longer hoped to change his mind. He was already trying to learn to cope with life without him. Though that was supposedly what Julian had wanted, the reality of Alexander no longer needing him was an unanticipated blow to his self-esteem. It made him realise guiltily quite how badly hurt he would have been if it had been Alexander rather than him who had ended their friendship.

After that, Julian's anguish waxed as Alexander's waned and died.

During Long Leave, his mother's puritanical bossiness grated on him far more than before, though there was no unusually harsh manifestation of it, until he began to suspect he actually hated her. He at least longed to defy her. He had long ago heard enough snippets of information about other boys' mothers to think himself unlucky, but now the unfairness of it seemed unbearable. If it had been her rather than his father who had confronted him about Alexander, should he really have submitted to her admonishment? He undoubtedly would have, just as he had over his *Mayfair*, but why? What did he seriously have to lose from standing up to her? Had not cowardice always been his greatest problem in life? He rather thought that if she attacked him unfairly again, he might explode and fight back.

When they went back to school, Julian noticed that Alexander was entirely his old self again, happy and exuberant. Sometimes, in the dining-room, Julian could not help gazing longingly down the table to where Alexander sat caught up in animated conversation with his friends, often smiling or laughing. Occasionally, a look of quiet melancholy would come into his eyes, but Julian could see it was only because one of his friends was telling him about some bad experience, and then Julian would remember miserably the warmth and sincerity of the

304

younger boy's sympathy. Once Alexander caught his gaze, and though Julian turned away quickly, he took in that Alexander was just mildly surprised. Evidently, he no longer shared any of his sadness at all.

The next morning, Julian passed him outside the dining-room. Alexander glanced at him without any change in his expression at all, and then Julian knew that he had disappeared altogether from his emotional existence. He pined for Alexander every day and wanked over him every night, but he himself was nothing to him, and entirely through his own fault.

He regretted then having taken things so far. He need not have done as his father told him quite so literally. Surely he could at least have kept up greeting him, and then there would at least not be this agonising silence when they met, as if he had never been more to him than say Cowburn.

The more he thought about it, the more he came to think that if they could at least be a little friendly when they met, it would not hurt so much. Deep down, he doubted it would help very much, but at least concentrating on the problem of how to get back on greetings terms diverted him a little from his misery. Once he had achieved that, then he would think again if more could or should be done.

He could not face saying even "Hi" to Alexander in their house. So far, no one had commented on how they had suddenly stopped spending their spare time together, but other boys must have noticed. If he were to try greeting him and Alexander cut him, or even worse, made some scathing but only too well-deserved retort in front of another boy, the pain and humiliation would be unbearable. The word would spread in no time that it had been Alexander who had dropped their friendship.

The only way forward he could see was to contrive to pass Alexander in the street. That meant knowing where he was going and he thought of the Eton Calendar, a booklet that listed every boy's divs with their times and schoolrooms. It cost 85p. and few boys saw much point in buying it. It was even more of an extravagance for him, but working out between which school buildings Alexander would be walking at different times of the day mattered more than buying food for his solitary teatime.

305

He bought it from Alden and Blackwell on his way back from his first div one Monday morning and spent After Nine working out Alexander's timetable. He decided to go into action that very morning. As soon as his third div was over, he ran to Judy's Passage and waited there with a thumping heart for Alexander to approach on his way to James Schools.

As Alexander came into view, Julian started walking towards him, but initially on the other side of the passage so as to retain an element of surprise until he was close.

"Hi Alexander!" he said, smiling nervously, just before they passed one another.

"Hi," said Alexander. His greeting did not sound heartfelt, but perhaps he was too surprised for that. At least the ice had been broken!

After that, Julian dared to greet him every time they passed in their house. At first, Alexander looked at him a bit disdainfully, but gradually his responses became almost friendly, though nothing like as warm as in those far off November days before they had ever chatted.

One afternoon, he came out of their house to see James Crichton chatting to Alexander in the alley. James was being his usual charming self and Alexander was listening to him wide-eyed and with evident pleasure. He did not like to interrupt them. Unless he was loud, they might not even notice his greeting, so he resigned himself to slinking miserably by. He was so stung with jealousy he could not stop hatred for James surging up in him until, just as he passed them, James noticed him and flashed him a warm smile over Alexander's head, and Julian guiltily swallowed his unworthy thoughts.

So far from being unusual, it was now an almost daily occurrence to see Alexander in animated conversation with much older boys. His self-assurance seemed to have blossomed magically until he far outshone the Alexander who had before so impressed Julian with his daring. He exuded an inexplicable happiness that infected those around him and drew them to him like a magnet, so that he had rapidly become one of the most popular boys in the house. One would call him cocky the way he held his own with eighteen-year-olds if he was not so obviously friendly and unpretentious. There was also a new and striking sophistication in his demeanour, which made him appear grown up compared to the others in his block and made Julian feel distinctly awkward. It disturbed him too that he could not explain it.

It was totally unfair that he alone could not talk to Alexander in just the normal friendly way that most of the older boys now did. He must put this right. It would hardly amount to being real friends with him, which was all he had promised his father to stop. Going to his room might be crossing the boundary though, and anyway he dared not. So how was he to get back on speaking terms? He shrunk from trying to initiate a chat elsewhere in the house, where they were likely to be interrupted at once by any number of boys with whom Alexander was nowadays much friendlier, so resuming use of Alexander's timetable, he decided to intercept him on his way back to Peyntors.

He waited around a corner he knew Alexander would pass on his way back after their last div until he saw him.

"Alexander!" he called out. Alexander stopped hesitatingly and looked at him quizzically, as he approached. "Did you hear what happened this morning about Angus Macdonald?" he asked, smiling determinedly to hide his discomfort at Alexander's coolness. Macdonald ma. was so well-known as the stingiest boy in their house that the others made jokes about him being a national hero in his native Scotland; Julian had latched onto the newest story about him as the only amusing thing he could think of that Alexander might not have heard.

"No."

"Well, Robert Williams and Oliver Fisher had a £ 2 bet as to whether he was stingy enough to pick a ½ p. coin out of the urinal, so Robert threw one in and hid in the bath cubicle during Chambers to see if anyone picked it up. He stood on the bath and every time someone came in, he peeped over to see who it was, and sure enough, when Macdonald came in he waited until he felt sure he was alone and snatched it up." Julian had to try hard to make his little tale sound amusing, his nervousness threatening to show in his voice and cause it to fall flat.

"Yuck, how disgusting!" said Alexander, chuckling. His coolness forgotten, he began to tell Julian another story he had heard about Macdonald. Julian had already heard it, but was certainly not going to let that ruin their first chat for a month. They were interrupted when they reached the turning to their house. As he moved towards it, Julian was disconcerted to see that Alexander was not following and was intent on going straight on towards the High Street.

"Where are you going?" asked Julian.

"Oh, I've got to deliver an essay to a beak," replied Alexander awkwardly.

The next morning, Julian tried again. This time, he rushed up to join Alexander in Common Lane, giving them five minutes before they would reach their house. They chatted amicably enough as they walked, then Julian saw a tall, young beak coming the other way and about to pass them. They raised their hands to cap him and Julian's attention was caught by an unusual pause by Alexander in lowering his. Then he saw him and the beak smile at each other as they passed. It was only for a moment, as if they did not want others to notice, but long enough for Julian to take in that their smiles were much the warmest he had ever seen a boy and schoolmaster exchange. Alexander's reminded him poignantly of the one bestowed on himself the day he had stood up for him against Cowburn. The beak had not even noticed Julian capping him. No beak had ever smiled at Julian like that. He felt a pang of jealousy the intensity of which he could not quite explain.

"Who was that?" he asked.

"Mr. Cavendish. He's my English beak. He's incredibly nice," answered Alexander with even more than his usual enthusiasm, though Julian thought there was something incongruously a little hesitant about the way he said it.

"Oh, I see." Julian supposed he must be quite a new beak. He had noticed him on the street before though. He stood out from most people with his dark, good looks and warm, dashing smile. Julian did not know why, but he suddenly felt more depressed than he had for a long time.

He used his copy of Alexander's timetable to intercept him yet again the next day, but this time Alexander looked at him oddly as if he had begun to suspect their meeting was not a coincidence. Clearly, he could not keep up the pretence much longer. The only way he was really going to get friendly with Alexander was by going to his room to talk to him, but if Alexander accepted him there, that would be tantamount to resuming their friendship and breaking his promise to his father. He could not bear the thought of his father too feeling cheated by him, but nor could he bear to renounce his new friendliness with Alexander. It had relieved his misery a little with a tiny glimmer of hope. Also, though thinking about his father made him feel guilty about his longing for Alexander, thinking about his mother made the boy even more enticing as forbidden fruit. He now found it thrilling to contemplate something that would outrage her if she knew about it.

In his loneliness, he reflected at agonising length over the question that had troubled him before: had an ingrained preference for boys always been in him despite his former unconsciousness of it, or was he rewriting his life history in so wondering? He finally arrived at a deeper truth: his former feelings would always elude him because they were subjective. What really mattered was not the past, but the future, which his unfulfilled longings were severely curtailing. He could now only think about boys despite knowing there was no future in it. If he could not just once do the thing his imagination told him was the most fulfilling conceivable, to possess Alexander, his unfulfilled desire would torment him for the rest of his life and he would never be able to recover any taste for girls.

Finally, Julian decided he would at the very least do everything in his power to persuade his father to relieve him of his promise, if only he could first establish that Alexander was willing to be friends with him again. Whatever happened, he would not go behind his father's back. Once he knew Alexander was willing, he would have to admit to his father that he had lied to him, that he had been in love with Alexander all along and could bear it no longer. His father would be upset and worried, but he also had a big heart and Julian was sure of his love. He did not want to think now about what he might do if his father really refused to back down. There was no point yet.

He was very nervous about going to see Alexander in his room, especially considering what he would have to say, even more nervous than when he had made himself do so before they became friends. In those long-distant days, it had been important to try to find Alexander alone, but now it was essential. If it happened like then that somebody else was with Alexander, he would have to say quite bluntly that he needed to ask him something in confidence, and ask him for a time to come back.

He was now so sickened though by all he had done to ruin his life through cowardly procrastination, that he refused himself all possibility of respite. He went to his room soon after lunch the day after his decision, and knocked on the door, quietly at first, then loudly, but there was no answer. It was a dreadful anticlimax slinking back to his own room after that, but he showed himself no mercy and went back again twenty minutes before tea-time and yet again ten minutes before supper, but all in vain. At supper, Julian ate slowly, waiting for Alexander to appear. Though he would not be able to talk to him there, following him out and catching him then would be his last chance of the day. There would be too little time between Prayers and nine o'clock, after which arose the dreadful possibility of Hodgson suddenly emerging. Alexander rushed into the dining-room only ten minutes before the end of the meal. Julian followed him out, only to find him chatting to a group of boys in the lobby.

The next day, there were afternoon divs, so no significant spare time until tea. He knew from the list in the first-floor kitchen that Alexander had gone back to messing with Drysdale and Churchill in the latter's room. He was too dispirited to collect the things for his own lonely one-boy mess, so he just sat in his room, trying vainly to read his French novel, while remembering miserably what fun it had been when Alexander messed with him. When the time finally arrived by which he thought tea-time must be over, he again went to Alexander's room and knocked with a firm fist but thumping heart. Silence.

He returned twice again before supper and twice again before tea-time the following afternoon. He was getting less nervous each time, as his hopes sunk of an answer to his knocking. It was very odd. How did Alexander manage to do all his E.W.s, if he was never in his room in his spare time? Walking back gloomily from it again after tea-time, he slowed down as he passed Churchill's room, listening hopefully for the sound of Alexander's voice, in case he had stayed on there, but he could hear nothing. Deciding suddenly he must do something to clear up the mystery, he knocked on Churchill's door.

"Come in!" answered Churchill.

"Hi Simon," said Julian, closing the door behind him. Simon, thankfully alone, looked up with a friendly expression, for since Julian had become Alexander's friend, he had always called him Simon instead of Lusty and was the only boy always to do so apart from Alexander. "You don't happen to know where Alexander is, do you?"

"No, no idea."

"Was he here for tea?"

"No, he never comes back on half-days."

"Where does he go then?" asked Julian, trying hard to make his question sound light-hearted.

"Well, I know that when he does come back for tea, he always goes off to the libwawy stwaight afterwards, because I asked him why he never dwops off his books in his woom. So that's pwobably where he is now." Simon saw the question in Julian's expression. "He's got obsessed wecently with doing weally well in Twials" he added helpfully.

"I see... But the library closes at five, doesn't it?"

"Yes, that's twue..... Perhaps he's gone on the wiver."

"Oh, what, with Rupert?"

"Yes. Er no, he can't have, because Wupert was here for tea. Is it vewy urgent?" asked Simon, looking at him curiously now.

"No, no, it's nothing important. I just wanted to ask him something," said Julian dismissively, but Simon looked even more curious.

"Actually, thinking about it, it's only School Libwawy that closes at five. He must go to one of the other ones, the Porson Libwawy perhaps."

"Oh right, well, it doesn't matter anyway. Thanks," said Julian, determined to set off there without delay. His spirits rose

311

immensely. He could pretend to go there on his own business, and in a little library like that there was an excellent chance of having a long chat with Alexander, uninterrupted by anyone they knew.

He was therefore intensely disappointed when he found Alexander was not there. He tried the Marten Library for good measure, and then the Porson again. Then he remembered Alexander's skill on the piano and tried the Music Schools, but he was nowhere to be found. Surely, he could not be in College Library, where the school's extremely valuable books were kept? One needed special permission to work there, so Julian could not go and check anyway.

After supper that night, Julian at long last found Alexander in his room, and alone too.

"Yes?" asked Alexander, seated behind his burry and looking definitely taken aback.

"Oh, I haven't come about anything in particular," said Julian, hoping his pain at the implied demand to explain his coming was not obvious. "I just wondered how things are going?"

"Fine," said Alexander warily. Then he seemed suddenly to relent and added "and with you?" in a much friendlier voice.

Julian was just beginning to wonder if he might after all be able to open his heart and express something of his terrible remorse, when there was a loud knocking. Drysdale, Bell and Parker rushed in as soon as Alexander answered, immediately chatting boisterously. When they took in Julian's presence, they glanced at him quizzically, but carried on talking without interruption. There were only twenty minutes to Prayers and Julian realised his chances of a private chat with Alexander had been ship-wrecked.

"See you," he said quietly to Alexander as he slunk out of the room miserably, but he doubted Alexander even heard.

Having found Alexander in his room had of course done nothing to explain the mystery of whither he had been disappearing for three days. Though he could not explain to himself why, thinking about it gave him a terrible sinking feeling. The only way to get rid of it was to find out, and the only sure way of doing that was to follow him.

The next day, having confirmed that Alexander had come back to the house for tea, he waited downstairs in the lobby, pretending to read the notices posted there. Sure enough, before long Alexander rushed past him holding a book and a folder, just as Churchill had led him to expect. As soon as the boys' entrance door swung shut, Julian opened it and quietly followed. He was only just in time to see that Alexander turned right out of the alley way towards the High Street rather than left towards the rest of the school.

He dared not follow too closely, which made it difficult to keep Alexander in sight, as there were quite a number of people walking up and down the right side of the street that they were on. Suddenly, he could not see him any more at all. He stepped into the middle of the street, supposedly to cross it, but really to get a clear view down both sides of it. There was no doubt the boy had disappeared, and he was fairly sure he had done so without crossing over himself, but that still left several houses where it could have happened. Most of them were shops, at least on the ground floor, and he peered through the windows of each of these until sure Alexander was not within. One of them was a cavernous bookshop, which he had to enter and pretend to browse around in order to be certain. That seemed to leave only flats that he could have gone into, but there were simply too many possible ones.

Deciding to wait until Alexander emerged, he crossed back over to get a better view. For nearly an hour, he pretended to be looking in the shop windows there, while frequently looking over his shoulder. Finally, all the shops had closed, he could no longer keep up the pretence and went back to his house with a sinking heart. He kept telling himself not to jump to wild conclusions, but he could not help feeling that whichever place Alexander had disappeared into was not only the key to the mystery, but a secret with potentially terrifying implications.

The next day, he followed Alexander again after lunch. This time he went along the other side of the street and not so far behind. Suddenly, Alexander pushed open a dark blue door and disappeared. Crossing straight over, Julian went up to the door and saw that it was number 135. There could only be three flats, one on each floor of the little, Georgian, brick house. The addresses section of the school fixtures should tell him who lived in each of them, but long before he reached his room, he already had a dreadful suspicion of whom it might be. As he walked back, he remembered Alexander's awkwardness that first time he had intercepted him going back to their house and, seeing that Alexander was heading down the high street, he had asked where he was going. To a beak, he had said. Then he remembered the exchange of smiles the next day that had rent his heart.

He looked straight for Mr. Cavendish in the fixtures. Sure enough, his address was Flat 2, 135 Eton High Street. Julian's heart pounded with anguish. Nevertheless, he went through the rest of the addresses, hoping fervently that there might be some other beak living in the building whom Alexander knew, anybody rather than that handsome young man. Mr. Butler in Flat 1 was an economics beak, whom Alexander, as a boy in F, could not have been up to. Mr. Lloyd in Flat 3 taught Classics, but Julian knew that Alexander had always been up to Mr. Trotter for that.

He tried telling himself that Mr. Cavendish was only one of Alexander's beaks. Perhaps he just gave him some extra tuition, and Alexander would soon be back, but in his heart he did not believe it for a moment. At half-past seven, Julian went back and positioned himself a little further down the other side of the street. He waited and waited, hoping against all his gut instinct that Alexander would not emerge through that blue door, that he was long gone. Time was running out for supper and his hopes were just beginning to seem a little credible when the familiar figure of the one he pined for suddenly emerged and sprinted gracefully back towards their house. He had been nearly six hours in Mr. Cavendish's flat.

It was no use pretending they were just an ordinary schoolmaster and pupil. Julian was sure he had never heard of a boy and beak spending so much time together. And why had Alexander lied to Simon, telling him that he went to a library on half-days? That could only mean that they had something to hide. It looked very much as though they were together every day, but did not want anyone to know of it.

314

Julian searched desperately for any reason why they should be hiding the truth other than the one he dreaded, then tried to reassure himself that Simon had misunderstood, that Alexander had not really lied to his friend, but try as hard as he might, he could not hold at bay agonising visions of the golden boy he loved lying in the handsome man's arms.

One of the most interesting boys in the house, at least in Julian's opinion, was an American called David Edwards. He had lived in various countries and had unconventional ideas about all sorts of things. A lot of boys could not stand him because he was so uncompromising in his quirky opinions and tastes, but as those boys tended to be the squarest, it only enhanced his appeal in Julian's eyes.

David's latest fad at this time was burning incense sticks, a stock of which his businessman father had recently brought back from the Far East. Most of the boys had never seen or smelt incense sticks. Whenever David opened his door, a strong waft of them would escape into the corridor and arouse some curiosity.

Just before After Two the next afternoon, David went up to his room followed by Henry Moody, who lived further down the same corridor. David opened his door just as Henry passed.

"What the hell's that smell?" asked Henry, surprised.

"Just an incense stick," replied David cheerfully.

"What's it for?" he asked. David explained.

It was typical of Edwards to have something weird like that, thought Henry, but he rather liked the smell and it was an interesting novelty he would like to show his friend Eddie Craven. "Can I have one?"

"Yes, okay," said David and handed him one.

"Thanks," said Henry and picked up Edwards's box of matches to light it.

"Hey, don't do that yet, not if you're going to go anywhere near a fire alarm!" exclaimed David.

"Why on earth not?"

"Because it will set it off."

"Oh come on, a little thing like this?"

315

David was scientifically minded and embarked on a lengthy explanation of how fire alarms used smoke detection to work, but Henry understood little of it and believed less.

"Don't be ridiculous. I'll bet you 50 p. this thing can't set the fire alarm off."

"I don't mind betting, but on your head be it. Don't say I didn't warn you."

"Right, let's go!" said Henry, lighting the stick, and he opened the door and turned down the corridor towards the nearest alarm. David watched from a distance as Henry went right up to the little metal and glass box and waved the stick in front of it. When five seconds had passed, David began to wonder if he could possibly be wrong, and Henry was just getting ready to say "I told you so", when the alarm went off at an ear-splitting volume and Henry froze in shock. It was so loud that as he stood there helplessly, he could barely hear the stampede of fifty boys rushing excitedly down the stairs from all parts of the house.

Julian was astonished when the alarm went off. They had a fire practice once every Half and Hodgson kept secret when it was going to be, but it was always in the middle of the night, not at five past two in the afternoon, as now. Perhaps there really was a fire, he thought excitedly as he joined in the rush out of the house and towards the garden shed, which was the appointed place to hold roll calls for fire practice. When they arrived there, he gathered from the excited chatter that the others thought it might be for real too, but they could not see any signs of smoke coming out of the building.

Suddenly the news spread through the crowd almost as fast as wind that it was all a stupid mistake, that Moody had set off the alarm with an incense stick despite being warned against it. It was simply too good to be true. They roared with laughter.

"Moooooody! Moooooody! Moooooody!" they all shouted.

Julian looked out for Alexander. It was a good opportunity to chat him up when everyone was in such a jovial mood, but he could not see him anywhere. It was strange, because it was absolutely obligatory to turn up for the roll call whatever one might believe was the cause of the alarm and everyone else seemed to have arrived several minutes ago. Anthony Burrows appeared with a house list and began the roll call. Only two boys failed to answer: Moody and Aylmer.

Suddenly, Henry emerged from the house and walked towards them. They roared with laughter again, almost falling over each other.

"Moooooody! Moooooody!" they started chanting again. Poor Henry tried to speak and flailed his arms in the air to try to get their attention, but the chant went on and on and there was no hope of being heard. Eventually he put his hands over his ears and ran back into the house. Only one boy apart from him was not laughing. Julian was thinking miserably that he could guess where Alexander was.

The next morning, Julian was desperately finishing one of his E.W.s during After Nine, when he heard the stampede of boys leaving the house recede into dead silence and he realised he was going to be late. He rushed down the stairs, out of his house and towards College Chapel, as fast as he was able. The street was virtually empty and as he approached the entrance to School Yard he saw a small stream of boys passing through it. He went through, but just as he reached the long steps leading up to the chapel, he heard the first chime of the school bells ringing out half past nine and the second came before he reached the top. The door was still open, and for a moment he thought he might get away with it, but as he went in, he saw a beak standing inside and looking at him. He knew at once that meant he was on Tardy Book again. Then his eyes adjusted to the relative darkness and his heart lurched. It was Mr. Cavendish standing there, a small note-pad and pen ready in his hands. Another late-comer ground to a walking-pace just behind him, both boys panting heavily.

"You're late. Your names and houses?" Mr. Cavendish asked them.

"Smith, Sir, in JRH." Julian saw the beak's expression change with sudden realisation and he knew at once that the man knew who he was. Mr. Cavendish hesitated for a few seconds.

"All right. Just go and sit down quickly, and don't do it again," he said quietly, looking at Julian thoughtfully as he put his pen back in his inner pocket. Julian saw the kindness in his eyes and it hurt him because he knew he would not be that kind if their positions were reversed. Was Mr. Cavendish not therefore a better person than himself, and more deserving of Alexander?

A boy soprano was singing solo. He was fair like an angel and his voice was fairer still. Coming to listen to the choir was the only reason why Julian often came to Chapel in the morning rather than to the more popular Alternative Assembly, where interesting speakers often came to address the upper boys. But now the haunting beauty of the song could not distract Julian from his anguished thoughts. The holiness of their surroundings only added to his pathos as he reflected wistfully upon the sin he longed so desperately to commit with a boy.

If Mr. Cavendish recognised his name, it could only be because Alexander had told him about him and his faithlessness. He must have opened his heart to him. Very likely Alexander had told Mr. Cavendish the story of his betrayal as they lay in bed together after making love. Mr. Cavendish had not looked at him with anger or disgust though. He had no need to fear Julian as a possible rival. Obviously his position as Alexander's lover was impregnable. No, if anything, Julian felt he might have detected pity in the man's gaze.

Julian thought about it intermittently throughout the day. He wondered how Alexander would react if he told him what had happened. He was fairly sure something in his reaction would betray their intimacy and he knew that every confirmation of it would hurt him deeply, but even so he felt compelled to know. Recounting the episode was also another excuse for conversation with Alexander the next time he managed to find him after supper. As it happened, he found him that very evening.

Alexander blushed as soon as he heard Julian pronounce Mr. Cavendish's name, and looked increasingly embarrassed as Julian went on, but it did not hide his obvious pride. "I'm not surprised," he said, when Julian finished his little story. "I told you he was nice."

Though the fullest ferocity of his jealousy was focussed on Mr. Cavendish, he found to his surprise that some of it was also directed towards Alexander. He not only desired him, but desired to be him too.

It was not at all that he wished himself in Mr. Cavendish's arms. Not only had he no desire for him, but, as a man himself, he could not imagine evoking any in him.

Society was profoundly ambiguous as to whether he at seventeen was a man or still a boy. He had noticed that in newspaper reports of crime, eighteen-year-old victims were usually described as boys, whereas sixteen-year-olds who beat up old ladies were invariably "men", but he himself had no doubt he was a man. It was a matter of physical fact. Besides his growth over the last year having been imperceptible, he no longer had the slender grace of a boy. His features were all hard, his hair coarse, his nose and chin big, his limbs and behind heavy and muscular and, most grotesquely of all, covered with hair, which also appeared as stubble on his face if he did not shave for a few days.

Imagining himself taking Alexander's place in Mr. Cavendish's bed made him shudder at once. The beak's reaction would surely be like that of the hero in the film *She*, when the beautiful young woman in his arms was quickly transformed into a hideous old one, for the difference between a pubescent boy and a young man as an object of manly desire was at least as great. It was also an affront to his own self-esteem to imagine himself trying hopelessly to forget his inescapable manliness so that he could take pleasure in accommodating that of another.

No, his envy of Alexander was less acute than it would have been if he had wanted the man as his lover, but much sadder. What he wanted was to be a fourteen-year-old in a handsome young man's embrace. Though he had spent much of the last two years longing to possess a beautiful boy, he had not given much thought before to what it would be like to be a boy at the receiving end of male passion. He had never been beautiful like Alexander, but he remembered from admiring his body in the mirror that it had been typical enough of a fourteen-year-old's for him to be able to imagine it exciting the lust of a man susceptible to boyish charm, and he felt a longing as terrible as it was impossible to go back in time and find a lover before it was too late.

He could imagine only too easily the excitement he would have felt at being lusted over and satisfying that lust. It would have been the proof of a love that could have brought him limitless happiness and self-confidence. He remembered only too well his sensitivity and terrible loneliness at that age, as an outsider at Eton. What joy it would have been to have somebody he was truly special to. Somebody to protect him, comfort him, and answer all his fears and doubts. If a handsome young man had only loved him as he was, he would not have cared a toss what the other boys thought of his background, and he would have fought back fearlessly at Cowburn and the others if they mocked him.

As with most boys in JRH, their housemaster's invariable riposte to anyone's enunciation of the words "too late" echoed in his mind, as he imagined all that could have been and never would:

"Too late. The saddest words in the English language." How very true.

Not a waking hour now passed in which Julian was not sick with worry that Alexander and Mr. Cavendish were lovers, and his nights were disturbed by erotic nightmares of them together, waking from which he sometimes passed hours in silent misery before he could get back to sleep. He still sought desperately for some proof he was wrong, trying to postpone acknowledgement of their affair as certain and escape the blackest depths he knew his mind would then descend to. After Alexander's absence during the roll call on the Wednesday, he resolved to wait until the next After Two on the Friday, and use his presence or absence then as a final test of whether or not his suspicions were well-founded. It might not be a big thing in itself, but he felt he had to fix on some point beyond which the accumulation of evidence was such that further evasion of the truth would finally be futile.

He approached Alexander's door with a sinking heart at half past two on the Friday and stood silently before it for several moments, hoping forlornly for sounds of occupancy within. He knocked gently then, and did not wait more than two seconds for a reply: he knew in his heart there would be none, well before he opened the door to confirm the room was empty.

320

Even all of Alexander's spare time was not enough for Mr. Cavendish. He took every possible moment of Alexander's existence. In effect, Alexander was only ever in their house during meals, After Nine and at night. Presumably if the house wasn't locked up at night, he would be off to his lover then too!

As half of B block were about to leave the school, an election to the Library had been held that week and, rather to his surprise, Julian had been chosen together with James Crichton and Oliver Fisher, who were already spoken of as likely future captains of the house and games respectively. The most immediate change this brought to his life was that he started messing in the Library and spending as much time as he liked socialising with the others there. Ever since his introduction to the old house books in December, he had been longing to delve into them again. Now at last he could read them as much as he liked, after pretending to come across them by chance his first day there. Within a few days, he had read the whole lot. He found more written in the same vein that had first gripped him, though disappointingly nothing juicier still.

His curiosity now turned to how the others would react if they were to read the more sensational bits. He was fairly sure none of them had, for the others' interest in the books was limited to what had been written about themselves and their friends and foes, and he was perhaps the first boy ever to have read all the old books. He was wary of drawing attention to his special interest, but thought he could brush it aside now that everyone supposed his special friendship with Alexander was over.

After tea on the same Friday afternoon he had found Alexander absent again, he found himself alone in the room with Oliver Fisher and could no longer resist the temptation to try it out, though for an interesting reaction Oliver was hardly promising, with his conventional outlook and limited imagination.

"Have you ever read these really old house books?" asked Julian, holding up one.

"No."

"It's just unbelievable what some people wrote. Listen to this, for example: 'Percy. Recently voted prettiest boy in F by the

321

Library. Russell and Troughton are having a three-guinea bet as to who can seduce him.'"

Oliver looked momentarily shocked and perhaps even a little disgusted, which increased Julian's slight dislike of him. "Oh, it must just be a joke," he said almost angrily.

Julian decided to wait for a chance to ask his friend James. That should be much more interesting. That night, when most of the house had gone to bed, he suggested having coffee in the library. They found it empty as he had hoped. He had already decided which excerpt to try out, a milder one in the light of Oliver's reaction. He took out the book and pretended to open it at random while they sipped their coffees and James read a newspaper.

"Christ, listen to this, James," he said after two minutes had elapsed. "This is from the library book of 1954. 'Mordaunt. Another pretty little chap. Obviously gets on well with Adams, his fag-master. Everyone suspects hanky-panky, but Adams isn't letting on.'"

"Hmm."

"Do you think the writer really meant it about finding the boy pretty?"

"Well, why not?"

"Wouldn't everyone think he was a pervert?"

"Oh, I doubt it. I should think that sort of thing must have happened quite often. What do you expect with no girls around?"

"Yes, I suppose so." There was a slightly tense silence, finally broken by James.

"Actually, to be perfectly honest, I had rather wondered earlier in the Half whether you might not have had something a bit like that going with Alexander Aylmer," he said gently, blushing a little.

"Me? No, that's definitely not my sort of thing," flustered Julian in shock. "I mean I liked him a lot, I still do, but not like that."

"Oh, right, I understand. I wouldn't have blamed you anyway. Alexander's just as pretty as any girl I've had the luck to meet." He smiled affably.

Julian returned his smile, but his mind was in turmoil. He

ought to be thrilled, he thought, that James was open-minded to such an unexpected degree, and he was of course pleased that it was so. However, it made him realise more than ever that all along he had worried far too much about what other people would think. James was after all the boy he liked most in his own block. If only he had known before, he might well have behaved differently. The agony of his regret at having missed his opportunity with Alexander intensified yet more.

It was that night that Julian first thought of exposing Mr. Cavendish's love affair with Alexander. It did not feel like a fresh thought and he realised guiltily that he must have been holding it at bay in his subconscious in the three days since he had discovered their being secretly together. He sat in the armchair in his room in silent darkness, as if the light might expose the rottenness of his soul. He tried vainly to persuade himself he should not contemplate such a course of action, that he was not bad enough for it, but nothing brought him any closer to being able to accept having lost Alexander to another. He knew he could indeed do it, and he wept silently for his consequent loss of respect for himself.

His tears reminded him of Alexander's the day he betrayed him, and that at last made him see things from Alexander's point of view. What he had done to the one he loved was not really forgivable, but he had not yet asked for forgiveness or even acknowledged the need for it, and now he was contemplating adding devastating injury to devastating injury. What if Alexander was willing to forgive him? Was it possible even now, if he showed how sorry he was, that he might win him back? He did not think so, but even he could not stoop as low as he had been contemplating without making sure. He would have to visit Alexander in his room once more and plead frankly to go back in time, to cancel the last six weeks as a terrible mistake. It was too late tonight, but tomorrow. He would follow him out of the dining-room after lunch, catch up with him long before he reached Mr. Cavendish's flat and demand a hearing, even in the street.

Julian went to lunch on the morrow quite certain, for once, of what he was going to do, but, to his astonishment, Alexander did not appear. Attendance at lunch was compulsory. Mr. and Mrs. Hodgson were there. His absence would surely be noticed. Was he taking his meals with Mr. Cavendish too? He must have taken leave of his senses.

He decided to go and ask Simon Churchill, who must certainly have noticed. When he had questioned him about Alexander a week before and got strange looks, he had decided he should not do it again, but now he did not care.

"Oh, didn't you know?" said Simon. "Alexander's father is getting wemawwied today, and he's been given special permission to stay out until eleven."

Julian's head spun. He had never heard anything about it. What an indication of how far apart they now were, he thought miserably, and resigned himself to waiting one more day.

One thing Julian had in common with David Edwards was a great dislike of Geoffrey Hay, who was widely regarded as a pompous ass. He was exactly the sort of person to whom David was incomprehensible and was himself calculated to arouse all of the American's rebellious instincts.

Geoffrey's most obvious foible was his intense and long-standing desire to be elected to Pop. He had spent years trying to ingratiate himself with the boys in his block who were most expected to reach those dizzy heights and had quite convinced himself for some time that his election was imminent. He had been disappointed several times, but his hopes remained high that they would finally be realised at the election due on the penultimate Sunday of the Half. Even he realised that it was his last chance, as in the next Half they would start to elect boys in the block below. Sadly for him, however, he was just about the only boy who thought he had any chance at all. He did not know that the boys in Pop regarded him as a tiresome sycophant and had even nicknamed him "the Pop Shadow."

Geoffrey was also oblivious to the fact that Julian knew and bitterly resented his earlier role in marshalling opinion against his friendship with Alexander. Julian having apparently submitted to common sense and given up his unsuitable liaison, Geoffrey imagined that the matter was forgotten and Julian ready to succumb to his obvious charm. He had even taken to inviting him occasionally to his room for games of chess in the forlorn hope of improving his own performance at it.

Julian was there beating Geoffrey yet again, soon after his conversation with Simon, and the afternoon before the election, when in came Pedro Gonzalez, another boy in C. Pedro was a nearly friendless boy who had latched on to Geoffrey as his only hope for his own promotion to the Library. Evidently Geoffrey was confident of Julian's goodwill, for he promptly told Pedro to tell him the latest tidings. It soon transpired that for at least the last week, Pedro had been assigned to hang around and eavesdrop on gatherings of the boys in Pop, so that his controller could better assess the situation.

"Are you really going to be elected to Pop, Geoffrey?" asked Julian in an innocent voice.

"Well, put it like this Julian, it's a virtual certainty."

When Julian relayed this conversation to David a little later, he knew it was like setting alight a tinder-box.

The next morning after chapel, Geoffrey went back to his room, where he paced up and down anxiously. The Pop election was being held right now. As soon as it was over, the members of the august body would stream through the school to search out the five or so successful candidates in their respective houses. The initiation ceremony was a rowdy affair. On entering each house, they would start chanting boisterously as they rushed past the awestruck boys, not at all accustomed to seeing such abandon on the part of these revered persons: boys in Pop were normally to be seen calm and utterly self-assured, strutting like peacocks in their dazzlingly colourful waistcoats. When they finally reached the glorious initiate's room, they would break eggs or other food over him and generally wreak havoc.

Geoffrey carefully stowed away his most precious possessions and began to listen intently as the expected moment approached. Suddenly he could hear the distant chant "Hoi, hoi, hoi." It was growing louder every moment and his heart soared with joy and relief. He had always known he deserved it. It was ridiculous of Hodgson to have made Anthony Burrows house captain instead of him. At any rate, to be in Pop was incomparably more glamorous and it was him rather than Anthony whom the whole house would be admiring enviously now. He could imagine their faces as he strolled nonchalantly into the library at teatime, their eyes glued on his new waistcoat.

"Hoi, hoi, hoi." It grew louder and louder until Geoffrey knew that they were right outside his door. Any second they would burst in, and he tried hard to adopt an expression of surprise, as if he had had no idea this was going to happen.

Then he registered that the noise was receding. At first he could not believe it, but within seconds there was no question about it. They had gone past his room. He could no longer hold his eyes wide open with feigned surprise. Instead he went to his door and listened carefully. Surely they could not be electing Anthony? No, Anthony hardly knew anyone in Pop well. Some idiot must have given them the wrong directions for his room and they would soon be back, he reassured himself, but he could not pretend he did not have miserable doubts.

Suddenly the chant stopped altogether. David and the excited rabble he had roused for the occasion had returned to the first floor and collapsed in laughter, but Geoffrey could not hear them. After a few minutes, he could no longer bear the suspense and went out into the corridor. John Haigh, another boy in B was already out there, equally mystified.

"What was all that about?" asked John.

Geoffrey was too shocked and miserable to attempt pretence. "I don't know," he said. "I thought for a moment I might've been elected to Pop."

The story whipped round the house in no time and Julian rushed off to Alexander's room, just in case he was there. He longed to be the first to break such hilarious news to him, but unsurprisingly he was nowhere to be found and his thoughts turned sour. At least he would have to come back for lunch soon, and the story might put him in a more receptive mood for the important thing he had to say.

An hour later, he saw Alexander leave the dining-room, one of the first to go, and he got up to follow him. When he reached Alexander's room, he found him already leaving, his door closed behind him.

"Where are you going?" he asked, struggling not to sound crestfallen.

"I've promised to go to see someone in another house."

326

"Oh, who?"

"Just a friend. No one you know," answered Alexander exasperatedly.

"Did you hear what happened to Hay this morning?"

"Yes, Rupert told me. That was really horrid of Edwards. I feel so sorry for Hay. I don't know why people think he's so awful. He's always been kind to me. Well, I've got to go."

"Okay. See you later," said Julian sadly, thankful he had not let on about his own role in the affair, as he had been planning. He had been feeling a little drawn out of his misery, but no more.

On Sundays, there were no Prayers before which he might find Alexander, and later than that was too dangerous in view of Hodgson's habit of visiting the F boys then, so Julian knew he would have to wait one more day. That was all though. He could not stand it any longer. He would not even wait until lunch and risk then being brushed aside again. He would go to his room during After Nine, when he was surely bound to be there, and they were also least likely to be interrupted. The small risk of being caught would just have to borne. Hodgson would probably sack him from the Library, but the humiliation of that would be a trifle compared to the agony he was already in.

As soon as all the boys had gone to their rooms after returning from their first div, and the house had fallen quiet, Julian crept out of his, went down to Alexander's and knocked quietly on the door. Alexander answered immediately, looking surprised and a little apprehensive when he saw Julian. He must have surmised that only some unusual purpose could have brought Julian to his room at this hour.

"Can we have a talk?" asked Julian nervously.

"Can't it wait until another time?"

"I've been wanting to have a proper chance to talk to you for ages, but you never seem to be around," said Julian, realising miserably, as he finished saying this, that he had failed to keep a peevish tone out of his voice.

"Okay then," said Alexander with a resigned sigh.

"It's about us," said Julian, wishing he could sound less strained. "We used to have such fun together, and I know it's all

327

my fault that it went wrong, but I regret it now, and I wondered if we couldn't go back to being friends again."

Alexander hesitated, evidently feeling a conflict of emotions. "Yes, I suppose so," he finally said with another sigh. "There's no point in us not being friendly together. But I really must finish my E.W. now. I've got a French vocab test coming up." His tone was amicable enough, though brisk, but Julian was no longer to be put off. Everything was at stake.

"Yes, but what I meant was, can't we be special friends like we used to be?" he steeled himself to ask at last. "I'm sorry I broke my promise and treated you like that, but I'm ready to go back to the way things were between us and I'll never do that again, whatever anyone says," he said in a voice shaking unmistakably with emotion.

"No, it's too late," replied Alexander without the slightest hesitation, as if he were almost horrified by the suggestion. "We can be ordinary friends if you want, but it could never be like that again." Julian thought he detected disdain in his tone and was cut to the quick.

"Okay. I see. It's up to you. I'll see you later then," said Julian anxious to be alone with his misery as soon as possible.

That's that then, decided Julian on his way back to his room. He could stand it no longer. He would stop their affair this very day. The only way was to get them caught and it was obvious how. It would be easy. He knew what would happen then, because it had happened before, when he was in F. An old housemaster called Mr. Berry had been found to be having an affair with one of his boys in D, and had been sacked at once. It had been given out officially that Mr. Berry had had a nervous breakdown and resigned, but before long the whole school knew the real reason.

All the same, it was a drastic step to take and he had to fight against his doubts. The most obvious one was that he had no evidence Alexander and Mr. Cavendish were having an affair at all. He had only definitely traced Alexander to the beak's building once, and even if he did go there every day, it did not prove they were lovers. It was just circumstantial evidence and his gut instinct that told him it was so.

These doubts were quite easily allayed though. He would anyway have to follow Alexander to Mr. Cavendish's flat again in order for his plan to work, so he would be doing nothing without having confirmed they were together. As for any doubts that their being together meant that Mr. Cavendish was the boy's lover, if he was not, then he obviously could not be caught being so, so Julian would have done no harm.

His more anguished doubts were of course about doing such harm to two people who had never done anything bad to him. The only way of bypassing these doubts was by reminding himself how unfair it was that he found himself in such a miserable plight. He had loved Alexander long before Mr. Cavendish had even set eyes on him. It was incredibly unfair that he had been made to give up his friendship when they had done nothing wrong, but Mr. Cavendish could get away with having a full-blown affair with him. It was one thing for boys stuck at school together to have affairs when there were no girls around. That ought to be allowed, but it was more understandable if people didn't want to put up with fully adult men doing it.

He realised that was not quite honest, and a dangerous conclusion to draw for himself. It could only be about six years until he was Mr. Cavendish's age and he no longer believed that by then he would prefer women to boys. He put himself in Mr. Cavendish's shoes. Why shouldn't a young man and a boy do what they liked together if they were both happy? Perhaps the most he could truthfully say was it was even more unfair of people to object to two schoolboys doing things together.

Anyway, being sent away was not such a terrible fate for Mr. Cavendish after all the bliss he had unfairly enjoyed. At his age, it was high time he started thinking about finding a wife. Probably he would, once he was sent away from the school and could not see Alexander any more.

Once Mr. Cavendish was out of the way, why should he not be able to win Alexander's heart again? Everything that he had had to offer him before, he still had, only this time he would be a truer and better friend. It might take time, but with enough determination and no more cowardice, he must at least have a chance. If Alexander was badly upset at losing his lover, it might even speed things along. He would be able to console him. If Alexander opened his heart to him and cried, he would take that as his cue to hug and kiss him. He would innocently ignite a physical affection he would then take care to kindle.

And once he decided that Alexander was willing enough, he would not again make the mistake of delay. He would bed him as soon as possible. No more fear. He had learned his lesson. The stakes of happiness were too high. His heart lurched with renewed misery when he remembered that Alexander was now infinitely more experienced in bed. Perhaps it would end up with Alexander showing him what to do, what had already been skilfully and lovingly done to him by the handsome usurper. It was agonising over this that finally steeled his determination.

After lunch he again followed Alexander out of lunch, but to his surprise, the boy stopped in the Common Room to bid in Nick Dashwood's auction of his belongings. It was only for a few minutes though. Soon Julian saw him sprint out of the house. He followed him until he disappeared through the same blue door, then he went straight into action without allowing time for further miserable reflection. He went back to Peyntors and typed an anonymous note to Hodgson on his waiting machine. He had already decided what it would say. He knew exactly what Mr. Cavendish did to Alexander even less than he knew they did anything amorous at all, but he did not really doubt that they went all the way. Anyway, if he was going to drive Hodgson into action, it was no use suggesting any uncertainty.

2:08 p.m., 2 July

Dear Mr. Hodgson,
     This is to tell you that you should go as urgently as possible to Flat 2, 135 Eton High Street, home of D. E. Cavendish, who is there at this very moment buggering your pupil A. M. C. Aylmer. This is also what was happening when your firm alarm went off on 27 June.

He put it in an envelope on which he typed "EXTREMELY URGENT. For J. R. Hodgson Esq." and circled the print with a thick, red highlighting pen.

Then he went quietly downstairs. No one was about because two o'clock had passed and they were all in their rooms. He opened the door that separated the boys' side of the house from the housemaster's and looked round it listening intently to make sure no one was around. Then he tiptoed in large silent strides towards Hodgson's private front door nearby, dropped his letter in the metal tray marked "Inbox" and stepped outside, pulling the door quietly closed behind him. No one was in the alley, so he pressed his index finger hard on the doorbell while he counted steadily to four. Then he ran round the building, back through the boys' entrance, up the stairs and was soon safely in his room without having encountered a soul.

Jack Hodgson noticed the garishly marked envelope as soon as he got to his front door. When he opened it and saw that no one was about, he immediately connected the mystery to the letter. Decidedly alarmed, though not enough to break his meticulous habits by tearing the envelope open, he returned to his study, sat down and slit it with his paper knife.

Appalled by what he then read, he wished fervently it was not true, but he suspected it was, and the more he thought about it, the more certain he became. He remembered that when he had asked Aylmer where he was when the fire alarm went off, Aylmer had not looked him in the eyes, and for the first time ever, he had had the disappointing feeling that the boy was lying.

He thought glumly that this was just the sort of minor stain on his career that could make all the difference as to whether he got a headmastership. Like many other Eton beaks, he had hoped that his housemastership would prove to be the stepping stone to one. The headmastership of Winterbourne, the school in Lancashire he had been to himself, was expected to come up in a year or two. It was only a very minor public school, and he knew many at Eton would sniff at even calling it that, but he had fond memories of the place and it could have led on to even greater things. The school governors would be bound to hear about this affair when the time came to make their choice.

"Make speed, not haste" was one of the little endlessly repeated sayings with which he liked to admonish his boys, but it was not one that he lived up to now, once he rose from his chair. By the time he arrived at Aylmer's room and threw open its door to confirm that it was indeed empty, he was dreadfully flustered. Realising this, he pulled himself together by taking slow paces back downstairs while he collected his thoughts.

All sorts of things fell into place. The most obvious was the Rosebery Prize. He remembered how surprised he had been by Aylmer winning that. He knew he was one of the more brilliant boys in his house and impassioned with ancient history, but all the same writing a prize-winning essay required gifts of composition and organisation for which maturity and experience were bound to be enormous advantages, so it had seemed extraordinary that he had beaten scholars up to two years older than him. Doubtless Cavendish had written the whole thing and Aylmer had just copied it out. The same presumably applied to the whole flood of Show Ups that Aylmer had been bringing for him to sign on an almost daily basis over the last month.

He knew he would inevitably get some of the blame for the sordid affair. He was "in loco parentis" and would be held to have failed in his duty of care in not having somehow averted it, but how much he would get blamed depended considerably on how long the affair had been going on, for that would be a measure of his negligence. Cavendish was a new beak, so it could not at least have started before this Half. That still left an appallingly long time.

Then he remembered furiously the Sent Up For Good that Aylmer had got at the beginning of the Half. It had been Cavendish himself who had given it for that story. He must have written that for Aylmer too. That must have been when he seduced him. He must have picked on him the first day he met his div. Presumably he had only become a schoolmaster because he had an illicit interest in boys. He would have seen that Aylmer was his best-looking pupil and fortuitously vulnerable thanks to his mother's still quite recent death. It would have been easy to pretend to be sympathetic and use it as a pretext to invite him to his flat. Then, once he had made the boy believe they were friends, he must have offered to "help" him with his short story and send it up for good in tacit exchange for sexual favours.

XIII: Triumph and Nemesis

All that's bright must fade,-
The brightest still the fleetest;
All that's sweet was made
But to be lost when sweetest.
  Thomas Moore, *National Airs*

Alexander lay forward in Damian's arms, relaxed but fast regaining his energy after his lover had drunk from the fountain of his boyish essence, the man gently fingering the boy's lustrous hair. They were completely in tune with each other's bodies now. Damian could sense from the slight tensioning of the boy's when he was growing restive and ready for further play, and Alexander knew the same way when Damian was about to react to that.

Alexander was completely self-confident with his lover now. Both acknowledging and giving sexual pleasure were a matter of pride to him, and embarrassment about them a forgotten concept. He knew he brought Damian unmitigated joy and that his body was attuned to Damian's in how to do it, so he felt no need to hold back whenever he thought of a new position that might bring them new joy, and he had thought of one this morning that he was looking forward to surprising Damian with.

When he felt that Damian was about to rise up from their embrace to anoint his organ in readiness for its passage of joy, he did not draw back his legs ready to rest them on the man's shoulders, so they could look into each other's eyes during the act of love and interrupt it with long kisses. Nor did he turn over onto his side to be entered from behind by Damian lying parallel, the best position when they wanted the act prolonged and relaxed, as Damian could use his free hand to bring Alexander to orgasm again or even twice more before his own climax came. Nor did he kneel down on all fours with his bottom raised submissively for his lover to mount him kneeling behind, which was most exciting when harder suited their mood. Nor did he adopt any of the other positions they had already tried.

Instead, he sat up and gently placed his hands on Damian's shoulders as if to tell him to lie still. When Damian looked into

333

his eyes quizzically, he giggled happily. He took the bottle of baby oil from the bedside table and poured some onto the palm of his right hand. Then he sat between his lover's legs and with his left hand he gently played with the man's balls until his body quivered with excitement. Next he pulled his cock towards him with his fingers round its base until it was as vertical as could be in its totally rigid state and slid his oily right hand slowly up and down the shaft, savouring its soft silky texture and simultaneous rock-like hardness. He stopped then for it would not do to waste Damian's excitement on a pleasure so inferior to that he planned.

He got up on all fours over him and brought his lips down to meet the young man's. He kissed him at length out of the boundless love he felt, conscious also that this would calm them both a little for more prolonged joy to come.

Then he rose up on his knees and flashed a smile at his lover as he felt for the huge, live poker behind him and nudged its head into place, resting in delicious hardness against his orifice. He leaned gently back. He was in control of his body now and anticipated his own gasp of pleasure, which thus coincided perfectly with the yielding of his sphincter, as Damian slid in. Then he leaned gradually back and ever further back until finally he was sitting completely impaled by his lover's organ, his knees either side of the man's stomach. He sighed and paused for a few moments, happily taking in his lover's look of disbelief that such ecstasy was possible. Then he slowly drew himself up and up and felt Damian's organ pulling out. This time it felt much longer than in their previous love-making and he was surprised at finding himself a bit tired by the time he reckoned he had risen up the right amount, with Damian's glans still safely wedged inside him, but most of the shaft outside.

Damian felt himself straining in eager anticipation of full re-entry, and could not help thrusting upwards as he felt the pressure of the boy's sphincter again slide deliciously down his shaft until he was once more entirely enveloped in the warm passage.

Except in those very first moments when Damian had deflowered him, Alexander had never known any discomfort being fucked, but as he rose up again, he reflected that riding one's lover cock was quite a tiring way of doing it. He spurred himself on by imagining himself as a boy riding his stallion. He was Alexander riding Boukephalos, and with each spasm of pleasure as he fell back to bring the full length of Damian's mighty shaft into himself, a surge of triumph went through him that he felt must be akin to that the Macedonian boy had felt as the hooves of his newly-mastered stallion thundered under him, bringing him closer to the cheering army.

His last inhibitions with his lover had disappeared, so he allowed himself to moan with ecstasy and growing exhaustion at each thrust. When he found himself beginning to pant, he decided to sing softly instead. It was a love song in rich, old-fashioned language by a popular Irish folk singer that expressed with a beauty that had sometimes made Alexander cry the singer's triumph at having won her love. Though the words came from the song, he felt that the triumph they expressed came from the depths of his own heart. He sung of his victory, the victory of love, freedom and joy over loneliness, constraint and despair.

As the song reached its euphoric finale, Alexander's pleasure at each sliding plunge intensified until there was no more room in his thoughts for exhaustion or any sensation but pure bliss. His nostrils flared, his lips drew back and his whole body writhed with delight.

Damian recognised the convulsions of the boy's sphincter rippling ecstatically along his shaft that meant he was about to come. Apart from his own orgasm and perhaps that special jolt of pleasure he always felt as he first slid into Alexander, these hugs on his cock gave the most intense pleasure he imagined it was possible for a man to feel and his familiarity with their rhythm gave him a precisely timed understanding of Alexander's zenithing ecstasy. They would begin gently, steadily quicken up to the moment of the boy's orgasm, then suddenly change to longer and much tighter hugs that coincided with his spurts.

He had been trying desperately to hold himself back until Alexander was ready to join him, but no more. He tightened his hand's hold on the pulsating boy's silky shaft, and just as his beloved's hot, crystal liquid shot up in great arcs onto his chest, his own shot deep into the boy, wave after wave.

335

Alexander too now had an instinctive understanding of what the tensioning of his lover's muscles signified. He was therefore ready for the intense spiritual joy he always felt when the pulsing of his lover's cock told him that he was being inseminated, and fully able to relish its coincidence with his own climax.

He felt suddenly as overwhelmed by his exertions as they had fulfilled him, and allowed himself to collapse exhausted onto Damian, his head lying on the latter's shoulder. Limp and as happy and relaxed as he had ever been in his life, he soon fell fast asleep.

Damian ran his fingers through his soft blond locks, tenderly stroking his head. He gazed with awe at the beautiful body lying on him, and in which he still lay. Then he drew his finger down from the boy's hair along his neck and the hardness of his backbone, slowly all the way until he met the contrasting softness of the crevice between his firm, little buttocks and on further until he touched his own hard organ where it disappeared into its soft, snug home, now tangible proof of their union.

As happened so often when Alexander lay in his arms, he felt yet another surge of fierce determination to protect him, which soon led to pride that he had already successfully done so, that he had changed the sad, lonely boy who had first come to his flat into one bursting with exuberance and confidence.

He felt himself beginning to drift happily off to sleep, when suddenly there was a loud knocking on his front door.

He extricated himself gently from the sleeping boy, who stirred only a little, got up and quickly dressed. As he did so, the knocking was repeated more loudly and he sensed possible trouble from its urgency. A knock on his door usually meant a pupil come to see him and he had always been able to deal with whatever business it was in the doorway, but surely no boy would presume to knock that loudly and impatiently. He went out of the bedroom, closing the door quietly behind him. As he reached for his door-latch, he reassured himself that it must be an impatient postman or tradesman. Just then, the knocking resumed and he had readied an expression of growing exasperation for his visitor by the time he confronted him through the half-open doorway. Then he froze in shock.

Mr. Hodgson stood there looking red and puffed-up, his eyes bulging angrily. Damian's heart lurched, as the link to Alexander struck him as almost certain. He had long ago been briefly up to Hodgson in Philosophy, but they had rarely spoken since he came back to Eton as a beak, so nothing else could explain his appearing in this manner.

"Mr. Hodgson!" he said shakily. "What is it?" worrying as he spoke that he had made Alexander and himself more vulnerable by not instead saying calmly "Good afternoon, Jack! What can I do for you?" The collegiate spirit amongst Eton beaks allowed that once two beaks had been properly introduced they could call each other by their Christian names, but in his terror Damian had fallen back on his schoolboy habit.

"I think you know very well what it is!" boomed the housemaster, deciding that Damian's rather dishevelled appearance confirmed yet again the accuracy of the mysterious letter.

"I'm afraid I don't know what you're talking about, but I'm in too much of a hurry just at the moment. Could we discuss whatever it is at Chambers tomorrow?" Damian rested his left hand firmly on the edge of the door, both as if to confirm that there was no possibility of admitting a visitor at this time, and to steady himself.

"No, we could not!" replied Hodgson, immediately responding to Damian's gesture by pushing firmly past him, his gaze already fixed on the bedroom door the other side of the sitting-room.

"Mr. Hodgson! You have no business ...," began Damian, panicking and following the intruder. He realised that he must at all cost stop him opening the bedroom door, and tried to seize his arm, but too late.

"We shall soon see about that!" Hodgson interrupted him, as he flung open the bedroom door.

Alexander, finally awakened by the repeated knocking, had also panicked wildly as soon as he heard the booming voice of his housemaster, and had leapt from the bed, from the far side of which he crouched helplessly, the sheet pulled revealingly hard down towards him.

"Aylmer! How dare you try to hide from me! Get up at once!" shouted Hodgson. The terrified boy stood up shaking, and gripping the sheet, which only partially hid his nakedness. Hodgson's eyes widened with outrage, even though it was exactly what he had expected. He glanced around, briefly took in the bottle of baby oil on the bedside table, its cap open, and guessed its significance at once. Self-satisfaction that he was too wise to miss such unobtrusive clues mixed with his fury.

"Get dressed immediately! You are coming with me," he spluttered at Alexander. Suddenly reddening with embarrassment at the sight of the boy's nakedness, he turned away to confront Damian, who was standing and looking aghast from the other side of the doorway.

As Hodgson bore down on him, Damian retreated a few steps to allow him back into the sitting-room. He instinctively wanted Hodgson to come away from Alexander and hoped he would come far enough in to allow him to pass round him and stand protectively between them, but Hodgson, with an equal instinct to keep the illicit paramours apart, did not come far enough into the room for this.

"Mr. Hodgson," said Damian and paused, lost for words.

"I suggest you reserve whatever you can think of to say for the Head Master," he replied scathingly.

Just then, Alexander rushed past them both. He was still entirely naked, having been unable to dress because he had left his clothes in a bundle by Damian's sofa. He pulled on his pants and trousers and picked up his shirt, only to throw it back on the ground as he suddenly realised being fully dressed would remove an obvious impediment to his being taken away. He came to stand behind Damian, his hands on the young man's hips, looking round his shoulder at their adversary.

"Please Damian, do something, do anything, but don't let him take me away, let me stay with you, please!" he cried frantically.

"Mr. Hodgson," repeated Damian in an agony of indecision. His boy's plea could not have been better calculated to stir the strongest emotions imaginable in him, for the one cause he knew he would willingly lay down his life for was Alexander's

338

protection, but he could not think of anything to say or do that offered the slightest hope. His thoughts veered absurdly between assaulting Hodgson and pleading to him on his knees. In the end, he just let his heart speak. "Please. Try to understand a little. He needs me. And I love him…"

"Great Scott, man!" exploded the housemaster, puffing up with outrage. "You must have completely lost your grip on reality, as well as having a moral blank in your character! Do you seriously imagine I might let you just carry on with this corrupt liaison?"

"Yes! Why not?" cried Alexander defiantly, suddenly in tears born of fury and shock as much as despair. "We're not doing any harm to anyone. It's not corrupt, and anyway it's no one else's business. Why can't you leave us alone?!"

His outburst shook Hodgson and he stared bemusedly at the boy, who cowered behind Damian, his arms now clinging round his lover's waist, and stared back at him as if he were a vicious wild beast about to spring at them.

For a moment, Hodgson saw himself from his pupil's point of view and was moved. Aylmer was the last boy in his house he wanted to be regarded by as an enemy. He would never in his life forget how awful it had been having to tell him his mother had died. It had been much his worst experience as a housemaster. There was clearly no way, at least in the short term, of making him see that he was not now acting to injure him grievously. Indeed, he was not at all sure he could make himself see that. Things having already gone this far, would the boy's life not in fact have turned out for the better if the affair had never been discovered? Just supposing that were so, would it not also have been better if he had turned a blind eye to the accusations in the anonymous letter?

Then he remembered that that would have made him complicit in the sordid business, and he recoiled in horror from his train of thought. He must not allow himself to think like that. He had not really done so. It had been mere idle speculation. There had never been any doubt where his duty lay. All the same, he should not be any harsher than strictly necessary.

"There is much that you do not understand, Alexander," he said gravely, "I urge you to believe I am not your enemy.

Whatever you may imagine, it is my unquestionable duty acting in loco parentis to report this matter without delay to your father, as well as the Head Master. However, if you will at least do as I am ordering you, that is get dressed and come back to the house right now, I shall at least endeavour to ensure that they both understand your view of things."

Alexander looked up questioningly at Damian, who sensed his gaze without seeing it. Damian was dumb with dread and despair.

"I can assure you," resumed Hodgson, "that you will only be making things very much worse for Mr. Cavendish if you do not do as I tell you."

Alexander remembered Damian telling him that if they were discovered he would be sent away and could even go to prison. Was the difference between the two what Mr. Hodgson had in mind? In that case, he really had no choice. As long as the Head Master really did get to hear of all the good Damian had done him and how it truly was between them, it was surely inconceivable he would want to send him to prison. Perhaps he could even be made to see how unfair it would be to sack him. However unrealistic that might be, as long as there was any hope that reason might prevail, they had better try using it.

"Shall I go?" he asked Damian, stepping out to his side.

"We have no choice," replied Damian in a low voice, heavy with grief, turning his head enough for the boy to see his face for the first time ever with the light gone out of his eyes.

Alexander had expected that dread reply, but he would not leave his lover's side without hearing it and could not help feeling overwhelmed with despair when he did. He went to put the rest of his clothes on. His hands trembled as he buttoned up his long, white shirt, and he interrupted the process to wipe away more tears that had appeared in his eyes. Then he forced himself to try to pull himself together. He needed to think urgently of whatever could be done to save them, while he slowly did up his collar and tie, then put on his socks, shoes and waistcoat.

He reminded himself that it was hardly more than a week to the end of the Half. Even if there was no hope the Head Master could be persuaded not to sack Damian, there was surely nothing they could do to stop them meeting in secret during the holidays. Perhaps they could run away together. They could decide about that later. In any case, the critical thing was that they meet again to make a plan before Damian was made to leave. The trouble was Hodgson was bound to try to stop them. How could he escape?

Suddenly, he remembered the coal room window in Peyntors. He would climb through it again tonight! In only a few hours, they could be together again. With a surge of relief, he put on his tailcoat and turned towards Damian, longing to tell him with his eyes that he would be back soon, but all he could read in his lover's eyes was a hopeless despair that terrified him. It reminded him that though he had of course told him about giving Miranda a present, he had not said how early it had been or therefore how he had got out of the house while it was still locked up. Damian had no idea that he could come to him if only he would stay until tonight.

"Whatever happens, you will wait for me, won't you?" he said urgently, crossing the room back to Damian and ignoring Hodgson, who looked on indignantly.

"I. ..... I'll try," answered Damian miserably, his implied uncertainty frightening Alexander yet more.

"Now, that is quite enough of that," said Hodgson, opening the door for the boy to leave.

Alexander gave him a fearful glance and turned his gaze back to Damian pleadingly. Surely, Damian would not be made to leave this evening? He could not pack up all his stuff by then. Whatever happened, he must not. He was terrified he would though. He longed to tell him how he would be able to escape, but it was too late. They were being stared at angrily by the one person who must not know

"Aylmer!" thundered Hodgson.

Alexander finally tore his tearful eyes away from Damian's woeful gaze and moved to the door. As soon as he had passed through it, he turned to give him one last, beseeching look, then Hodgson closed it firmly behind them.

Mr. Allenby, the Head Master, was deeply troubled. It was the most upsetting case of its kind he had yet encountered in his career, not because of what had apparently happened, but because of what was now going to happen for the first time due to radical changes in society in the last few years.

As might be expected of the head of such a prestigious school, he was extremely assiduous in keeping himself informed of everything that could possibly enable him to carry out his duties better. Even teaching for its own sake was not considered a worthwhile use of his precious time. He only ever did it to gain a greater insight into the thinking of the boys, so he could better perform his role of improving the excellence and smooth running of the school. He knew every beak and far more of the boys than anyone else. He had also thought about and was much better and more broadly informed than anyone else on the most sensitive issues that affected the school.

It was only five months since he had interviewed Cavendish and he had decided immediately that he was the right man for the job. He had already known him quite well from his earlier days as a member of Pop and a house captain. Cavendish had evidently continued to distinguish himself at Cambridge, but on top of all that he had that peculiar quality which was hard to define, but by which any really good headmaster just somehow knew he had before him an outstanding schoolmaster. It was a genuine enthusiasm to teach more than anything, but it ran deeper than that. He also had character, almost indispensable for fitting in at Eton, though it could have unforeseeable consequences, sometimes unfortunate as now. In any case, he had already, in the headmaster's mind, become a future housemaster and likely to go on to dizzier heights. Now he was to be ruined for ever and more terribly than most people would understand was inevitable.

He also knew Aylmer, which was rather an oddity, for he did not meet many of the lower boys. Eton had a Lower Master who deputised for him with them, and it was generally only the most promising who crossed paths with him, as indeed in this case. Throughout his career as a schoolmaster, his extraordinary memory and iron-willed determination to remember his boys' names had ensured that he almost never forgot one, even years after a single meeting; his meeting with Aylmer over the Rosebery prize had by extraordinary coincidence been barely more than a week ago. He had of course been struck by his remarkable good looks too, so he was not surprised that he should be the choice of a man inclined to indulge in immorality, not that he had ever felt remotely tempted by that vice himself.

Sadly, though, what he remembered more than the boy's looks was his promise. Hodgson seemed to think Cavendish must have written his essay for him. If it was true, that would disappoint him in the man as much as the buggery did, but he did not believe it for a moment. Cavendish may well have encouraged him, that was what schoolmasters were for, but he cannot have done much more than that. He had seen the boy's enthusiasm and self-assurance when talking about Alexander the Great. He had been moved to see a young boy so impassioned about a figure from the ancient world. It was just the sort of odd thing that Eton hoped to inspire. From what Hodgson had told him of the affair, it seemed certain that the boy was already suffering dreadfully. He knew that worse was soon coming for him too.

Deeply as he felt sorry for Cavendish for what he was about to endure, he did not feel inclined to condone to any degree what he had done. He knew he stood at the head of his profession because others believed in his unwavering sense of duty to uphold the highest moral as well as educational standards in what was thankfully still a Christian school. He and all the teachers under him had been placed in a position of trust by the boys' parents and Cavendish had abused that trust.

Besides, Allenby was a genuine Christian. He believed that all sex outside marriage was at least a mistake, if not wrong. He had most certainly been a virgin himself when he had married at the age of twenty-six. Before then, during the war, he had served in the navy, which had brought him into proximity with lower-class men of his age for the first time, and he had been truly shocked by what he learned of their promiscuity.

At the end of every Half in which there were leavers, he gave them a final lecture, mostly homely advice on how they should conduct themselves now that their schooldays were over and they were going out into the world with all its promises and temptations. His main point never changed, year after year.

343

"You may also find yourself tempted by opportunities to sleep with young ladies before you get married," he would say, "and many people nowadays will tell you there is nothing wrong with doing so. But I urge you to believe that the greatest happiness in life is to be found in marriage, and that your chances of enjoying a truly successful and happy marriage will have been spoiled if you and your wife have not kept yourselves pure for each other. Again, some people may tell you that you will benefit from sexual experience, but I can assure you from personal experience that if you wait until you are married, you will very soon learn together and make up for lost time." During this last statement, he would allow his normally austere features to relax into a slight smile and a twitter of surprised amusement would rumble through his audience. Boys always listened to him respectfully, but they were taken aback by hearing him admit to appreciation of anything as earthy as the pleasures of the flesh. He could sense then their approval too, and though many would doubtless fall by the wayside, if just some took his advice to heart, he would have done his duty to them well.

Buggery was a distasteful vice, he thought, but then people did do the most extraordinary things, and that was not the point. He understood that allowing other people to do things one found repugnant oneself was, so long as they did no harm to others, the basic foundation of any free country, of any civilised society at all. What mattered to him was his pastoral duty to guide the boys towards happy and useful lives, and he knew that both homosexuality and fornication were obstacles to this. He had always taken just as hard a line with fornication, even a little harder, as bringing girls back to the school for sex was a newer and perhaps greater threat to discipline that needed to be nipped in the bud. He had always expelled boys caught doing that, while he had allowed the buggers to get away with caning until it was abolished.

In truth, homosexuality was not considered such a great threat any more because the battle against this most ancient of boarding school vices had at last largely been won. He knew it to be one of the greatest victories of recent times, but it could not be celebrated, because that would involve admitting to the public how very rife it had been before.

344

Only a handful of people as well-read as himself in the history of the school were aware of the most disturbing thing about buggery in the old days, namely that until the nineteenth century it had just been accepted as an inevitable part of school life. The only recorded case of anyone, master or boy, getting into trouble for it before then was one of his own distinguished predecessors, Nicholas Udall, who had in 1541 been convicted by Henry VIII's Privy Council of buggering some of his pupils by his own confession, and he had only been exposed because he refused to yield to blackmail from two choirboys whom had been caught stealing silver candlesticks from College Chapel.

Well into the nineteenth century, the seventy College boys had all slept together in the infamous Long Chamber, where they were locked up without supervision from eight p.m. until the morning without the slightest concern being shown for the wild revelry and open indulgence in vice this resulted in. Things were hardly better in the oppidans' boarding houses, where surviving correspondence revealed that boys of often dangerously disparate ages were encouraged to sleep naked in the same beds to keep themselves warm during the winters. It was hard to fathom whether his predecessors had simply been incredibly naïve as to the inevitable consequences or whether they had operated in a sort of moral void.

Only in the middle of the nineteenth century had the school authorities finally awoken to the need to fight the vice determinedly, and the resistance they had met from both boys and occasionally even masters had initially been rather stronger than in most public schools. One Eton master's wife was recorded as displaying a shocking astonishment at the fuss made over an exposed affair.

"It's the traditional, ancient, aristocratic vice of Eton," she said. "What do they know of it in those modern, sanitary, linoleum schools?"

Until recently, the methods resorted to for its extirpation had often been regrettably crude and only partially successful. Though public displays of affection between boys or masters and boys that had once been thought harmless soon became unthinkable, veiled warnings had proven woefully inadequate in achieving more. Boys caught were therefore humiliated, brutally

345

caned and often expelled. Masters were quickly dismissed. The sleeping arrangements were gradually changed until finally every boy had his own room. A taboo was developed against friendships between boys more than a year apart in age. The blocks were made rigidly age-based to stop the stupid older boys from being in the same divs as twelve-year-olds, as had happened when performance in Trials had been the only criterion. Boys' free time was severely curtailed in favour of compulsory sports and the School Corps, both designed to encourage manliness, and the little time they had left subjected to heavy surveillance.

Despite all these efforts, many of them applied in all public schools, homosexuality had still been rife in his own school days at Shrewsbury, and he knew from his subsequent career in other public schools that it had remained so until half a generation ago.

Its reduction since then was dramatic indeed. The nicest irony was that the most lethal blow to the vice had been dealt by its loudest advocates. It was precisely the legalisation of adult homosexuality in 1967 and consequent open emergence of a gay identity in society that had changed the average schoolboy's view of it from a naughty or immoral but understandable indulgence to an intolerable and ineffaceable slur on a boy's normality and masculinity. This new stigma applied by the boys themselves to any questionable friendship was far more effective than the housemasters' attempts at suppression in the days when boys had often approved of romantic friendships. It helped too that the school was opened up more to the outside world and increased contacts with girls. Even the regrettable sexual possibilities offered by those contacts since the upheaval of the sixties had its flip side in thoroughly heterosexualising the boys.

It was therefore ironic that just when they had finally succeeded in bringing homosexuality under control, the school was becoming subject to undesirable and unnecessary interference over it from outside. New guidelines from the Department of Education recommended notification to the police of all known cases of "child sexual abuse", as it termed any sexual contact between a child and someone significantly older.

It was yet another example of the ever increasing and mostly harmful interference of the government in the school's affairs.

For more than six hundred years the cream of the English nobility had sent their sons there, more recently foreign Kings had too, and now even the future King of their country was down for it, and all because they knew that Eton offered the best education the country, or perhaps even the world, could provide. Yet despite that, increasingly, year after year, the school's hands were being tied by petty-fogging government bureaucrats, and all on the instigation of semi-educated social activists who would not know Plato from Nietzsche, but thought they knew better.

If it had been up to him, he would have disregarded this reporting of abuse recommendation, but curiously, despite the prestige of his post, he had less authority at Eton than he had had at the minor public school he had been headmaster of before. He could not effect any policy changes without the Provost and Fellows, who were by no means the mere rubber-stamping authority the governors of some schools were, but took their responsibilities very seriously indeed. Unfortunately, they were in his opinion overly concerned with the school's reputation and too eagerly swayed by public opinion, perhaps because they were themselves public figures.

He had argued that the welfare of the boys should be their overriding concern and so the police should not be brought in unless a boy or his parents wanted it. Where a master was involved with one, they should continue the old policy of requiring his resignation for "health reasons" and immediate removal from the school. He knew from long experience that what the boy needed in these cases was the help of his parents and housemaster in getting back to normal schoolboy life as soon as possible, without anyone else knowing. Buggery had been going on at Eton for four hundred years before the police or social workers were invented, so what could they understand about such things? The trauma a boy was likely to suffer at their hands was probably far more harmful than his corruption into vice.

Though the Fellows had thankfully dismissed without serious debate the idea of reporting affairs between older and younger boys, as the government apparently wanted, a majority of them had overridden him where masters were involved. The Provost had led them in arguing that the risk to the school's reputation

347

was too great. Constant vigilance had to be exercised in its protection: anything to do with the school was considered good copy by the press and a sex scandal would be a rare coup for any newspaper, especially the gutter press, which was generally quite hostile to the school and willing to pay large sums to anyone ready to leak a juicy tale. In that case, if they had not followed the government's recommendations, they would quickly be accused of covering up sexual abuse or not taking it seriously. Child sexual abuse had over the last few years become the greatest cause célèbre on which the public expended its fury and this was the crux of the problem. If the sacked master somehow managed to secure another teaching position and repeated his offence, and it then emerged that Eton had concealed his former wrongdoing, public outrage with the school would be terrible.

It had not been the first time they had allowed their concern for the school's image to come before what he strongly believed was the welfare of the boys. They had clashed most strongly over caning, which they had insisted on abolishing three years ago out of concern for the barbaric image of Eton it gave the public once popular opinion had turned against it. He was relieved that the days when housemasters and even house captains could cane boys were over, but he believed that as administered by only himself it had remained an extremely useful penultimate sanction against serious misbehaviour. Fear of pain was a deterrent to any boy and brought his shame home to him without having any long-term adverse effects. Expulsion, which was often the only alternative, did not deter every boy as much and was extremely damaging to his future. The punishment of buggery was a particular case in point. He had always caned the culprits and they had been able to continue their careers at the school without interruption, their peers generally unaware of what had happened. They could hardly be rusticated with all the attention that drew to their immorality, so now they had to be expelled.

This was the first case of buggery he was going to have to report to the police. It sickened him to have to do it, because he knew it was not in the boy's interest. Hodgson had made it clear beyond doubt that Aylmer was utterly infatuated with

348

Cavendish, and he could hardly bear to think how he would react to the police trying to get him to help them incriminate the man. All he could do to limit the damage to him was make telephone calls to certain highly placed persons who would hopefully be able to ensure that his anonymity was preserved.

He thought what was going to happen to poor Cavendish was also way over the top. He was bound to go to prison for a very long time, and one heard terrible things of the treatment there nowadays most especially reserved for child sex offenders. It would surely have been more than enough punishment that his hitherto promising career was stopped in its tracks, as had generally been the only fate of those caught in recent centuries. Even Udall had been sent to prison for less than a year and went on to become headmaster of Westminster thirteen years later. And yet people now talked of Henry VIII's reign as a paradigm of brutal repression! Since then, discreet expulsion had always been the satisfactory answer.

Affairs between masters and boys were much rarer than those between boys. There had only been two discovered in his time as headmaster. The first one had been very much like the present, except that there had fortunately not been so much passion involved. The boy's housemaster had been duly solicitous in helping him get it in perspective and he had got over it in time. None of the other boys had had a clue of what had happened, so his anonymity and their innocence had both been preserved. The master had gone on to become a theatre critic of considerable merit.

The last case three years ago had been the worst scandal at the school in living memory. A housemaster fell for one of his charges, a boy called Minto, and carried on an affair with him for more than a year. Typically of the way the vice corrupted, when Minto was in D, he sought simultaneously to build his own little harem. He was caught in bed with a boy in F. The house captain grew suspicious that he had not been punished and rather bravely bypassed the housemaster by coming straight to him. He summoned Minto at once. It was at that point that the scandal had turned into an outrage, for Minto himself revealed his affair with his housemaster and had the brazen effrontery to threaten to go public with the details if he was expelled. It soon emerged that Minto had the full backing of his father, who owned one of the national dailies and threatened to publish the story. In an emergency meeting, the Provost and Fellows quickly capitulated to save the school's reputation, which was ironic in view of their later insistence on protecting it by exposing affairs. The housemaster had of course been sacked, but although further investigation revealed that Minto had buggered two other thirteen-year-olds, he was allowed to stay on, albeit boarding out with a master in Willowbrook. There was widespread disgust, for this scandal proved too great to contain and soon spread around the school. Nevertheless, libel law prevented it getting into the public domain, and from the point of view of the three F boys, the damage had again been limited as much as possible by discretion.

It was a pity Hodgson was such a useless housemaster. If he had paid proper attention, this affair could surely have been nipped in the bud. He had been an impressive classics beak, so his failure to get properly involved with the boys in his house had been a great disappointment. There had been complaints from parents about his negligence before, and it had even been discussed by the Fellows, but he had been given tenure as housemaster and, unless he did something really bad, there was simply nothing they could do to be rid of him, beyond dropping hints which he ignored. As he picked up the telephone, he wondered vaguely if the present crisis might finally give them enough cause.

When Hodgson closed the door of Damian's flat behind Alexander and himself with a firm thump and click, and total silence descended on the premises, Damian felt at first as though the door had been closed on his existence, so lifeless was the place. It was hard to believe that only an hour earlier, it had been filled with laughter and joy. He stood still, staring stunned at the door for several minutes. Unlike Alexander, he was not quite young and innocent enough to believe there need be any hope against the odds. His beloved was gone and Damian knew that he would likely never see him again, and certainly not so long as he remained the boy who so desperately needed him.

350

Finally, he forced himself to move a little. He intermittently sat on his sofa, numb with shock and misery, and paced around his flat, trying to clear his mind.

Should he have thought more about the possibility of this happening? He found he did not really believe so. He had known his affair with Alexander was no one else's business and for that very reason had thought quite reasonably that no one was likely to find out about it. He still could not understand how Mr. Hodgson had. Someone, a neighbour perhaps, could have wondered why Alexander went into the building so often, but the jump from that to Hodgson's apparent certainty that Damian was his lover was still huge and inexplicable.

From the only similar incidents he had heard of, he expected that at any moment this afternoon he would be told by the headmaster that he had lost his job, should remove himself from the school premises within so many hours and never be seen within them again. Very likely it would also be pointed out to him that what he had done was a criminal offense, which was only not being brought to the attention of the police because it was in no one's interest to do so, and he would be threatened that further such action could be taken if he attempted to communicate with Alexander ever again.

Perhaps he should already be packing his belongings, but his mind was in too much turmoil, and his nervousness was increased by the expectation that at any moment he would be interrupted by the harsh ring of the telephone summoning him to see the Head Master. He was just a little worried that the matter might be dealt with over the telephone, but he thought that unlikely. He very much did want an interview with Mr. Allenby, because he had important things he wanted to say that were best said soon and in person. He had no intention of trying to hide or obscure any of the truth, far from it, and he knew there was not the faintest chance he would not be sacked, but it was nevertheless terribly important to him to set the record straight.

He desperately tried to marshal his thoughts. He did not know how long the Head Master would be prepared to listen to him, so it was important that he stuck to the important points he wished to make. Finally, he worked out what they were. There were really three things that needed to be said, of which he

351

would have to leave the most important to last, because if it was to do any good he needed to try to regain whatever modicum of respect for himself might be possible by saying the other things first.

First, he would say, he was genuinely and profoundly saddened to have caused the school or the Head Master to feel let down, because he had the greatest respect and admiration for both. Such had been the opposite of his intentions. He had been immensely grateful for being given the job and had looked forward to performing his duties to the best of his abilities. He understood why he must feel let down, in that Damian had broken the most serious of the rules that he had been trusted to preserve. Tragically though, adhering to this particular rule had clashed with what he perceived as his primary duty of answering the needs of a boy who had placed his happiness entirely in his hands.

Secondly, it was simply not true, as might be supposed if nothing was said to the contrary, that his affair with Alexander was the outcome of a man knowingly attracted to boys allowing himself to get close to one and then losing self-control. Less still had it been a planned seduction. Nothing could have been further from the case. He would explain that he was not saying this to defend himself, but simply so that the Head Master need not fear that his judgement in giving him his post had been so poor as to fail to detect someone who was applying for it for the wrong reasons.

At the outset, he had simply liked the boy and felt sorry for him. He had found that Alexander was in desperate need of caring attention as a result of miserable circumstances that were no one's fault, and he had felt sure he was doing the right thing in giving it. As their friendship had developed, he and Alexander had grown to love one another, but they had done so without any idea of a sexual outcome. He had come to love Alexander as much as he thought it was possible for one being to love another and he believed Alexander felt the same about him. It was only after each discovered the other felt this way that they had felt irresistibly drawn to physical fulfilment of their love. Even in giving in to this passion, he had acted in good conscience, for he felt absolutely certain that the love he had given Alexander, including the physical love, had made the boy happy and otherwise greatly benefited him, and therefore he could not in all sincerity believe it was not right, however differently other people might feel bound to see it, and although he of course understood that the Head Master had no option but to dismiss him for it.

Thirdly and most importantly, there was an urgent need to bring forth anybody at all who could be found to give Alexander genuine warmth, friendship and support: he knew him better than anyone and feared for him more than he could express if he did not get them soon and in abundance. He would really like also to get through to the Head Master that he doubted either Alexander's father or his housemaster were up to doing this nearly adequately, but he could not think how he would be able to do that without sounding insufferably presumptuous and putting him off. He could not in fact think of anyone who might bring the boy more than a minuscule fraction of the comfort that he could, which brought him full circle to indignant thoughts about the iniquitous unfairness of society's attitude. Mr. Allenby must at least be brought to understand the desperate straits in which Damian had originally found Alexander, his sensitivity and loneliness, which would now be far worse than before. This was his overriding fear.

Damian suddenly realised that each time he got up to pace or sat down again, he was really trying to distract himself from his knowledge of the misery the boy was going through and his terrible inability to do anything about it, as it was to this that his thoughts kept returning. He felt his own appallingly acute loss too of course. The loneliness of life without Alexander was so dreadful a prospect that he could not hold back his tears each time he let himself try to imagine it.

He had of course always known they could not love one another for ever in this way. Within a few years Alexander would have grown out of being his boy and their friendship would have evolved in something much less intense, though surely still deep. Once he had asked himself if such intense love invested in a temporary union was not foolishly misplaced, but then he had realised that the knowledge that it was theirs to enjoy for limited time only heightened its intensity, and that same knowledge now increased his heartache over the premature and unnatural termination of their union.

He thought too a little about the loss of all his hopes and ambitions as a teacher. He knew that having left Eton suddenly and after such a short time, there would always be suspicions about him which he would never be able to allay by producing a reference, so his career was in ruins. He found though that he could think about that quite calmly compared to his dread of the days after countless days to come when he would be sitting around miserably lonely, longing for the beautiful boy who had lit up his life with warmth and joy and knowing that he too was longed for, but that there was nothing they could do about it. Always though, these miserable thoughts were interrupted by his real and immediate terror of the idea of Alexander abandoned, rather as if he was coming up from a deep dive to find himself stranded in the middle of an ocean with nothing in sight.

Suddenly there was a loud knocking on his door for the second time that afternoon. He went to it with a beating heart, thinking that the Head Master must have sent a messenger to summon him instead of telephoning. He opened it and blanched as he saw standing there four men staring at him with cold and menacing dislike, two of them in police uniform.

"Detective Inspector Hatchet, C. I. D.," announced the older of the men in plain clothes, holding up his identification. "Are you Damian Edwin Cavendish?" he asked, almost spitting out the words.

"Yes," replied Damian, his voice shaking with the new shock.

"I am placing you under arrest on suspicion of indecent assault of a male child under sixteen years of age," said the Inspector, his moustache bristling with contempt. "You do not have to say anything unless you wish to, but what you do say may be taken down in evidence."

XIV: Too Late to Save

Children of the future age
Reading this indignant page
Know that in a former time
Love, sweet Love, was thought a crime!
   William Blake, *Songs of Experience*

Alexander and Hodgson walked back from Damian's flat in silence. Hodgson was in front as they reached the door to the street and caught the boy's tearful look of suppressed animosity as he opened it to let him through. It was more than enough to convince him that there was little chance of regaining any of his trust at all soon.   Though he knew it was his special responsibility to bring his charge to terms with what was happening, he suspected deep down that he was not up to it, and that frightened him. How was he to begin, when he knew so little of the boy's hopes and fears and had lost his confidence? It would be an immense relief if everyone concerned were to agree on sending him home for a few days, ideally for the remainder of the Half. Only then did he remember that Hal Aylmer had just got married and was presumably away on his honeymoon. The timing was incredibly bad luck. All the same, if the boy showed he badly needed his father, perhaps the latter might come home early and arrange another family member to take care of him in the meantime.

Hodgson glanced at his watch as they approached Peyntors and realised that there were only twelve minutes left until Alexander's next div.

"Now," he said, as soon as he had closed the door to his study. "Do you think you are up to attending your divs this afternoon?"

"Yes, Sir," said Alexander sullenly.

"Very well then," said Hodgson, rather relieved. He needed to get onto the telephone urgently, and could not think what else he could do with the boy at such short notice. "But you must come to my study after tea, say at a quarter past five. I do understand how traumatic this sorry business must be for you, and we need to talk about it a great deal more. I think it might be best for you

355

if someone in your family were to take you home this evening, at least for a few days."

"But I don't want to go home, Sir," said Alexander, a look of sudden panic in his eyes, "and I can't anyway because my father's on holiday."

"Indeed. I imagined so. Where is he?"

"In Bali, Sir," said Alexander almost triumphantly.

"Do you know how I may contact him there?"

"No, Sir," he said, adding to himself that he certainly would not tell him if he did. The one thought that was sustaining him in his misery was how to meet up secretly with Damian so they could frustrate any plans to keep them apart.

"I see. I expect I can nevertheless find some means of contacting him. He may want to come home early when he understands your distress, and in any case he may in the meantime want to arrange for you to be with someone who can comfort you. You have older brothers, do you not?"

"But Sir, I have to prepare for Trials," said Alexander with new anguish.

"Well, you must run along now, or you will be late. We shall discuss this further at a quarter past five. But I must also forewarn you that any attempt to contact Mr. Cavendish again can only have dire consequences for him. Is that understood?"

"Yes, Sir."

Hodgson's telephone conversation with the Head Master ten minutes later was a dreadful ordeal, though he dreaded the one he must make to Hal Aylmer even more. He knew he was being subtly grilled on why he had known so little of what was going on in the life of one of his more obviously vulnerable boys, and could sense his superior's unspoken indignation. He had been hoping to raise the possibility of sending Aylmer home, but gave up all idea of that when Allenby remarked in a distinctly scathing tone that he expected he would be busy in the coming days bringing solace to his charge.

Calling Hal Aylmer to inform him that his son had apparently been sodomised for weeks by one of the schoolmasters was an even more intimidating prospect, and it was little comfort that he could still disclaim knowledge of the sordid details. When he telephoned Hal's chambers, he found his secretary so reluctant to put him in touch with the judge that he was half tempted to give up.

"Though I do have a number for absolute emergencies, Lord Justice Aylmer left strict instructions he was not to be disturbed on his honeymoon," she said. "Has Alexander been in an accident?"

"Not exactly, no. I fear I cannot divulge the nature of the crisis, but crisis there is, and I must speak to him urgently."

"Well, if Alexander hasn't been hurt, I think the best I can do is to leave a message at his hotel for him to call you."

Hodgson was to be teaching for the last div of the day, and it was a relief to set out for James Schools and temporarily distract himself with consideration of the numerical breakdown of the ancient Athenian population into their different classes. He knew his analysis of this question was brilliant, probably the best-thought-out ever, and as he walked back to his house afterwards, gravely pondering the problem of Aylmer again, he felt it almost to be an unfair intrusion. What had he done to deserve having to deal with this?

He had just sat down to tea with his wife and was on the point of unburdening his soul to her, when the doorbell rang; its second sonorific disruption of this afternoon, he thought irritably. She kindly went to answer it, so he sipped his tea thoughtfully and prepared a cleverly caustic comment for her on their unknown intruder, a comment he quickly forgot when she came back to announce that two policemen were waiting for him in his study.

"Good afternoon, Sir. I'm Detective Sergeant Greenop, Thames Valley Police," said a podgy-looking man in his late thirties in plain clothes, holding out his identification for Hodgson to see, "and this is Constable Yates," he added, indicating a tall, young policeman in uniform. "I expect you know what we've come about."

"I may well be able to guess, but I think you had better tell me," said Hodgson cautiously, still recovering from his shock that things had gone so unexpectedly far.

"I understand that you have a boy in your house here, a lad called Alexander Aylmer, age fourteen, and that you have reason

357

to believe that he's been sexually abused by a teacher here named ... Damian Edwin Cavendish," finished the Detective Sergeant after checking his notebook.

"Yes. I am afraid that is so."

"In that case, Sir, we'll be needing to hear all you can tell us about it, and afterwards we'll have to question the lad."

"Are you sure that's really necessary? I can assure you that this boy would prefer that the matter were not pursued."

"I'm afraid that's out of the question, Sir. Indecent assault of a child under the age of consent, and especially a boy under sixteen, is a very serious criminal offence, which we're bound to investigate."

"I see. Well, as it happens, Alexander should be coming here in about twenty minutes," said Hodgson, glancing at his watch.

"Good. That should give us just enough time. If you could tell us everything you know about Mr. Cavendish's er, involvement with the lad."

When it came down to it, Hodgson was rather embarrassed by how little he could find to say about it. He felt briefly a little less dejected when he sensed that the Sergeant was, as he had expected, impressed by his detailed observations on what he had seen that afternoon. Then the Sergeant and P.C. Yates exchanged knowing glances which reminded him uneasily that every bit of his own cleverness was simply making things worse for Cavendish. It was hardly in keeping with what he had told Alexander. Had he really needed to go so far in doing Mr. Plod's job for him?

"To the best of your knowledge, Sir, have there ever before been suspicions of paedophilia raised about Mr. Cavendish?" asked Greenop.

Hodgson recoiled at the word paedophilia, which offended his zeal for verbal accuracy. Mentally, he put a firm line through it in red ink. As a classicist he knew Cavendish's feelings for his pupil were perfectly described by the old English word pederasty, which came straight from the Greek and implied precisely the love of a pubescent boy. So why use a new and vague word which rather conjured up images of men gratifying themselves with sexually immature children without regard to their gender? It was not just a minor inaccuracy either. It was bound to lead to the affair being misjudged, and he began to feel pity for Cavendish, who seemed headed for a fate much worse than he really deserved. It was not his job though to educate policemen.

"No, Sergeant," he said, "but I am not the person to whom suspicions of that nature would normally be referred. That is the role of the Head Master."

"I see, Sir. Have you informed the lad's parents yet?" asked Greenop.

"No, regrettably not. Alexander's mother died a few months ago, which is why I am particularly anxious he should not be subjected to further stress now. His father has remarried and is right now on his honeymoon the other side of the world. I have of course tried to contact him, but so far in vain."

"I see. One other thing, Mr. Hodgson," said the Detective Sergeant. "We'll be needing to conduct a medical examination of the lad. Normally we would ask the parents for permission, but seeing as his can't be contacted yet, I assume you give us your permission, acting in loco parentis?"

"Can this not wait until Alexander's father can be consulted?"

"I'm afraid not, Sir. That might defeat the whole purpose. Also, any delay would mean we would have to detain the lad in a designated place of safety in the meantime. That wouldn't exactly be in his best interest, would it now?"

"What on earth do you mean by a designated place of safety?" asked Hodgson, shocked.

"I can't say for sure in this case, but if he has to be kept overnight, we might send him to a Community Home or such like, any government-run place where he can be cared for in isolation until ..." They were interrupted by a knock on the door.

"Wait just a minute," boomed Hodgson into the distance.

"We obviously don't want to keep him any longer than necessary, so if you could give your consent, we should have him back here in a jiffy," continued Greenop more quietly.

"Do you mean you want to take him away? Surely you can question him here and arrange for him to be examined in this house?"

"No, Sir. We need to take his statement in the station, and the medical could only be done there too."

359

Hodgson let out a long sigh. "Very well, but presumably I must be allowed to accompany him in lieu of his father?" he asked, his heart sinking at the prospect of an evening lost in the grim tedium of a police station.

"My instructions are that we're to be as discreet as possible in our comings and goings here, so it would be helpful if you could bring him to Maidenhead police station yourself. We can take your own statement at the same time, but we'll need longer with the lad. You can stay on with him, Sir, if you insist, but I'd really advise against it. There's no point, and it could well be more distressing for the lad to have to talk about the dirty details of what he's been subjected to in front of someone he knows and respects. Though Judges' Rules say children should be interviewed in the presence of a parent or guardian whenever practicable, in this case, with your agreement, we can easily say it's not."

"Hmmm. Well, we'd better see what Alexander thinks of the matter," he suggested, careful to disguise his relief at the likely reprieve. "Are you ready for him now?"

"Yes, Sir."

"Come in!" Hodgson called out loudly.

Alexander had spent the intervening two hours completely wrapped up in hopes and fears of what he and Damian might or might not do. He had gone through the essential motions of pretended attention during his divs, but his mind had been far away.

He hoped most of all that Damian would agree on their running away together. They would probably have to put up with being apart for the rest of the Half, but then they could surely do as they had planned during the holidays. Sometime before their end, he would find the means of getting his passport off his father and they could slip off abroad together. In the worst case that he could not get his passport, he had seen a film about a man on the run who had got a little boat to take him across the Channel.

He did not mind how they survived. If they were being looked for, then at first they could perhaps become fishermen or live in a forest together like cavemen. He would be happy whatever they did because they would sleep together and be together all the time. People would stop looking for them after a while, and then they could go off for the most amazing adventures. After all, there was no one to really mind. His father would make a great fuss at the outset, but though everyone he knew would suppose he minded terribly, in fact it would surely suit him well to have his remaining son gone from home like his brothers. He would be able to get on with his life with his new family undisturbed.

He feared though that Damian would find reasons they could not take such drastic action. In that case, they could still meet up in the holidays, but next Half they would be reduced to slipping off in Damian's car for a couple of hours on the odd afternoon. Depressing as that sounded, knowing it could at least be done would be a relief compared to the deepest fear that was gnawing at his heart: that until he could see Damian again in private and agree on what they were going to do, he could not actually be certain he would ever see him again. They had not even had a chance to exchange addresses. They surely knew enough about each others' families to be able to find one another somehow, but still he would never know a moment's peace until he did meet up with Damian.

During tea, Rupert and Simon found Alexander so absent-minded that they exchanged glances several times, but Alexander did not even notice and continued to act almost as if in a trance until he opened the door to Hodgson's study. Then he saw two strange men, one of them in police uniform, and his head spun.

Alexander had only ever spoken to a policeman once in his life, when he was nine. Early one morning before his parents were up, he had answered the door to a bobby who had come due to a malfunctioning of their new burglar alarm. He probably only still remembered it because his parents' exasperation when he went to their bedroom to tell them had inspired him to stage a fake repetition of the scene on the next April Fool's Day.

"Now, Alexander, these two officers from the Thames Valley Police need to ask you some questions," said Hodgson. Alexander noted both his affirmative nod to the older man in

361

plain clothes and his irregular use of his Christian name, which for the first time struck him as deceitfully friendly.

"Hello, Alexander!" said the plain-clothes man with a reassuring smile. "I'm Detective Sergeant Greenop. There's nothing to be alarmed about, lad. We just want to have a chat with you down at the station."

"But what about?" asked Alexander to gain time to think, his mind in turmoil. Why were the police involved? He had done as the housemaster told him. He became aware that he was trembling all over, but he could not stop himself.

"About Mr. Cavendish," said Hodgson, after exchanging further knowing glances with Greenop.

"But I don't really have anything to tell about him, Sir," replied Alexander in a shaking voice, mustering with difficulty the courage to fight his ingrained habit of trusting and obeying his elders. The police could only be here to make trouble. He reminded himself that everything between him and Damian was private and none of their business. They could not make him talk about it. Evidently, they thought they could though, and he steeled himself to stand up to them, terrified that he might fail. "He hasn't done anything wrong."

"In that case, he won't be in any trouble. We just need your help to establish that by coming down to the station for an interview" said Greenop. "It's in everyone's best interest," he continued encouragingly. "Don't worry about it. Your teacher here will bring you along, and he'll come to collect you as soon as we've finished."

"Though if it is what you really want, I could stay with you," interrupted Hodgson.

"I don't think we need to bother Mr. Hodgson to stay, do we, Alexander? We can sort this all out together without troubling him."

Alexander hesitated only a few moments. Until this day, he had always liked Mr. Hodgson and he still grudgingly respected him, but he resented him intensely as the one who had brought all this trouble by his unfair interference, and he no longer trusted him. The sergeant, on the other hand, looked kind and reasonable, and the younger policeman also gave him a smile when he glanced nervously at him. He would surely be better off

362

on his own getting through to them that Damian had done nothing wrong. Surely they must be able to understand?

"No, there's no need, Sir," he said coldly to Hodgson.

It felt peculiar being driven in a car by his housemaster for the first time, the possibility it theoretically opened of informal, private conversation in conflict with Mr. Hodgson's stiffness and his own new antipathy to the man. The latter seemed equally ill at ease, sweating more than the warm afternoon called for.

"You must understand that all of us are under an obligation to tell the police the truth," he eventually began awkwardly, "but that does not mean you cannot defend Mr. Cavendish to them, if you so wish. If you really believe he has done nothing wrong, you should tell them so."

"Yes, Sir," said Alexander sullenly, and they lapsed into silence for the rest of the journey.

Despite his resentment of Mr. Hodgson, Alexander's heart lurched when they parted at the police station reception and P.C. Yates led him down a long succession of plain, white corridors. He had never been in a police station before, or indeed in any building nearly so grim. They passed a few other policemen on the way. Each time one of them glanced at him, Alexander imagined he was wondering what crime a boy like him could have committed. Eventually they stopped before a door with a frosted glass window, just below which he read the word "interview" on a plastic plaque.

"Just sit down there," said Yates, indicating a large square table with a chair either side of it, such being the only furniture in the quite large room. "The Inspector will be here in a moment." He himself remained standing slouched against the wall.

A few minutes passed during which Alexander tried to distract himself from his nervousness by looking around the room, but there was nothing on the grey walls except one round clock. The walls appeared to be made up of large concrete blocks. For lack of anything else to do, Alexander wondered at contrived length whether the grooves that suggested this might not instead be the painter's attempt to provide some decoration to what was otherwise the plainest room he had ever been in.

There was a light knock on the door. Yates briefly half-opened it, blocking Alexander's view of whoever had come, then brought to the table a can of Coca-Cola and a plate with two biscuits.

"There you are!" he said. Alexander saw that the biscuits were Jaffa cakes, which he didn't like much, but he started to nibble one out of boredom, which was now competing with trepidation in his mind, when suddenly the door swung open and two men in suits came in. The one behind was Sergeant Greenop, but it was the other, a bald, portly man with a moustache, who spoke.

"Good evening!" he said with a strained smile. "I'm Detective Inspector Hatchet, and you are Alexander Aylmer, I take it?"

"Yes."

"You've already met Sergeant Greenop," continued Hatchet in a strong accent that Alexander thought was probably Midlands.

"Hello again!" said Greenop cheerily, before turning to Yates. "Okay, Steve," he said with a meaningful nod. The constable left the room, while Hatchet sat down opposite Alexander and leant back with the back of his head resting against his hands.

"I believe you know we need to talk to you about one of your teachers, Mr. Cavendish. I want you to understand that this is a very serious matter and it is very important that everything you tell us is the absolute truth."

He stopped and there was an awkward pause which Alexander felt impelled to end by saying "Yes."

"Do you promise to tell us the truth?"

"Yes," said Alexander, his voice shaking a little.

"Good. Now I understand that this afternoon at about 2:40 your housemaster, Mr. Hodgson, came to Mr. Cavendish's flat and found you naked in his bedroom. Is that correct?"

Alexander's mind reeled. He instinctively distrusted the rather aggressive detective and he realised from the man's approach that he was going to try to get him to tell him things about Damian that could land him in serious trouble. On the other hand, they obviously already knew what Mr. Hodgson had seen, and he must not make this man angry if he was to have a chance of explaining why Damian had done nothing wrong.

364

"Alexander, I am asking you a very simple question. Were you or were you not naked in Mr. Cavendish's bedroom this afternoon?" asked Hatchet in a slow and exasperated tone.

"Yes," said Alexander miserably.

"Why were you naked?"

"Because I'd taken my clothes off," said Alexander quietly after a pause.

"Yes, I had worked that out," said Hatchet sarcastically and sighed. "Why did you take your clothes off?" A full minute's silence ensued, in which Alexander stared down at the table. "Did Mr. Cavendish tell you to?"

"No," said Alexander firmly, relieved to be able to speak the truth.

"Was it the first time you'd been naked there?"

"No," answered Alexander in a reluctant murmur.

"Has Mr. Cavendish ever been naked when you've been with him?" After another long, silent interval, Hatchet put his hands on the table and leant forward aggressively.

"If I might put in a word, Sir?" interrupted Greenop, and then, taking the Inspector's grimace as assent, continued in a reassuring tone to Alexander: "You're safe now, lad. We've got Mr. Cavendish locked up in a cell, and there's nothing he can ever do to you. You can tell us the truth. You've no need to be afraid."

"But he hasn't done anything wrong and I'm not afraid of him at all. You don't understand. He cares about me more than anyone else in the world does and he's done nothing but good to me."

"You'll have to let us be the judge of that, lad," said Greenop gently. "If you tell us everything he's done to you, and none of it is wrong, then we'll let him go, but first we need to know what he's done."

Greenop sounded so reasonable that Alexander could not believe him incapable of grasping the real point. "But nothing he's done to me could be wrong because everything we've done I wanted to do," he pleaded. "He's never made me do anything. It was all my own choice."

"That'll do, Greenop," said Hatchet impatiently. "Now look here. Let's stop beating about the bush. We have reason to

365

believe that Mr. Cavendish has perpetrated serious criminal acts and you are going to tell us everything he has done to you so that we know if our suspicions are correct. Is that understood?"

"Why should I tell you anything I don't want to?" protested Alexander, becoming seriously frightened.

"Because it is your duty to. Otherwise you are obstructing the police in the course of their enquiries," said the Inspector loudly.

"No. It's not your business. I haven't done anything wrong, nor has Mr. Cavendish" said Alexander, shaking his head defiantly. The detectives exchanged knowing glances, both aware that the boy was near tears.

"You are going to tell us, even if we have to sit here all night until you do." They sat in stony silence for over a minute, Hatchet only continuing when it was obvious Alexander was not going to reply. "Look," he went on at last, "the sooner you tell us what we need to know, the sooner you can go back to your school. We'd like to be getting home as much as you. Why not save us all a lot of trouble?"

Alexander looked fixedly down at the table, trembling all over, but remained defiantly silent, while Hatchet got up and paced around the room, thinking and calming himself, before sitting down opposite the boy again, brushing his moustache thoughtfully with the back of his finger.

"We do understand you know," said Hatchet at last in a suddenly much softer tone. "This sort of thing has happened before, to other children. It's not surprising that a nice-looking boy like you should be one of them. I should think it made you feel proud. You couldn't know it was wrong, so it's not your fault that you gave him what he wanted and you don't have to feel ashamed."

"I'm not ashamed," said Alexander.

"Good, then there's no reason to mind talking about it. You didn't do anything anyway. You couldn't. You're still too young to be able to have sex. Mr. Cavendish was just using you to gratify himself."

"Of course I'm not too young."

"No, I can't believe that. What could you possibly do?" said Hatchet gently with an expression of amused disbelief.

Alexander flushed deeply, lost for words. Before he could find any, however, he caught the Sergeant shooting his superior a fleeting but premature glance of tentative congratulation. "It's not your business," he said at once, hoping the Inspector could not tell how frightened he was.

Hatchet got up angrily again. If it had been another boy, he would have given immediate vent to his fury. Perhaps he might have grasped his face, finger and thumb digging menacingly into his cheeks, and threatened him that he would see no one and have nothing to eat or drink until he told all. He was not an ordinary boy, however, though the reason he was not only made it more irritating. He remembered the conversation in the Superintendent's office a couple of hours earlier.

"I'm handing this case to you," the Superintendent had told Hatchet, "but I'm warning you to be very careful how you handle them both, especially the kid. However you feel about it, you can't use all the interrogation techniques that you're used to."

"Orders from above to protect their own kind, Sir?" the Inspector had asked sardonically.

"Don't be a bloody fool, Hatchet," the Superintendent had replied wearily, long familiar with the Inspector's social chippiness. "The teacher and the kid are likely to have the same sort of connections, so it could make no difference to the outcome, but a lot of powerful people are going to be watching how we get there. All I'm telling you is to stick very strictly to the rules, so no one can call a foul. Even more than you always stick to them" he added just a little sarcastically.

Still, he could get a bit tougher with the child, toff or not.

"You know just because you tell us what Mr. Cavendish did, you don't have to say you let him willingly," Hatchet told him, his voice hardening.

"But it's true. I've already told you he never made me do anything I didn't want to," protested Alexander.

"Do your mates know you're gay?" he asked sneeringly.

"I'm not gay," said Alexander furiously.

"What do you suppose they'll think if we have to make further enquiries at the school because you won't tell us the truth, and as

367

a result they find out that you willingly let a man use you like a girl?"

Tears filled Alexander's eyes then, but they were tears of fury as much as grief. "I'll never ever tell you anything," he said defiantly.

"In that case we'll have to proceed with a medical examination. The police doctor can soon find out exactly what's been done to you."

"No. I refuse."

"I don't need your agreement, young Sir," said Hatchet, unable to resist mimicking the boy's posh accent for a moment. "Unless you want to co-operate by making and signing a statement right now telling me everything that Mr. Cavendish has done to you, I'll have no choice but to order one, whether you like it or not."

"No. You can't," said Alexander, wiping away his tears, but he was trembling and very much afraid Hatchet could.

"So be it. Greenop, would you go and tell Dr. Turtle that the child abuse victim is ready for him now and fetch Constable Yates back here."

"Can I have a word first, Sir?" asked Greenop anxiously.

"Very well," conceded his superior grudgingly and led the way to the door.

"Are you sure it's wise to force the lad to have a medical, Sir?" said Greenop in an urgent undertone as soon as the door was closed again.

"Yes, I am. Justice must take its course. We must obtain the evidence by all authorised means available. We're just doing our duty."

"Don't you think the lad's been through enough? Besides, it somehow doesn't seem quite right that we're having the teacher up for doing things to him that he didn't resist and then we're forcing him to have something a bit similar done to him again."

"Do I detect some sympathy for them, because the teacher wormed a sort of consent out of the boy?" said Hatchet impatiently.

"Whoa, Sir!" protested the Sergeant quite angrily. "I never said I sympathised with 'them'. It's true I feel sorry for the lad, but not that despicable teacher. My own kids are around the same age as the one he's been fiddling with, and if it wouldn't land me in deep trouble, I'd like to do what any normal, decent bloke would and beat the shit out of him, the dirty pervert."

"All right, I understand, but look. We're faced with a participating victim. You've seen we can't get anything out of him, and you don't want to let his molester off the hook. There's a good chance a medical will help settle the matter and get him locked away for five or ten years where he won't be able to harm any more children."

"Yea, I suppose you're right, Sir," said Greenop reluctantly.

Alexander and the Inspector waited in grim silence for the two minutes until Greenop and Yates reappeared.

"Right, Alexander. Can you come with us?" said Greenop chirpily, hoping his intervention might make the boy more amenable.

Alexander followed Greenop out, Yates behind him, but as soon as they headed in a different direction to that he had originally come from, he tried to run off. Yates reacted fast and overtook him just as he got round the next corner and held him tight until Greenop caught up.

"Come along now, lad. There's nothing to be afraid of," coaxed the Sergeant, but Alexander did not stop trying to pull away and the two policemen had to force march him all the way to the examination room.

As they pulled him into the hospital-like room, Alexander caught sight of a mild-looking man in his fifties, bizarrely dressed in a white medical coat and black bow tie, who merely raised his eyebrows when he saw him struggling. Greenop went over to talk to the doctor in an undertone, leaving him sitting on a couch in the grip of Yates alone. He stopped struggling, beginning to hope that the plump little doctor would not really be willing to use force against him.

After a few muttered exchanges, Greenop came back towards him and the doctor went over to a table the other side of the room. It was only when the doctor turned round a minute later and came towards him that Alexander saw horrified that he had armed himself with a syringe. He tried with all his might to tear himself away, but it was too late. Somehow Greenop already had him pinned face down on the couch by his arms, his ankles were also in a vice-like grip, and he felt his trousers being pulled down.

"It's all right, Alexander. It'll soon be over," he heard the Sergeant say as he felt the needle jab sharply into his thigh. He struggled as hard as he could, even as his mind clouded over.

An hour later, the Superintendent summoned the Detective Inspector to his office again.

"How's the interview with the boy going?" he asked.

"Badly. He hasn't exactly been co-operative, but the medical examination's been more promising."

"He agreed to that?"

"No, Sir," said Hatchet irritably, "he did not, but it was the only means of establishing the truth."

"Oh Christ! I've just had the Chief Constable on the phone. The kid's father is a Lord Justice of Appeal. I told you to stick strictly to the rules, so I hope you're not going to tell me you didn't seek parental consent?" asked the Superintendent almost frantically.

"We got consent from the boy's housemaster acting in loco parentis. Lord Justice or not, I'm sure the father will be as keen as anyone for us to nail the slimy queer who's been molesting his son, and he'll understand that as the boy's a participating victim, we had no choice."

"I don't like this at all, Hatchet. How do you know the medical's promising? You can't possibly have a report yet."

"No, but Dr. Turtle kindly let on that we're going to get what we were hoping for. I understand we'll have forensic evidence of recent buggery."

"Thank God for that. I wouldn't like to be in your shoes if it had been for nothing. I don't mind telling you the Chief Constable said he's going to take a keen interest in our handling of this case. You make damned sure we do get a conviction, but from now on you handle that boy with kid gloves. Is that clear?"

"Yes, Sir," said Hatchet morosely, silently abandoning his plan to carry on questioning Alexander when he woke up.

"In fact it would probably be better if you keep out of his way and leave it to the social services to try to get more out of him."

"Very well, Sir." Hatchet departed grumpily, switching his concentration to the problem of how to extract a confession from the teacher, whom he was now ready to begin grilling.

Alexander awoke slowly, unaware at first that the nightmare he thought he was having about the day's events was real. It was the uncomfortable feeling in his posterior and the unfamiliarity of the operating table on which he was lying, which finally made him realise that he was awake. The deep depression he felt was soon mixed with a growing and seething fury that he had been violated, that his most intimate parts, only ever before explored lovingly and with his eager consent, had been forcibly desecrated by his enemies. He felt dirty, contaminated and humiliated to a degree he had never before come remotely near.

As he struggled to shake off his drowsiness and sit up, a policewoman popped her head through the door and withdrew. A minute later the Detective Sergeant appeared.

"Are you feeling all right, lad?" he asked cheerily, then turned and muttered to the policewoman standing behind him in the half-open doorway. "Constable Bartrum here is going to bring you a nice cup of tea," he added, coming over to Alexander to help him up, but Alexander shied way from him and managed shakily to get on to his legs. "You just sit down here until you're feeling better," continued Sergeant Greenop, handing Alexander's tweed jacket over to him. "There's no need for hard feelings, lad. I'm sorry about what we had to do, but we were just doing our duty, see."

The policewoman returned with a mug of tea and some biscuits which she placed on the little table in front of Alexander's seat. "Tah, Yvonne," said Greenop.

Alexander did not move. He sat tensely, looking downwards. He would not look at them, these people who must both have joined in his unbelievable humiliation, have watched him being violated and thought they were right to do it. He felt a surging hatred towards them that was such a new experience that he doubted he could ever again be the same person he had been.

"I don't want anything from you!" he shouted suddenly, and swept the mug and biscuits off the table to smash on the floor. Then he could no longer hold back his tears and wiped frantically at his eyes, desperate not to humiliate himself further before them.

Greenop and the policewoman exchanged worried glances. "Come on, lad," said Greenop. "There's no need to take it like that," but Alexander continued to sit trembling silently, looking the other way. "Your housemaster is busy right now," added the Sergeant after a pause, "so he's asked us to drop you back at your school. We'll be leaving in just a minute or two."

Soon Yates reappeared, much to the evident relief of Greenop, who said they could be off. They drove back to Eton in almost total silence, Yates behind the wheel. Greenop in front, and Constable Bartrum in the back beside Alexander, kept glancing at him with a view to friendly conversation, but Alexander stared fixedly away and out of the window.

"You are a lucky boy, going to a school like this," ventured the policewoman enthusiastically as the police car began to drive through the school, but Alexander ignored her, and she did not try again. They parked unobtrusively down the High Street and the plain-clothed Greenop alone walked Alexander back to the front door of his house. Hodgson answered the doorbell and led them into his study.

"I'm afraid he's had rather a distressing time," the Sergeant told Hodgson in an undertone, looking uneasily sideways at the smouldering boy. "He didn't take kindly to being examined medically, so we had to sedate him. I expect he'll be all right after a good night's sleep. Good night, Alexander!" he concluded genially and withdrew.

Alexander said nothing and just glowered with open hatred at Hodgson. This ugly, balding man with a bulbous nose and face that reminded him a little of a garden gnome was his greatest enemy. If he had not implied in Damian's flat that Damian would be treated more leniently if they co-operated with him, he would never have left the flat so easily. Perhaps they could have run away together then and there. As it was, how could they have been treated more harshly? Hodgson had betrayed him completely. It had been a shabby lie that the police would give him a chance to explain that Damian had done nothing wrong.

"Well now," said Hodgson looking at him embarrassedly and abandoning his tentative plan for a proper discussion,

372

"it's past your lights out. I shall be ready to discuss anything you wish tomorrow. In the meantime, I suggest you go to bed."

"Yes, Sir," said Alexander and left forthwith, not giving him a chance to bid him good night.

Alexander sat in silent darkness in his room. He was not going to get undressed as he would be going to Damian's flat, and he thought he would be left alone with his light off, but after ten minutes he was interrupted by a knock on the door. It was the dame, who had been told he was back and wanted to know if he had had anything to eat. He saw her off, but the intrusion reminded him that it would be safer for him to go to bed. He must not do anything that might jeopardise his escape to any degree. He remembered he should go in his tails too, as he might need to get back in the morning without provoking questions, so he got undressed after all. He decided he had better wait until midnight, so he lay in bed miserably until the hour approached and his grief gave way to mounting excitement.

He crept silently through the slumbering house and down to the coal room. He took his time to open the window noiselessly. The High Street was deserted and he reached Damian's door without mishap.

He sensed as soon as he went in that the flat was empty, but with sinking heart he opened the lights in each room all the same. Both bedroom and sitting-room were in a mess Damian could never have borne. Papers were lying about everywhere, and he could tell that Damian's books had been pulled out of their shelves too, for although they had been put back, they had been pushed unevenly in as far as each would go, that sloppy way he had learned from Damian to find unsightly. The sheets had been torn off the bed and had disappeared, leaving the mattress bare.

He understood the implications at once, that their private temple of love had been ransacked by the police with a view to getting them further into trouble, but still he could not help hoping that Damian might come home. He cried out silently for him to do so, trying to persuade himself that a telepathic message might somehow get through if it was heartfelt and urgent enough. Surely the police would have to let him go when they had finished questioning him? He might appear at any moment.

He knew he could wait until a quarter past seven before he must leave, and decided he had better turn out the lights. He went back into the bedroom, turned on the bedside lamp and drew the curtains.

As he sat down on the bed, he noticed his short story continued by Damian lay strewn and creased on the floor. He wondered whether the police had bothered to read it. He read it himself, and could not help crying as he read what Damian had written about him. The saddest thing was that it was after all his story that was true to life with its message of despair and not Damian's tale of hope.

He had no idea how many hours of dwindling hope had passed, when to his horror he saw that it was getting light. Looking at Damian's alarm clock, he saw that it was nevertheless not yet five, but the fright concentrated his mind. He must think carefully what to do if Damian did not come. An hour later, he finally composed a note.

6 am., 3ʳᵈ July

Dear Damian,

I don't know where you are or when you will get this. I've been waiting for you here all night, but I'll have to go back to my house as soon as it opens. I didn't get a chance to tell you that I know how to get out of it after lock-up.

I hope you are okay. The police have done horrid things to me and tried to make me tell them all about us,

374

but I don't think I told them anything that matters and I refused to sign anything.

I promise that nothing that anybody says will ever change my mind one bit about loving you, but I'm very frightened without you and need to talk to you urgently. Can you call my house's public phone 07535 63892 and pretend to be my brother? I'll meet you anywhere you tell me.

Remember we agreed to stick together whatever happens. If you say we can run away together, I'll be very happy to go. I don't mind what we do as long as I'm with you. Please make contact soon, because I can't stand it without you.

If we really can't meet up before the end of the Half, please, please call me at the beginning of the holidays. The number is 01 352 9536. If my father or step-mother asks who you are, you could say you're an older friend from my house, Julian Smith perhaps. My address is 36 Old Church St., London SW3 5BY.

With all my love,
Alexander

xxxxxxxxxxxxxxxxxxxxxxxxxx

He had given up hope of Damian coming by the time he lay his letter carefully half-upright on Damian's pillow, but he stayed on in the flat until the last moment he dared, taking in a last sight of all the things that made up this place where he had been more fulfilled than any other, all except the man who had made them special.

When Hal Aylmer had received his secretary's message that morning, he had been thoroughly baffled.

"But it's only three days since we saw him, and he looked happier then than I can remember seeing him for ages," he protested to Janet over breakfast. He was not convinced by her suggestion that Alexander might have broken some rule terrible enough to get expelled or rusticated, because it had not sounded like that. Nevertheless, he was sufficiently worried she could be right, that he calculated the time difference carefully and telephoned Hodgson as soon as he thought he must be up.

At first, he was speechless in reaction to the news, then outraged. It was only when Hodgson suggested he come home urgently to take care of Alexander, instead of in the planned six days' time, that he suddenly calmed down.

"But I..., I can't possibly come home now. It's out of the question. I'm on my honeymoon. The flights are booked. I very much doubt it would be possible to change them." He paused then, searching frantically for reasons that would show his concern for his son's happiness. "Has Alexander said he wants us to come home?"

"No, he has not, but I fear he is not in a state of mind to know what is for his own good."

"But I really don't see what possible good it could do," replied Hal with relief. "Surely the best possible thing is for him to get on with life as normal, to be kept busy?"

Hodgson wanted to insist that Hal at least find a family member to take immediate charge of Alexander, but he could not do that without the backing of the Head Master whom he had a horrid feeling would say very much the same thing as Hal if asked. In the end he got nothing more useful out of Hal than his number to call if there should be further worrying developments.

What frightened Hodgson was his fear that he had lost all control over the boy and had no idea what he might do or might already be planning. Alexander's evident hostility towards him was especially unnerving because he had always before been such a warm, friendly boy. He could no longer cope with the responsibility.

When Sergeant Greenop had telephoned him the evening before about returning Alexander to the school, he had forewarned him to expect a call from the Windsor social services's child welfare officer, who would want to interview the boy soon. Hodgson next pinned his hopes on this person agreeing it was not in Alexander's interest to remain at school. She called at last late that afternoon. They agreed Alexander would go to her office at two the next day and that she would inform him straight afterwards if she agreed the boy should go home.

On the strength of this, he finally mustered the courage to call the Head Master to ask to be allowed to insist on Alexander being sent home if the social worker thought it unwise he be left at school. Again, he sensed rather than heard spelt out the reproach that he himself was, by his own admission, not up to bringing the necessary comfort to his charge.

Alexander passed through that day in a daze, his misery mercifully dulled by his utter exhaustion after missing a night's sleep. The afternoon was worse than the morning because it was a half-day, which he had become totally used to spending with Damian. He did not anyway dare leave his house in case Damian telephoned and he missed his call. He could not face talking to anyone and kept to his room until Prayers. Just afterwards, there was a knock on his door and his heart leaped, hoping Damian had called at last.

When Julian came through the door instead, he could not hide his intense disappointment or concentrate on what he was saying. He was too tired and his mind was too much elsewhere, though he sensed that Julian was trying hard to be nice. After a while, he could not bear it anymore.

"Please. Not now. Just leave me alone," he said wearily. He felt guilty when Julian had gone. Julian was only being kind to him, and it wasn't fair to take his anguish out on him.

Soon afterwards, he fell into exhausted sleep, for the first time ever before lights out.

The next morning, Mr. Hodgson suddenly appeared in his room during After Nine. Alexander stood up, but nothing else in his demeanour suggested the respect Hodgson was used to. The housemaster did not react, though it pained him.

"It has been arranged for you to meet a social worker in Windsor at two o'clock this afternoon," he said.

"What for, Sir?" he asked, ready to rebel. He had no idea what social workers were for. Why should he have to go to see someone else who very likely wanted to inflict further harm? "I need to revise for my Trials," he added virtuously, as if to remind Mr. Hodgson that study was what he was at Eton for, not jaunts to meet people who were nothing to do with him.

"I am sorry about what happened to you in the police station. I assure you that I did not want the police to get involved at all. It was not my decision, but once it had been made, the police officers had to do their duty, which is to investigate breaches of the law. Social workers are different. This one, Miss Johnson is her name, is a child welfare officer, which means her job is to help you."

Alexander felt churlish then. It was the first ray of hope since he returned from Damian's flat and he could not help reaching out for it, conscious as he was that he should not again put too much trust in Mr. Hodgson.

"How can she help?" he asked carefully.

"I do not know precisely. I do not want to give you false hopes. I believe she is bound to listen to your point of view and to act in your best interest, though her view of that may well not be the same as yours. If you convince her, you may perhaps be able to lessen Mr. Cavendish's troubles, though I fear you cannot hope to extricate him from them altogether."

It was only when Alexander arrived for his English div later that morning that he heard the excited rumours that something mysterious had happened to their beak. Boys in Mr. Cavendish's other divs had reported that he had suddenly disappeared from the school, but no one knew why. Many of the boys in their div looked disconcerted. Alexander heard four of them readily agreeing that Mr. Cavendish was their favourite beak.

Soon Mr. Pease, another English beak, appeared and said he

was taking over for this very last English div of the Half, as Mr. Cavendish was indisposed. The boys exchanged glances until Michael Stanhope, the boldest boy in the div, put up his hand.

"What's happened to Mr. Cavendish, Sir?" he asked.

"All I can tell you is that he won't be returning this Half," replied Mr. Pease in a tone intended to deter rejoinder, and began talking about their revision for Trials. He seemed nice enough, but Alexander soon noticed with pride that most of the boys were finding his teaching very dull after what they were used to.

Alexander could not have concentrated anyway, though he was no longer hopelessly mired in misery. He told himself not to get carried away in his hopes, but he could not stop his excitement mounting that he was finally going to meet someone who would listen to his point of view and might well try to meet his wishes. He was getting nervous too. Though he did not think it should be difficult to make someone reasonable see that neither Damian nor he had done any harm to anyone, it was a daunting responsibility. He knew now that Damian was in seriously deep trouble and that it was up to him to try to get him out of it.

Alexander arrived punctually at the address in Windsor Mr. Hodgson had given him directions for. The social worker's office was on the ground floor of a beige concrete block in an ugly modern zone of the town he had had no idea existed before.

The fat receptionist led him to a door which she knocked on and opened for him as soon as there was a reply. Alexander saw a short woman in her early thirties with mouse-coloured hair and a kind, earnest expression sitting on a swivel-chair behind a formica desk in a non-descript little office.

"Hello. You must be Alex," she said with a smile.

"No, Alexander," he replied. He hated it when people slaughtered his name, but he managed to smile back all the same.

"Oh, okay, Alexander. I'm Linda. Do sit down."

"How are you today?" she asked, as she rearranged the files on her desk.

"Okay," he said quietly, not bothering to give a real answer to what had not been a real question.

379

"So," she continued in her whiny version of the local accent, "you're Alexander Aylmer, you were fourteen on the 27th of May and you're a student at Eton College?"

"Yes."

"That must be nice," she said.

"Yes," answered Alexander in a weary tone that apparently made her decide to give up on small talk.

"Well, Alexander, do you know why you're here today?"

"Yes," said Alexander more enthusiastically.

"Could you tell me in your own words, please?"

Alexander hesitated, frustrated by her manner of talking to him as if he might be an idiot. He longed to get into detailed explanation of the facts. "To talk about Mr. Cavendish and me," he said finally.

"Yes, that's right. Now, before we go on, I must ask you if you understand what the truth is?"

"Yes, of course I do," he replied indignantly enough that she seemed to change her mind about what she had been going to say next.

"And do you promise to tell me the truth now?"

"Yes," he said cautiously. "But can I ask you some things?"

"Yes. Go ahead."

"Is what I've been told true? That the purpose of all this is just to help me, and that you'll listen to my explanation of how things really are?"

"Yes. That's exactly what I'm here for," she said with a much friendlier smile that left him feeling greatly relieved, and thankful he had managed not to show his irritation at her manner. "So do you know why we need to talk about Mr. Cavendish?"

"Yes. Because no one understands how it is between him and me, and that he's done nothing wrong."

"It's because he's done things with you sexually that he's done terrible wrong, Alexander."

He considered denying the sex for a moment, but he knew she would not believe him and he needed her on his side. She was their last chance. "It wasn't wrong. Everything we did together was what I wanted. It was my choice."

"Alexander, you've got to understand that you're safe now.

Everyone understands that you couldn't do anything about it before and that you're not to blame, but now it's okay to tell. He's locked up and there's nothing he can do to you. We can help you."

"You're not listening. I told you everything I've ever done with him was my choice."

"You're much too young to be able to make a choice like that. You don't have the necessary maturity and experience. That's why there is a law to protect you. Sadly, Mr. Cavendish broke it and victimised you."

"But it was me that got him to break it because it's unfair. He made it quite clear when he first started loving me that there was no chance he would ever ask for anything like that, and I'm sure he never would have. Can't you understand it was all my idea?"

"It may well seem like that to you," said Linda with a wry expression, "but I suspect it was really Mr. Cavendish who put that into your head. In any case, he's an adult and you're not, so he's responsible for whatever happened."

"But what's wrong with what happened? All we did was make each other happy. It never affected anyone else."

"It's absolutely wrong because you're underage," she said, adopting a much severer tone. "You're really much too young to be having sex with anyone, though it wouldn't be so very bad if it was with someone your age, even another boy. It is quite acceptable to be gay when you're an adult and mature enough to decide that is your orientation. What's really wicked in this case is that you're a child and Mr. Cavendish is an adult. There's a power imbalance."

"You don't understand," he said, becoming seriously worried that she might never. "I wouldn't want sex with a boy my age." He paused, exasperated and lost for words. He tried briefly to imagine what sex would be like with Rupert, but the image conjured up was so hollow compared to the overpowering happiness he had experienced in Damian's arms that he found himself suddenly obliged to fight back tears, he missed him so badly. Linda had got completely the wrong end of the stick. How could he make her see that it was continually consummated love, not just sex, he needed? And why did she and the police assume so annoyingly that it was to do with being gay, when he would a hundred times rather go to bed with Miranda than any boy?

"It's nothing to do with me preferring males to females," he continued. "It's just to do with loving Damian and wanting to be as close to him as possible. Only he takes care of me, explains everything to me and answers all my questions."

"Maybe Mr. Cavendish has been doing some good things, I don't know, but the bad he's done *far* outweighs them."

"He is the only person in the world I can trust completely and I'm sure it wouldn't have been possible for us to be that close without the sex. Only he understands me." He said the last sentence in a much wearier tone, as if finally confirming to himself what he already knew.

"That's what your mum's for."

"My mother is dead," said Alexander. It felt like saying "check" at last, and she looked so nonplussed that for a moment he could not help hoping she might even concede checkmate.

"Well in that case, your dad," she said flustered. So, she did not even have the grace to concede she had lost a castle in their tussle.

"My father's not that interested. There's no way he could understand me like Damian does. Anyway, he would never have the time." This time, Linda did not look at all surprised.

"Well, if you have problems you can't talk about to your dad, you need to see a special kind of doctor called a psychiatrist" she said. "That is what they're for. To help you sort out your problems. I can help arrange it for you."

"But it's only you and the people on your side who are my problem!" he said furiously.

She paused, containing her irritation and wondering how best to continue. "Look," she said eventually with an impatient frown. "We're getting side-tracked. Let's go back to what matters, which is what exactly Mr. Cavendish, Damian if you prefer, did to you sexually. I know it's hard to talk about, but we need to know the details. When did he first touch your private parts?"

"Why do you want to know?" asked Alexander, suddenly realising she was not to be trusted one bit. Apparently, she had been lying when she had said her only purpose was to help him, though she had only been confirming what Mr. Hodgson had told him. It looked as though she really only wanted to help the

382

police get Damian into further trouble.

"Damian has committed a serious crime," she said, her patience visibly strained. "You're too young to understand the harm he's done you, which is why others have to act on your behalf. In order to do that, we need to know exactly which laws he's broken and when and where."

"Can't you understand these unfair laws are just modern inventions?" pleaded Alexander. She had still not answered his demand to know what harm had been done. He had to have a last go at making her understand there could be other ways of looking at it. "It doesn't have to be like this. It wasn't in ancient Greece. Everyone there understood that it was good for a boy to have a man as his lover. Most boys did and that's why so many of them grew up to do great things." He could at once tell from her blank and increasingly impatient expression that she had heard nothing of this.

"This is nineteen-eighty-four, Alexander," she said very slowly as if talking to an imbecile, "and we're in the U.K. I don't know or care if the ancient Greeks let men abuse their children. We've made progress since then."

For the first time in his life, Alexander resented being addressed by his Christian name. He had always before disliked being called by his surname. It was so cold. At his prep school, only his very best friends had called him Alexander, and though many more boys did at Eton, none of the beaks had except Damian. But this woman was doing so in order to impose an unwanted familiarity on him. For the first time, he understood why his father got so indignant when he was called Hal by people he had not accepted as friends. The intimacy of his personal name was nullified and his privacy desecrated.

He knew now there was no hope of getting through to her and his temper was rising. Though he had always relished Damian's rebuttal of the snobbery typical of his father's social circle, at heart he was still proud to be the scion of an ancient, noble family and a pupil at the best school in the land. Linda's arrogant assumption that she could decide what was best for him was perfectly calculated to excite his own arrogant disgust at everything she stood for. How dare this whiny oik, too stupid to engage in logical debate and so uneducated that she was

383

unashamed to know nothing of classical civilisation, presume to sit in judgement on his lover, who came from one of the greatest families in their island's history, had attained the highest levels of distinction at the best places of education, and was as good, wise, cultivated and charming as she was the opposite? It was intolerable.

"You know nothing!" he said, and though the words were only three, the anger and contempt with which he uttered them expressed volumes. "And I'm telling you nothing."

"I know you've had sex with this Damian because you've told me so several times today. The police will be able to put that together with whatever they've found out themselves," said Linda coldly, though her own face was glowing hot.

"You mean you're going to tell them?" he asked, stunned by such a frank admission of treachery. "You told me the only purpose of my coming here was for you to help me."

"Yes, and whatever you think, I will be helping you and other children too by telling the police so that he is appropriately punished and can't do any more harm." Seeing his fury about to erupt and realising that she was not going to get more out of him, she remembered that there was another matter to be broached.

She opened the top file in front of her and drew out a sheet of A4, which Alexander saw to his horror was a photocopy of his letter to Damian. He froze.

"It was very wrong of you to go to Mr. Cavendish's home and write this letter," she said severely. "You've got to understand that he's abused you and you're never going to see him again. You were told not to try to see him. You've only made things worse for him as well as yourself by your disobedience. Because of this letter, which the police found, Mr. Cavendish is going to be kept in prison until his trial. If you hadn't made everyone concerned that he might run off with you, he'd have been let out."

Alexander stood up then. "You cheating liar! I hate you!" he shouted, tears filling his eyes, and stormed out of the room.

"You come back here at once!" she shouted angrily, getting up to follow him, but by the time she reached the reception room, the only person there was the fat lady behind the desk, now standing helplessly, and the swing door to the street was slowly closing. She followed Alexander out, but he had disappeared.

Back in her office, her anger soon subsided into weariness. It was a classic case of the willing victim, almost straight from the child abuse textbooks she had read. The child having consented to his own abuse was perhaps the most pernicious thing about it. The paedophile teacher had corrupted his mind completely, probably beyond remedy. He clearly needed psychiatric care and she would have to telephone the school now to tell them to arrange it urgently, but in her heart she doubted that even months of therapy could redress much of the damage. In effect, the paedophile had murdered the boy's soul, which was just as bad as physical murder, possibly worse. At least her report should help to put him behind bars for many years, so he could not do the same to other children. It was sadly too late to save this one.

Alexander ran he knew not whither, propelled by fury. As it subsided into despair, he slowed down until he came to a bench on a little green beside a quiet suburban crossroads, and sat down.

He was still seething at the injustice. He realised that although he had known about the age of consent, deep down he had hardly believed until now that it would really be enforced, and certainly not so brutally. Besides being so unreasonable, it ran counter to everything his father had always taught him. His father had often extolled the special freedom of the English since Magna Carta seven centuries ago, and as his father was an important judge, he had thought he must know more about it than almost anyone.

He believed it now though. He let his tears flow freely and they flooded down his cheeks, but when they began to subside, he did not feel any of the customary relief, but only a bleak despair. There was no hope because no one would listen to reason. None of them were at all interested, neither Hodgson nor the police nor the social worker nor anyone, even though they were all apparently supposed to be helping him.

The social worker had not really listened to any of the things he had told her, less still had she tried to understand them. She had never intended to do either. She had absolutely no interest

385

in how his relationship with Damian worked. Even if she had understood how good it was, she would not have cared. She was only interested in whatever he had to say in so far as it might fit in with her fixed ideas and objectives. He remembered that whenever he had raised a new point, she had answered him straight away as if the answer to whatever he might say was already laid down in some simple manual.

He looked up and saw that a little old woman with a dog had stopped a few feet away to stare at him. A moment after he caught her gaze, she took a doddering step towards him and he realised from her kindly expression that she intended to come and comfort him. He knew very well though that there was nothing she or anyone else could do to help him. He did not want to hurt her feelings, but he could not bear the thought of talking to anyone at all except the one person they would not let him be with, so he got up hastily and walked away.

Would Damian even want to talk to him though, if he knew that it was all his fault that he was being kept in prison until his trial? On top of that, he had now just let on to vile Linda far more clearly than he had to the police that he and Damian had had sex together. If only he could go back in time little more than a day, Damian would now be free to escape with him. Just a few hours earlier still and they could have avoided being caught. Looking yet further back, he remembered again that it was himself who had led them into making love. Damian never would have done anything otherwise.

He tried to imagine what Damian would say if he were able to confess to him how much of the ruin overwhelming him was his fault. Would he forgive him? Yes, he found he was sure of that, though it did not stop him feeling guilty. He was probably already direly regretting their affair though and that thought hurt terribly. Should he himself be regretting it too? Obviously he regretted that they had been caught, but try as he did, he could not find it in his heart to regret the affair itself. What was the point in life if one had to renounce one's deepest longings for no better reason than the wish of strangers to interfere?

However Damian felt, he was unavoidably going to waste his life away in prison, and he himself would return to an unbearable loneliness thinking every day of Damian suffering just for having loved him. He had no idea for how many years Damian would go to prison, but to him only a few seemed an eternity. By the time he came out, he himself would be grown up, a different person. If they met, it could not be as old intimates whose friendship had gradually evolved according to their needs, which was how he had hitherto imagined their future. It would be more as if they were both attending a memorial service for their long murdered love.

He tried to imagine what he might do in the meantime. Was it possible to simply carry on? Could he go back to Peyntors and start revising for his Trials? Only two days earlier he had been bursting with enthusiasm to excel as never before, but now he decided he would rather not shine than do so unseen by the only eyes whose admiration he pined for. The idea even of walking the streets they had both known so well, going into the familiar buildings, worst of all passing the flat where they had been so happy together, and knowing that Damian was not there and never would be, was more than he could bear. Nor, with all his hopes for his own life gone, could he face going home and trying to fit in with his father's new family.

Was he overreacting? He had long since realised that was what he had done when Julian had let him down. Swiping himself with his penknife had been more an act of exasperation than anything. He had wanted to protest against the way the game of life was being played rather than to end it. But now he was calm and knew his despair to be of an entirely different order. Though he was utterly repelled by a world in which they had gained such terrible power, he was no longer angry with the police or even Linda. He no longer cared about their disregard for truth or reason any more than anyone but his imprisoned lover cared about him.

As he approached the High Street, Windsor Castle loomed into view above him. He saw the Round Tower in the middle, looking down on the rest of the huge fortifications and remembered standing there with his mother long before he went to Eton. She had pointed out College Chapel gleaming splendidly in the sun half a mile away and told him that one day he would go to services there. He had been so happy and excited.

387

Suddenly he knew what he was going to do. There was no need to go back to the school or anywhere else ever again. It could all end here, where it would be so easy.

He walked towards the castle entrance. At the ticket booth, he pulled a bank note out of his wallet and handed it to the woman at the counter without looking at it. Then he walked on in a daze.

"Excuse me.... Hey, the kid there!" she shouted after him. He turned his head confused. "You've forgotten your change." He paused a moment, wondering if he had to go back to get it, then he did. She looked at him sharply, irritated by his indifference, then drew her breath sharply when she saw the pain in his eyes.

He followed the straggle of tourists walking towards the Round Tower without noticing them. As he climbed the steps, he felt he was no longer wholly part of the world around him, barely able to hear the loud whining of the uncouth child passing him or the angry threats of its loutish father. As he strode across the top of the tower towards the battlements, some of the Japanese tourists crowded together taking photographs turned to watch him, their attention caught by his beauty and air of purposeful oblivion to everything around him, but he did not notice them either.

At the edge, he paused for a while and remembered Miss Flaherty's words about his mother being in heaven, wishing they were true. Then he would very soon be with her. She would have unlimited time for him now that his father did not need her any more. He would explain to her all about him and Damian. He was sure that in the end, she at least would understand. Together they would wait for him, however long it took. He knew he had never really believed in an after-life, but he did not want to think about that now. He did not want to have to think about anything any more.

He stepped trembling onto one of the openings in the battlements, his hands on the merlons either side. Sudden giddiness threatened to overcome him as soon as he glimpsed all the way down, so he gripped the stone momentarily harder and closed his eyes.

Then he jumped.

He felt a brief rush of air and then a split second of searing agony which evaporated into darkness and he felt no more. Only some of the people around heard the dull thud as his beautiful body struck the ground and smashed instantly into hideous pieces. His head opened and bounced a little as whitish stuff came out which soon turned red as a pool of blood spread slowly out.

A woman started screaming loudly in great, long bursts, then another joined her and soon there was pandemonium.

XV: Full Circle

As Clover looked down the hillside her eyes filled with tears. If she could have spoken her thoughts, it would have been to say that this was not what they had aimed at when they had set themselves years ago to work for the overthrow of the human race. These scenes of terror and slaughter were not what they had looked forward to.

George Orwell, *Animal Farm*, Chapter VII.

Alfred was on his way home from work when he saw the news.

"ETON BOY IN DEATH LEAP" screamed the billboard in front of the old man selling *The Standard* outside Whitechapel underground station. Alfred stopped stunned and picked up a copy to buy.

Teacher charged with sex attacks on top judge's son
ETON BOY JUMPS TO DEATH FROM QUEEN'S CASTLE
An Eton College boy jumped to his death this afternoon from Windsor Castle in front of scores of horrified tourists. Alexander Aylmer, 14, son of Lord Justice of Appeal Sir Henry Aylmer, and a pupil at the £4725-a-year school, climbed the royal residence's Round Tower, mounted the battlements and plunged to his death before anyone could intervene.

Mitsuhiko Hasegawa, a visitor from Japan, was right there. "I saw this cute-looking kid walking across the tower as if he was in a trance. He stopped purposefully right by the edge and I was just beginning to think there was something odd about it when he suddenly carried on walking as if into thin air."

Detective Inspector Jim Hatchet of the Thames Valley Police revealed that Damian Edwin Cavendish, 23, a teacher at the school, had been remanded in custody yesterday, charged with sexual abuse of the boy.

"It seems reasonable to suspect that this child's tragic death is linked to his having been sexually assaulted," said the Inspector. "The circumstances are still being investigated however."

Alfred recognised the boy's name straight away, though he had only heard the surname once. He tried vainly to fathom how the information might fit with what he knew from Julian. He had deliberately not mentioned his son's younger friend in any of their conversations since Julian had agreed to drop their friendship. He had assumed that Julian had done as agreed, though he could not see how Julian doing so or not doing so could be linked to Alexander being assaulted by a teacher. In any case, poor Julian could hardly fail to be in the most horrific emotional turmoil at the moment.

Alfred had only just got home when the telephone rang. He ran to answer it, hoping it was Julian. He longed to know how he was and to comfort him. Instead, it was Denise, telling him excitedly that she would not be home until very late, and to watch BBC Two at 10:30. In view of the public outrage there was bound to be about the suicide at Eton, there was to be a special presentation on what do with child sex offenders on *Newsnight*. She had been invited to appear on it as one of the best-known campaigners against child abuse.

After that, Alfred was too worried about Julian to concentrate on anything. He was sorely tempted to telephone him, despite having always given in to Julian's old entreaty not to, but he kept reminding himself that Julian could call him any time he wanted.

Alexander's death was the first item on the nine o' clock news after the usual update on the miners' strike.

"It has now been established that the boy killed himself only half an hour after being interviewed by Linda Johnson, a social worker in Windsor, whom police believe was the last person to speak to him," said the reporter against a backdrop of Windsor Castle. "I have been speaking to her. Miss Johnson ...," she said, as the scene switched to outside an office block. "I'm sorry. This must be very distressing for you."

"Yes, it is. It's the most upsetting case I've ever had to deal with," she replied with a taut and flustered expression.

"Can you tell us why this boy, who according to his school was promising and well-liked with everything going for him, should have taken his own life?"

"I'm sorry, I cannot comment. The matter is sub judice."

"The police have already suggested it may be linked to his having been sexually assaulted by a teacher at Eton College. Can you at least confirm that's what he came to see you about?"

391

"I can't comment on this specific case at all … All I can tell you is that it's sadly very common for sexually abused children to feel suicidal. Usually we can help them come to terms with what's been done to them enough to stop them, though the psychological scars remain with them for life. Sometimes we can't though."

The scene changed to show an earnest-looking, bearded man in his fifties sitting behind a large desk.

"I asked the Director of Berkshire Social Services for comment," said a voiceover from the reporter. "Mr. Grimshaw," she continued live, "What lessons should we be drawing from this horrific tragedy, if the sex abuse allegations are proven?"

"I hope it makes the government and the general public aware of how devastating child abuse is. Much more needs to be done in both prevention and deterrence. Everyone involved with children needs to make it difficult for possible paedophiles to come into contact with them and to ensure that signs of abuse are detected early. The problem there is that victimised children won't normally speak out. The penalties for sex abuse are unacceptably light too, considering the harm it does."

Next the reporter turned to the police.

"I can confirm that Mr. Cavendish has been charged with buggery of a boy under 16, for which the maximum penalty is life imprisonment, and that thorough investigation of the case is continuing," said a grim-looking Inspector Hatchet.

"But even if he is found guilty, he won't really get life, will he, Inspector?"

"It would be highly unusual, regrettably so in my view."

Denise had been looking forward to her interview with tremendous excitement ever since she had been contacted. It was going to be her night of triumph. This case was going to get massive publicity, making it easily the best opportunity she had ever had of getting her views across. She had already made a list of the points she most hoped to make.

In the first place, it was the perfect opportunity to remind the public that no one was immune to the scourge of paedophilia. It was everywhere, even in the most expensive schools and homes.

392

She wondered whether she should give what she had to say a personal touch by revealing that her child was a pupil at the very same school as the victim. That would certainly take them by surprise. It was an amazing coincidence. Perhaps Julian even knew the boy, though that was unlikely as he was three years older. She did not like to telephone to make sure, as he had made such a point of asking her not to and she had been finding him particularly difficult recently. Finally, she dismissed all idea of disclosing her link to Eton. Too often when the school was mentioned in the press, allusion was made to its fees, which would hardly sit well with her fund-raising activities for child protection.

Fantastic progress had already been made over the last few years, she reflected proudly. The general public was at last becoming alert to how widespread and devastating the sexual abuse of children was. Amazing to remember, only a few years ago, she had had to explain to people what a paedophile was. She would never forget how irritating it had often been getting people to take the subject with appropriate seriousness.

Just three years ago she had got herself invited to a dinner party that looked like a good opportunity to meet an M.P. potentially interested in helping needle the government into giving her organisation more funding. Her husband had stayed at home to look after their son. The M.P. was reputed to be a "wet," as Conservatives with social consciences were known, but she had found him facetious, and the rest of the company just as disappointing.

They had started making fun of Americans. She liked Americans. They were so much more socially concerned and responsible, and the men far more respectful and sensitive towards women than the British. She was always thankful she had not married an Englishman. Fred was much more considerate and responsible than most that she knew, even if a little morally lax on some issues. At least he never made personal jokes about people or mocked them when they were trying to do the right thing in that typically British, puerile way. The conversation that evening had been a good example.

"Have you heard about the latest fad in America?" a young man evidently considered a wit had exclaimed in an amused drawl. "They've become convinced that everyone wants to have sex with their own children, even babies! There was one poor chap recently who quite innocently took some photos of his three-year-old daughter having a bath. He took his film off to be developed, went back home, and the next thing he knew the police were knocking down his door and some social workers came and took his daughter away."

"Good Heavens! How frightful!" the M.P. had exclaimed. The company had let off an outraged titter, and she had seethed with silent fury, knowing there was no point in trying to correct them. It would have been no use trying to explain to the male chauvinist pigs that Americans were rightly concerned. They would have listened to her in polite boredom, and tried to change the conversation. When she had talked to the M.P. later, she had even had to pretend to agree the photo business was overboard in order to have a good chance of eliciting his support.

But her time had come. No one would laugh about that sort of thing now. It was encouraging how fast society could be changed on occasion.

She thought back further into the past. She had always been politically progressive, the one thing she admitted owing her father, a London Underground ticket collector and union activist, but ironically in her youth she had not seen the obvious link between the oppression of women and their sexual exploitation by men.

Girls of her generation were brought up to keep themselves for marriage, but she had been well ahead of her time. She had rejected that oppressive, paternalistic way of thinking in her mid-twenties, as soon as she was old enough to be able to make responsible decisions. That had been in the fifties, well before the sexual revolution.

But though she had been ready for sex in appropriate circumstances, a suitable partner had not presented himself. She had begun to worry that she might never find one. Finally, when she was thirty-two, she had thought it was going to happen. Her new boss, Des, had started inviting her out for meals. He was a nice-looking man just a year older than her, respectful, sensitive and progressive in his opinions, or so he had appeared. She had just reached the point of deciding that she would accept if he invited her to have intercourse with him, when his invitations out suddenly dried up. It had been a fortnight before she could understand what had gone wrong. Then she had gone into his office, thinking he was out, and found the new secretary, a young girl of nineteen, sitting on his lap in a deep embrace. After that, they had made no secret of their affair. They even seemed to be flaunting it, and there had been nothing she could do about it. It was disgusting. She had never been so deceived as to someone's character. They had got married a month after that, but she had already successfully applied for a transfer.

It was a pity they couldn't get the age of consent put up to twenty-one for girls as well as boys. But that was only to be expected, as Parliament was mostly made up of men, and if the truth were known, half of them would probably like to exploit a young girl if they could get the chance. Exploitation would never really end until society was controlled by women, well emancipated women like herself who understood what had to be put right, at least until men had been completely re-educated.

She had been thirty-six when she had finally met Fred and had sex herself, and that had been mostly because they were getting married and planning a baby. As she had long suspected, sex for women was greatly overrated.

Everything had worked out for the best anyway. If she had not met and lost Des, she would not have switched to the Bermondsey social services, and it was from her appointment as their women's welfare officer that all her later successes stemmed. It was in the ensuing years that she had gradually discovered how many women's lives had been ruined by sexual abuse during childhood.

The more she probed, the more cases she encountered of socially dysfunctional women admitting to being victims of childhood abuse they had previously denied. In most cases, they had been abused in their early teens and simply had not seen anything wrong with it until she explained the harm it had done them. Occasionally, though, the abuse had taken place at such an early age that their memories of it were confused, and it was only through her help that they were able to recover them. The richly rewarding thing was that in every case, the more she showed them that problems they had imagined were their own fault all ultimately derived from their abuse, the more relieved and empowered they felt.

When she had been working in Bermondsey for fifteen years and was still struggling to get anyone to take her findings seriously, strikingly similar discoveries began to gain publicity in America. She waited just long enough to be confident the people who ran the NSPCC must be aware of the storm brewing the other side of the Atlantic, and then went to them with her own neglected reports. That was the moment her career had taken off. They had taken her on in no time.

Soon she was being sent to seminars in the States. The first one was with the New York Police Department's new special unit for dealing with child molesters. They had taken her to meet real child victims, and she would never forget how harrowing it had been seeing innocent young children shaking fearfully as they reluctantly described to their rescuers the revolting abominations that men had inflicted on them. She had known only too well that the damage was lifelong.

Over the next few years, the NSPCC had come to rely on her to keep them abreast of the latest developments: the discovery that child abuse had been perpetrated on a scale far greater than anyone had imagined, and the new methods of detecting likely victims, of getting them to come forward and to understand that what they had been subjected to was abuse. Most usefully for the NSPCC as an organisation, she had learned new ways of fundraising and bringing the problem to public attention. She had worked tirelessly giving lectures to police forces and social services up and down the country.

Finally, it had paid off. Paedophilia had gripped the public imagination, donations coming into the NSPCC had mushroomed beyond their wildest dreams, and four months ago she had set up her own charity, Child Rescue, which had been an immediate success. Now tonight she might finally begin to be publicly known in her own right.

Alfred watched with mounting excitement, as the circumstances of the Eton suicide were briefly recapped by *Newsnight*'s auxiliary presenter. Then, suddenly, there she was: his own wife

396

was sitting in the BBC studio, looking very authoritative, with Peter Snow, the presenter, and two other men.

"This heart-rending story raises the question of how we should treat people who sexually abuse children," began Snow. "How can we make our children safe from them? I am joined tonight by three experts in different fields of child abuse prevention. Dr. Gerald Hartman," he said, turning to an affable-looking man of about forty, "You're a psychiatrist who specialises in treating paedophiles. Could you explain to us how you do this?"

"Yes, I use what's called aversion therapy. My patient sits in a chair with his penis connected to an instrument called a plethysmograph, while I show him nude slides. The plethysmograph measures his arousal in response to them. Whenever he responds to the image of a child, I administer an electric shock, but I allow him to become aroused by the pictures of nude men or women. Eventually, the patient develops such a horror of erotic images of children that he won't be aroused by them, and his sexual interest is diverted to adults."

"And does it always work?" asked Snow.

"In the end it always stops the patient becoming aroused by children, at least if he keeps up the treatment."

"So it's voluntary for them?"

"Oh yes. Most of my patients are referred to me while awaiting trial. Their chances of avoiding long prison sentences are improved if they can be shown to have voluntarily undergone treatment."

"Is this the only cure for paedophilia?"

"It is the only treatment which leaves the patient free to develop a sexual interest in adults and lead a normal life. The only alternative is chemical castration, which involves the weekly injection of drugs to suppress the sex drive. It has undesirable side-effects though. It increases body fat and causes the patient to grow breasts, sometimes so large they have to be cut off surgically. There are indications it may cause cancer too."

"I think many people would say we shouldn't make any concessions to the wellbeing of paedophiles while the safety of children is at stake," commented Snow drily.

"Yes, of course, but then not all of my patients are paedophiles. Some of them have got into trouble over willing young men of eighteen or nineteen, which is hardly paedophilia. And many of them are decent people who've..."

"Excuse me!" interrupted Denise, visibly boiling. "We're talking about men who've had sex with children. That's abuse, full stop. You are condoning it by confusing the issue with talk about nineteen-year-olds, which has nothing to do with it."

"It is to do with it because the law ..."

"No, it's not, because it's not child abuse."

"I promise you I've twice had patients in my clinic who'd been charged by the police after having oral sex with nineteen-year-olds in public toilets, and were otherwise decent, law-abiding men. I'm just saying it's not all black and white. Sodomising a fourteen-year-old is obviously a quite different matter."

"You're twisting the subject. We're here to talk about child abuse, which is black and white."

"Dr. Will Dalrymple, what do you have to say about this?" intervened Snow to the evident relief of a shaken Dr. Hartman. "I understand you've been involved in the special unit for sex offenders at Wormwood Scrubs."

"Yes, I've examined hundreds of cases," replied Dalrymple, a short, balding, bespectacled man of nearly fifty, "and with all respect to Dr. Hartman, I have to say that aversion therapy has no effect in the long-term. It is purely temporary."

He thought for a moment of the most disturbing finding by a colleague who had experimented with plethysmographs at Wormwood Scrubs. They had tried them out on both child sex offenders and "normals", as they termed the other inmates, and the proportion of normals who had been stimulated by images of children was huge, almost as high as the offenders. There was no point in mentioning that now though.

"Chemical castration also lasts only as long as the treatment is given," he continued. "The hard truth is that paedophilia is completely incurable and the only solution is real, surgical castration. Society has got to face up to that if children are to be safe. The only other choice is that they are locked up for the rest of their lives. Castration should therefore be in the best interests of the paedophiles too, as the only way they can be let out of prison safely."

"Denise Smith, you founded the charity Child Rescue to alert the public to the problem of child abuse," said Snow, turning to her at last. "Which do you think is the better way of dealing with sex offenders?"

"I agree with Dr. Dalrymple that the safety of children must come before any other consideration, but I think we're getting diverted from the more important issue, which is prevention. Once an offender is caught, a child's life or several children's lives have already been ruined. In most cases it could have been avoided if the proper measures had been taken, but the government has for years now been taking no heed of advice from those who know."

"What measures are those?" asked Snow.

"Most urgently, we need checks on teachers and everyone else working with children. We need special police units trained in detecting child abuse and handling the victims so that they're not afraid to testify. It's a disgraceful situation compared to the United States, where every county has its own child protection unit. We need many more trained social workers too. Charities like Child Rescue cannot cope with a problem on this scale without far greater funding. The public has become concerned, as we've been seeing from the generosity of their donations, but the funding of something so vital should be what the state is for. It is really the stinginess of the present government that is putting British children at risk."

"Do you think that the publicity over the suicide of the Eton boy might finally persuade the government to do something?"

"Yes, I think there may be some hope at last, just because this boy went to Eton. The many Old Etonians in the government may realise now that their own children aren't safe from the scourge of child abuse, and it's not just a problem for ordinary people".

He was lying gagged and naked on his back, spread-eagled on a steel operating table, his arms and legs tightly bound with straps to the metal bars that rang along its sides. Another pair of straps around his thighs ensured their immobility. His thick, dark hair was moist with sweat and his normally handsome features were distorted by terror. His cock lay shrivelled by his fear and fixed against his belly by strong sticky tape, leaving his scrotum nicely exposed for the imminent operation. The doctor and nurse came back into the room where they had left him ten minutes earlier.

Only his head could move and he bent it forward as hard as he could, his hazel eyes fixed in abject terror on those of the middle-aged doctor, who briefly reassured him in a matter-of-fact tone that the operation was painless and would be over in less than ten minutes. He could watch if he really wanted, but it would be much easier for him if he just lay back and closed his eyes. But the horror that engulfed the patient's mind did not allow him to consider this.

As the doctor leaned over him and lifted his scrotum a little with his gloved hand to inspect it, the patient could only see the man's bald pate and the horse-shoe of fading ginger hair around it. The physician soon stood up straight again and the nurse handed him a steel tray, from which he removed a scalpel that flashed a reflection of the overhanging light across the room as he turned its gleaming blade. The doctor adjusted the round spectacles on his great beak of a nose. As he pulled the scrotum tight with his left hand, the patient writhed desperately and jerked his head from side to side. The doctor told him not to squirm. At best it was fruitless, and at worst it would be his own fault if he lost his penis too as a result.

The only thing that rivalled his terror was his despair. He knew his future, his essence, half the value of his life was about to be torn from him and destroyed for ever and he could sense from the doctor's expression and gestures and the nurse's approving looks that they thought it was a disgusting, contemptible thing they were going to dispose of.

As the doctor bent down again and his expert hand carefully made a neat midline incision across the scrotum, the patient's eyes widened in terror and he emitted a long series of hoarse shrieks through his gag. It was not possible for an observer to tell whether this was because he guessed from the doctor's movements that the scalpel had begun its fatal work or whether they had not left enough time for the local anaesthetic to numb him completely against the searing agony.

Once he judged the incision long enough, the doctor replaced the scalpel on the tray and took instead a pair of little forceps with which he prised open the scrotal sack until he could peer inside and find a grip on the right testicle. Then he moved his left hand back to the tray and picked up a pair of long, slender scissors. The patient jerked as violently as he was able with each snip on his spermatic cords, though again it was not possible to tell if that was because the anaesthetic was inadequate to mask the excruciating pain or because of the revelatory sound that accompanied each severance, akin to that of crushing frozen celery.

At last the doctor was able to extract and hold up the severed testicle. It looked for all the world like a tiny whitish meatball in a slimy reddish sauce, a residue of the spermatic cords hanging from it like short, fine noodles. The visible proof of his own emasculation induced a new fit of horror and despair in the patient beyond anything he had imagined possible and he vomited violently, drenching his face and the fringe of his hair in muck.

The doctor dropped the testicle into a glass on the far end of the nurse's tray, the forceps making a little tinkle as they struck the glass's edge. Then he proceeded to repeat what he had done with the other testicle and emitted a sigh of satisfaction as he finally dunked it in the glass beside its twin. The nurse looked at the doctor quizzically. He caught her glance and nodded, so she picked up the glass with an expression of familiar distaste mingled with relief that its contents could finally be thrown away.

As the doctor sewed up the incision, he reflected that he had had a long day and was looking forward to a long, hot bath followed by a brandy before dinner. He could still count that it was the thirty-seventh pair of offensive testicles he had consigned to oblivion since assigned this responsibility. Of all the surgical operations he performed, it was the most rewarding in its finality, the feeling that he had served humanity profoundly by irreversibly terminating yet one more possibility for its pollution.

Alfred woke up with a violent start. He sat up and knew at once that he could not stop himself vomiting. He jumped out of bed, rushed into the bathroom and threw open the lid of the lavatory just in time to empty himself into it. He knelt there groaning with nausea for ten minutes after his last retching. Then he washed his face in the basin, drunk some water and stumbled back to his bed, his chest heaving and his mind blanketed in a dread despair he could not yet explain.

The mutilated boy in his nightmare was his dear old friend Otto and Alfred had never thought to see him so vividly again in this life, even in a dream. He had also never realised he still missed him so much. Now that he was fully awake, it seemed particularly poignant that Otto had still looked so young and fresh, still a tender fourteen, whilst he, once the same age, had become a hoary, aging man of fifty-six.

He remembered it all now with a clarity he had vainly hoped he had escaped for ever. Otto and his lover had been caught. The commandant had taken a very dim view of the matter indeed. He chose not to sully his own reputation by exposing the guard, who had been one of his personal appointees, but had him consigned to the Eastern Front.

As for Otto, it was never spelt out whether the fate he was accorded was due to his crime of willingly submitting to deviant passion, for which many pure-blooded Aryans suffered a similar fate at Sachsenhausen, or whether it was just a tiny part of the Reich's broad scheme of preventing sub-humans from perpetuating their filthy genes, towards the most efficient implementation of which drastic experiments were carried out on the genitals of even larger numbers of Jews. The timing of it strongly suggested the former, but it made no difference.

Otto had told him about it slowly and in graphic detail the day after he was unmercifully released from the hospital ward, his body breathing weakly and his spirit utterly broken with hopeless despair. Soon after that, he had died painfully of an internal bleeding no one was both capable of, and interested in, stopping, and Alfred's spirits had sunk to their very lowest ebb.

Alfred found no consolation at all in the realisation that the doctor in his nightmare resembled the Dr. Dalrymple of the BBC discussion rather than the real concentration camp Dr. Redick Otto had told him of, but whose appearance he had never described. Quite the opposite. He had had nightmares of Sachsenhausen before, but always when he had awoken in his

402

comfortable bed in Wandsworth, he had exhaled with relief that he had escaped and his breathing had become steadier as he reassured himself that he really was safely in England, the gentle and peaceful land of his childhood dreams.

This time, however, no relief came. His chest continued to heave and his mind remained wide awake. He was indeed in England, but not safely so. He was in an England that until recently he would have refused to believe existed, one where a respected doctor could calmly recommend mass castration of human beings to millions of television viewers without anyone batting an eyelid.

As the day dawned, he gave up trying to get back to sleep. He sat morosely in the kitchen drinking coffee until he heard the newspaper being dropped through the door.

"ETON PERVERT AND VICTIM BOTH DIE" announced the headline on the front page of *The Daily Express.*

Alfred hurried through the first half of the article rehashing Alexander's suicide to get to the startling new information:

It is strongly suspected the boy was in distress due to months of sickening sex abuse by Damian Edwin Cavendish, 23, a teacher at the prestigious school.

Cavendish had earlier been remanded in custody in Wormwood Scrubs prison on charges of buggering a child. By a bizarre coincidence, he also met a violent end yesterday, beaten to death by disgusted fellow inmates.

Police confirmed that Kevin Black, 32, held on remand for suspected murder and George Edward Sheath, 35, convicted of illegal possession of a firearm, were being questioned on suspicion of murder.

Two prison officers reported coming into the kitchen at lunchtime after hearing cries, to find Sheath, armed with a wooden table leg, and Black beating and kicking Cavendish, who was lying on the floor. By the time the officers were able to pull them away, Cavendish was already unconscious, his face a bloody mess. He was taken to the prison hospital, but died soon afterwards without regaining consciousness.

It is suspected that his alleged child sex crime was the cause of the attack, as Black was heard shouting "Die, you f***ing nonce!" as he kicked his face. The suicide of Cavendish's victim cannot have been an extra motive, as the assault on Cavendish took place first.

403

His death is bound to be seen as quick justice by many, but Ian Dunbar, Governor of Wormwood Scrubs, expressed dismay: "The rule of law extends to our prisons as much as anywhere else and those responsible will be brought to the same justice as if they had murdered any other person."

Asked why Cavendish had not been put on Rule 43, the protective segregation of sex offenders and other prisoners despised by their fellow inmates, he said: "There did not seem to be any need. There had been no publicity about his case. We do not know how his alleged offence became known."

In the meantime, the widespread revulsion caused by the child suicide is leading to calls for harsher measures against paedophiles ...

Suddenly he saw it all again. The memory he tried hardest to shut out of his mind during the day, but that still disturbed his sleep: the Night of Broken Glass. He was ten years old again. He and his little sister had been woken up in the middle of the night by a crashing sound followed by angry shouts. They had crept out of their bedroom and into the hall, to see two big men yelling at old Herr Gomperz. Alfred had no idea why Herr Gomperz was there. Their old nanny, Frau Gomperz, had come alone that evening to babysit for them, and now she came over to grasp Alfred and Gerta in her trembling arms. The elder of the men glanced briefly at them with an expression of disgust and demanded to know if there was anyone else in the flat.

"Nein, mein Herr," squeaked Herr Gomperz. The younger intruder immediately stormed off to check the other rooms, kicking their doors open, returned and shook his head. The first man threw what must be Herr Gomperz's identity papers on the floor, strode over to the terrified old man and grabbed him by the throat.

"Wo ist Professor Wertheimber?" he asked, but got only a frantic shaking of the head in reply.

The thug let out a host of expletives, of which Alfred only understood filthy Jewish swine, before slamming Herr Gomperz against the wall, and repeating his question still more menacingly. Fear seemed to have robbed Herr Gomperz of speech. His interrogator let go of his throat and instead landed a heavy punch straight in his face, sending him sprawling to the feet of the other man, who kicked him in the groin. Alfred

404

caught his expression of loathing and contempt as he did so. It shook him to the core. How could anyone so hate a sweet, gentle old man like Herr Gomperz? They could not possibly know anything about him.

The interrogator repeated his question for what he promised was the last time. Herr Gomperz struggled slowly to sit up.

"Ich weiss das nicht" he pleaded. Rather than making the elder man even angrier, as Alfred expected, this reply seemed to make him come to a decision that calmed him. He gave his comrade a knowing nod and looked on with satisfaction as the latter went to the broken front door and picked up a sledgehammer that lay beside it. Alfred could feel Frau Gomperz's fingers suddenly digging hard into his shoulder.

The younger man swung the sledgehammer straight at Herr Gomperz's head. The old man was still dazed and only drew back at the last moment. Instead of killing him outright, it caught the front of his face, instantly pulverising his nose. As his scream of agony rent the air, Alfred watching in silent terror saw from the ghastly hollow socket that one of his eyes had been knocked out. His attacker raised the sledgehammer back again, noted with satisfaction that his victim was no longer capable of movement, and swung it again with a contemptuous grimace. There was a sickening cracking noise. All that seemed to be left of Herr Gomperz's head was a shapeless mess of blood, bone and brain.

Alfred's terror had mounted yet further as he realised that at any moment the attackers' attention would be diverted from their motionless target, and it would be the turn of the rest of them, but after a few moments of silence, the two men left without a word.

He did not want to imagine Cavendish's death, but it was too easy to do. He picked up the newspaper again, wondering if anything in it might tell him if anyone else shared his nausea, and found it was the subject of the main editorial:

Child abuse is a brutal form of torture committed against the most vulnerable people in society and deserves the harshest penalties. Nevertheless, in Britain a person is innocent until proven guilty and we cannot tolerate anyone taking justice into their own hands. Even if Cavendish's guilt in this case were certain, his assailants would have been cheating justice by giving him an easy and early way out of the long prison sentence he should have suffered.

He remembered that when Parliament had debated restoring capital punishment the previous year, there had been a pious editorial about the cruelty of the death penalty. He sighed, wondering what anyone was supposed to make of people who denounced the death penalty as inhumane, but then showed the true blackness of their hearts by wishing that someone could have suffered more than it.

Just as he put the paper down in disgust, he heard Denise go into the bathroom from her bedroom. He was not in the mood to offer her the congratulations he knew she would expect, so he scribbled them on a note he left on the kitchen table and went off to work early. He had a busy day, but still found it hard to concentrate, his anxiety about Julian not abating at all. It was already longer than usual since Julian had telephoned. Finally, he made a bargain with himself that if he hadn't done so by half past seven that evening, he would call him.

He left work earlier than usual and again bought himself a *Standard* at the tube station, in case there was any further news. There was only a letter:

The death penalty is not enough for paedophiles like Damian Cavendish, the teacher who caused a young boy's suicide. It might pay him back for the innocent child's life that he stole by molesting him, but what about his debt to society? The only way scum like him can pay that back is if they are used for medical experiments. Pharmaceutical companies could pay to use them as guinea pigs until they died, and that way some good might eventually come of their lives to counterbalance the harm they have done.
Robin Dobbs, Guildford.

Not long ago, Alfred would have thought Mr. Dobbs a deranged maniac and his letter unprintable in a decent British newspaper. He was obviously proved wrong on the latter point, and once he had thought about it, he realised wearily that he was probably wrong on the former too. Very likely Mr. Dobbs thought of

406

himself as a kind and thoroughly decent member of society, was sincere in his beliefs and keen to do all the right things. He probably helped old ladies cross the road and sang in his local choir.

Since Alfred had come to England, he had heard endless people aver that the sort of men who killed Herr Gomperz were just Nazi fanatics, that they had nothing to do with ordinary German people who would never have supported them if they had realised what they were up to, but Alfred had always known that was not true.

The morning following Herr Gomperz's death, when their own street was quiet, Frau Gomperz had escorted them across the town. Their route took them over a large boulevard where there were several shops owned by Jews. A crowd was watching and cheering as stormtroopers smashed yet another shop window. Alfred saw two fashionably dressed women clapping their hands and screaming with glee, while an ordinary-looking mother held up her baby to see the fun. Worst of all, they caught sight of Herr Hoevel, the nice owner of the sweet shop they went to most often, looking on with interest. He had always had a friendly word for them. Did he know their father was a Jew?

Alfred had also heard people in England express disbelief that ordinary German people could really have believed that Jews were as bad as the Nazis said, but he knew that was not true either. Those attracted by Hitler's anti-semitism were utterly sincere in their conviction that Jews were evil.

Months before the Night of Broken Glass, his father had taken them to the Bavarian Alps for a fortnight. It was their very last holiday together, and just after his mother had deserted them. Alfred spent the first week playing with a local girl his age. They happily explored every nook and cranny together until, one morning when they met, she seemed troubled. It was not really true, was it, she asked, that he was a Jew? She could not believe it. Alfred was a bit confused as to exactly what a Jew was, but he knew by then that most people considered his father as one, and that his mother was not. He wanted to be like his father, not his mother, so he said yes.

407

"But you killed God!" she said, horror and mounting fear apparent in her face. He called to her as she ran back down the hill, but she would not stop to listen.

Eddie Craven answered the phone in Peyntors when Alfred finally rang, and ran to fetch Julian.

"Some strange, German-sounding man wants you on the phone," he told him bluntly, and Julian blushed, though he felt more angry than embarrassed.

"Hello, Julian," said Alfred when Julian got to the telephone a minute later. Julian heard the tenderness in the familiar voice and fought to hold back the tears he feared were coming. It had been a little earlier than this on the previous day that he heard the wild rumour sweeping through the stunned school, a rumour confirmed by an ashen-faced Mr. Hodgson at Prayers, and he had avoided speaking a word to anyone in all that time.

He could easily guess why his father had called in this unprecedented way, but he was not ready to talk even to him, and certainly not then and there. The telephone booth was only partially hidden from the lobby. He could see Craven there talking animatedly to the group of boys hanging around, including Cowburn and Leigh, who both glanced with interest in his direction. It would be hard to disguise tears and anyone walking past would be able to overhear him.

"Hello, Dad. What's up?" he said with an attempt at cheerfulness.

"Julian, I had to call because I've been so worried about you. I have read the news, you know."

"Dad, I'm sorry, I can't talk now. Please understand," he pleaded. "There are people around," he added almost in a whisper. "I promise I'll call sometime tomorrow, okay?"

"Okay," said Alfred, and they exchanged goodbyes sadly.

"Hey, Julian!" called out Oliver Fisher, as Julian passed through the lobby to go back upstairs. "Who's your Kraut friend?" Julian had heard him before boast about the war-time exploits of his father, a much decorated submarine commander. The others looked at Julian curiously, Cowburn and Leigh with slightly mocking expressions.

408

"My father," said Julian loudly, glowering briefly straight at Cowburn before striding quickly up the stairs.

Julian returned to his room and sat down in front of his biology notes. Trials were beginning the next morning. He knew he was not prepared. He was going to do badly, so badly that he would be moved down divs next Half and no one would carry on considering him possible Oxbridge material, but he could not begin to concentrate on revision now any more than before.

He had regretted everything the moment he went into Alexander's room on Tuesday night, the last night of Alexander's life. When he saw his haggard face drained of all expression except pain and the once vivacious eyes so dull, the extent of the harm he had done was at once obvious. Julian realised then that Alexander's love of Mr. Cavendish was pure and unassailable and there had never been the slightest chance he could take his place. Hopes he had had that he might be able to offer Alexander a physical comfort that could assume erotic undertones dissipated into self-disgust. Shame at the selfishness of his lust extinguished it. He knew then that selfish and unworthy as his love for Alexander had often been, it had been genuine too, for now he could say truthfully that he had no physical designs on him, and yet he still longed more than anything to make him happy again. He wanted desperately to abolish the past and offer sincerely to Alexander every possible benefit of altruistic love, to try to make up just a little for what he had done, but his culpability for all of Alexander's suffering made such an offer too shabby to articulate. In any case, the little he had found to say in that final conversation had fallen so flat that Alexander had just looked mildly irritated by the distraction and soon asked him to go.

Since hearing of first Alexander's death, then Mr. Cavendish's, Julian had not doubted that he deserved to die too, but he was never tempted to kill himself. He was not deterred by any hopes for the future. Not only had he destroyed what he had most badly wanted, but he could see no end of the tunnel for his guilt, his self-hatred and his loneliness. He could not imagine coming close to anyone again. A recently growing doubt that he could

409

one day like a woman enough to get married grew to certainty the morning after his father's telephone call.

He had a free period to study in his room before his first Trials. Incapable of resisting the possibility of new information, he turned to *The Times*, and an article therein finally enlightened him as to the true nature of his mother's work. Complimentary as it was, his revulsion with her and everything she stood for deepened with every sentence. He soon understood that she and her kind were claiming Alexander's death was Mr. Cavendish's fault, while he was rapidly coming to understand that apart from his own role in betraying Alexander into their hands, the fault was entirely theirs.

Though he could no longer imagine loving a woman, Mr. Cavendish's fate had removed any illusion he had had that this world could be anything other than a living hell for a lover of boys. In any case, after what he had done, he could never think of acting as if worthy of even a poor reflection of the boy he had betrayed.

As he could see so little hope of happiness in life, he assumed initially the only reason he was not inclined to suicide was his cowardice. Without doubt, the idea terrified him, but gradually he perceived that it was not that simple.

Alexander had taken his own life knowing that it was his and that he owed nothing to anyone except the lover from whom he had been irreparably torn. Julian, in contrast, was heavily in debt. He owed Alexander and Mr. Cavendish the lives he had stolen from them, and though he could not yet see any way of ever repaying even a morsel of that debt, to abandon his life before exploring every possible avenue of expiation would be an act of fraud and unrepentant evil. However miserable his life might be, he was bound to carry on in the hope that somehow some day he might do something that would win their applause, if their spirits were looking on, or, if not, would at least be in the spirit of what they stood for. Perhaps he could find some means of making the world understand how pure and profound he felt sure their love had been. Meanwhile, enduring this bleak, grey world would be his richly-deserved penance.

After lunch, Julian was passing through the lobby, his depression increased by his performance in his first Trials paper,

410

when he caught sight of Leigh ahead grinning stupidly at someone evidently just behind him. He whipped round to behold Cowburn clicking his heels together, his arm raised in a Hitler salute. Cowburn lowered his arm a second before Julian's fist smashed hard into his face, knocking him onto the floor. Cowburn slowly sat up and clutched a hand to the left side of his face, but Julian strode away through the crowd of astonished boys who parted silently to let him pass.

He went straight to his room. He wondered briefly what might be the consequences of his loss of temper. He had probably given him a black eye, so it was hardly likely to remain a secret from the authorities, but he soon decided he did not give a damn about either that or Trials or anything else in the little world of Eton. He had had enough. Instead of going to his next exam, he began to pack up his belongings.

Denise's head was so spinning with elation that she walked out of the Labour Party's Central Office straight into the street, forgetting she had parked her new BMW in the car park the other side. She had been invited there following her television appearance.

She had often been asked why she did not go into politics, and recently new friends in the Labour Party had expressed confidence that she could get herself selected as a candidate in one of its safe seats. She was exactly what the Party was looking for. There were only twenty-three women in Parliament, a measly 4%. To the chagrin of the leadership, which had long been pushing for greater representation by women, there were even fewer Labour women MPs than Conservative ones. The problem was simply that not enough good women candidates were putting themselves forward. She had been tempted, but put off by the long hours of tedious work she would have to put in as a constituency MP before she could hope to do anything nearly as useful as she currently was with child protection.

Now it had been made clear to her that not only could she be selected for a safe seat when one came up in a by-election, but that she would then find herself on a fast track to the shadow cabinet, perhaps in time to join the government if Labour won the next election. Neil Kinnock himself had watched her on *Newsnight* and had made enquiries.

Suddenly she remembered where she was supposed to be going, and walked back to her car. She felt newly elated as she got into it. It was not just that the BMW was such a vivid reminder of her new independence and wealth. She could hardly help feeling proud of that when she remembered how her own mother had spent most of her life tied to a kitchen sink in a decrepit house in Southwark. It also finally put paid to those jibes she had heard over the years from jealous colleagues and even her own brother, the sexist bastard, that she had been neglecting her family by devoting herself so much to her career. No one would say that about a man who worked hard. What had hurt most was the insinuation that her career was not worthwhile because it was Fred who brought in most of the money as well as looking after Julian.

The BMW was a highly visible reminder that she was now the principal breadwinner. Soon that would become even more obvious. There had been an endless string of phone calls and promises of donations to Child Rescue over the last two days. Clearly she was going to have to take on new employees, which meant a larger office. The obvious solution was to buy a very much larger house, in Islington perhaps, to be shared between Child Rescue and her family. Fred should perhaps stay at home as a househusband. Her work was now much better paid as well as far more worthwhile.

As she drove home, her mind turned again to the future. If it was seriously possible that she might be in the government in a few years, it was surely not impossible that she become Prime Minister one day. No one had seriously thought Maggie Thatcher might be until a few years before she had, and she herself would be so much a better one. How she hated that woman, who had joined the party of privilege and patriarchy, and had been at the pinnacle of power for five years without doing a thing for women's rights. Worst of all, Thatcher's rise to power had given people the comfortable illusion that sexual equality had been achieved, and that was so untrue. There was so much yet to be done.

Yes, she would definitely go for it. Prime Minister or not, she would play an important role in building the first truly compassionate society, one with feminine values and with both

412

women and children fully protected from men. It would be a safe society where all were cared for, and laws protected everyone from being willingly manipulated or exploited, as well as forced. That was not all. She would not only help build a better Britain, but, in partnership with their American friends, a better world in which the same values were exported everywhere. No country should be allowed to perpetuate barbarities under the guise of religious or cultural differences. Now was not merely the dawn of a new age. They were in the midst of the greatest social revolution in recorded history.

Alfred had told Denise at breakfast that he was staying at home that day. She had looked at him rather oddly, but decided not to comment. He had clearly been unsettled since she had been on television and the news that she had an appointment at the Labour Party Central Office seemed only to have made him worse. She supposed it might be his male ego that was suffering, but she was wrong. The truth was he could not break out of his gloomy foreboding over Julian. He was not therefore thinking about her, as she fondly imagined, while she was having her momentous interview, but worrying about their son.

When the doorbell rang, Alfred guessed instinctively who had come. Nevertheless, as he went to the door, he tried to reassure himself that his supposition was silly, and his heart still lurched when he opened it and beheld Julian, the school trunk and two large cardboard boxes resting on the doorstep beside him. He guessed too what they signified, that it would be useless to try to persuade him to go back to Eton before it was too late.

Julian was looking down, and for a few moments Alfred fought against the despair that was overwhelming him, the knowledge that his life had been futile. Perhaps all was not yet entirely lost; might there not yet be some remedy to the apparent finality of Julian's decision to reject all that had been built for him? Then Julian looked up and met his gaze. And Alfred understood. His dream was over.

Sadly, he picked up the trunk and followed Julian wordlessly into their lounge.

"It's time to tell me, Julian. I need to understand," he said gently, though he could not disguise the agony in his voice.

413

Julian replied by sitting down and bursting into tears, his hands over his eyes. "It's about Alexander and that teacher, isn't it?" prompted his father, when Julian seemed unable to speak.

"I killed them both," he cried, uncovering his face in full flood. Gradually, he calmed down, and began to tell his story, pausing only occasionally to wipe away his tears. There was no one else he could confess to, for there was no one else he trusted, even though it meant hurting and abasing himself before the only living person he loved.

He told his father the whole story, neither embellishing it nor evading any hard truths. He began with how he had fallen in love with Alexander when he first saw him, explained how and why he had lied to his father and everyone else, and concluded with his treachery, showing how it had led to Alexander and Mr. Cavendish's deaths. He had read the news and knew what was being said about Mr. Cavendish, so he also did not flinch from insisting on the single truth that had once hurt him most: that from all he had seen of Alexander over the last month, he was now sure he had been deeply in love. Strangely, asserting this now made him feel better. He no longer resented it any more than Mr. Cavendish himself, whom he had belatedly come to admire. He found doing so a cathartic part of his penance. When he finally ran out of words, he remained on the sofa weeping silently, while his father paced around the room, apparently lost in gloom.

"No, Julian you didn't kill them, or rather, you did in a way, but not alone," said Alfred finally. "You were only one of many. Alexander killed himself. He did so straight after seeing a social worker, presumably because she did something to make him think there was no point in his life. You also know he would be alive now if the police hadn't arrested Mr. Cavendish. The police couldn't have done that if Mr. Hodgson hadn't told them. He didn't have to go that far. All those people have blood on their hands. I killed Alexander too by persuading you to end your friendship with him. If I hadn't, he would have remained your dearest friend and never have had an affair with his teacher. Deep down, I knew at the time it was wrong of me. But though I'll always deeply regret it, the real guilt isn't yours or mine. It is every man and woman's."

He paused to glance at Julian, not sure if he was taking in his words, but Julian was looking straight at him, interest strangely mixed with his tearful despair, rather as a man about to be executed for his crimes might listen to his confessor explain why his soul was not necessarily bound for the eternal fires of hell.

"Alexander really died because Parliament had passed laws instructing the police and social worker to do what they did. And Parliament wouldn't have passed those laws if that hadn't been what most people wanted. Most people in this country know about Alexander and Mr. Cavendish now and I bet you almost all of them approve of their affair being smashed. They're delighted that Mr. Cavendish has died miserably for it. If they regret anything, it's that he didn't suffer more. Don't think it's just the British public either. Believe me, I know, people are the same unreasonable and cruel beasts everywhere, though it's taken me until now to understand that."

Alfred was sure Julian had told him the true story. It all made sense at last. It ought to be obvious to anyone who knew their story that Alexander and his lover had done nothing but good to one another and no harm to anyone else, but he knew there was no hope Denise would understand that. She was not burdened with the doubts that would allow her to consider the circumstances objectively. Like others long before her, she delighted in a world in which all moral questions were being answered with final certainty thanks to progress.

He himself could see that Alexander and Mr. Cavendish had died for no better reason than his own father and sisters had, and that Denise was no different to the thousands of officials of the Third Reich who had genuinely believed that Jews were evil.

Captain Holland had been wrong when he said something like the Holocaust could never happen in England. Recognised atrocities like the Holocaust itself could not be repeated as long as they were remembered, but new ones always could as long as people could not or would not see them for what they were. Alfred had believed Captain Holland because he wanted to, and as a result he had lived his life according to an illusion. That everything he had dreamed about and worked so hard for now lay in ruins had always been inevitable.

415

From the ancient Israelites, who had exterminated the Amalekite men, women and children by divine command to the Khmer Rouge cadres, who killed millions of their own people to build a utopia free of reactionary thought, people throughout history had been cruel, and as often as not they had believed themselves most virtuous whilst being so.

Moreover, every generation was hypocritically ready to denounce the cruelty of its predecessors while remaining blind to its own. Had not the same Romans that invaded Britain partly in order to wipe out the cruel and uncivilised human sacrifices of the druids soon afterwards unashamedly fed to the lions the early Christians whom they believed to be evil? And had not the same mediaeval monks who denounced the cruelty of the Roman emperors and were eager to do good themselves, tortured and burned heretics to save their souls? And had not these heretics who damned the Inquisition for unparalleled cruelty gone on to burn and torture witches for the common good?

Denise was a mere instrument of a pervasive human evil always ready to manifest itself. There was no point in contesting the arguments specific to her cause, as they were mere camouflage for the real reason they were accepted: people's need to believe in some evil so that they can feel good about combating it. A mysterious combination of fears and ambitions was responsible for any society's particular choice of bogeyman, but once he had been firmly chosen, any protest was like flailing one's fists against the juggernaut of the spirit of the age.

Julian was not the only one weeping now. His father had had as tough a life as any man. He had not cried since he was separated from his sisters more than forty years ago and he had thought he was inured to tears, but they were flowing down his cheeks now and he did not try to stop them. He wept not just for the ruination of everything he had striven for, but also for his final loss of innocence, for the cruelty and self-deceit in man's heart and for the darkness of it that would never go away.

Made in the USA
Lexington, KY
05 March 2013